Philip Bourke Marston, Louise Chandler Moulton

The Collected Poems of Philip Bourke Marston

Philip Bourke Marston, Louise Chandler Moulton

The Collected Poems of Philip Bourke Marston

ISBN/EAN: 9783337408237

Printed in Europe, USA, Canada, Australia, Japan

Cover: Foto ©Andreas Hilbeck / pixelio.de

More available books at **www.hansebooks.com**

THE COLLECTED POEMS

OF

PHILIP BOURKE MARSTON

COMPRISING

"SONG-TIDE," "ALL IN ALL," "WIND-VOICES,"
"A LAST HARVEST," AND "AFTERMATH"

With Biographical Sketch

BY

LOUISE CHANDLER MOULTON

AUTHOR OF "SWALLOW FLIGHTS," "IN THE GARDEN OF DREAMS"
ETC., ETC.

BOSTON
ROBERTS BROTHERS
1892

University Press:
JOHN WILSON AND SON, CAMBRIDGE, U.S.A.

TO PHILIP BOURKE MARSTON.

Since now at end of pain thou liest dead,
  How shall I dare to utter moan for thee?
  Doth any grieve for prisoner set free?
Or shall our tears upon his brow be shed
Who after long starvation full is fed?
  Nay, rather, clamor bells exultantly, —
  Like wedding chimes ring out your harmony,
Since saddest Life to gladdest Death is wed.

Thou, whose whole life was sorrow! In thy grave
  Doth not strange joy possess thee, and deep rest, —
    Such rest as no man knoweth, having breath?
Dost thou not hear from far the old blasts rave
  That long pursued thee with relentless quest;
    And know them mocked, at last, by Thee and Death?

L. C. M.

CONTENTS.

———⊷⊶———

CONTENTS.

CONTENTS.

b

CONTENTS.

TO PHILIP BOURKE MARSTON.

Sweet Poet, thou of whom these years that roll
    Must one day yet the burdened birthright learn,
    And by the darkness of thine eyes discern
How piercing was the sight within thy soul, —
Gifted, apart, thou goest to the great goal,
    A cloud-bound, radiant spirit, strong to earn,
    Light-reft, that prize for which fond myriads yearn
Vainly, light-blest, — the Seer's aureole.

And doth thine ear, divinely dowered to catch
    All spheral sounds in thy song blent so well,
    Still hearken for my voice's slumbering spell
With wistful love? Oh, let the muse now snatch
My wreath for thy young brows, and bend to watch
    Thy veiled transfiguring sense's miracle!

DANTE GABRIEL ROSSETTI.

BIOGRAPHICAL SKETCH

OF

PHILIP BOURKE MARSTON.

———◆◆◆———

" No ominous hour
Knocks at his door with tidings of mishap, —
Far off is he above desire and fear."

TO write of PHILIP BOURKE MARSTON is to speak of
one at whom, through all his life, Fate seemed
to mock ; and yet I have sometimes felt, while reading
his noble and beautiful verse, that many a man on whom
Destiny has smiled would have considered such inspiration and such achievement, as were the consolation of
our blind poet, cheaply purchased at cost of a life of
commonplace happiness.

He was the son of Dr. Westland Marston, himself
both a poet and a dramatist, and a lineal descendant
of John Marston, the play-wright of the sixteenth cen-
tury.   Philip was heir, it would have seemed, to an
inheritance of good fortunes.   His beautiful dark eyes
opened on a world fair with love and hope.   Philip
James Bailey, the author of " Festus," was his godfather ;
and Dinah Maria Mulock (Mrs. Craik) was his god-
mother.   There were already two sisters — Eleanor and
Cicely — to welcome the baby brother born into their

home on the 13th of August 1850. This newcomer
was the idol of them all, and he began to be " Philip, the
King, ' long before he could speak.

There were three years during which all the promises
of Fate were fair. Then came that accident — a blow
received while playing with some little companions — in
consequence of which I should have said that he wholly
lost his sight, save that he has so often insisted to me on
the difference between seeing, as he did in his boyhood
(though dimly as through a mist), the fires that lit the
sunset sky, the glow on the winter hearth, the trees
waving with the wind's breath, the vague, phantom
shapes of men and women walking like ghosts, and seeing — as was the case after he was twenty — nothing.
Who can possibly measure the calamity of the loss of
vision to a predestined poet?

Philip, of course, could never learn to read. His
education came to him through the books that were
read to him, and the talk of the clever and gifted people
who were the guests of the household. There are few
homes, indeed, to which such visitors came as to that
London house near Regent's Park, where Browning and
Thackeray and Dickens and Rossetti and Swinburne,
and many more of the best and brightest men and women
of the time were frequent visitors.

Philip began to write — or rather to dictate to his
mother, who was, as long as she lived, his loving and
faithful amanuensis — when he had scarcely outgrown
his pinafores; and by the time he was fifteen he had
written some really note-worthy verse that was afterwards
included in his first volume. While he was beginning
to arrange the poems for this first book, and when he
was scarcely twenty, his mother died. He has talked

to me sometimes of his passionate sorrow at her loss. He felt, then, as if the whole world "had gone to pieces;" and for a while after that he could think of nothing but the love that had been, and was not.

It almost seemed like a miracle of mercy when he met Mary Nesbit; and her sweet young voice lured him back to a fresh interest in this world. He loved her, as poets love, — suddenly, romantically, and with an adoring and idealizing devotion that at once expressed itself in the fifty-seven sonnets which form the first division of his earliest book, "Song-Tide, and Other Poems." The poems, the love, the lover — who knows what? — touched the girlish heart he sought to win, and moved it to response; and Mary Nesbit pledged herself to share the young poet's darkened life. In 1871 — soon after this betrothal — "Song-Tide" was published, and dedicated to the memory of Philip's mother. It was an immediate success. The best critics welcomed it with their approval; the "Examiner" even declared that, by virtue of this volume, the author should "take an equal place alongside Swinburne, Morris, and Rossetti." I have seen letters on letters of praise addressed to the young poet from such masters of song as Swinburne and Rossetti. In one of these, Rossetti wrote: "Only yesterday evening I was reading your 'Garden Secrets' to William Bell Scott, who fully agreed with me that it is not too much to say of them that they are worthy of Shakespeare in his subtlest lyrical moods."

Remembering the long sadness of Marston's life, I love to pause for a moment on just this height of being, — to see him, at twenty-one, young, happy even in spite of his misfortunes, loving and beloved, welcomed by noble poets as among their own high kindred, full of eager hope, triumphant, as it seemed, against his fate! But, alas, it was not for long that he stood upon this summit of his fortunes.

In the November of 1871 Miss Nesbit died of swift consumption; and then, indeed, the last gleam of light departed from the eyes that wept for her such bitter tears. Henceforth they beheld no more of the pageantry of sunset, or the hearth-fire by which he and his sorrow sat, desolate, at night. But no! I must not speak of him as quite desolate; for Cicely remained to him. His sister Eleanor was, by this time, married to Arthur O'Shaughnessy, himself a poet; but Cicely, henceforth, until her own death, gave herself to be eyes and hands for her stricken brother. It seemed almost as if his heart beat, his brain throbbed, in her body, so entirely was it the business and the pleasure of her life to do his will.

The house, near Regent's Park, where the family had lived so long, and which during the life-time of Mrs. Marston had been the scene of so many brilliant symposia, was given up, and Philip and Cicely henceforth abode together. They lived in London (which was Philip's birthplace and his lifelong home), but they travelled many times to France, and one golden year to Italy, — that fair "woman-country," which forever after haunted Philip's memory, as for many a longing year it had haunted his dreams. They worked together, too, and no sightless man can ever have been served more faithfully than was Philip while this sister of his mind as well as of his heart was spared to him.

It was perhaps a year after Miss Nesbit's death when her bereaved lover made the acquaintance of Oliver Madox Brown, the author of "The Dwale Bluth," "The

Black Swan," and several other remarkable tales. He was the son of Ford Madox Brown, the well-known artist, and was himself a painter, as well as a novelist and a poet. His friendship was one of the supreme joys of Marston's life. The two met almost daily; and when anything kept them apart they wrote to each other. They planned conquests of art and of literature; they sympathized with each other's ambitions; they were friends in the uttermost sense of the word. At last Oliver became ill, from blood-poisoning; but though Philip was full of anxiety during this brief illness, the news of his death came with an awful shock of surprise and horror.

It was in 1874 that Oliver Madox Brown died; and before his illness he had read some of the proofs and all the manuscript of "All in All," — Marston's second volume of poems. "Song-Tide," as I have said, had been inscribed to the memory of Philip's mother. "All in All" was dedicated to his father, though all the poems it contained — with the exception of one to his sister Cicely, with which the book concluded — were consecrated to the lost love whose young life had been pledged to his own.

A book so heart-breaking could scarcely win the ear of the pleasure-loving world as had the gayer music of "Song-Tide," written when life was at its full. Critics and poets, indeed, appreciated the sad dignity, the poignant pathos of "All in All;" but the world at large craves sunshine and not shadow. No thoughtful reader, however, could ignore the nobility of many of these poems.

His life was eventful only in its sorrows and in its friendships. He was but fourteen years old when he

was first taken to see Swinburne; and at that time —
wonderful as the achievement seems — he actually knew
by heart the whole of the First Series of " Poems and
Ballads." The friendship begun on that memorable day
was a pride and a joy to Marston for all the rest of his
life. Later on he came also to know intimately Dante
Gabriel Rossetti, and to love him with adoring enthusiasm. One of Rossetti's latest sonnets was addressed to
Marston. Another well-beloved friend was Theodore
Watts, — a poet whose noble work won for him the lifelong and intimate friendship of Rossetti and Browning
and Lord Tennyson, and was the first link in that
chain of more than brotherly love which binds him
to Swinburne, his housemate at present, and for many
past years. William Sharp, poet and novelist; Herbert
E. Clarke, the poet; Coulson Kernahan, the brilliant
author of "A Dead Man's Diary;" C. Churchill
Osborne; the Hon. Roden Noel; A. Mary F. Robin-
son; Olive Schreiner; Iza Duffus Hardy; Mrs. W. K.
Clifford; E. Nesbit, — these were a few only of the
group of literary friends who cheered with their sympathy and appreciation the last sad years of Marston's
darkened life.

I myself first met him in 1867, on the first day of
July, — just six weeks before his twenty-sixth birthday.
He was tall, slight, and in spite of his blindness, graceful. He seemed to me young-looking even for his
twenty-six years. He had a noble and beautiful forehead. His brown eyes were perfect in shape, and even
in color, save for a dimness like a white mist that ob-
scured the pupil, but which you perceived only when
you were quite near to him. His hair and beard were
dark brown, with warm glints of chestnut; and the color

came and went in his cheeks as in those of a sensitive girl. His face was singularly refined; but his lips were full and pleasure-loving, and suggested dumbly how cruel must be the limitations of blindness to a nature hungry for love and for beauty. I had been greatly interested, before seeing him, in his poems, and to meet him was a memorable delight.

He and the sister who was his inseparable companion soon became my close friends, and with both of them this friendship lasted till the end.

In Cicely's case the "end" was not far distant. She came to see me, on the morning of July 28, 1878, and complained, when she came in, that her head ached "desperately." I persuaded her to lie down; but suddenly she sprang to her feet, called my name, and fell back again, stricken with the "foudroyant apoplexy" of which she died in the mid-afternoon of that same day. Philip and his father were travelling in France, just then; and as they were moving from place to place on their homeward way, we did not even know where to reach them with a telegram. They returned to London, therefore, in utter ignorance of their loss, to find the daughter and sister so beloved awaiting her burial.

I have always felt that this was the cruellest bereavement of Marston's life. When his mother, his betrothed, and his friend died, in sad and swift succession, there had always been Cicely to comfort and console him. But when Cicely went, there was no such survivor. His other sister was not only married, but was even then a chronic invalid. His father's health, also, was broken; and devoted as he was to his son, he could not give him what Cicely had given him of day-long companionship and constant service. It was after this loss of his sister that many of the new friends I have mentioned came into Philip's life; and to the list might be added various Americans, — such as Mrs. Laura Curtis Bullard, and three of our well-known poets, Edmund Clarence Stedman (who had spoken of Marston with earnest appreciation in his "Victorian Poets"), Richard Watson Gilder, and the Southern poet Paul Hamilton Hayne. From this time forth a large proportion of Marston's work, both in prose and verse, was published in America, and won a wide audience among the best American readers.

As years went on he needed the comfort of friendship more than ever, for sorrow upon sorrow assailed him. His sister Eleanor died in the February of 1879; and his brother-in-law, Arthur O'Shaughnessy in the January of 1881. In the April of 1882 Dante Gabriel Rossetti — the enthusiasm of the blind poet's life — died in his turn, and in a sonnet to his memory Marston spoke of him as transcending all other men, and leading "the train of love."

Marston's third volume of poems — "Wind-Voices" — was published in 1883; by Eliot Stock, in London, and by Roberts Brothers, in America. It was certainly a distinct advance on the two preceding volumes in variety, and on the whole in strength; though no lyric in it surpassed "The Wind and the Rose," and perhaps no sonnet excelled two or three that might be selected from the previous volumes. That "Wind-Voices" was dedicated to myself, as a proof of its author's friendship, does not, I am sure, affect my judgment of it. I am convinced that it contains work which generations to come will value, as we value now the lovely legacies of song bequeathed to us by singers of old days. The best critics in England and in America reviewed it with such cordial praise that I like to remember the pleasure their words gave to him whose pleasures in those days were so few.

From that very time — the autumn of 1883 — Marston's health began sensibly and visibly to decline. He was gay still, when his friends were with him; for no man ever confronted the sorrows of his life more bravely, or made less claim on the compassion of his fellows. He wrote once : —

> Of me ye may say many a bitter thing,
>   O Men, when I am gone, gone far away
>   To that dim Land where shines no light of day.
> Sharp was the bread for my soul's nourishing
> Which Fate allowed, and bitter was the spring
>   Of which I drank and maddened, even as they
>   Who wild with thirst at sea will not delay,
> But drink the brine and die of its sharp sting.
>
> Not gentle was my war with Chance, and yet
>   I borrowed no man's sword: alone I drew,
>   And gave my slain fit burial out of view.
> In secret places I and Sorrow met ;
> So when you count my sins, do not forget
>   To say I taxed not any one of you.

This sonnet was no idle boast. He had a delicate pride that always led him to prefer to confer favors rather than to receive them. Many of the sonnets in "Wind-Voices" were self-revealing to a degree that only those who knew him well could fully divine. In one — "A Question" — he asks himself whether the prevision of Death would have been ghastlier, had Life been full for him of joy; and he answers his own question thus : —

Harder seems this, — to die and leave the sun,
And carry hence each unfulfilled desire.
I heard one cry, " Come where the feast is spread,"
But when I came the festival was done;
Somewhile I shivered by the extinguished fire,
And now retrace my steps uncomforted.

And, once again, he wrote : —

Still the old paths, and the old solitude,
And still the dark soul journeying on its way.

The journey was not to be long; yet the three years after the publication of " Wind-Voices " were so full of loneliness and of sadness that I cannot bear to think of them; though always and up to the very last, he could be blithe whenever there was any one with whom to make merry, — and small things sufficed to please and cheer him. He founded, during those years, a Club, to which he gave the name of " The Vagabonds," which used to meet for a monthly evening. This club survives him. It is " The Vagabonds " still; and there have been numerous additions to its members. Marston's memory is its religion.

Philip clung, if possible, more closely than ever to his friends, because a low voice was forever whispering in his ear that his time for friendship was brief. He often said to me that his future would be short; but I could never quite believe it. How could I think that with so much affluence of life in the world, life would be snatched from these young lips that thirsted for it so eagerly?

In the autumn of 1886, while in Brighton with his father, he was stricken with brain fever, and one of his delusions was that from his window (which looked upon a stone-paved yard) he could see great ships, with all their white sails set, sailing, all of them, to America, whither he had always hoped to go. "They will stop for me soon," he used often to say. A ship stopped for him soon, indeed, — too soon; but it was to bear him to a farther shore than the one of which he dreamed, over a sea unfathomed, to a port unknown.

I saw him in the autumn after this illness; and I was curiously and painfully struck with the vividness of his memory of things long past, and his frequent forgetfulness of the engagements and the interests of the day. How often he said, "Why should I want to live? I really do not know why?— but I shrink from that great mystery beyond. If I only knew!"

Through the winter of 1886-7 his letters — which came to me regularly, almost until the end — were far briefer than usual, and inexpressibly sad. He wrote that he was too weak to sit long at the type-writer, which, after Cicely's death, he had learned to use for himself. How unutterably pathetic those mid-winter letters seem to me, when I recall them now! How they come back to me, — vain cries out of the dark! "If I only *could* sleep!" he wrote, again and again; and now sleep laps him round.

It was the last of January that he experienced what then seemed only a slight shock of paralysis. On the first day of February he telegraphed his friend Herbert Clarke to come to him. Even then he could speak only with great difficulty, though he managed to say that he wanted to live, and hoped to get better. After that day he never spoke at all. His father wrote me how agonizing were his attempts to make himself understood; but this was at first. After a few days he gave up the struggle, and subsided into a gentle quietude; until, at last, "he almost slept into Eternity."

He died in the morning of February 14, 1887. Had he lived till the 13th of the next August, he would have been thirty-seven years old. He was buried at Highgate Cemetery on the 18th of February. It was a gray and foggy day, — as if the Earth, herself, were in mourning for him, her lover. Many friends wrote me how strangely beautiful was the dead poet's face; and one of them spoke of its extraordinary likeness to Severn's portrait of Keats. The coffin was heaped with wreaths of flowers, sent by friends near and far. Even before his funeral — on the very day after his death — Swinburne had written so memorable an expression of his sorrow for his friend's loss that I must quote it here : —

> The days of a man are threescore and ten.
>   The days of his life were half a man's, whom we
>   Lament, and would yet not bid him back to be
> Partaker of all the woes and ways of men.
> Life sent him enough of sorrow: not again
>   Would anguish of love, beholding him set free,
>   Bring back the beloved to suffer life, and see
> No light but the fire of grief that scathed him then.
>
> We know not at all: we hope and do not fear.
> We shall not again behold him, late so near,
>   Who now from far above, with eyes alight
> And spirit enkindled, haply toward us here
>   Looks down, unforgetful yet, of days like night
>   And love that has yet his sightless face in sight.

Theodore Watts quoted, in the "Athenæum," this tribute of Swinburne's, enshrining it in a prose memorial of his own, so beautiful that by no one who read it could it be forgotten; and in addition Watts himself wrote a sonnet to the memory of the blind and sad-fated poet

without which I should feel that this record would be
sadly incomplete : —

> The shorn lamb shivers, but the woolly sheep
>   Feeds on and fattens thro' the untempered storms.
>   Felt thro' a curly fleece, the east wind warms,
> While far away shines heaven, — an azure steep.
> We loved thee, Philip, but we could not keep
>   The wind away, nor quell the pitiless harms
>   Such sorrow fans from hell.   We had no charms
> For those blind eyes that lived, but lived to weep.
>
> Yea, weak to heal is Love ; but Death is strong,
>   Balming the sorest heart that travaileth,
>   As under bloody wheels of Jaganneth, —
> Even such a heart as thine, even such a wrong ;
> Soother of sorrow is he whose deathless song
>   Keeps all the choral spheres revolving, — Death !

The illustrated papers published Marston's likeness,
accompanied by sketches of his sad and too brief life.
Praises were lavished on his work, as flowers had been
upon his tomb ; and he — he, who had so loved the
sympathy and appreciation of his fellow-men — was he
deaf to it all, I wonder, down there where he was
laid ?

He had always so welcomed the spring, had sung
its praises in so many a rhyme, — and now the spring
came on apace without him. As his friend Clarke
wrote, in a " Monody " too long for quotation here : —

> The March wind buffets the blithe daffodils ;
>   Snowdrop and crocus the rough season dare ;
> A rumor of vague joy is on the hills ;
>   Gladness of expectation holds the air ;
>   And in the bright cold sunshine forth I fare.

c

And lo! a silent shadow at my side, —
A sad and silent shadow everywhere, —
Like to another self, goes stride for stride,
A wraith that with its desolate presence fills
The year's house, bare and wide.

I think that others, who were Philip's friends, recognize, sometimes, this silent shadow at their side. It almost seems as if he were but veiled from us by some unfriendly cloud, and that he must know, still, all that concerns his fame, — yes, even these poor words I write.

He had published a good many stories, — he used to call them his pot-boilers; and after his death a volume of them was collected by his friend, William Sharp, and published under the title of "For a Song's Sake, and Other Stories." Some of these tales are so original and so interesting as to persuade us that a veritable and note-worthy success in fiction might have been easily possible to him had the conditions of his life been more favorable. Such stories as, for instance, "Miss Stotford's Specialty," and "Bryanstone and Wife," justify the praise that has been bestowed on Marston's prose by so distinguished a critic as Edmund Clarence Stedman. It is always the prose of a poet. Looking at his published and his unpublished work, — a manuscript novel (his first attempt at fiction), his stories short and long, his brief essays, his critical reviews (chiefly published in the "Athenæum"), and his many poems, I am filled with amazement at the numerous and varied achievements of this young and blind man who fought his battle of life against such terrible odds.

Three other books, beside the volume of his stories, have been compiled from Marston's works since his death. For the first of these — "Garden Secrets" — I was responsible. It had long been a favorite project of Marston's to publish, sometime, as he used to say, "a little book" with only the Garden poems in it, — the secrets the flowers had whispered to him. With this his long-cherished wish in mind, I arranged the volume, in the spring after his death ; and it was published, in 1887, by Roberts Brothers, Boston. Later on Mr. Sharp compiled for publication in the "Canterbury Poets" series, a book of selections from Marston's three previously printed volumes of poems. It represents his work fairly enough, perhaps, for the general reader; but does not, in my opinion, detract from the desirableness of a collected edition of all the verse which is this poet's legacy to the world. The third volume, also edited by myself, and entitled "A Last Harvest," was composed of poems not included in the previous books. They were the fruit of the three sad, last years of Marston's life. They were not wholly sad, however, — though, in those last years, sadness rested upon him like a pall.

The present "Collected Edition" includes "Song-Tide and Other Poems" (with the exception of a few numbers which seemed to me, and to several critics abler and more impartial than myself, to be unworthy of preservation in a volume which contains poems of such almost matchless beauty as "The Rose and the Wind," such power as "A Christmas Vigil ") ; "All in All ; " "Wind-Voices ; " "A Last Harvest ; " and, in addition to these four previously-published volumes, a number of poems, under the general title of "Aftermath," not hitherto printed in any book.

Surely in years and centuries to come, this collection must be dear to whoever loves what is loveliest and truest in literature ; for Philip Bourke Marston was not " the idle singer of an empty day," but a poet who spoke to the deepest hearts of men, and whose words have a claim upon our hallowing memory. If in these poems the minor chords of life are oftenest struck, I do not think their charm or their interest is thereby lessened. Even those who are happy may care, sometimes, to listen to the passion and the pathos of a sorrow they themselves have never known; and to the heavy of heart there is a gleam of comfort in the knowledge that other hearts have ached with a kindred pain, — that they are not pioneers in the desolate path of grief. Swineburne was not at fault, when he wrote, in that February darkened by Marston's death, —

" Thy song may soothe full many a soul hereafter."

But indeed, I must quote the whole of the noble poem, which though written almost before the sod had been heaped upon Philip's grave, appeared, for the first time, in the " Fortnightly Review " for January, 1891.

LIGHT: AN EPICEDE.

TO PHILIP BOURKE MARSTON.

Love will not weep because the seal is broken
    That sealed upon a life beloved and brief
Darkness, and let but song break through for token
    How deep, too far for even thy song's relief,
    Slept in thy soul the secret springs of grief.

Thy song may soothe full many a soul hereafter,
    As tears, if tears will come, dissolve despair ;
As here but late, with smile more bright than laughter,
    Thy sweet, strange, yearning eyes would seem to bear
    Witness that joy might cleave the clouds of care.

Ten days agone, and love was one with pity
  When love gave thought wings towards the glimmering
    goal
Where, as a shrine lit in some darkling city,
  Shone soft the shrouded image of thy soul;
  And now thou art healed of life, art healed and whole.

Yea, two days since, all we that loved thee pitied;
  And now with wondering love, with shame of face,
We think how foolish now, how far unfitted
  Should be from us, toward thee who hast run thy race,
  Pity, — toward thee, who hast won the pitiless place:

The painless world of death, yet unbeholden
  Of eyes that dream what light now lightens thine
And will not weep. Thought yearning toward those olden,
  Dear hours that sorrow sees, and sees not shine,
  Bows tearless down before a flameless shrine.

A flameless altar here of love and sorrow
  Quenched and consumed together. These were one,
One thing for thee, as night was one with morrow,
  And utter darkness with the sovereign sun;
  And now thou seest life, sorrow and darkness done.

And yet love yearns again to win thee hither, —
  Blind love, and loveless, and unworthy thee;
Here where I watch the hours of darkness wither,
  Here where mine eyes were glad and sad to see
  Thine that could see not mine, though turned on me.

But now, if aught beyond sweet sleep lie hidden,
  And sleep be sealed not fast on dead men's sight
Forever, thine hath grace for ours forbidden,
  And sees as compassed round with change and night;
  Yet light like thine is ours if love be light.

If the dead know anything, then surely this poem,
written by a poet who had been the very earliest object

of Marston's boyish enthusiasm, must have thrilled his silent heart to pride and joy. And if the dead know anything, glad indeed must have been the welcome which Dr. Westland Marston received — on the fifth of January, 1890 — from the son who had preceded him to the Stranger's Country by a month less than three years. Few fathers, surely, ever mourned for a son as that father mourned. His days and nights were passed in seeking for some sign that the dead had not forgotten him. And sometimes, in answer to his yearning, he seemed to hear a voice, to which all other ears were deaf, that whispered to him, from out the unknown world, of love that was immortal.

Father, mother, sisters, and brother, — surely they are all together, now, somewhere. For them is peace after tumult, rest after weariness, plenty after famine. To us the memory of a joy and a sorrow, the echo of a song.

LOUISE CHANDLER MOULTON.

1892.

SONG–TIDE.

PRELUDE.

Hear'st thou upon the shore line of thy life
  The beating of this song-tide led by thee,
  As by the winds and moon is led the sea?
The clashing waves conflicting meet in strife,
  Bitter with tears of hopeless love they roll,
  And fall, and thunder, between soul and soul.
Strange things are borne upon their foaming heights,
Through wild, gray, windy days and shrieking nights;
O'er rocks and hidden shoals, round beacon lights,
  Their foam is blown, till on thy shores at length
  They burst, in all the trouble of their strength.

Sad things, O love! upon thy shore they cast, —
  Waifs from the wreck of that fair dream of joy
  With which the winds of Fortune love to toy,
Whereto the waves seem kind; until at last
  The tempest burst upon it in its might —
  Though through the utter darkness of the night
The happy haven lights shone calm and clear,
Of that loved land so far and yet so near.
No voice was left to call, no hand to steer;
  It fell before the tempest blind and strong,
  To float a wreck upon this tide of song, —

This bitter tide, by winds of passion moved;
  This stormy tide, that wraps and bears its dead;
  This tide, from all strong springs of sorrow fed,
Flowing between my soul and thine, beloved;
  This tide, that knows no moon by night, by day
  No burning sun to flame upon its way;

This passionate, strong tide, whose waste waves roll,
And call from one soul to another soul;
This tide that knows the tempest and the shoal,
  The utter darkness, and at best such light
  As comes between the day-fall and the night.

Dead hopes, spoiled dreams, sad memories that ache,
  Desires whose hopes were vain; poor, sterile prayers,—
Such things as these to thee this tide upbears.
Hear where the song-waves roar, and where they break,
  Let the sharp sound of woe assail thine ears,
  Even as his who on some midnight hears
Upon a close and yet night-hidden strand
The roused sea calling to the silent land,
The strong sea stricken of the storm-wind's hand;
  And as he listens, feels himself the pain
  Of shipwrecked men, who battle with the main.

Hear it again, in some less stormy mood,
  As one who, waking from a dreamless sleep,
  Hears the complaining of a moonless deep,
And feels its vast and endless solitude,
  With sense of wants untold, his heart oppress;
  With terrible, strong yearnings to express
All life's untold, unmeasurable woe;
To look past unrevealing stars, and know
Whereto at length men's prayers and yearnings go.
  Once, only once, with purged and holy eyes,
  To see, and know, the promised Paradise.

O love! my land whereto I may not come,
  Is not my spirit to thy spirit set?
  Hear once, O love! then, if thou canst, forget,
For when death makes my lips and thy lips dumb, —
  When thou hast done with pity, I with grief,
  When no hope comes to comfort or deceive,

This tide shall flow unchanged upon its way,
And men who catch its beat will surely say,
" When comes such love to us, in this our day?
What must have been the soul that thus could move
One human spirit to such mighty love? "

Small music in its voice this song-tide has, —
Not strength enough, perchance, to stir one heart ;
No sun, no moon, their light to it impart,
No happy stars above it shining pass ;
The summer wots not of it ; and no spring,
With winds that sigh, too full of peace to sing,
Can hope to ease it from the tempest's blast.
Between the future and the distant past
It roars and rolls ; its waves fall thick and fast,
Whirled madly by wild winds, and only warm
With pulse and passion of the viewless storm.

A GREETING.

RISE up, my song! stretch forth thy wings and fly
  With no delaying, over shore and deep!
  Be with my lady when she wakes from sleep;
Touch her with kisses softly on each eye;
And say, before she puts her dreaming by:
  "Within the palaces of slumber keep
  One little niche wherein sometimes to weep,
For one who vainly toils till he shall die!"

Yet say again, a sweeter thing than this:
  "His life is wasted by his love for thee."
  Then, looking o'er the fields of memory,
She'll find perchance, o'ergrown with grief and bliss,
  Some flower of recollection, pale and fair,
  That she, through pity, for a day may wear.

THE LAST BETROTHED.

IN places that have known my lady's grace,
  Seeing how all my soul and life lay there,
  I sat; when lo, so sitting, I was 'ware
Of breath that fell in sighs upon my face,
While like a harp wherethrough the night-wind plays
  A sorrowful, delicious, nameless air,
  A voice wherein I felt my soul had share
Made music in the consecrated place.

Then, lifting up my eyes, I looked, and lo!
  A fair sad woman sitting all alone
  Where Love brief while ago had made his throne:
Against her pale still breast I leant my brow,
"Thy name," I said, "is Grief; take then my vow
  That I and thou henceforward be as one."

SONNET III.

WEDDED GRIEF.

AND now we walk together, she and I ;
  She sits with me unseen where men are gay,
  And all the pleasures of the sense have sway ;
She walks with me beneath the moonlit sky,
And murmurs ever of the days gone by ;
  She follows still in dreams upon my way,
  She sits beside me in the fading day,
And thrills the twilight silence with a sigh :

So on we journey till we gain the strand
Whose sea conjectures of no further land ;
  There, where the past is fading from my view,
To this my sorrow I will reach my hand
  And say : " O thou who wert alone found true,
  Forgive if now I must forget thee too ! "

SONNET IV.

UNUTTERED THOUGHTS.

HAVE I not bared my soul, O love, to thee,
  And told thee of the things that sorrow said,
  When joy went out from life, and hope was dead ?
I would that this life's song of mine should be
A song to cleave unto thy memory.
  I have not made my soul a peaceful bed,
  The worms of sin upon its dust are fed,
And hell makes mirth at its mortality.

I have not spared to cloud thy heart with dole ;
  But in my breast strange secret thoughts there lie
  Whereof no song of mine shall testify.
Then by the song and silence of my soul,
  The thoughts that live and pass without a cry,
Know thou of this, my love, the very whole.

A LAKE.

O soul serene ! like some fair, placid lake
 'That flows on silently 'neath day and night,
  What if my spirit, dazed with heat and light,
Drop, drowned in thee ! shall a leaf falling make
Thy surface troubled, or a light wind shake
  Thy tranquil depths that ever flow aright?
  O cold and lovely lake ! what tempest's might
Shall ever thy smooth currents part or break?

Thy great, calm beauty can reflect the sun ;
The stars are mirrored in thee, and the moon
  Beholds her image in thy waveless flow,
So cold, and yet so fair to look upon ;
So cold that, even in love's hottest noon,
  Thy depths untroubled are more cold than snow.

ANTICIPATION.

How shall it profit me to love thee so?
  What shall I gain for all my love, save tears,
   To make more grievous still my grievous years?
Or shall the bliss of half a year ago
Comfort my spirit, when it comes to know
  How all breath·taking hopes, all joyous fears,
  Are buried deep where no man sees or hears,
While on their grave no gladdening blossoms blow?

Before this fatal love o'erwhelm me quite,
  Be something different, sweet, to what thou art ;
Alter, or hide thy beauty from my sight,
  Reverse thy nature, or release my heart ;
   Let not grief gather strength by long delay :
   O love, what thou hast made canst thou not slay?

SONNET VII.

TOO NEAR.

So close we are, and yet so far apart, —
  So close, I feel thy breath upon my cheek ;
  So far, that all this love of mine is weak
To touch in any way thy distant heart :
So close, that, when I hear thy voice, I start
  To see my whole life standing bare and bleak ;
  So far, that, though for years and years I seek,
I shall not find thee other than thou art !

So, while I live, I walk upon the verge
  Of an impassable and changeless sea
  Which more than death divides me, love, from thee ;
The mournful beating of its heavy surge
    Is all the music now that I shall hear :
    O love, thou art too far, and yet too near !

SONNET VIII.

THE LAST LOOK.

My soul, before we altogether quit
  This land wherein we once had hoped to dwell,
  Take one last look, — yea, take one brief farewell.
    There shine the paths that now her spirit's feet
    Shall tread alone : since, soul, it was not meet
That thou shouldst walk with her : yet why rebel?
Such things we know must be, and who shall tell
What might have been, had she to save thought fit?

Turn round, my soul, and look upon the sea
  That we must cross : " Is not the harvest past,
    The summer ended !   And we are not saved ! "
    Strange hands to us across the sea are waved,
Strange voices rise and call tumultuously,
  And hell laughs out for joy, and cries, " At last ! "

SONNET IX.

A VAIN WISH.

I WOULD not, could I, make thy life as mine;
   Only I would, if such a thing might be,
   Thou shouldst not, love, forget me utterly;
Yea, when the sultry stars of summer shine
On dreaming woods, where nightingales repine,
   I would that at such times should come to thee
   Some thought, not quite unmixed with pain, of me, —
Some little sorrow for a soul's decline.

Yea, too, I would that through thy brightest times,
Like the sweet burden of remembered rhymes,
   That gentle sadness should be with thee, dear;
And when the gates of sleep are on thee shut,
I would not even then, it should be mute,
   But murmur, shell-like, at thy spirit's ear.

SONNET X.

LOVE AND FORGETFULNESS.

CAN I not find in sleep some hidden place
   Whereto, upon some midnight, I may bring
   The image of my love; some dark, deep spring
Wherein no stars are mirrored, and no rays
Of moonlight fall; and there a little space
   Look long into her eyes, imagining
   Some strange and now impossible sweet thing?
Then, turning, put one hand before my face,

And with the other seize her image fair,
   And cast it down into the water deep,
And see my old dreams pass me voiceless by,
Ended, as is some dead man's dying prayer:
   And so returning from the land of sleep,
Rise up, be glad, nor know the reason why?

SONNET XI.

A SUMMER DREAM.

THERE was a man who through long winter days
  Walked sadly, without hope, until the spring
  Came back to make the whole world shine and sing ;
And then he found one day a gracious place
Girt round with trees ; while over waving ways
  Of deep green grass the gusty winds did bring
  Soft, subtle scents of sweet flowers blossoming,
With sound of wild birds singing face to face.

There he lay down, and dream'd a dream most fair,
  And, as he slept, through all his dream he felt
  The golden beauty of the summer melt.
    How long he slept he knew not, till one day
    He woke, and, when his long sleep ebbed away,
Rose up and shivered in gray winter air.

SONNET XII.

KNOWN TOO WELL.

Lo ! now how well I know the thing thou art ;
  Not more the color of thine hair and eyes
  I know, than all thy various tones and sighs ;
The laugh half-song, half-moan, that comes to part
The low clear voice, as placid as the heart,
  Which, being stainless, needeth no disguise, —
  Serene and pure as moonlit seas and skies
Wherethrough no thunders roll, no lightnings dart.

The music of thy voice by heart I have ;
  Yea, every tone, and semi-tone, I know ;
    The sound of taken breath, divinely sweet,
    The touch of fingers, and the fall of feet ;
I know thee better than the wind the wave,
  The sun the heavens, or the Alps the snow.

EXPIATION.

O LOVE ! if I have ever in thee wrought
　　The slightest grief, or for the smallest space
　　Troubled the happy calmness of thy face,
Then may my soul be blasted by the thought :
May it be made my curse, till I am brought,
　　Through nights of anguish and through bitter days,
　　To stand at length before God's judgment place,
Where all man's strength comes utterly to nought.

　　Then, though on earth I had grown good as Christ,
　　Done all fair, righteous things, and sacrificed
Myself for man, God shall no mercy show,
　　　But damn me utterly ; and should Christ turn
　　　To plead, His intercession I will spurn ;
And say, " Nay, God, 't is just ; Lord, even so ! "

BITTER GIFTS.

My captive soul knelt at my lady's feet,
　　And said, " O queen, what are thy gifts to me ? "
　　All strong and pale and mute, it knelt, and she,
Seeing its capture utter and complete,
Sighed just a little and looked down on it,
　　And said, " I would that I could make thee free,
　　For, lo ! the gifts that I must give to thee
Are bitter gifts indeed, and no way sweet."

Then, with a robe the folds whereof were fire,
She clothed my soul in unfulfilled desire,
　　And crowned it with a crown of grief, and said,
　　　" Rise up ! go forth, and labor in thy day."
　　So crowned with grief, with torture garmented,
　　　My soul arose and, speechless, went its way.

LOVE'S DESPERATION.

Since, sweet, you cannot love me, and we twain
  Must live and die apart ; and since I know, —
  Though you, through pity, will not own it now, —
Sundered, your soul from mine will not retain
The memory of love, as strong as vain ;
  That soon you will forget to grieve, and so
  Forget for what you wish to grieve ; and lo !
Once gone, you will not think of me again ; —

O loved, unloving love ! let not this be.
  Rather, O my love, hate me, with the whole
  Deep strength of that unfathomable soul —
With hate as strong as is my love for thee ;
    Let it a brand upon my soul be set.
    O love, do all things else, but not — Forget !

A POEM.

Lo ! even now, on this wild winter night,
  Yielding to wishes looked far more than said,
  My lady of her spirit-sweetness read,
In tones that ever soothe my soul aright,
Peaceful and full and tender as the light
  Down the dim isles of old cathedrals shed,
  That sweetest poem, that her voice first made
Sacred to me, in days when skies were bright.

And, as she read, the vanished June returned,
  And in the tranced, gold, sultry, summer weather,
  Once more in our old place we sat together.
O days of joy ! before my heart had learned
    The bitter, bitter truth, whereby at length
    I know love's grief, the passion of its strength.

SONNET XVII.

A MESSAGE TO THE SEA.

RISE up, my song, and plume thy wings for flight!
    For I will have thee fly to a far place,
    Sad with the joy of unreturning days;
There, evermore, 'twixt storm-scarred height and height,
Calm sighs the sea or thunders in its might, —
    Go down unto those whirling water-ways;
    And where the winds the fiercest tumult raise,
And waves upon the loudest reefs are white, —

    Cry out, O song, to all the sea and say:
    " Lo! even he who sent me bade me pray
That thou once more beloved of him wouldst be,
    And comfort him again, in the old way;
That from this new love thou his heart wouldst free,
Wash clean his soul, and be again the Sea."

SONNET XVIII.

LOVE'S STRENGTH.

HAD you but loved me once as I love you,
    With all my strength of body, heart, and brain,
    Till nothing, save our love, in life was plain,
I well had borne all else God had to do, —
Whether He made you false to me, or drew
    The soul forth from the body in slow pain,
    And set Death like a gulf between us twain, —
I still had said (though what God made He slew):

" Though she be false to me, or cold and dead,
    Is not my soul yet glorious from her love?
    If life be cold now, is there not enough
To keep my spirit warm till life is shed?
        All strength save Death's upon the past is vain,
        And in the past do I not live again?"

SONNET XIX.

LOVE'S WEAKNESS.

I KNOW if I had loved you, as saints may,
  I had kept mute this love within my breast;
  So high I think you are above the rest,
That what to other women had been play
Made you just something sorry for one day, —
  One day, not more; but great love unexpressed,
  Such love as makes death dark and life unblessed,
Is hard to bear, whatever saints may say.

It doubtless had been strong of me and great,
  If I had let you pass and said no word,
    When all my heart was as the heart of one
From whom, as old tales tell, the mystic bird
    'Turned slow and sadly, seeing life was done,
As turned your soul from mine, my love, my fate!

SONNET XX.

A DAY'S SECRET.

ABOUT the wild beginning of the Spring
  There came to me, and all the world, a day
  To prove the Winter wholly gone away.
I said: " O Day, thy lips are sweet to sing,
But surely in thy voice some sweeter thing
  Than thy mere song I find; lo! now I pray,
  Before thou goest, turn to me and say,
Why round thee so my heart keeps wandering? "

Then, as a man who having loved and lost,
  Still in his dead love's kindred seems to see
Something of what on earth he treasured most;
  So looking on that day, my memory
    Was filled with thoughts of April days wherein
    Love's joy, too young for pain, did first begin.

SONNET XXI.

PERSISTENT MUSIC.

Lo! what am I, my heart, that I should dare
 To love her, who will never love again, —
 I, standing out here in the wind and rain,
With feet unsandalled and uncovered hair,
Singing sad words to a still sadder air,
 Who know not even if my song's refrain —
 "Of sorrow, sorrow! loved, oh, loved in vain!" —
May reach her where she sits and hath no care.

But I will sing in every man's despite;
 Yea, too, and love, and sing of love until
My music mixes with her dreams at night;
 That when Death says to me, "Lie down, be still!"
  She, pausing for my voice, and list'ning long,
  May know its silence sadder than its song.

SONNET XXII.

SIX MONTHS AGO.

Six months ago, and what thing is the same?
 Here in this garden, where the sweet June day
 Sank into sleep, while starry stillness lay
Like peace on all, last night the winter came,
With stormy winds made strong to smite and maim
 The well-loved trees, whose boughs, now bare and
  gray,
 Toss helplessly from side to side and pray
Once more to feel the summer's touch of flame, —

Six months ago, when, half afraid, I said,
 "Can God's heart be relenting? Ere I go
  Shall even I stand face to face with bliss?"
 Now all the meaning of that hope I know:
  My soul, since consciousness but sorrow is,
I would, O soul, thou wert asleep, or dead.

SONNET XXIII.

LOVE'S CONQUEROR.

BEHOLD, O Love ! thy conquest is complete ;
  Through every sense thy subtle forces stole,
  Until they won possession of the soul,
Where all is sad and branded by defeat.
Lo ! Peace lies slain, and Hope, with weary feet,
  Returns to me, not having gained the goal.
  Here, all the spring is bloomless, and the whole
Deep music of the sea no longer sweet.

But only, Love, be glad a little space,
  For one, far mightier than thou, shall come
  Who makes the piteous mouth of sorrow dumb.
Lo ! he shall cast thee down from thy high place ;
    No warder when He comes may keep the gate :
    Till then, rejoice : for me, behold I wait.

SONNET XXIV.

THE WIND'S MESSAGE.

I SAID : " What wouldst thou with my soul to-night,
  O wild March wind that wailest round the land ?
  Tell'st thou of some new grief even now at hand ?
Or dost thou in thy swift and sounding flight
But chant a requiem for a past delight ?
  Like moan of billows on a distant strand,
  Thy message which I fain would understand,
Comes down to me from Heaven's starless height."

Then sadder wailed the wind, and sadder yet,
  And swept with a great sudden rush of dole
  Across me, till I cried : " My lady's soul
Is stirred by Pity, and its currents set
    To me-ward, and to me she bids thee say,
    ' Those prayed in vain, grieve more than those
        who pray.' "

2

SONNET XXV.

BRIEF REST.

O Love ! O lord of all delight and woe !
   For all who hear, thy voice is still the same ;
   Thy hands cast down the body of wretched shame ;
Still to thy chosen children thou dost show
The marvellous, sacred images that glow
   Within thine inmost shrine where one deep flame,
   Intense and clear, of color without name,
Lights still the carven altars where they bow.

Brief rest is all I ask, O Love, of thee ;
A space wherein to look contentedly
   Upon the beauty of my lady's face,
   And mouth whereof the voice is its best praise ;
     To feel the joy, and not the bitterness,
     Of all her deep and silent loveliness.

SONNET XXVI.

AT DAWN.

Here, at this day's dawn, desolate and gray,
   Whose light divides the wan and watery skies,
   Seeing with troubled soul and sleepless eyes,
I think upon my love so far away.
Sees she, as I, the dawning of this day,
   Around whose birth the wind presaging sighs?
   Or roams her soul the twilight land that lies
'Twixt life and death, wherein all ghosts have sway, —

Wherein the pallid lips of days long dead
   Unclose and murmur as they hover round
   The souls that thread Sleep's mysteries without sound?
Lo ! even now, some day remembered,
   May to her heart be saying all I fain
   Would say myself, that she may hear again.

SONNET XXVII.

DIVINE PITY.

I WONDER when you gain the happy place,
   And walk above the marvel of the skies,
   And see the brows of God, and large sweet eyes
Of Christ look lovingly upon your face,
And find the friends of unforgotten days, —
   Will you, some time in that fair Paradise,
   While all its peaceful light around you lies,
To greet your lover lost, your dear eyes raise?

And when at length this thing you come to know, —
   How he, forbid to pass the heavenly bourne,
   Through undreamed distance roves with shades for-
      lorn, —
Will you be sorry, and, with eyes bent low,
   Wander apart the sudden wound to hide,
   And, meeting Mary, turn your face aside?

SONNET XXVIII.

TWILIGHT VIGIL.

HERE in the stillness of this fading day,
   Moveless, with lips apart and folded eyes
   Lovely in dreamless calm my lady lies;
And as one who, by some long weary way,
Has gained the land he longed for, will delay
   His sleep at night, because in heart he tries
   To walk once more 'neath bleak and unloved skies,
And lose this azure in their distant gray,

That he may start with rapturous surprise
   To find anew his bliss, — so, even now,
      From looking on her loveliness I turn
   To fancy that the seas between us flow.
      O foolish heart! dost thou not still discern
That gulfs impassable between us rise?

REMEMBERED WORDS.

Lo ! 'mid the fall and ruin of my days,
 One thing is sweet for my remembering, —
 Those words which once my strength of love did
  wring
From out my lady's soul, when face to face
We stood together for a little space.
 She felt my spirit to her spirit cling ;
 From every look she saw love's longing spring.
While all my soul was shaken to its base ;

Then from my passion turning half away,
Her heart conceived, and her lips found to say,
 The words whereby my soul is comforted ;
 Whereby my unbelieving heart was led
  To know at length her soul believed the love
  That had no way whereby its strength to prove.

DE PROFUNDIS.

Out of the depths, love, have I called to thee ;
 Love, hear my voice ; consider well, O love,
 The voice of my complaint. If prayers could move
Thy heart, O love, then wouldst thou pity me.
Look thou deep down into my soul and see
 The way in which I love thee ; test and prove
 The spirit's passion and the strength thereof.
O my beloved ! through change of years to be,

My life henceforth for thee anew begins.
 If I in heaven should thy rapture mar,
 I 'gainst myself the gates of peace would bar ;
  But shouldst thou have a whim to save my soul,
  Then will I strive indeed to reach the goal,
And thou shouldst me redeem from all my sins.

LOVE'S YEARNINGS.

I would I could believe the words men say,
   And think, despite of all, there ruled above,
   Some sure strong God, compassionate enough
To hear and pity spirits when they pray ;
That so from day to night, from night to day,
   In passionate strong praying I might prove
   The height, breadth, depth, and length of all my love.
So when soft dreams upon thy spirit lay,

I, sleepless, had devised sweet things for thee,
   Poured forth my soul in prayer, nor let God rest
     Till he had heard my prayers, and answered all.
     Prayers have I, but no God, at need, to call.
Then, in the absence of all Deity,
   Still show me, love, how I may serve thee best.

VAIN LOVE.

I would the wide waste waters of the deep
   Had met above me ere my eyes had seen
   The face of her who is my spirit's queen ;
Or would that Death had met with me in sleep,
And taken me where none may laugh or weep,
   Ere I had felt her hands on my hands lean :
   From out the fields of life shall I not glean
One year of joy, while others harvests reap ?

I would some snake about my life had wound,
   Ere in the calm, ineffable and sweet,
     Of that strange voice my soul had lain a space,
Faint, trembling in a Paradise of sound.
   How shall I bear once more her look to meet
     And feel we walk apart in separate ways ?

SONNET XXXIII.

ASSOCIATIONS.

Sweet is the voice that sings, and sweet the air;
　　But only sweet to me, because they bring
　　Back perfectly to my remembering
A tune as sad and passionate as pray'r, —
A tune I heard when life and love were fair;
　　When all the strong, sweet perfumes of the spring,
　　Did so about my lady's presence cling,
They seemed her very loveliness to share.

So, when I hear this tune, that other strain
Revives within me, and I see again
　　My lady's face; yea, then I do rejoice,
　　Recalling half-lost beauties of her voice;
　　　A little then the present off I cast,
　　　And walk 'mid lovely ruins of the past.

SONNET XXXIV.

BEFORE SEVERING.

There, let me gaze upon you ere I go, —
　　The supple body and the perfect face,
　　Half known before we met, through old sweet lays;
Or wondered on, with ecstasy and woe,
In some great picture such as dead years show;
　　But now, found fairer, in all gracious ways,
　　Than those which lacked the special, unnamed grace,
That makes your face the fairest man may know.

Speak once again, that I may hear your voice,
　　And madden on the beauty of each tone.
O love! be sorry for these poor dead joys!
　　Be sorry, O my sweet, for fair dreams flown!
　　　You had a little what in me was best,
　　　Now let all vile things fatten on the rest.

SONNET XXXV.

RETROSPECT.

OH, strange to me, and terrible it seems
　To think that, ere I met you, you and I
　Lived, both, beneath the same all-covering sky;
Had the same childhood's hopes and childhood's
　　schemes;
And, later on, our beautiful false dreams:
　The funerals of my dead joys passed me by,
　And things, expected long, at length drew nigh.
The joy that slays and sorrow that redeems

Were ours before that day whereon we met,
And all the weary way that God had set
　Between us was past over, and my soul
　Knew in your fatal loveliness its goal.
'T was mine to love, 't was yours, sweet, to forget;
　For you the haven, and for me the shoal.

SONNET XXXVI.

BODY AND SOUL.

ALL know the beauty of my lady's face,
　　The peace and passion of her deep gray eyes,
　　Her hair wherein gold warmth of sunlight lies,
Her mouth that makes as mockery all praise,
Her languorous low voice that hath such ways
　　Of unimagined music that the soul
　　Stands poised and trembling; breathless till the
　　　whole
Ends in an unhoped symphony of sighs:

But who as I my lady's soul shall know,
　　The deep tides of her nature that bear on
　　Till all the line of common life seems gone,
To hearts that weary of their boundaries grow, —
Then must I turn, O love, from thee to go
　　Through ways, to places, of thy soul unknown?

SONNET XXXVII.

DISTANT LIGHT.

Oh, when, love, do I think upon thee most?
  When life looks blackest, and when hope seems dead,
  When darkness over all the past is shed,
When, as men hear upon some darkened coast
The distant tumult of the ocean's host,
  I hear the future sound in places dread
  Through which full soon my spirit must be led.
Then does my soul, through sorrow well-nigh lost,

Look up to thy soul shining from afar,
As men at sea look up to some fair star
  Whose saving light may point the wanderer home.
   O love ! bear with me for a little space,
   Bear with the roar and tumult of my days,
  Till I am past the reach of wind and foam.

SONNET XXXVIII.

WHY DO I LOVE?

What is the thing for which I love thee best?
  It taxes me to say ; but this I know,
  Thy tender regal beauty moves me so
That my heart beats and leaps within my breast,
As might the sea 'twixt narrow shores compressed —
  Haply for this, or smiles that come and go
  About thy mouth, or music sweet and low
Of thy clear voice, wherein is perfect rest,

Or for high intellect, that as a light
  Kindles the mind that straight illumes thy face,
   Or for thy soul's deep tenderness that flows
  Through every tone, and lingers in thy gaze, —
For these known things I love with all love's might,
  And for the things beyond which no man knows.

SONNET XXXIX.

BEFORE MEETING.

So we shall meet within a little space,
   And on the face wherein no love has birth,
   Where nought is clear save beauty and the dearth
Of passions good or ill, I long shall gaze.
We shall not speak at all of vanished days,
   Of years that might have been, and made the earth
   All fair to me ; but words of little worth
Shall pass between us, standing face to face.

Too well I know the voice that I shall hear
   When her lips, parting, give forth sound more sweet
Then ever fell before on mortal ear —
   O heart of mine, be strong until we meet !
     Fill well thy *rôle* before her, O my heart,
     Till death shall end the playing of thy part.

SONNET XL.

WASTED STRENGTH.

AND has my love then no more use than this, —
   To waste its strength in waves of sterile song
   Upon life's shore, while heart and hand are strong
To dare for love's sake every ill that is?
O God, the dying patriot's final bliss,
   Who, though he see his land not free from wrong,
   Knows, as he stands above the shrieking throng,
He serves her dying, without crown or kiss !

The Pagans joy when for their gods they die
As Christians for their Christ : I, only I,
   Must worship what I may not serve at all.
     O thou, my land, my Christ, my God, my love !
     Find some sure way whereby love's strength to prove,
   Ere love and life in one vast ruin fall.

SONNET XLI.

LOVE'S SELFISHNESS.

AND have I no more share in thee, O sweet,
  Than any of the other men who gaze
  Well pleased upon the beauty of that face,
Whose eyes are glad, indeed, thine eyes to meet? —
I, who have laid my soul beneath thy feet ;
  I, who upon the ruin of my days
  To thee an everlasting shrine will raise,
That men in coming years with song shall greet ;

I, even I, whose pride it is to bear
  The cross which thou hast laid upon me, love ;
Who give thee bitter songs, as men give prayer
  To high and unknown gods, whom no prayers move, —
    I, who must long for thee through my life's night,
    More than the blind man ever longed for light.

SONNET XLII.

LOVE'S MAGNETISM.

O LOVE ! though far apart our bodies be,
  I think my soul must somehow touch thine heart,
  And make thee, in the dusk of slumber start,
To feel my strong love beat and surge round thee,
O one sweet island of my soul's waste sea !
  Serene and fair, and passionless thou art ;
  Why should my sorrow of thy life make part,
Or shade the face burnt in my memory ?

And when I dreaming pace the tawny sand,
If thou wert on the opposite fair strand,
  And my heart should with love to thy heart yearn,
  I do believe thou couldst not choose but turn
    And look across the sea, my way, until,
    Not knowing why, my soul should burn and thrill.

SONNET XLIII.

LOVE'S SHRINES.

ALL places that have known my love at all
  Have grown as sympathetic friends to me,
  And each for song has some dear memory;
Some perfume of her presence clings to all;
How then to me, O love, shall it befall,
  When I no longer in my life shall see
  The places that through love have grown to be
Of buried dreams the mute memorial?

Then surely shall I seem as one who stands
Exiled from home in unfamiliar lands,
  And strains, across the weary sea and long,
His desolate sad eyes, and wrings his hands,
  While round him press an undiscerning throng
  Of strange men talking in an alien tongue.

SONNET XLIV.

SEVERED FOREVER.

O LOVE ! when the great gulfs between us are,
  When all is said that you or I can say,
  When you have made your choice and gone your way,
While in strange lands, unlit by any star, —
But full of storm and flame, and all the jar
  Of shrill, strained music such as fiends may play,
  When on some soul, long waited for as prey,
Their hands the gates of hell in thunder bar, —

I walk, and heap new nights and barren days
  Upon my weary soul to keep your face
From rising up to look at me, and daze
  My sense once more with its beguiling grace, —
    Then you may know, across a dead soul's grave,
    How love is strong to slay as well as save.

SONNET XLV.

LOVE PAST UTTERANCE.

I AM a painter, and I love you so
   I cannot paint your face for very love.
   My heart is like a sea that tempests move,
Wherein no ship its certain path may know;
I can but gaze upon you till you grow
   Lonely and distant as the skies above:
   How then to man shall I my worship prove,
And unto coming worlds your beauty show?

I am a poet; but my love is such
   I cannot tell the marvel of your voice,
Or show the laugh that thrills me like a kiss;
The very recollection of your touch
   O'ercomes me like a sudden tide of joys,
   And my heart gasps for breath 'twixt waves of bliss.

SONNET XLVI.

UNSOLVED.

MAIMED from my birth, and nowise fair to see,
   The soul aflame in me was keen and strong
   To shape my sorrows into burning song;
Such was I when she first discovered me.
O face, O voice, O one sweet memory!
   Her touch I thought a trifle kind and long
   For mere indifference; but I did her wrong
To think upon a thing that could not be.

I said, " 'T is only pity makes her kind,
   I will not vex her by a useless pain;"
   And turned me from the sunlight of her face:—
Now I am old, not only maimed, but blind;
   I cannot guess if love did wax or wane,
   And God alone her spirit's veil shall raise.

SONNET XLVII.

HOPELESS LOVE.

SHE came to me as comes sometimes in sleep
  A mystic midnight vision, strange and fair;
  The beauty of her presence tranced the air;
And as she came I felt my soul up-leap
'To see her face, and for pure passion weep;
  She paused a moment, and swept back her hair.
  And looked upon my face, as seeking there
Some little sign in after years to keep.

Then, mad with love and strong with love's despair,
  With open arms to bar her path I strove:
    But "I must pass," she said; so I gave way,
And then I felt the barrenness of prayer,
  The fearful bitterness of hopeless love —
    My God, which thing is worse, to love or pray?

SONNETS XLVIII., XLIX., L.

SONNETS TO A VOICE.

I.

ROSSINI and Beethoven and Mozart,
  And all the other men of mighty name,
  Together joined their previous work to shame;
The subtlest mystery of their god-like art
To that most magic voice they did impart.
  Oh, from what kingdom of rare music came
  A voice on which alone might rest such fame
As never yet made glad one mortal's heart?

A star of sound, set far above the din
    And dust of life, a shade wherein to lie
  Faint with the sudden ecstasy of bliss,
A voice to drown remembrance of sin,
    A voice to hear and for the hearing die,
  As Antony for Cleopatra's kiss!

II.

A CLEAR voice made to comfort and incite,
   Lovely and peaceful as a moonlit deep, —
   A voice to make the eyes of strong men weep
With sudden overflow of great delight ;
A voice to dream of in the calm of night ;
   A voice — the song of fields that no men reap,
   A treasure wrung by God himself from sleep !
A voice no song may follow in its flight ;

A queenly rose of sound with tune for scent ;
   A pause of shadow in a day of heat ;
     A voice to make God weak as any man,
     And at its pleadings take away the ban
'Neath which so long our spirits have been bent, —
   A voice to make death tender and life sweet !

III.

THERE is no other sound in heaven, I trow ;
   God and His angels bow from their high place
   To hear the smallest word which that voice says ;
And they do well, indeed, to listen so,
For they can hear it, though its tones are low ;
   They must have learnt by heart its gracious ways,
   Its fluctuant languor, and low laughter's grace, —
Such tune as man again shall never know.

O winds ! O birds ! O rushing streams and seas !
   And all things that make music for a space,
     Be still, grow mute ! for one who hears that voice
     Can no more in your lesser sounds rejoice.
O voice of rest ! O amplitude of peace !
   Sound deified, — a bliss that beggars praise !

SONNET LI.

A VISION OF DAYS.

THE days whereof my heart is still so fain
  Passed by my soul in strange and sad procession :
  And one said, " Lo, I held thy love's confession ! "
And one, " My hands were filled with golden gain
Of thy love's sweetnesses now turned to pain ! "
  And one, " I heard thy soul's last sad concession ! "
  And one, " For thee my voice made intercession ! "
And one, " I wept above thy sweet hopes slain ! "

Then followed, in a long and mournful band,
  Days wreathed with cloud and garmented with gray ;
  And all made moan upon their weary way : —
But one Day walked apart ; and in her hand,
Before her face, she held a sorcerer's wand ;
  And what she said I heard, but may not say.

SONNET LII.

PARTING WORDS.

GOOD-BY, O love ! once more I hold your hand :
  Good-by, for now the wind blows loud and long ;
  The ship is ready, and the waves are strong
To bear me far away from this your strand :
I know the sea that I shall cross, the land
  Whereto I journey, and the forms that throng
  Its palaces and shrines ; I know the song
That they alone can sing and understand.

But promise me, O love, before I go
  That sometimes, when the sun and wind are low,
You, walking in the old familiar ways
Thronged with gray phantoms of the buried days,
  Will, looking seaward, say, " I wonder now
How fares it with him in the distant place ? "

SONNET LIII.

PRESENTIMENT.

WHEN, after parting long and sore, we twain
   Met, and stood soul to soul as face to face,
   While yet her hand in mine was, and her gaze
Made the blood burn and leap through every vein, —
When thus, 'twixt risen joy and fallen pain,
   We stood with Love in his own time and place,
   My soul had foresight of the coming days
When, parted, we should never meet again.

O days expected long, and are ye here?
Come ye with clouded brows and eyes austere,
   Or with blithe faces making glad the sight, —
I know your song for curse, your laugh for jeer :
   Which, then, is worse, — your mockery of light,
   Or the dumb darkness of the hopeless night?

SONNET LIV.

LOVE AND HOPE.

A VOICE within me whispered, " Hope is sped :
   He will not stir again, so still he lies.
   Alas ! for all his sweet false prophecies,
Love sits and weeps above his silent bed ;
His life is ended as a tune outplayed."
   But while the voice was speaking in this wise,
   My lady came and said, " Forbear thy sighs,
For sleep, not death, upon this hope is laid."

Thereat hope rose, and smiled a little space ;
   But after this came love to me, and said,
   " No sleep but death now on thy hope is shed."
Then came my lady, and with steadfast gaze
Looked on me and passed by with bended face.
   And so I knew that hope at last was dead.

SONNET LV.

LOVE'S MUSIC.

LOVE held a harp between his hands, and lo !
    The master hand, upon the harp-strings laid,
    By way of prelude such a sweet tune played
As made the heart with happy tears o'erflow ;
Then sad and wild did that strange music grow,
    And like the wail of woods by storm gusts swayed,
    While yet the awful thunder's wrath is stayed,
And Earth lies faint beneath the coming blow, —

Still wilder waxed the tune ; until at length
    The strong strings, strained by sudden stress and sharp
        Of that musician's hand intolerable,
And jarred by sweep of unrelenting strength,
        Sundered, and all the broken music fell.
Such was Love's music, — lo, the shattered harp !

SONNET LVI.

SUMMER'S RETURN.

ONCE more I walk 'mid summer days, as one
    Returning to the place where first he met
    The face that he till death may not forget ;
I know the scent of roses just begun,
And how at evening and at morn the sun
    Falls on the places that remember yet
    What feet last year within their bounds were set,
And what sweet things were said, and dreamed, and done.

The sultry silence of the summer night
    Recalls to me the loved voice far away ;
    Oh, surely I shall see, some blessed day,
In places that last year with love were bright,
        The face of her I love ; and hear the low,
        Sweet, troubled music of the voice I know.

SONNET LVII.

FINIS.

My lady has no heart in her for love :
　Her soul can understand the mountain's peace,
　And the blue quiet of the summer seas,
Or scented warmth of the dim, thick-leaved grove
That hears the low lament of one lone dove ;
　But when the skies grow black and winds increase,
　And rains and sudden lightnings charge the trees,
And seas at length in strife begin to move, —

She joyless stands, amid the flame and noise
　Of storms that rend the night and lift the main ;
Her griefs are pale, and flameless all her joys :
　How should she know, then, love's great bliss and
　　　bane ?
　O love ! has all my singing been in vain ?
My songs are ended ; hast thou heard no voice ?

GARDEN SECRETS.

THE DISPUTE.

The Grass.

I FELT upon me, as she passed, her feet.

The Beech.

'Neath my green shade she sheltered from the heat.

A Rose.

She plucked me as she passed, and in her breast
Wore me, and I was to her beauty prest.

The Wind.

And now ye lie neglected, withering fast,
And the grass withers too, and when have pass'd
These golden summer days, O Beech, no more
She 'll sit beneath thy shade; but I endure,
To kiss her when I will; so more than ye
Am I made blest in my felicity.

WHAT THE ROSE SAW.

The Rose.

O LILY sweet, I saw a pleasant sight.

The Lily.

Where saw you it, and when?

The Rose.

Here ; when the night
Lay calmly over all and covered us,
And no wind blew, however tremulous,
I heard afar the light fall of her feet
And murmur of her raiment soft and sweet.

The Lily.

What said she to you when she came anear?

The Rose.

No word, but o'er me bent till I could hear
The beating of her heart, and feel her blood
Swell to a blossom that which was a bud.
Alas ! I have no words to tell the bliss
When on my trembling petals fell her kiss ;
Sweeter than soft rain falling after heat,
Or dew at dawn, was that kiss soft and sweet.
Then fell another shadow on the ground,
And for a little space there was no sound.
I knew who stood beside her — saw his face
Shining and happy in that happy place —
I knew not what they said ; but this I know
They kissed and passed : where think you did they go?

THE ROSE AND THE WIND.

Dawn.

The Rose.

When think you comes the Wind,
The Wind that kisses me and is so kind?
Lo, how the Lily sleeps ! her sleep is light ;
Would I were like the Lily, pale and white !
Will the Wind come?

The Beech.

Perchance for you too soon.

The Rose.

If not, how could I live until the noon?
What, think you, Beech-tree, makes the Wind delay?
Why comes he not at breaking of the day?

The Beech.

Hush, child, and, like the Lily, go to sleep.

The Rose.

You know I cannot.

The Beech.

Nay, then, do not weep.

(*After a pause.*)

Your lover comes, be happy now, O Rose!
He softly through my bending branches goes.
Soon he shall come, and you shall feel his kiss.

The Rose.

Already my flushed heart grows faint with bliss;
Love, I have longed for you through all the night.

The Wind.

And I to kiss your petals warm and bright.

The Rose.

Laugh round me, Love, and kiss me; it is well.
Nay, have no fear, the Lily will not tell.

MORNING.

The Rose.

'T was dawn when first you came; and now the sun
Shines brightly and the dews of dawn are done.

'T is well you take me so in your embrace ;
But lay me back again into my place,
For I am worn, perhaps with bliss extreme.

The Wind.

Nay, you must wake, Love, from this childish dream.

The Rose.

'T is you, Love, who seem changed ; your laugh is loud,
And 'neath your stormy kiss my head is bowed.
O Love, O Wind, a space will you not spare ?

The Wind.

Not while your petals are so soft and fair.

The Rose.

My buds are blind with leaves, they cannot see, —
O Love, O Wind, will you not pity me ?

EVENING.

The Beech.

O Wind, a word with you before you pass ;
What did you to the Rose that on the grass
Broken she lies and pale, who loved you so ?

The Wind.

Roses must live and love, and winds must blow.

THE GARDEN'S LOSS.

A Lily.

HE will not speak to us again :
No more the sudden summer rain
Will fall from off his trembling leaves :
Even the scentless Tulip grieves.

Ah me ! the loud noise of that night,
And that fierce blaze of blinding light
That slew him in the midst of bliss —
Reach out, O Rose, and let us kiss !

The Rose.

He was a friend to all indeed ;
Even the wild unlovely Weed
Loved him and clove unto his root :
When next winds blow he shall be mute.

The Lily.

He was the noblest of all trees.

A Tulip.

Your sorrow cannot bring you ease.

The Lily.

Still we must mourn so great a one.

The Rose.

I would the summer-time were done !
The birds we loved sang in his boughs,
And in his branches made their house ;
All graciously he bowed and swayed,
And, when of winds we were afraid,
How tenderly his boughs he moved,
A loving tree and well beloved.

An Elm.

He was a noble tree and vast ;
His branches revelled in the blast :
I always took him for our king.

Yet better that he was so slain,
In midst of his loved wind and rain,
Than some sharp axe should lay him low.

The Rose.

Better! but now I only know
He shall not speak again to me —
Nor, Lily, shall he speak to thee.

POEMS.

A CHRISTMAS VIGIL.

ROUND the vast city draws the twilight gray;
     I know men say
This evening is the eve of Christmas Day;
But what has Christmas-time to do with me,
Who live a shameful life out, shamelessly?
A creature now that doth not even yearn
      From sin to turn;
Too blind, perchance, it may be to discern
God's mighty mercy, and the boundless love
That those paid, praying preachers tell us of.

Here he lies dead, with whom my shame began!
     This is the man,
Through whom my life to such dishonor ran.
His was the snare in which my soul was caught;
Oh, the sweet ways wherein for love he wrought!
Yet God, not he, my wrath of soul shall bear,
      God set the snare!
God made him lustful, and God made me fair.
O God! were not his kisses more to me
Than Christians' hopes of immortality?

O lovely, wasted fingers, lithe and long,
     So kind and strong!
O lips, wherein all laughter was a song,

All song as laughter !   Oh, the cold, calm face,
The speechless marble mouth, that had such ways
Of singing, that for very joy of it
      My heart would beat
Almost as loud as when our lips would meet,
And all love's passion, hotter for its shame,
Set panting mouths and thirsting eyes on flame.

Thus, would I part his hair back from the brow;
      But look you now,
What thing is left for me, save this, to bow
Myself unto him, as in days gone by,
To stretch myself beside him, and to die ;
To crush my burning, aching lips on his,
      In one long kiss ;
And know how cold and strange a thing death is?
His lips are cold, but my lips are so hot,
That all death's fearful coldness chills them not.

Fast falls the night, and down the iron street,
      Loud ring the feet
Of happy people, who pass on to meet
Fair sights of home ; I hear the roll and roar
Of traffic, like a sea upon a shore.
One dying candle's pallid light is shed
      Upon the bed
Whereon is laid my beautiful, cold dead, —
Mine, altogether mine, for two brief days !
Are not these hands his hands ; this face his face?

And now I can recall the time gone by,
      The pure fresh sky
Of spring, 'neath which we first met, he and I,
The smell of rainy fields in early spring,
The song of thrushes, and the glimmering

Of rain-drenched leaves by sudden sun made bright ;
> The tender light

Of peaceful evening, and the saintly night.
Sweet, still, the scent of roses ; only this,
They had a perfume then which now I miss.

Yea, too, I can recall the night wherein
> Did first begin

The joy of that intoxicating sin.
Late was the day in April, gray and still,
Too faint to gladden, and too mild to chill ;
Hot lay upon my lips the last night's kiss,
> The first of his :

I wandered blindly between shame and bliss ;
And, yearning, hung all day about the lane,
Where, in the evening, he should come again.

Now, when the time of the sun's setting came,
> The sky caught flame ;

For all the sun, which as an empty name
Had been that day, then rent the leaden veil
And flashed out sharp, 'twixt watery clouds, and pale,
Then, suddenly, a stormy wind upsprang,
> That shrieked and sang ;

Around the reeling tree-tops, loud it rang,
And all was dappled blue, and faint, fresh gold,
Lovely and virgin, wild and sweet and cold.

Then through the wind I heard his voice ring out ;
> And half in doubt,

Trembling and glad, I turned, and looked about,
And saw him standing in my downward way,
Full in the splendor of the dying day.
Silent I stood a space, and then at last
> Strong arms were cast

About me, and his burning spirit passed
Into my spirit, till the twain as one
Shone out together under passion's sun.

I felt that joy unnamable was near;
A great sweet fear
Fell all around me, and no thing was clear
To me save this, — that in his arms I lay,
And felt his kisses burn my soul away.
I heard the wild wind singing in my hair,
And saw the fair
Green branches tossing in the stormy air;
And, through the failing light, I heard a voice
That cried, " O soul, at least this night rejoice ! "

Ah me ! the shameless, limitless delight
Of that spring night !
The magic ways wherein, 'twixt dusk and light,
I wandered, dazed and faint with joy's excess —
Ah, God ! what human creature shall express
That night's dear joy, the long thirst quenched at last,
All shame outcast,
The haven entered, and the tempest past?
O shameful, sacred night, whereby alone
I bear with life till life's last day be done !

But when the feverish night had passed away,
And faint and gray,
On wet, chill April fields calm broke the day,
I rose, and in an altered world had part;
Love, marred by shame, lay bitter at my heart.
Through all my daily rounds that day I went,
Till day was spent ;
And with the night once more came sweet content,
And joy that shut out every thought of shame,
And made of infamy an empty name.

Then quickly came the waste, gold, summer days,
The blinding blaze
Of burning sunlight, and the sultry ways

Of breathless nights, wherein the moon seemed strange,
And with the scent of roses came the change ;
Yea, when as naked blades sharp-edged and bright,
'Neath blasting light,
Sharp flashed the streams ; when every coming night,
Solemn with moonlight, or with stars thrilled through,
Or quite unlit but passionately blue,

Was sweet as rest, — 'mid song and scent and flame,
To me there came
The sense of loss, and bitterness of shame.
Surely between his kisses he had said,
" O love ! before the summer-time has fled
I will return, and thou with me shalt come
To a fair home."
My kisses answered, for my voice was dumb.
Ah, God ! those terrible June days, wherein
No rapture came to hush the cry of sin.

O sickening perfume of those summer days !
O tree-girt ways
Wherein we wandered !   O the happy place
Where first I burst on love, and love on me !
O sleepless nights when tears fell bitterly !
So died the Summer, and the Autumn sweet,
With languid feet,
And recollections of the by-gone heat
Came down to us ; but still he came no more,
And then I knew my destiny was sure.

I know not how, at length, when hope was gone,
And shame had grown
Too sharp a thing to be endured alone,
I left the peaceful country far behind,
And to the mighty city came to find
Some opiate for pain, and found it, too.
Fresh passions grew
Within me ; and a little while I knew

The bitter joys that set the blood on flame, —
So grief slays joy, and wretchedness slays shame.

But still, through every feverish night and day,
     The old love lay
Hot at my heart, though he had gone his way,
As I had mine; sometimes of him I heard,
And how the world was by his spirit stirred.
Then came the news, how he lay dying here!
     I shed no tear,
I only felt the time at length was near,
When meeting I should see his face again,
And feel, through all, I had not lived in vain.

And now it is two nights ago, since first
     With eyes athirst
To see his face, resolved to know the worst,
I came in here, and stood beside his bed.
No look he gave me, and no word he said;
But I said, bowing down, and speaking low, —
     "Two years ago
You slew my honor; and I come here now
To tell you, whether yet you die or live,
Lost as I am, I love you, and forgive."

He turned, and then I knew that he would speak;
     Against my cheek
Hot beat the blood; I stood there dazed and weak.
He said: "O face and voice that I remember!
'T was July then, and now it is December;
Poor dove! that all God's hawks for prey have got.
     Ah me! how hot
This fever burns, and she remembers not
The ways of love wherein last June we trod! —
They work their will, this woman and her God."

Thus, as towards ending of his speech he drew,
     I only knew
Some other bitter mem'ry had come through

His thoughts of me, and set his soul adrift;
Then, as he backward fell, I saw him lift
Bright hollow eyes unto the wall, whereon
                  A picture shone, —
A picture now that from the wall has gone;
A portrait of a woman strange as fair,
With calm gray eyes, and wayward golden hair.

The pale, calm face, immovable and sad,
                Such beauty had
As well might make with love a strong man mad.
The long sweet hands upon her breast were laid,
The full throat just a little back was swayed,
Its firm white beauty better to expose;
                The mouth kept close
The spirit's secret of all joys and woes.
So calm and still he lay I thought he slept,
Till, bending nearer down, I knew he wept.

And then he said, as one who speaks in dreams, —
            "O face that gleams
Upon me when in sleep my spirit seems
To walk with thine! O long-loved love, O sweet,
O vanished eyes, O unreturning feet!
O heart that all the tempest of my love
             Could no way move!
O death, is not the end now sharp enough, —
To love her, and to lose her, and to die,
While she knows not how life is going by?

"Could she know all, I think she would arise,
            And let her eyes,
Wherein the very calm of heaven lies,
Fall on my face; yea, too, I do believe,
So sweet her sweet soul is, that she would grieve

A little space, in silence sitting here,
        To see draw near
Death's sea o'er which no light and land appear;
Yea, too, with words and touches she might make
The death-ward path smile as a flowering brake."

Then all his love came on him, and he cried, —
        " O death ! divide
My soul from thought of hers; O darkness ! hide
The passionless cold face, and speechless mouth
By mine unkissed, that waste my soul with drought !
O love, and must I die unkissed by thee ?
        What man shall be
The chosen one to come 'twixt thee and me ? "
Then forth into the air he stretched his hand,
As one who, drowning, strives to reach the land.

Upon his brow a trembling touch I laid,
        And tearless said,—
" Lie down and rest."   Then, as the rain is shed
When awful thunder-storms break up the heat,
My kisses on his lips and eyelids beat,
My fingers met and closed within his hair,
        He was so fair;
And, like the unhoped granting of a prayer,
Such prayers as dying men for life must pray,
At length upon my hand his kisses lay.

Then by him, bowed with all my love, I fell,
        And cried, " 'T is well,
Live yet, and in thy presence let me dwell ! "
He smiled, and said, "O tender hands and kind,
O lovely, worshipped hands that now I find
So sweet, so sweet ! O love, that bringest bliss,
        What joy is this
To gain at last the heaven of thy kiss ? "
And then he turned himself, gave thanks and sighed,
Nor spake again; and in the dawn he died.

My lips sealed up his eyes, my hands were spread
                              Beneath his head.
I stretched the lovely limbs upon the bed,
Folded the wasted hands upon the breast;
As there he lay in calm and frozen rest,
The drawn and rigid lips looked cold and stern,
                              That seemed to spurn
All joys and griefs; no soul was left to yearn
Within the hollow, dreamless, lampless eyes,
Whose death-look said the dead soul shall not rise.

I know not whether I did wrong or right,
                              But in the night
I came into his room, and raised the light
Unto the pictured face upon the wall
That looked on his, and was not moved at all;
I took it down, — the face indeed was fair, —
                              But, standing there,
I spurned it with my foot as God spurns prayer;
And lacking strength, not will, to spoil the face,
I cast it forth where none might know its grace.

And yet I think sometimes if he could know,
                              Loving her so, —
As men, O God, can love and bear with woe, —
He might be angry for the face downcast,
And for it come to hate me, at the last.
But now the heavy tread upon the stair
                              Of men who bear
Some strange thing up; they come, they will not spare.
O God! they come, and now the door goes back;
They smell of death, the thing they bear is black.

4

SHAKE HANDS AND GO.

COME now, behold, how small a thing is love;
   How long ago is it since, side by side,
   We stood together, in that summer-tide,
   And heard the June sea, blue and deep and wide,
Murmuring as one that in her dreams doth move
   To thoughts of love's first kiss and beauty's pride?

How long is it?   But one brief year ago, —
   One autumn, and one winter, and one spring;
   Now, as last year, the birds awake and sing,
   Once more unto the hills the hill-flowers cling.
How is it with you?   What heart you have, I know,
   Changes with every comer and fresh thing.

And yet, I think you loved me for a space;
   At all events you loved my love of you:
   Whether to me or that your love was due
   I know not.   While it lived perchance 't was true;
But you forget each season and each face,
   And love the new as long as it is new.

Scan o'er that time, as at the close of day
   One thinks what he has done or left undone;
   Know you those days when noontide heats of sun
   Smote full upon us, and we strove to shun
Their flaming force and took the sheltered way
   'Neath shading trees, with green leaves softly spun

There in an island of dim green and shade
   We paused, while round, like a great silent sea,
   Lay the blue, blinding, burning day; but we
   Knew nothing save our own life's melody,
And there, until the day was done, delayed;
   Then homeward wended o'er the dewy lea.

Know you those moonlit nights upon the sand, —
  The golden sand beside the lucid deep, —
  Where soft waves rippled as they sang in sleep;
  How there we sowed what I alone shall reap?
Nay, feign not thus to draw away your hand,
  Nor droop your lids; I know you cannot weep.

O pliant crimson lips and bright cold eyes, —
  Lips that my lips have pressed, and fingers sweet
  That lay about my neck, or soft, would meet
  Around my eyes to screen them from the heat;
Where are your words, where is our paradise?
  Your love was warm as summer — and as fleet.

And yet, behold, with some how strong is love;
  How helpless is the dupe that boasts a heart!
  I know you now, and yet regret to part.
  Fairer than ever, in the marriage mart
You 'll fetch your price; time's dealings that are rough
  With nature, leave untouched the works of art.

Well, kiss once more as in the gone-by time;
  Let your hair mix with mine; take hands again.
  Your kiss is sweet — and do you only feign?
  There, look once more on jutting cliff and main;
And now go hence, while I in some sad rhyme
  Weave our love's tale, — brief joy and lasting pain.

Go, go thy way; return not to the gates
  Of the fair past, forsake the dear dead days;
  I know thou wilt. I to some distant place
  May wander, and forget your voice and face.
Ah, let us say " Good-by ! " I know one waits;
  He paid his price, and for his purchase stays.

TO A CHILD.

I KISS you, dear, and very sweet is this,
To feel you are not tainted by my kiss ;
   Cling with your warm soft arms about me so,
   Give me one small sweet kiss and murmur low,
In speech as sweet as broken music is.

How long shall God my Lily darling give
Untainted by the shrieking world to live? —
   I cannot tell ; but this my wish shall be,
   Longer at least than God has given me.
Ah, sweet, be glad ; as yet, you need not grieve.

There, see, I put the hair back from your face,
And if my lips in kissing should displace
   Your sunny hair, you will but laugh, my child, —
   A babbling silver laugh and undefiled :
God keep it so, through the all-ruling days.

But, I, who in the darkness sit alone,
With heart that, once rebellious, now has grown
   Too weak to strive with foes that smite unseen,
   Will only ask you once your head to lean
Upon this heart which grief has made his throne.

I will not tell you of the things I know ;
I cannot bar the path that you must go ;
   God's bitter lesson must be learnt by all ;
   But, living, I will listen to your call,
And stretch to you a hand that you may know.

You feel the wind against you as you run,
And love its strength, and revel in the sun.
   So once did I, and but for this last blow,
   Of which none other knows, so might I now ;
But now for me the light of life is done.

These little hands that lose themselves in mine,
May some day haply in a man's hair twine,
　　While 'neath their touch his heart shall palpitate ;
　　Then will your soul with triumph be elate,
And mix sharp poison in a maddening wine?

But see you keep your lips from tasting sweet ;
For it begets within us such a heat
　　As cooling waters never can allay.
　　We see, through mists of blood and tears, the day,
Until we sicken for the nightfall's feet.

There, there, you 're weary, and I let you go ;
But this kiss, softer than a flake of snow,
　　I will remember when alone I stand.
　　I wonder will you ever understand
The reason why I loved and kissed you so.

BEFORE BATTLE.

HERE in this place, where none can see,
　　Lean out your throat, and let us kiss ;
Who knows? — to-morrow I may be
　　As far from any joy like this,
As is my own sea-beaten strand
　　　　　　　　From this fair land.

She put the hair back from her face,
　　And kissed him on his eager mouth ;
Her kiss was warm, and long her gaze,
　　He felt the passion of his youth
Burn fierce through every thrilling vein,
　　　　　　　　Till it was pain.

He filled for her a cup of wine,
　　The sparkling wine as red as blood ;
She quickly drank, and for a sign
　　He kissed its edge, as saints the rood,
Before Death plucks their souls away,
　　　　　　Too faint to pray.

He said, " O love, the wine is sweet,
　　But, sweet, thy kiss is sweeter still ! "
She flushed, with sudden joy and heat ;
　　She said, " O love, then take thy fill
Of both these things, for both thine are,
　　　　　　Before the war."

Another cup of wine he quaffed,
　　Then in his arms her form he pressed.
He murmured low ; she sighed and laughed, —
　　And they clung fiercely breast to breast :
While all her hair fell round his face,
　　　　　　Her love to grace.

She thrilled with passion, till her lips
　　Could nothing do but kiss and cleave ;
Their souls were like sea-driven ships.
　　He felt her swelling bosom heave ;
His lips her lips with kisses flaked,
　　　　　　Till both lips ached.

His face above her fair, flushed face,
　　Now seemed a thing to wonder on ;
Her soul was ravished by his gaze,
　　Her warm, wet eye-lids shook and shone,
Till, leaning back, for pure delight,
　　　　　　She laughed outright.

He wrung her long sweet fingers out ;
  He drained the passion of her mouth ;
Her hair was all his face about, —
  O life to life ! O youth to youth !
O sea of joy, whose foam is fire !
          O great desire !

But, suddenly, a sharp, shrill sound
  Cut like a sword their dear delight.
Once more his arms about her wound ;
  They felt their pulses beat and smite.
At last he said, in accents low,
          " The foe ! the foe ! "

Then quickly from her arms he sprang ;
  For all the night-black winding street
With clash of deadly weapons rang,
  And sudden storm of passing feet.
She heard the thunder of the drum, —
          Her lips grew dumb.

" O one night's love ! Good-by ! " he said,
  And kissed her on the lips, and passed.
She heard his quick, departing tread ;
  She saw the torches glare at last ;
She saw the street grow light as day,
          And swooned away.

A long hour afterwards, or more,
  With stormy music, loud and strong,
With light behind, and light before,
  The men marched down, an armèd throng ;
And as they passed, he saw her light
          Still burning bright.

She from her chamber-window leant,
    Deep down into the street to gaze ;
Her head upon her hands was bent :
    He looked, but could not see her face ,
But still he thought, through sound and flame,
                    She cried his name.

She watched the torches fade away,
    She listened till the street grew still,
Then back upon her bed she lay,
    Of her own thoughts to drink her fill ;
And afterwards, when others wept,
                    She only slept.

Next night she revelled in the dance,
    She quaffed her wine, she sang her song ;
While he, with soldier's eyes askance,
    And heart with lust of slaying strong,
Leaped laughing into battle's hell,
                    And struck and fell !

UPON THE SHORE.

ALL, love, is as it was this time last year,
    When we together stood as now we stand,
    By the same sea, on the same curving strand ;
And, as last year we heard, so now we hear
The rippling of the water cool and clear !

The old grief still goes with me near and far,
    Like the sweet burden of a mournful air
    Full of the sadness of unanswered prayer ;
Not sad with discords strange that strike and jar,
But sad as early autumn twilights are.

And you?　You know I do not blame you, sweet ;
　My lot was sore and had but little ease,
　And his was smooth and soft, a path of peace, —
Ah, well it was, love, that the path was smooth
For your soft beauty and your untried youth.

Let us recall the past a little space, —
　That night of summer storm, when on the shore
　We heard athwart the sea the thunder roar,
And sound of rising wind, and saw the blaze
Of lightning all about the sea-girt place.

That night you leaned your head upon my breast,
　As now upon another breast you lean.
　O days gone by, O days that might have been !
To love is good, no doubt ; but you love best
A calm safe life, with wealth and ease and rest.

Gifts he will bring you, dear, each mood to please ;
　And make life soft and pleasant for your feet ;
　But will he give you love like mine, O sweet,
From which my heart can never know release
Till death and darkness bring me perfect peace ?

Nay, let us once take hands before we part ;
　You bore — half prized — my love a little while, —
　'T was something that long summer to beguile !
There, see, I kiss the hand that cast the dart ;
You gave me grief, and I gave you my heart !

WAITING.

WHEN shall I see that land where I would tread;
That shrine where I would fain bow knee and head?
In autumn — ere the autumn pass, I said;
In winter — ere the winter-time is sped;
In spring — ere yet spring's fair sweet feet are fled;
In summer — ere the summer-time is shed, —
And now I say, perchance when I am dead.

IN PRAISE OF HER.

WHAT thing is there on earth to which I can
    My love compare?
So far she is beyond all praise of man,
    That speech is bare
    To say how fair
She is beyond comparison.

Her nature seems like some warm summer sea,
    That bears alone
The utmost glory, and the majesty
    Of all the sun,
    Till day be done,
Then takes the stars for company.

As children who for cooling waters crave
    On some hot day,
And in the ebb of the retreating wave,
    Are glad to play,
    And feel the spray
Their gleaming, panting bodies lave, —

So in the shallows of her nature we
           Are glad to move :
I know not if on earth a man there be
           Found strong enough
           The depths thereof
To reach, in calm security.

Yea, all the music of a summer deep
           Her tones possess ;
Such melody as comes when light winds sleep,
           And souls confess
           Joy's keen excess
In tears that are most sweet to weep.

O deep, kind sea ! O passionate, wild sea !
           Thy strong tides flow
'Twixt God's vast life and our mortality ;
           Yet who shall know
           Where thy waves go, —
Who say where the far strand may be ?

IN GRIEF.

WITH thee so vanished, our life's light has flown ;
   A sudden night has fallen on the day, —
A cheerless, moonless night, with no white way
Of stars that lead to lands of men unknown ;
   A night wherein the winds of grief are loud ;
   A night made black with sorrow as a cloud ;
   A night that wraps its darkness as a shroud
Around a world now sad and cold and gray.

God fashioned thee and gave thy spirit birth,
   To ease a little our sore load of pain ;
   More sweet to us thy love was than the rain
Is, after long hot days, to the parched earth.

Thou wert a refuge in a stormy deep;
From thee there flowed a peace like conscious sleep.
I will not sow sweet things, who may not reap;
I will not strive, who nothing here may gain.

As is, to one within his dungeon's gloom,
A sudden burst of music and of light,
Cleaving the darkness, trancing ear and sight, —
Making resplendent what is still his tomb, —
So, living, to my prisoned soul thou wert;
Now all once more is dark about my heart, —
No light, nor any sound its depth shall part,
And there shall be no daybreak to this night.

Now all is done; no more is left to do.
A space we stood together on life's shore
Waving weak hands to those who went before;
Thou knowest now if heavenly skies are blue;
Thou knowest if the after-world is sweet: —
Dost thou tread light or darkness 'neath thy feet?
When with weak hands upon the gate we beat,
Will it be opened, or closed evermore?

And shall we meet with lips that yearn to kiss, —
Meet soul to soul as face to face on earth?
And shall there be an end of death and dearth?
Yea, shall there be a harvest-time of bliss;
And shall we stand together side by side,
Never again to sorrow or divide?
And shall at length our hearts be satisfied,
Full of the wonder of the second birth?

Shall this life past be as a dream outdreamed, —
The ghastly fancy of a fevered brain?
Shall we at all remember the old pain,
So great it past all human bearing seemed?

If angels tell us of that mournful time,
Will it then sound but as an empty rhyme
Made by a boy in some forgotten clime?
Ah, shall we say we have not lived in vain?

Shall we stand up before the face of God,
Stand up and sing a loud, glad song of praise,
And bless him for the sorrow of our days,
And kiss with pure cold lips the burning rod
Wherewith he hath so stricken us, that we
Might fare at length within his home to be,
Traced in the light of his divinity,
And blinded by the glory of his face?

O strange and unseen land whereto we come,
Are thy shores shores of day, or shores of night?
As we draw near shall we indeed see light,
And shall we hear, through lessening wind and foam,
The voice of her we love sound from the land,
And, looking shorewards, shall we see her stand
Girt round with glory on a peaceful strand,
Smiling to see our dark skiff heave in sight?

I cannot know; there is no man who knows.
We are, and we are not, — and that is all
The knowledge which to any may befall;
We know not life's beginning, nor life's close, —
'Twixt dawn and twilight shine the sunny hours
Wherein some hands pluck thorns and some hands
flowers;
'Twixt light and shade are shed the sudden showers;
Yet night shall cover earth as with a pall.

Sadder than all thou art, O song of mine,
Because thou callest vainly on her name;
Because thou fain wouldst rise, and sudden flame
Before God's face and her face most divine,

And tell her of the bitter grief we feel,
And pray her by some sweet sign to reveal
The land which God and darkness so conceal, —
Say where our sorrows lead and whence they came.

O saddest of sad songs by sad lips sung,
  Fresh hopes may rise, fresh passions snake-like hiss,
  Or fresh illusions find fresh rods to kiss ;
But joy is fleet, and memory is long, —
    And on the fair sweet reaches of the past,
    Lovely and still, for evermore is cast
    A sad and sacred light which shall outlast
The fierce and short-lived glare of summer bliss.

Alas, poor song, all singing is in vain ;
  What thing more sad is left for thee to say?
  Oh, weary time of life, and weary way,
Can dead souls rise, or lost joys live again?
    Now by the hand of sorrow are we led ;
    Though sweet things come, they come as joys born
      dead :
    Let us arise, go hence, for all is said,
And we must bide the breaking of the day.

PAST AND FUTURE.

O Love, once more if we
  Should meet, and once more stand
  Upon the golden strand,
  Between the sea and land,
The green land and the sea,

Should we speak of the past,
  But two brief years gone by,
  When, 'neath the summer sky,
  Was born what shall not die
While life with me shall last !

Shall I recall that day,
 My last of perfect peace,
 When through the branching trees
 The gusty summer breeze
Moved singing on its way,

And far off lay the main ;
 But we together stood
 Within that well-loved wood :
 Then life looked to me good,
It looks not so again !

Yes, far off lay the sea ;
 And, vaguely and half seen,
 We caught its tender sheen
 Of blue that mixed with green,
As I would mix with thee,

And hold thee for a space
 Within my arms, O sweet,
 Till heart to heart should beat,
 And our glad lips should meet,
As in the dear gone days, —

A space wherein to sigh
 With love, and bow my head
 Down to thy face, and shed
 My soul for thee to tread
Beneath thy feet, then die !

But strong is fate, O love,
 Who makes, who mars, who ends,
 Whose strength with weakness blends,
 Who joy with sorrow sends, —
Just little joy enough

To mock us, crying — lo,
    What might be, and what is !
    Yea, often falls the kiss,
    The long-desired bliss,
On lips that nothing know.

O love, what did we say?
    I know thou canst not tell ;
    But I know, ah, too well,
    Each little word that fell
From thy lips on that day !

Yea, I shall see till death
    Thy face, thy deep blue eyes,
    And hear the soft short sighs
    That take, with sweet surprise
Of sound, the rapid breath !

Thy lot is sweet for thee ;
    Fair, flowery is thy way ;
    With thee 't is always May.
    My life is cold and gray
As any winter sea !

Perchance thou mayst recall
    That mute warm summer night,
    When with the moon's clear light
    The sea was calm and bright,
And no wind was at all !

And hardly could the deep
    Get strength to kiss the strand, —
    The sea-wet shining sand ;
    A spell lay on the land
As of great love and sleep !

Still, love, my sad sight sees,
　　As in the days that were,
　　Those eyes that would not spare,
　　That light of golden hair
As flame blown by a breeze !

Oh, sound of vanished feet,
　　Oh, sad remembering
　　In winter of the spring !
　　My lips now only sing
Sad songs, and no more sweet !

I shall live on, and see
　　Fresh people and fresh days ;
　　But none the reason trace
　　Why one name of one place
Is more than tune to me !

But when I call the name,
　　The reason thou mayst find, —
　　O fair land left behind !
　　O sea of summer, blind
With light of summer flame !

Yea, love ! no more may we
　　Together walk or stand
　　Upon the golden strand,
　　Between the sea and land,
The green land and the sea !

BALLAD.

" O MOTHER, the wind wails wearily ;
  The twilight gathers round the shore
        And on the sea ;
  Oh, loud he cries, ' Love come to me,
        And weep no more ! '
Alas ! my love, I am not free,
        And my heart is sore."

" Be still, my daughter, and have no fear,
  'T is but your fancy's idle play,
        No sound ye hear
Save winds and breakers roaring near
        From the vexed bay ;
Be still, my child, my daughter dear,
        Wait for the day."

" O Willie, the night is bleak and bare,
  No moonlight shines upon the main.
        In my gold hair,
And on my shoulders white and fair,
        I feel the rain.
Willie, my love, where are you, where?
        Do you call in pain ? "

"Oh, ask me not too much, my love,
  The starless night is like a pall
        Your truth to prove ;
Will you not come through bay and cove,
        Love, when I call. —
Thro' waves that white and whirling move,
        Each wave a wall ? "

She girt her raiment to her knee ;
 She left the barren cliffs behind,
  And to the sea
She set her face right silently.
   " Love, I am blind,
Oh, guide me as I come to thee,
   Clothed with the wind :

" Blind with the force of beaten foam ;
 Blind with the driven rain and sleet, —
  O love, I come !
O love, await me in thy home ;
   Love guide my feet ! "
She spake no more ; her lips grew dumb, —
   Red lips and sweet.

AFTER MANY DAYS.

In autumn's silent twilight, sad and sweet,
 O love, no longer mine, alone I stand ;
Listening, I seem to hear dear phantom feet
 Pass by me down the golden wave-worn strand :
  I think of things that were, and things that be ;
  I hear the soft low ripples of the sea
That to my thoughts responsive music beat.

My heart is very sad to-night and chill,
 But hushed in awe, as his who turns and feels
A mournful rapture through his being thrill,
 When music, sweet and slumb'rous, softly steals
  Down the deep calm of some cathedral nave,
  Then swells and throbs and breaks as does
   a wave,
And slowly ebbs, and all again is still.

And is it only five years since, O love,
  That we in this old place stood side by side,
Where in the twilight once again I move?
    Is this the same shore washed by the same tide?
      My heart recalls the past a little space,
      The sweet and the irrevocable days;
I knew not then how bitter life might prove.

I loved you then, and shall love till I die;
  Your way of life is fair, it should be so,
And I am glad, though in dark years gone by
    Hard thoughts of you I had; but now I know
      A fairer and a softer path was meet
      For treading of your dainty maiden feet:
Your life must blossom 'neath a summer sky.

The twilight, like a sleep, creeps on the day,
  And like dark dreams the night creeps on that
      sleep;
If you should come again in the old way,
    And look from pensive tender eyes and deep
      Upon me, as you looked in days of old;
      If my hand should again of yours take hold, —
How should I feel, and what things should I say?

Ah, sweet days flown shall never come again;
  That happy summer-time shall not return,
When we two stood beside this peaceful main,
    And saw at eve the rising billows yearn
      With passion to the moon, and heard afar,
      Across the waves, and 'neath the first warm star,
From ships at sea some sweet remembered strain.

I can recall the day when first we met,
  And how the burning summer sunlight fell
Across the sea; nor, love, do I forget
    How, underneath that summer noontide spell,

We saw afar the white-sailed vessels glide
  As phantom ships upon a waveless tide,
Whose shining calm no breezes come to fret.

And shall I blame you, sweet, because you chose
  A softer path of life than mine could be?
I keep our secret here, and no man knows
  What passed five years ago 'twixt you and me, —
    Two loves begotten at the self-same time,
    When that gold summer tide was in its prime:
One love lives yet, and one died with the rose.

I work, and live, and take my part in things,
  And so my life goes on from day to day;
Fruitless the summers, seedless all the springs,
  To him who feels December one with May:
    The night is not more dreary than the sun,
    Not sadder is the twilight, dim and dun,
Than dawn that still returning shines and sings.

Fed with wet scent of hills, through growing shades,
  To the white water's edge the wind moans down;
The lapping tide steals on, while daylight fades,
  And fills the caves with shells and seaweed brown.
    Ah, wild sea-beaten coast, more dear to me
    Than fairest scenes of that fair land could be
Where warm Italian suns steep happy glades!

Farewell, familiar scene, for I ascend
  The jagged path that led me to the shore;
Farewell to cliff, cave, inlet, — each a friend, —
  My parting steps shall visit ye no more:
    Dear are ye all where soft light steals through
      gloom.
    Here had my joy its birth; here found its
      tomb.
Here love began; and here one love had end.

OUT OF EDEN.

AGAIN the summer comes, and all is fair;
A sea of tender blue, the sky o'erhead
Stretches its peace; the roses white and red,
  Through the deep silence of the trancèd air,
  In a mute ecstasy of love declare
Their souls in perfume, while their leaves are fed
With dew and moonlight that fall softly, shed
  Like slumber on pure eyelids unaware.

O wasted affluence of scent and light!
Each gust of fragrance smites me tauntingly;
Yon placid stars have rankling shafts for me;
  My great despair, by its own fatal might,
  Converts to pain the loveliness of night.
Ah, would I could from all this beauty flee,
And, 'neath some gray sky on a cheerless sea,
  Let drift a life that cannot end aright.

Vain flower of fame from which is gone the scent,
Vain crown no longer glorious in mine eyes,
Vain hopes at which, years back, my joy would rise
  Like melody within an instrument
  When skilled hands touch the strings. All now is
      spent,
And what is gained? Lo, I have won my prize,
And here neglected at my feet it lies;
  It meant so much, — ah, what was that it meant?

For thee, lost love, I shall not see again;
The pale sad beauty of thy tender face —
Once lamp and light of this now starless place —

Comes to me in my dreams, and I am fain
To hold thee in my arms, and so retain
Thy phantom form in one long wild embrace ;
A flush illumes the features of dead days,
But fades before the lights in heaven wane.

I am as one who, in a festive hall
Ablaze with glow of flowers and cresset fires,
Hears from a hundred joy-begetting lyres
A storm of music roll from wall to wall,
Yet feels no joy upon his spirit fall ;
For all the while his wandering heart desires
One small sweet waif of sound those pealing quires
May scorn, may drown, but never can recall.

Yea, seem I like that fabled king of old
Who gained his wish, and woke one morn — and lo !
With gold his bed and chamber were aglow,
And when his glad arms did his child enfold,
He clasped but to his heart a form of gold, —
Gold roses in her breast, no more of snow,
Gold hair upon her golden, polished brow,
Hard, bright the hands of which his hands took hold.

But from her trance of gold he saw her wake,
Saw life and bloom return to all the flowers ;
Green grew again and fresh the wind-stirred bowers,
And from its golden frost was freed the lake ;
But, though I drain my heart for my love's sake,
She will not come to make my waste of hours
Fruitful as earth beneath warm sun and showers,
Nor quick with scent my scentless roses make.

Dear soul, to-night our wedding-night had been ;
And death has come to you, and fame to me.
The summer's breath makes music in the tree,
Its kiss with over-love has charred the green ;
Through quivering boughs I catch night's starry sheen,

A sense of unborn music seems to be
In air and moonlight falling tenderly, —
　　And yet I draw no sweetness from the scene.

O love, sweet love, my first, my only love,
How can I find those flowering meadows sweet,
That feel no more the kisses of your feet !
　　O silent heart that grief no more can move,
　　O loved and loving lips, whereto mine clove
Till hope, long stanch, with thy heart's muffled beat
Furled his lorn flag and made his last retreat,
　　And all was void below, and dark above !

Pale shape, they should have clothed thee like a bride ;
Have twined a bridal chaplet round thy head,
And decked thy cold grave as a marriage-bed ;
　　For, though the envious darkness strive to hide,
　　I still shall find thee, sweet, and by thy side
Lie peaceful down, while hands and lips shall wed,
And winds, attuned to lays of love we said,
　　Float o'er the stillness where we twain abide.

But now the gulf between us, love, is deep :
I labor yet a little in the fight,
And bear the outrage of the joyous light, —
　　I toil by day, and in the night I sleep,
　　And then my heart gets ease, for I can weep ;
But you, in starless, songless depths of night,
With dreamless slumber shed upon your sight,
　　Rest where none need to sow, or care to reap.

A GARDEN REVERIE.

I HEAR the sweeping fitful breeze
   This early night in June;
I hear the rustling of the trees
   That had no voice at noon.
Clouds brood, and rain will soon come down
To gladden all the panting town
With the cool melody that beats
Upon the busy dusty streets.

But in this space of narrow ground
   We call a garden here —
Because less loudly falls the sound
   Of traffic on the ear,
Because its faded grass-plot shows
One hawthorn tree, which each May blows,
Whereon the birds in early spring
At sun-dawn and at sun-down sing —

I muse alone. A rose-tree twines
   About the brown brick wall,
Which strives, when Summer's glory shines,
   To gladden at its festival,
Yet lets, upon the path beneath,
Such pale leaves drop as I would wreathe
Around a portrait that to me
Is all my soul's divinity :

A face in nowise proud or grand,
   But strange, and sad and fair ;
A maiden twining round her hand
   A tress of golden hair,

While in her deep pathetic eyes
The light of coming trouble lies,
As on some silent sea and warm
The shadow of a coming storm.

From those still lips shall no more flow
    The tones that, in excess
Of tremulous love, touched more on woe
    Than quiet happiness,
When my arms strained her in a grasp
That sought her very soul to clasp;
When my hand pressed that hand most fair, —
I hold now but a tress of hair.

How look, this breezy summer night,
    The places that we knew
When all the hills were flushed with light
    And July seas were blue?
Does the wind eddy through our wood
As through this garden solitude?
Do the same trees their branches toss
The undulating wind across?

What feet tread paths that now no more
    Our feet together tread?
How in the twilight looks the shore?
    Is still the sea outspread
Beneath the sky, a silent plain
Of silver lights that wax and wane?
What ships go sailing by the strand
Of that fair consecrated land?

Alas! what voice shall now reply?
    Not thine, arrested gale,
That 'neath the dark and pregnant sky
    Subsidest to a wail.

On dusty city, silent plain,
And on thy village grave the rain
Comes down, while I to night shall jest,
And hide a secret in my breast.

"MY LOVE IS DEAD."

'T is Spring, the fresh green glints in the brook,
The primrose laughs from its shady nook,
Winter away like a ghost has fled, —
Let it be Spring, then — my love is dead !

The Summer is come with burning light ;
The swallow wheels and dips in his flight ;
The Spring away like a ghost has fled, —
Let it be Summer, my love is dead !

Autumn is come, with its gold-tressed trees,
Far through the wood sighs the dirge-like breeze ;
Summer away like a ghost has fled, —
Let it be Autumn, my love is dead !

The Winter is come, with white, wan cheek,
The bare boughs toss, and the wild winds shriek ;
Autumn away like a ghost has fled, —
Let it be Winter, my love is dead !

DEAD LOVE.

I SEE that you are weary with the dance ;
  Inside the air is faint with scent and light,
But here, where many-colored lanterns glance
  Through trees whose branches quiver in the night, —
Here let us stand alone a little space,
As in the days departed, face to face.

Your hair is not less golden than of old,
   Your eyes are not less subtly sweet to snare
The souls of men, and still your curled lips hold
   The magic of a smile which was more fair,
Years back, to me than fairer things could be;
Yet now its charm with flameless eyes I see.

Oh, how your face thrilled through me, five years' since;
The touch of this small hand 1 hold in mine
Would warm my blood like fire, while lips would wince
   To feel your kiss; and as a shaken vine
That bows its straining branches to the wind,
So then to me you yearned, with love made blind.

Then our lips clove, as if they ne'er would part,
   Then hands were linked with hands, and eyes met eyes;
Thus quickly never beats again my heart
   As in the days of that lost paradise;
For now as tunes played out, as poems said,
The music ceases, the closed book is read.

Then all the ways of life with bliss grew bright,
   As when in spring the long-delaying sun
Breaks through the sky and floods the land with light,
   And all the heaven's glory is begun;
Though yet before October ends, the skies
Shall look as sad as life-resigning eyes.

So shone our love which, ere late autumn-time,
   Lay pale and dying with no breath for speech;
And now a withered rose, an empty rhyme, —·
   Ah, is this all that fate has left to each?
So tame love's fire, I gaze and snatch no kiss;
Alas! poor love, that it should come to this!

Let's sit beneath this lantern-fruited tree,
   That dances in the wind with jewelled light;
Let our souls backward look till they can see
   Some little glory of a gone delight:

Can you remember something of that time?
Or have you quite forgotten the old rhyme

I made, that day of days, when I and you
   Stood by the sea whose stormy shallows roared
On wastes of shell-strewn sand? The sky was blue
   As down the hot sun on the wet sand poured ;
Up steamed the sea-scent warm and sharp and sweet ;
We laughed to see the billows, thundering, meet.

None, save us twain, upon the shore was seen, —
   The gull cried loud his short, hard, stormy cry,
The blown foam crested all the deep sea's green,
   The summer sun burnt hot, the wind was high,
And, hissing, dashed the bright spray in our eyes
When a great wave broke with a great surprise.

But see how I have wandered from the verse
   Which I remember, though I see you doubt.
Laugh not, songs counted better I 've deemed worse ; —
   A little love-sick song, and all about
Your face and voice, where still the old charm lies,
Sweet waifs of laughter and soft tender sighs.

It was a sad and happy time, you say,
   Yet sweet as is an ever-changing tune ;
Ah me, the close of that still July day,
   When with the sun's excess earth seemed to swoon,
And we together wandered on the shore,
Half feeling we should wander there no more !

All round, the sea-wet shining nets were spread ;
Gold shone the cliffs, and all the sea was bright
As through its glowing depths the sun had shed
   His soul in one great ecstasy of light.
It faded ; mutely we awhile did stand,
   Then left forever that enchanted strand.

Your goal was Paris : there one eve we went,
   Your mother with us.   How she loved to see
Our love !   That night the moon from heaven leant,
   As leans some maiden from a balcony
Down looking to the lawn with eager eyes,
To see a loved form through the stillness rise.

Recall the jingling horse-bells, the whip's crack,
   The still, lit villages where all was peace,
The hedges in the moonlight strange and black,
   The voiceless cornfields and the fleeting trees,
The long hill, wild and steep, which, dashing down,
We saw the tree-girt, white-walled, shining town.

Rattling into its narrow streets we plunged,
   And left the dim, still country far behind ;
The coach-wheels strained and thundered, whirled and
     lunged ;
   At first the great light almost made us blind.
Ah, then, what laughs we laughed, what songs we sung,
While hands unseen, oft meeting, closed and clung.

As hot as ever Eastern desert was
   Grew Paris 'neath the blaze of August heat ;
The public gardens, sad with withered grass,
   Seemed but to say : " Time was when we were sweet,
Before the south wind left us, and the west ;
Oh, once more in some gray cloud's shade to rest ! "

But life hates joy.   The war-cloud burst at length ;
   The men of England girt themselves for strife,
Amongst them I : it tried my manhood's strength
   To kiss you the last time, perchance, in life ; —
That night of thunder I remember yet
   And how we parted I cannot forget.

The earth with imminent tempest seemed oppressed ;
   The torpid air shook shuddering to the sound
Of thunder booming slowly from the west :
   Long lurid light the vaporous grayness crowned,
And all things, with one stillness, ominously
Waited for that which was about to be.

The o'er-wrought heaven heaved and gasped in flame :
   Below, black clouds hemmed in the fading light ;
Incensed, the thunder cried aloud God's name,
   As one who warns the world ere he shall smite ;
When suddenly up sprang a gusty breeze
And spread a panic through the swaying trees.

Then fiercer lightnings clove the sky in twain ;
   Loud fell the thunder crashing through the sky ;
A pause : then like redemption fell the rain,
   And hissed against the cracking earth and dry,
Dark all around, save where the lightning's glow
Lit up the empty, tree-fringed court below.

Oh, the last kiss, the long last lingering look,
   The touch and thrill of hands that intertwined !
But when at length the storm the sky forsook,
   I heard your cry rise mixing with the wind, —
You say my voice was broken ; so it was,
But yet did not your own in grief surpass.

Ah, think of how we looked, and what we said ;
   Laugh as I laugh, — your laugh is sweet to hear.
Love was our sovereign then, rose-garlanded ;
   He gave us pain and bliss and hope and fear ;
Now he is dead ; yet know we not how slain,
But this we know, — he shall not live again.

Out in the past, there let him lie and rot —
  He had his time of birth and time of death;
Give him one thought now, then remember not
  That ever his pale lips were warm with breath.
Oh, I am glad to-night, yea, gay enough
To dance a measure on the grave of love.

Nay, now at our past follies we can smile;
  I wept hot tears who had not wept till then.
No second love shall thus our hearts beguile:
  It happens to most women and most men
To know one love, which as a sudden fire
Burns and consumes their hearts with great desire.

Then all earth's fairness in one fair face lies;
  Then all earth's music in one sweet voice is;
Then, 'neath the long rapt gaze of hungering eyes,
  Love leaps to find its vent in one long kiss,
While cold and sad seems every other fate, —
But we can smile now, only saying — wait!

You wedded joys that spring from wealth alone;
  I courted fame, — a bright and barren bride,
Whom from Death's arms I snatched to make my own,
  When roared the red strife like a stormy tide.
Oh, very strange to-night this meeting is,
So much to feel, and yet one feeling miss:

That comes not back. Speak on, still — sweet, your
        voice,
  Years back it hurt me with delicious pain;
Let us shake hands across our buried joys.
  The waltz strikes up: you catch the well-known strain?
When last we heard it 't was that year in France.
Let us go in; your hand for the next dance.

MISCELLANEOUS SONNETS.

BEREFT.

I WILL not mock thy memory, most dear,
  By striving to describe what soul was thine,
  A soul which never more shall look on mine.
I cannot talk of any higher sphere,
Nor can I make the utter darkness clear;
  I know no God, I worship at no shrine;
  I only bow before thy life divine!
I will not tell of voices that I hear;

I will not tell of secret bitter tears;
I will not tell of desolated years;
  Of sunless springs that come to ravaged lands;
  Of altered seas that break on altered strands:
    My heart has only room this thing to know,—
    Thou once wast with me, and thou art not now.

6

TO ———.

O YEAR ! while others crowned with pleasure sit
   To watch thee slowly, darkly pass away,
   To thee, so dying, I at least will say, —
O bitter year, that with remorseless feet
Didst tread down all whereby my life grew sweet, —
   Didst thou not turn the golden into gray,
   And snatch the very sunlight from my day?
Yet, now that thou art dying, it is meet

That ere thou goest quite, for one sweet thing,
   One, only one, I give thee thanks, O year ! —
   The knowledge of a friend, now found so dear
That she a little can bring back the spring
      To fields that seem forgotten of the light, —
      A star to bless my moon-deserted night.

DESOLATE.

I STRAIN my worn-out sight across the sea ;
   I hear the wan waves sobbing on the strand ;
   My eyes grow weary of the sea and land,
Of the wide deep, and the forsaken lea.
Ah, love, return ! ah, love, come back to me ! —
   As well these ebbing waves I might command
   To turn and kiss the moist, deserted sand !
The joy that was, is not, and cannot be.

The salt shore, furrowed by the foam, smells sweet ;
   Oh, blest for me, if it were now my lot,
      To make this shore my rest, and hear all strife
Die out, like yon tide's faint receding beat :
      If he forgot so easily in life,
   I may in death forget that he forgot.

FORSAKEN.

WOULD God that I were dead and no more known, —
  Forgotten underneath the deep cold main,
  Freed from the thrill of joy and sting of pain !
There I should be with silence all alone,
To weep no more for any sweet day flown :
  I should not see the shining summer wane,
  Nor feel the blasting winter come again,
Nor hear the autumn winds grow strong and moan ;

But time, like sea-mist screening the far deep,
  Should make each hated and loved object dim,
    And I should gaze on both with hazy sight ;
God granting this, I should no longer weep,
  But, wearied, rest beneath the clear green light,
    And surely lose in sleep all thoughts of him !

FIRST AND LAST KISS.

THY lips are quiet, and thine eyes are still ;
  Cold, colorless, and sad thy placid face ;
  Thy form has only now the statue's grace ;
My words wake not thy voice, nor can they fill
Thine eyes with light.   Before fate's mighty will,
  Our wills must bow ; yet for a little space,
  I sit with thee and death, in this lone place,
And hold thy hands that are so white and chill.

I always loved thee, though thou didst not know ;
  But well he knew whose wedded love thou wert :
    Now thou art dead, I may raise up the fold
That hides thy face, and, o'er thee bending low,
  For the first time and last before we part,
    Kiss the curved lips — calm, beautiful, and cold !

NOT LIVED IN VAIN.

HAVE I not worshipped thee in tender lays,
   And told in barren rhymes my love for thee ;
   And now I wish that I no more might see,
Or ne'er had seen that fair, alluring face,
Or as a tune felt that lithe body's grace
   Melt through my heart, that leap'd up eagerly
   With joy of hope : now hope no more may be ;
For hope lies dead, amid the dear, dead days.

Still, if the bitterness of unshed tears,
   And burden of a spirit sorely tried,
     Did e'er with joy of maiden's victory fill
Thy woman's heart, then surely these sad years
   Have been well lived, nor, sweet, would I have died
     Till thy heart had of mine its perfect will.

CHANGELESS.

THE Spring, a maiden beautiful and pure,
   Wearies of earth, and leaves the happy lea ;
   The stormy winds grow weary of the sea ;
The sailor lad grows weary of the shore ;
Tunes that charmed once fail, sometime, to allure.
   Weary we grow of grief, or too much glee ;
   We weary captive, and we weary free :
Suns set, moons rise, the stars do not endure.

Let this be as it is ; — but this I know,
   Though life, grown weary, parts at length from me ;
Though joy remembered turns to deepest woe ;
   Yea, though as one our lives may never be, —
Through life, in death, where none may reap or sow,
   My love, O sweet, shall weary not of thee.

ACROSS SEAS.

TO BJÖRNSTERNE BJÖRNSON, AUTHOR OF "ARNE."

I.

I, TOILING here through many weary days,
  Turn from the extreme bitterness of pain,
  As turns a journeying sailor from the main,
In middle sea to rest, a little space,
On some soft island where his hands may raise
  'Twixt land and sea a rough and rocky fane,
  Whereat his God to worship, ere again
Unto the stormy waves he sets his face.

So, ere I pass, a little yet I turn,
  And raise, apart from all, to thee a shrine,
    And render homage in these trembling lays,
Which, could they higher rise, and clearer burn,
  Might reach a little from my soul to thine,
    Not past man's worship, but beyond man's praise.

II.

FOR, looking downward from thy spirit's height,
  Things that we cannot see, to thee are clear;
  Music by us unheard, thou yet canst hear;
And, as men read the wonders of the night,
So dost thou read with clear unfailing sight
  These hearts of ours, and from thy higher sphere,
  Canst see in Spring the Autumn dawning near;
Canst in the darkness see the unborn light;

Canst see how love, ere yet men know its name,
  Fed with cool dews of dreams, begins to bud,
    Ere yet it break into a blossom bright,
Whose warm and trembling petals shine as flame, —
  A flower that fades not when the summer wood
    Lies chilled and leafless in the winter's blight.

III.

SWEETER than half-heard music is to one
  Who waits, upon a summer's night, and sees
  The warm, white moonlight slanting through the trees,
And smiles to think the glad time is begun ;
Sadder than, after summer-time is done,
  The autumn twilight, when the fitful breeze
  Sighs for the year's lost prime and sunny ease, —
So is to me the web thy soul has spun

Of dream-flowers plucked from pale, dim fields of sleep,
  Warm with no sun, wet with no rain of ours.
    Surely the web was woven well of these,
And, in the streams we know not, did God steep
  The opening blossoms, and the full-grown flowers, —
    Hopes born of griefs, and joys of memories.

IV.

So end these rhymes that lack the magic wing
  Which could alone bear up my thoughts to Thee,
  O soul unseen, though not unknown of me ;
Yet, as in winter thinking of the spring
Doth seem more near the distant May to bring ;
  As one who worships prone on bended knee,
  Then nearest seems unto his God to be :
So — with like hope — a little while I sing,

And bow in soul, and worship in this rhyme ;
  And from my land, to-night, I look afar,
    Until I almost deem that I can see
The snowy mountains of that northern clime,
  In midst whereof, as flames a winter star,
    Thy spirit shines in its divinity.

SPEECHLESS:

UPON THE MARRIAGE OF TWO DEAF AND DUMB PERSONS.

THEIR lips upon each other's lips are laid ;
  Strong moans of joy, wild laughter, and short cries
  Seem uttered in the passion of their eyes.
He sees her body fair, and fallen head,
And she the face whereon her soul is fed ;
  And by the way her white breasts sink and rise,
  He knows she must be shaken by sweet sighs ;
Though all delight of sound for them be dead.

They dance a strange, weird measure, who know not
  The tune to which their dancing feet are led ;
Their breath in kissing is made doubly hot
  With flame of pent-up speech ; strange light is shed
    About their spirits, as they mix and meet
    In passion-lighted silence, 'tranced and sweet.

TO SLEEP.

O TENDER Sleep ! queen over ev'ry queen !
  Our mother, since from thy deep womb we spring,
  And unto thee return, and to thee bring
Our weary limbs and wearier hearts, and lean
Upon thy breast ; thou who hast pitying seen
  Our woe on earth, and blunted life's sharp sting,
  And when we were in trouble did so sing,
That we forgot what was and what had been, —

Open thy gentle arms and take me in ;
  Hide me ! oh, hide me in thy mother-breast,
    Between thy bosom sweet, and long, soft hair :
  Yea, let me from thee drink the milk of rest :
Lay all my virtue level with my sin,
    So that I have no thought of days that were.

A MOOD.

BEHOLD ! How fair it is to see in Spring,
  The frozen river once more thaw and run
  Under fresh wind, and warm, soft, flickering sun !
Is it not good to dance and laugh and sing,
To feel somewhile the lips of pleasure sting?
  Lo ! now the fairness of a love well won ; —
  But then things pass, and some day Spring is done ;
And, since we see there are no joys that cling,

Would it not be far wiser to have none?
  Time's tide is dark and bitter with our tears ;
    Why should we swell it with the greater pain
  Of fair gone things ; a few, glad, golden years?
Of one sad color let our days be spun,
    So we may live, nor weep to see life wane.

LOVE'S ILLUSIONS.

A WOMAN, strange, and beautiful to see,
  With limbs of light, and hair of the sun's gold !
  Her fair hand did a mighty goblet hold ;
The bubbling wine thereof shone dazzlingly,
So that I said, " Now, give, even to me,
  Some of this wine that sparkles bright and cold."
  She gayly laughed, and said, " Thou art too bold,"
And went her way, and heeded not my plea.

But I said, " She will come again ; " and bore
  The present bitter for a coming sweet :
And lo ! she came, but passed me as before,
And came yet once again, but held no more
    The goblet filled with wine of life and heat,
    That stains now, and makes wet, God's hands and feet.

SLEEPLAND GLORIFIED.

By night my lady comes to me, to rest
   Contentedly in quiet vales of sleep ;
   And sometimes, those sweet eyes of her will weep,
And barren tears make wet each white round breast.
Once only were her lips to my lips prest ;
   Then in my veins I felt love's passion leap,
   And all the blood-red waves of pleasure sweep
Across my heart that might not be repress'd,

But found its vent in kisses thick and sweet,
   That fell upon her mouth and quivering eyes,
   While all her gracious body shook with sighs ;
And we were wedded then, as was most meet.
     No light shone round, no music breathed, save this :
     Love's moan of joy, and murmur of his kiss.

SLEEPLAND FORSAKEN.

O LOVE ! O sweet ! where art thou gone, my love ? —
   I tread the songless ways of sleep alone ;
   In sleepland's shadowy caves I make my moan.
O sleep's pale, waveless, voiceless seas whereof
She seemed a part — where is the syren gone?
   O whispering forests, tell me of the dove !
   O paths with lilies and with roses sown,
Where is my flower, the fairest of the grove?

O sweet, unanswering voice and feet so flown,
   In vain along the silent shore I rove
Where shadows of the moon-lit rocks lie prone,
   By tideless seas that never winds may move !
   Alas, my God, their depths are deep enough
To hide that face, and they shall keep their own.

JUSTIFICATION.

I CHARGE you lay on this dead man no blame.
  Had not God so his mighty spirit cursed,
  And set his hand against him from the first,
He now had had as great and pure a name
As ever flashed through all the world like flame.
  Had not his soul been wasted by this thirst,
  Until his o'erwrought heart was nigh to burst,
He had not drunk so deeply of this shame.

The hands of God are strong to make or mar;
And if He gather clouds about one star,
  Who says that star is least among the rest?
  I swear, by these blank eyes and tortured breast,
    Though I should take upon me God's worst ban,
    'T is God that I abjure, and not this man.

LOVE'S WARFARE.

" AND are these cold, light words your last?" he said,
  And rose, his face made pale with outraged love.
  She answered gayly, "Are they not enough?"
And lightly laughed until his spirit bled,
While snake-like on his grief her beauty fed.
  He looked upon her face once more for proof;
  Then through and through his lips the sharp teeth
    drove,
Till with the bitter dew of blood made red.

At length he said, "And so 't was but a jest, —
  A well-conceived, well-executed plan;
  Yet now may God forgive you, if God can!"
And, passing, left her calm and self-possessed.
    She watched him cross the lawn with eyes bent low,
    Where she had kissed his face one hour ago.

LOVE'S TRUCE.

SHE speaks no word, but, stretching out her hand,
  Touches him softly where asleep he lies;
  And he, too feeble now to feel surprise,
Awakes and faintly smiles : they understand.
But now her fragrant breath his brow has fanned ;
  He raises to her face large, hungry eyes,
  While like entrancing music fall her sighs
Upon his heart long exiled from joy's land.

For she, repenting of a deed ill done,
  Bows, kissing tenderly his white, chilled face,
    And in the dim gold twilight of her hair
  His eyes grow blind ; he feels her last embrace ;
    Then on her breast his head sinks unaware,
And life goes nightwards with the setting sun.

COUNSEL.

IT takes us such long time to understand
  That God is God, and man can be but man.
  We live and labor for a little span ;
We wait, and watch, and fertilize our land, —
And all for what ? — that war's all-wasting brand
  May spread its dearth according to God's plan ;
  And still we vainly strive beneath the ban,
And think against this God to set our hand.

Oh, all my brothers, rest a space from strife, —
Let each one with no murmur live his life.
  Will ye make glad our tyrant's eyes and ears,
  By sound of sighs and sight of bitter tears?
    Not so ; but rather spite the God on high,
    By showing Him how men can live and die.

IN BONDAGE.

OH, I have waited long for you, my sweet,
   In these cold dungeons far from light or day;
   And wondered if your eyes were blue or gray,
And how your face would look, my face to meet.
Yet his stern vengeance cannot be complete,
   Who holds me here as pris'ner in his sway;
   And, as a panther lurks about his prey,
Lurks he about us now, with noiseless feet.

Oh, kiss me once upon the lips, and bow
   The solemn beauty of your face to mine;
      Laugh as you laughed of old; but why turn pale,
      And why does such sweet, rising music fail?
Ah, he hath fill'd the cup to overflow,
   And I must drink your tears for my last wine.

TO A TUNE.

O WILD, sweet tune, of which my soul is fain,
   Through the loud sound of sea and tempest heard,
   Like the low moan of a wind-driven bird, —
O sad, sweet tune! O passionate, wild strain!
Full of past joy, dead hope, and present pain, —
   Once more I catch thee, and my heart is stirr'd,
   Stung sharply by that one great, simple word,
Gone as a dream that shall not come again.

Once more I see my lady's warm, flushed face;
   See her deep amorous eyes, and swept back hair;
      Yea, hear the tender sobbing of her breath.
   O tune, made sad with all sweet things that were!
O tune, keep back, or quite restore those days,
      That, past, crown life, or break our wills for death!

TO A DAY.

SHALL I sing of the earth or of the sea? —
   Of bright-wing'd Mirth, that stays its hour, and flies,
   On fickle wings, to far-off, alien skies ;
Shall I praise these, O Day, and not praise thee
That giv'st me rare, sweet gifts, — yea, was to me
   As sudden fire ; a rapture for mine eyes,
   That made my roused, stung heart to swell and rise,
Filling it with the joy of joys to be?

The year returns, but thee I see no more, —
   Gone as a man's first dream of goodness goes ;
   But, where less joys are as forgotten things,
When I draw near to the pale, shadow-shore,
   Be with me then, to fight against my foes ;
    Kiss me, and guard me ! hide me with thy wings.

STRONGER THAN SLEEP.

WEARY, my limbs upon my couch I laid,
   And dreamt ; and in my dream I seemed to see
   My lady, who was soon my bride to be,
Silently standing, gazing on my bed,
A crown of bright red roses on her head.
   I said, " O love ! this hour is sweet to me ;
   Stretch out your throat, and let us kiss." Then she
Bowed down her head, her fair brows garlanded.

" Reach out your hand and feel," her deep eyes said.
   I touched ; and through soft raiment felt her form
    Panting and glowing with the need of love.
Then all the waves of pleasure, deep and warm,
Burst through my veins. My eyes love's hot tears bled,
    And I awoke, too weak to speak or move.

SHAMELESS LOVE.

THY food my body, and my blood thy wine;
　My soul, too, thine, to tread beneath thy feet:
　While thus my hair is gold and my breast sweet,
Most rapturous is this shameful life of mine.
But time must come, between my life and thine,
　When I must leave the heaven of this heat,
　And through the cold, gray twilight go to meet
That night wherein no stars nor moon may shine.

A rose, then, withered by fierce passion's sun,
　Left soiled and trampled in the public way;
　　A broken wine-cup emptied of delight:
　Yet would I not, to triumph o'er that day,
　　Give up one wild, sweet moment of this night,
That finds once more love's tune of joy begun.

STRICKEN!

O LOVE, behold thy feet are shod with flame!
　Thy body clothed with torture as a dress;
　Too weak thy stricken lips are to express
Thy mighty grief, or call upon the name
Of Him who gives the sorrow and the shame.
　Thy lips have tasted the salt bitterness
　Of tears like blood, wrung out of thy distress.
Thy soul must reap a barren, bitter fame.

Fair lands beneath thee, and fair skies above,
　Thy heart falls blind, outside of that fair land
　　Whereto it may not come; all words are vain, —
It is the unattainable we love.
　But rest a little, and a friendly hand
　　Shall give thee peace, and ease from all thy pain.

ABOVE LOVE.

COME now, I will be frank with you, and say
    I have for you a strange and bitter love :
    Most strong it is, but no love's strong enough
From higher aims to make me turn away ;
Some short sharp pain, some idle night or day,
    Is all the hurt that I shall have thereof.
    I will not wed you, and I must remove
Your spell from off my path as best I may.

Your face would come between my work and me ;
    Your love would quite unnerve me for the strife ;
      Kiss me, forget me wholly, as I know
    I shall forget you in the whirl of life :
Nay, do not look ; I swear I will not see ;
      Take off your lips lest I should crush you so.

THE FIRST KISS.

SHE sat where he had left her all alone,
    With head bent back, and eyes through love on flame ;
    And neck half flushed with most delicious shame ;
With hair disordered, and with loosened zone, —
She sat, and to herself made tender moan,
    As yet again in thought her lover came,
    And caught her by her hands and called her name,
And sealed her body as her soul his own.

The June, moon-stricken twilight, warm, and fair,
    Closed round her where she sat 'neath voiceless trees,
Full of the wonder of triumphant prayer,
    And sense of unimagined ecstasies
      Which must be hers, she knows, yet knows not why ;
      But feels thereof his kiss the prophecy.

BOUNDED LOVE.

ALL ways of common love pall on me now ;
  No kiss the madness of my thirst allays ;
  Through all my wild warm dreams deep burns thy face,
And, when I wake, I hear thy love-laugh low,
As all the amorous blood is set aglow.
  Oh, for some hymn of unconjectured praise,
  Some unimagined splendor of new lays,
Wherein love, bounded, might at length o'erflow !

Oh, for an ocean of new deed and speech,
  Where, no more cramped, our spirits might toss free,
  As ships that revel in full wind and sea ;
That living, yet beyond life, we might reach
    To find some strange tide, deep and strong enough
    To bear the mighty burden of our love !

CONJECTURE.

I THINK, love, as I hold your hand in mine,
  If starless, cheerless, everlasting night
  Should settle suddenly upon my sight,
And I should no more see your eyes divine,
Or golden lights that in your tresses shine,
  Or that fair face, my measureless delight,
  Or sweet curved throat, warm, beautiful, and white,
Or soft, lithe arms that round about me twine, —

How should I bear to sit with you as now,
And if you looked upon me not to know ;
  To hear men praise your throat, mouth, eyes, and hair,
  Yet feel to me you were no longer fair ?
    To miss the blush that colors your swift kiss, —
    Slay me outright, O God ! but spare me this !

TO M. C., ON HER VISIT TO LONDON IN WINTER.

SHUT are the summer's golden gates, I said,
　Gone are the life and light, and gone the bloom ;
　Now turn we sadly to the winter's gloom,
Pale, silent lands beneath our feet to tread,
Cold wastes of gray sky stretching overhead.
　But, while afar we saw the winter loom,
　Fate came between us and the coming doom ;
Summer he claimed, but gave us thee, instead.

Then fairer glowed the earth than in June days,
　Sweet sounds, more sweet than sounds of summer be,
Hearing your voice, we heard.　The darkest place,
　If you but through it passed, grew light as day,
　And if again in spring we meet not thee,
　Then shall December triumph over May.

CAPTURED THOUGHT.

A THOUGHT came to my spirit as I lay
　Between two sleeps ; and through the silent night
　It looked at me, with sudden eyes and bright ;
Then, when I strove to touch it, fled away,
And bade me dream ; but at the break of day
　I, waking, saw, through gray, increasing light,
　My last night's thought ; but as, with greater might,
I strove to grasp it, only crying, "Stay !" —

It spread its wings for flight.　Then, as a snare
　I set my song, and snared the lovely thing,
And said, "O flying thought, thou art too fair
　For me to leave thee free and wandering !
Yet fret not for thy liberty, but where
　Sad souls can hear thee be content to sing."

7

SUPPLANTED LOVES.

WHEN first the music of your voice I heard,
   Methought love's mystic promptings did arise,
   And gathered strength beneath your gentle eyes ;
My being to its depths was strangely stirred ;
And you, I think, by look and tone averred
   Your heart was mine : yet, as a meek star dies
   When slow, resistless daylight fills the skies,
So softly waned that love, when one deferred,

Transcendent passion lit my life, — its sun !
   Upon your nature rose a kindred light,
      To quench my ray ; and yet our half-born fate
      Perchance no future can obliterate ;
But, bliss fulfilled recalling bliss begun,
   We four shall walk together in God's sight.

ALL IN ALL.

PRELUDE.

Love and Bliss wedded in one heart of peace,
   And offsprings of glad songs they had ; but lo !
   Bliss sickened soon, and died ; then did Love know
For her was no more any joy or ease.
And Sorrow, coming after Joy's decease,
   Laid hold of Love, and Love was linked to Woe ;
   And where Love goes, there, too, must Sorrow go, —
Forever more inseparable are these.

But, as Bliss brought to Love glad songs, so now,
   See the sad offsprings of this second troth ;
     Yet, as the mother, twice a wife, may trace
     In children of both marriage-beds her face,
And knows the twain have sprung from her, even so,
   Love sees her image equally in both.

INSEPARABLE.

WHEN thou and I are dead, my dear,
　The earth above us lain ;
When we no more in autumn hear
　The fall of leaves and rain,
Or round the snow-enshrouded year
　The midnight winds complain ;

When we no more in green mid-spring,
　Its sights and sounds may mind,—
The warm wet leaves set quivering
　With touches of the wind,
The birds at morn, and birds that sing
　When day is left behind ;

When, over all, the moonlight lies,
　Intensely bright and still ;
When some meandering brooklet sighs
　At parting from its hill,
And scents from voiceless gardens rise,
　The peaceful air to fill ;

When we no more through summer light
　The deep dim woods discern,
Nor hear the nightingales at night,
　In vehement singing, yearn
To stars and moon, that dumb and bright,
　In nightly vigil burn ;

When smiles and hopes and joys and fears
　And words that lovers say,
And sighs of love, and passionate tears
　Are lost to us, for aye, —
What thing of all our love appears,
　In cold and coffin'd clay ?

When all their kisses, sweet and close,
    Our lips shall quite forget;
When, where the day upon us rose,
    The day shall rise and set,
While we for love's sublime repose,
    Shall have not one regret, —

Oh, this true comfort is, I think,
    That, be death near or far,
When we have crossed the fatal brink,
    And found nor moon nor star,
We know not, when in death we sink,
    The lifeless things we are.

Yet one thought is, I deem, more kind,
    That when we sleep so well,
On memories that we leave behind
    When kindred souls shall dwell,
My name to thine in words they 'll bind
    Of love inseparable.

IN THE JUNE TWILIGHT.

In the June twilight, starless and profound,
She sits, and of the twilight seems a part.
No birds sing now, nor is there any sound
Of wind among the leaves: faintly you hear
The distant beating of the city's heart;
It doth not break the spell nor vex the ear,
But seems to make the silence yet more deep,
As though some giant whispered in his sleep.
Sometimes from little gardens lying round,
A voice calls through the evening; or you catch
The sound of opening windows, or a latch
Rais'd stealthily beneath, by those who keep
Love's trists, that often are too bitter found.

And lo ! one sits beside her ; does she know
How the least tone of hers, the slightest noise
Of soft, stirr'd raiment sets his heart aglow?
Yea, does she see how all the soul of him
Yearns to her in his look and in his voice?
Their faces in the failing light are dim ;
And now to ease his heart a little space,
He tells her songs, that Love, with sovereign grace,
Has given him to sing of her ; that so,
When Time, grown weary, casts his soul away
As a thing wholly done with, men shall say,
" How this man loved, and she his verses praise —
Such women come not twice God's grace to show ! "

And now he ceases ; and the common things
Of outer life go on : she does not move ;
Her soul is full of mystic whisperings.
Is this heart hers, to do with as she wills?
But men as well as women can feign love,
Or deem that love which time too quickly kills.
Has she, then, kindled in this man the fire
That only with his being can expire?
And starts he, when she looks at him, and springs
The violent blood through each dilating vein
When her hand touches his? Can love be pain?
Can love unloving hearts with love inspire,
And is her love the heaven of which he sings?

IN THE NOVEMBER NIGHT.

I WONDER, when the moonless night had come
    On that November day,
And the street's roar subsided to a hum,
    While winds upon their way
Sang of the coming winter, and the rain
Drove drearily against the window-pane,

How felt she, knowing she was loved at length,
    As men but love when young, —
With all the untamed ardour and the strength
    That overflow in song;
When the whole spirit has no hope but one,
Which, quenched, it grows a sky without a sun.

Was she more glad or sorry? Did she say, —
    " This love but lives to die?" —
And sit and watch the firelight fairies play
    About the room, and sigh,
Because her heart's surprise still left unproved,
Whether she pitied more, or more she loved?

Did she sit long that time, with gold brown hair
    Shed over shoulders white,
Recalling each intense, unspoken prayer
    Of his love-looks that night?
Did she think over words of his, it seem'd
That she in some past life of hers had dream'd?

Did she say smiling to herself, " The song
    He made then was of me? "
And as some rapt musician will prolong
    The tune he plays, did she
Think of the days gone by, wherein her soul
But guess'd in part, what now it knew in whole?

Did she recall the night they met on first? —
    Wonder, if even then
Love as a revelation on him burst,
    While lesser aims of men
Died in his heart before his love at once,
As light of stars expires in light of suns?

Or grew his love upon him as a tune,
    Which heard, we 'd hear again,
And once more having heard, find sure and soon
    Work in the heart and brain,

And dreaming of it, wake up in the night,
Half mad, because we cannot sing it right?

Oh, the soul's rapture when it has by rote
　　That melody complete ;
When the voice, clinging to each separate note
　　Of each particular sweet,
Loses no jot or atom till the soul
Rest at the full completion of the whole !

Did she lie long awake that night to hear
　　The wind among the trees?
Did she say over his first song of her?
　　And was it pain or peace
To know she was beloved so?　Who shall say?
But this I know, that, as deep natures may,

She shut that love of his within her breast,
　　Apart from vulgar eyes ;
Let those who will, by look and voice attest
　　Their lesser victories :
Whether she bade it live or turn to dust,
She kept his love as a most sacred trust.

FIRST KNOWLEDGE.

When in sad sweetness and delicious dole
　　Love whispered her, " Thou lovest," did she start,
　　Confronted with that knowledge in her heart?
Or, did she pause to comprehend the whole
　　Deep meaning of Love's speech, and no word say?
　　As some musician who, about to play
　　The sweetest tune his cunning can essay,
Sits with still hands among the harp-chords lain,
Seeming to hearken with his heart and brain
To the dear music, ere it breaks and springs
From out the thrill'd, expectant, shuddering strings.

Did she think over love of lovers dead,
  And say, " Is such our love? " Did she recall
  His steadfast look, his bitter sighs, and all
Sad words that at their parting he had said,
  Not thinking he might ever call her his?
  Did she smile tenderly in saying this, —
  " I, only I, can give to him the bliss
For which he longs ; I can his life make fair
By granting in this one his every prayer ;
And love permits me now, his soul to save,
Yielding it all the love that it can crave? "

Did she through summer twilight sit alone,
  Marking with those intensely peaceful eyes
  The sweet and gradual changing of the skies?
And as the birds stopped singing one by one,
  And all the sounds of day in lapsing light
  Grew silent, while the fast approaching night
  Shadow'd the world in peace, before her sight
Did he rise visioned in her solitude?
Ah, surely at such peaceful hours he stood
Before her, and her spirit saw his face,
Bright with the peace of the approaching days !

Did she the coming time anticipate,
  And murmur, " Through the deep'ning twilight come,
  O thou who lovest me, nor be thou dumb !
Call me again thy life, thy love, thy fate ;
  Pour out thy love before me, let me see
  The very passion of it filling thee :
  For so, ah, doubly blessèd it shall be,
To answer, as I then shall make reply, —
' Oh, heart that thought to live unloved and die !
If love can bring thee heaven, ah, surely then
Thou art no more unblessèd among men? ' "

Ah, very sweet for such a soul as hers
  It must have been to sit and think how soon
  His clouded morn should grow to glorious noon :
For sure the crowning joy that love confers
  On such high natures, is the sense supreme
  Of being solely able to redeem
  The heart beloved, fulfilling all its dream,
Making a sad life joyous, saying, " Stand
Henceforth within the boundaries of Love's land."
Ah, doubtless then she carried in her breast
The double blessing of two hearts at rest !

Unworthy of her love he was, I know, —
  He but a minstrel singing in the night
  Sad things and strange, unfitted for the light,
Made more for sombre shadows than the glow
  Of perfect morn transfiguring the sky.
  And if she heard from out the shade his cry
  Of bitter singing, and, approaching nigh,
Said softly, " Can you sing no song to prove
The bliss as well as sorrow of great love ? "
And made his heart to know, and lips to say,
How love has power to save as well as slay, —

Yea, if her act were such, and such her speech,
  Is it for me to shame, with words ill said,
  The soul her soul from out the darkness led,
To set in open daylight, in the reach
  Of winds and all sweet perfumes?   Time shall prove
  Whether or not he would have shamed her love.
  Till then I pray you that we stand aloof;
For darkness hides her now, and she has done
With loving any underneath the sun.
And he, he waits 'mid shadows sad and strange,
Till grief to rest, and life to death shall change.

SONNETS.

LOVE AND RESURRECTION.

I.

WHEN a man dies and wakes in Paradise,
  If Paradise there be, — for what man knows? —
  He hardly feels, at first, how all his woes
Of life are over; but, with awe-struck eyes,
Looks where the towers and heights of heaven rise;
  And as he looks, so great the glory grows,
  That eyes, as yet not strong enough, must close,
While he in speechless expectation lies.

But through the golden gate he hears the song
  The angels ever sing for joy of heart,
Yet dares not mix those shining forms among;
Till, lo! Christ, stepping from the circling throng,
  Says to him, "Friend, why standest thou apart?
  Enter, for one of these thou surely art!"

II.

So, when the joy for which I long had prayed,
  Was granted, and Love's gates stood open wide,
  With shining angels thronging either side,
I held a little back, with feet afraid
To dare the shining land before me spread;
  Though I had seen the faces glorified,
  Heard Love's own song of joy, felt all the pride
To know his very hands had crowned my head.

While thus I stood, my lady came, and said,
  "Come, now, and worship at Love's inmost shrine;"
  She spake with a compulsion so divine
That straightway I arose, and followèd.
  Now Love's continuous lights about us shine,
And by our voices is Love's anthem led.

SAVING LOVE.

I SAID, " Oh, thou who holdest in thy hand
    A rose-wreath'd lamp, whereof the mystic light
    Makes dim the floating glories of the night,
Surely thou comest from some unknown land :
Draw near and speak, that I may understand
    Thy will ; make weakness strong, make darkness
        bright."
    Then burn'd intenser glories on my sight,
And unseen wings the quivering stillness fann'd,

While a voice said, " Rise up, O weary heart !
    Poor heart that died in a too bitter strife,
    I am the Resurrection and the Life !
I am the Love, whereby redeem'd thou art."
        And then I knelt, and all love's light was shed
        About me as I knelt and worshippèd.

POSSIBLE MEETING.

ART thou afar or near, O Royal Day, —
    Thou Day that bring'st me to my love again?
    Must the sweet autumn moon be in the wane
Before I feel thy breath, and hear thee say,
" Behold thy love ? " or shall the skies be gray,
    Disturb'd by wind and sense of imminent rain,
    Before I hear thee cry, " Oh, not in vain
Thou didst beseech my coming in thy lay ? "

Or shall the leaden winter be begun,
And all the sky forsaken of the sun ?
Let this be as it may, my thoughts outrun
    The dull and hostile days that intervene ;
    They shall not bar thee, conqueror and queen,
    But be thy guards when thou dost, crown'd, pass in.

SAD SONGS REMEMBERED.

NOT of my lady be, this once, my lay,
　But of my songs of her be this my song ; —
　My songs, that stood, a strange and unseen throng,
About my spirit, ready to obey
The words that grief and love might have to say.
　In this one, all the pain of hope found tongue ;
　To this I said, " Go forth ! and be thou strong,
Some pity of my lady's soul to pray."

And now, poor songs, that they have done their best,
　Though weak their wings might be my love to bear, —
　Now that Joy's regal foot is on the stair
That Grief so often trod in long unrest, —
　I will not these my faithful songs despise,
　But look on them with reverential eyes.

LOVE'S ANSWER.

I SAID to Love, " Lo, one thing troubles me !
　How shall I show the way in which I love?
　Is any word or look or kiss enough
To show to her my love's extremity?
What is there I can say, or do, that she
　May know the strength and utter depth thereof?
　For words are weak, such love as mine to prove,
Though I should pour them forth unceasingly."

Then fell Love's smile upon me, as he said,
　" Thou art a child in love, not knowing this, —
　That could she know thy love by word or kiss,
Or gauge it by its show, 't were all but dead ;
　For not by bounds, but shoreless distances,
Full knowledge of the sea is compassèd."

A DAY OF PEACE.

BECAUSE the time was autumn, and the day
    Serenely sad as trusting souls may grow,
    That, having borne the uttermost of woe,
Take faith in God, for help upon their way,
And no more weep, but live, and watch, and pray;
    Because the warm moist wind blew faint and low,
    Seeming the secret of my heart to know,
While birds sang softly through the tender gray;

Because of these, my heart was glad forsooth;
    But only glad thereof, because my love
    With hands in mine, and sweet face hung above,
Said, as my kiss receded from her mouth,
    The words that give my spirit strength to rest
    'Till Love's full glory be made manifest.

THE ONE GIFT.

AND can I give thee nothing, oh, my queen?
    Have I no gifts to cast down at thy feet, —
    No crown which for thy wearing might be meet?
Yet, when thy hand my hands I take between,
When round my neck thine arms encircling lean,
    When 'neath thy quickening kiss, prolonged and
        sweet,
    My heart, on fire, seems audibly to beat,
And yearn to thine so distant and serene,

I feel that it is better as it is;
    Better that all the glory should be thine,
Than I, indeed, should give thee bliss for bliss.
    While things are thus, one gift may yet be mine;
        But couldst thou love me once as I love thee,
        Giftless indeed, belovèd, I should be.

MOVELESS MEMORIES.

Blow, autumn wind of this tempestuous night !
   Roar through this garden, and bear down these trees ;
   Surely to-night thy voice is as the seas,
And all my heart exultant in thy might !
Lo ! thou wast up before the morning light,
   And in the darkness thou dost take no ease ;
   But ever thy wild clamor doth increase,
As through thy waves the nightbirds wing their flight :

Roar thyself hoarse, thy rage is all in vain,
   Thou canst not from this garden, or this grove,
   Drive forth the undying memories of love,
Nor hush at all the sweet mysterious strain
     They sing, who never into sleep descend,
     But keep perpetual vigil to the end.

COMFORT IN ABSENCE.

Oh, love, remember when between us lies
   The bitter, barren sea, the dreary land,
   How utterly alone I then shall stand.
Lo ! not with thine, but with my sadder eyes,
Look thou upon the cold, unpitying skies ;
   Or, when glad birds beneath thy window band,
   As when we, silent, sitting hand in hand,
Watch'd the gray windless autumn morning rise, —

Since I would have my soul still beat in thine,
   Be sad for me, and in thy spirit say, —
   " How dark for him, and desolate this day,
From gray beginning unto gray decline."
   So shall I gather strength to go my way,
Feeling thy soul compassionating mine.

8

PRELUDES.

I.

Oh, ye whose hearts on happy things are set,
  Ye lovers who love well and have no fear,
  Come ye no farther, do not enter here;
This is the land where Love and Death are met, —
A land ye may not easily forget,
  Once having entered. When your eyes see clear,
  Oh, lover, into hers, and lips draw near,
And kisses multiply, and lids shine wet,

'T were ill if visions of this land should rise
  Between you, overshadowing your bliss;
  Live on and love, nor think each time ye kiss
This kiss may be the last, — for all joy dies!
  Think not on death, lest so love's peace ye miss,
Wasting your breath in unavailing sighs.

II.

Will ye come in, and sit in this dark house? —
  'T were better, as I think, for ye to go
  Where blackbirds sing and early violets blow,
And watch Spring dawning in the fields and boughs.
Here, with pale wreaths around their blanched, cold
     brows,
  Lie dead the days whereof ye nothing know.
  Ye say the dead are harmless; is it so?
Nay; uncompassionating Death allows

The ghosts of their dead selves to come again;
  And, if ye tarry, ye will see them rise, —
Dim shapes intangible, that wax and wane.
  Some gaze with pleading, some with wrathful eyes,
    "Mere ghosts," ye say; yet go, before ye cry, —
    "We have seen the immortal faces, and we die!"

III.

UPBRAID me not, O world, that I forbear
    To make this song of mine a sword to smite
    The wrongs of nations and defend the right ;
Nor that I fail, through some remoter air,
To follow proud philosophy even where
    Through soundless skies she tracks the lonely height.
    You say the world 's in darkness ; in the fight
Of creeds conflicting bid me take my share :

In truth I am no coward, but I say,
    Strive for the right you love so ; quell the wrong.
I cannot rise and join you in the fray ;
    All I could give you would not be for long,
And might avail you nothing ; go your way !
    The grief that weds my soul requires my song.

IV.

As looking on a river that progresses
    Through some loud, populous city, till it gains
    The acrid sea, — thought tracks it through the plains
O'er which it flowed, to innermost recesses
Of hills the earliest light of morn caresses,
    Where, nursed by Nature, fed by fragrant rains,
    Sung to by birds, swayed by all varying strains
Of winds the very soul of spring possesses,

It sprang a slender stream, which, gath'ring force.
    Grew to a river hurrying to the sea ;
    So, on this current of my song look ye.
Think not upon its dark unalterable course,
    Nor of drowned hopes that in its eddies be ;
But dream ye know and wander near its source.

V.

Not as who gives to some belovèd one, —
   Some dear belovèd one whose altered eyes
   May not the face above them recognize, —
The roses he has taken from the sun
To deck her cold, sweet body, saying, " None
   Shall give thee gifts hereafter," — one rose lies
   Upon the breast that doth not sink or rise,
And in the hand whose pressures are all done

Another rests, — not so to thee, my love,
   Give I these songs of thee ; I do but give
   Because I love, and for thy memory live ;
As swaying pines, that winds to dirges move,
     Give to the winds again what winds have given,
     Give I these songs to thee, my life, my heaven.

VI.

I said to you, my songs, in other days,
   Go forth ! and say now, in my lady's ear,
   " From love's intense and stormy atmosphere
Our life is given.   Where fierce passions blaze,
And great despair through the soul's echoing ways
   Rolls thunder-like, we circle : but are here,
   To say the storm shall cease, the heavens clear,
If so thou wilt have pity, in thy grace."

And as men read, the Saviour of mankind,
   When his disciples in their hour of dread
Called on Him, rose, and quell'd the waves and wind, —
   So at her answer all the tempest fled,
     And love's high heaven was filled from end to end
     With light no lesser heavens can apprehend.

VII.

AND yet again I said, " Go forth, and see !
  Your tones are glad and solemn as the strains
  To which men worship in their holiest fanes.
Proclaim the glory of the days to be,
When Love himself, in sovereign ministrelsy,
    From lands where he in visible godhead reigns,
    Shall wake that lordlier music which sustains
All souls to look on his divinity."

O songs ! my songs, did I not bid ye say,
  " Pardon, O queen, wherein we failed to show
The bliss that turns his night to glorious day ? "
    So did ye say, my songs ; and well I know
      She took your singing voices to be part
      Of the diviner music of her heart.

VIII.

Go down, my songs, now to the land unknown, —
  The starless kingdom that has Death for king, —
  About the silent porches close and cling.
Through windless air, where bird hath never flown,
Or waste, gray fields, wherein no flower hath blown,
    Hills from whose barren bosom wells no spring,
    Let your tones rise, and die in echoing ;
And by their sadness let my love be shown.

Then, like the echo lasting, it may be
  A voice shall answer ; but if otherwise,
Cease not ! nor strive to solve Death's mystery,
    For she *may* hear you, though no voice replies.
      Go then ! and say, " He follows in our wake,
      Who bade us hasten here for his love's sake."

NOT THOU BUT I.

It must have been for one of us, my own,
  To drink this cup and eat this bitter bread.
  Had not my tears upon thy face been shed,
Thy tears had dropped on mine; if I alone
Did not walk now, thy spirit would have known
  My loneliness; and did my feet not tread
  This weary path and steep, thy feet had bled
For mine, and thy mouth had for mine made moan:

And so it comforts me, yea, not in vain,
  To think of thine eternity of sleep;
  To know thine eyes are tearless though mine weep:
And when this cup's last bitterness I drain,
  One thought shall still its primal sweetness keep, —
Thou hadst the peace and I the undying pain.

NOT DEATH, BUT LIFE.

I am not dead, belovèd, would I were!
  My spirit has not ceased to beat with thine;
  Only my hope is dead; and Peace divine
Lies dead upon Hope's tomb, while black Despair,
Repeating ever an unanswered prayer,
  Gives me to drink his sacramental wine,
  And sacramental bread to eat, in sign
That I am his till death, his robes to bear.

I am not dead! I have not died with thee.
  This is no sleep, perpetual as time.
Dead lips are mute, and dead eyes cannot see
    Pale memories and half-dreamed dreams of bliss;
  Dead feet have rest, but living feet must climb
    The steep round which the eternal darkness is.

A YEAR AGO.

A YEAR ago, belovèd! Who shall say
  What smiles and tears were ours a year ago?
  Last year my heart was fain its love to show;
Then had I songs to sing, and prayers to pray,
And dreams to dream, in dawns and twilights gray, —
  Dreams of love's heaven, that I came to know
  For passionate realities; and, lo!
Realities turn back to dreams to-day.

O thou, my love, my saviour, living yet!
  I stand with folded hands before the gates, —
  Dark doors, whereof Death hath alone the key.
So, with strained ear to iron gratings set,
  His term of bondage spent, some prisoner waits
  The word that, long delayed, shall make him free.

DREAMLESS LIFE.

I HAVE a work to do, which being done
  I will go out from men, and sit apart,
  And give myself up wholly to my heart.
The winds, the moon, the ocean, and the sun,
And all the rain-vexed streams in spring that run
  To rest in the broad rivers; birds that start
  The fields with sudden singing, as they dart
Through eve aglow with fire, or dawns begun, —

These shall my hidden thoughts interpret right.
  So, when I walk far off from any strife,
  Folded in quiet of sequestered life,
Through some pale autumn evening's lessening light,
  My soul may catch her voice, discern her face,
  And, yearning, lapse in rapture of embrace.

LIFE IN MEMORY.

As when two lovers in one room have been
  Alone together for a rapturous space,
  Hand lock'd in hand, face resting against face.
She says, " Farewell ! " and, gone, the man, unseen,
Tarries behind, where sat with him his queen;
  There, of her love recalling all the grace,
  His arms her quivering body re-embrace:
Once more, his lips upon her dear lips lean, —

So in the past, left lovely from thy love,
  Lit by sad lights of memories that shine,
  Holy as lamps that burn before a shrine,
My spirit from the whole world stands aloof;
    Yea, and shall dwell so till Death takes it where
    No grief is bitter and no memory fair.

THE WATCHERS.

HERE in this room there is no light of day,
  Only dim light of funeral lamps is shed
  Upon my past, that lies here still and dead ;
Only Love hears the words I have to say;
Only he, watching, sees the gifts I lay —
  Sad gifts, indeed — upon the silent bed.
  Down distant passages I hear the tread
Of feet that from this chamber keep away.

Here sit we, I and Love, and keep one troth :
  Nor will I quit my sacred past at all,
  Till Death in his good time my name shall call,
Then shall one equal darkness cover both ;
    Then of this chamber shall Love seal the door,
    That, being closed, shall open never more.

LOVE'S JOURNEY UNENDED.

HUSH'D is this place, where now to live seems best, —
    Here in Love's journey came we, she and I ;
    Beyond me wind the dim, sweet paths, whereby
Of Love's high hill we should have gain'd the crest.
Here, something weary, did she stop to rest,
    But yet more weary grew, till with one sigh,
    One kiss that seem'd of a dumb grief the cry,
We parted, and deep sleep her soul possess'd.

The paths at end of which Love's temples shine,
    Glad feet of other lovers may essay ;
    But, as they, singing, pass me on their way,
Who place sad songs for flowers upon a shrine,
        Let them not ask how long waits he, and why,
        Lest sadder they should go for the reply.

LIFELESS LIFE.

SINCE we, for the last time, " good-by " have said ;
    Since I may never hold thy hands again,
    And prayers are useless, and all tears are vain, —
What do I here, when round thy soul are spread
Silence and sleep, and on my spirit shed
    The bitter, uncompassionating pain,
    Till my heart yearns for rest, as earth for rain,
When by the utter sun discomfited?

So, a blind man within some storied hall
    May hear men round him press, and one voice praise
    The deep enchantment of a pictured face,
One this sheer stretch of sea, and one the fall
    Of April sunlight on some green, wet place,
While he stands sightless between wall and wall.

FOREDOOMED.

No star upon thy course sheds any ray;
   Though thy bark bear for years the wind and foam,
   To no sweet haven shall it ever come.
The night shall see thee drifting, and the day
Behold thee as the night; thou shalt not pray,
   Nor utter any cry, but, cold and dumb,
   Watch the waves pass; and glad ships sailing home
Shall hail thee not upon thy trackless way.

The salt wave shall taste bitter to thy lip:
   Weary, yea, unto death, thy soul shall be
   Of winds, and the interminable sea,
     That does not bring thee nearer any goal,
But sweeps through changeless gloom the fated ship
     To its remote, inevitable shoal.

CHANGED MUSIC.

When I and she I loved walked side by side,
   With love beneath, around us, and above,
   I made her songs, whereof the soul was love.
My happy songs flowed to her as a tide
That shoreward sets when angry waves subside;
   And sweet it was to feel her life should move
   To music of my making, sweet enough
To please her heart, and leave it satisfied.

And now, if she, remote from griefs and joys
   ('Mid fields forlorn no reapers come to reap),
     Should catch this sadder music, she would seem
   Like one who fallen to glad strains asleep.
     And waking, as it were, from some long dream,
Finds the song changed indeed, but not the voice.

LOVE'S RANGES.

Not merely the sweet words that she has said;
  Not merely the too long unnoticed place,
  Transfigur'd by the presence of her grace, —
Least things she touch'd, least poem that she read,
And any soul on which her love was shed,
  Are dear to me, through love that in such ways
  Brings round me ghosts of buried nights and days
That watch, what time I sleep, about my bed :

But places that her eyes (not mine) have known,
  Wherethro' her feet have wander'd many a time,
Have in their names a music not their own :
  And now she makes her home in that far clime,
    Whereof the name is Death, is it not meet
    That I should find that name of all most sweet?

TO LOVE.

O Love, because when others praised thy name,
  And worshipped at thy shrine, I stood aloof,
  And said to men, " Why prate you so of Love,
And of Love's inextinguishable flame?
Lo ! Love is trodden under foot of Fame ;
  This light you boast of, burns it clear enough
  To guide you if the path you tread is rough?
Lo ! Love, at last shall bring you all to shame : "

Because I took thy holy name in vain,
  Kept not thy laws, nor followed in thy ways,
Can I hope any place with thee to gain?
Yet, as one came, and bade my lips refrain,
  And brought my soul to know thee, let these lays
  Lie now accepted at thy throne of grace.

SPRING'S RETURN.

A VOICE within me said, " Is not Spring fair?
 Is not the light she moves in very sweet?
 Sweet all the flowers that rise beneath her feet;
The songs of newly-mated birds that wear
Fresh plumage on their breasts; the lucid air
 Wherein wild scents ecstatically meet;
 Laughter of winds and waters, pulse and beat
Of Nature's heart, — hast thou in these no share?"

And I made answer, saying thus, "The bride
 Clothed in fair raiment, in her maidens' sight
 Looks fair to all, except that desolate one
Whose love upon the eve of marriage died —
 She finds more fair the grave, sequester'd nun,
 Seeing for both shall be no wedding night."

WEARY WAITING.

UNTO myself I say, "I am alone!
 Upon the bounds of further life I stand."
 I have passed very swiftly through Love's land;
But I have seen it, even I have known
The bliss of calling one beloved my own:
 And now, before my time, upon the strand
 Of the pale sea, with Sorrow hand in hand,
I wait until the weary time be done.

No boat as yet is at the water's side
 To bear me over; all its solitude
 My heart might bear with, but a multitude
Of ghastly memories track me to the tide;
 They sing, they weep, they sob with passionate
 breath,
 "Love lies behind thee, and beyond is death!"

I ABIDE IT.

Love, I abide it, come to me what may
 When this my life is done, whose tides now fall
 'Twixt shores wherefrom pale memories lean and
  call
On some sweet night, or dead, delicious day :
And as a gray sky makes the whole sea gray,
 So, 'neath this vast, impenetrable pall
 Of hopeless sorrow reaching over all,
My life rolls on its unbeholden way : —

Whether thou wilt in death dispel this pain,
 And give me sleep instead, or cry, " Arise !
 Prepare to meet her lips, her voice, her eyes,"
I cannot tell ; such things with thee remain,
  According to thy will, which, though thou hide it,
  I question not, but living, I abide it.

A LOST CHANCE.

When side by side we watched the darkening sky,
 With love-lit faces, leaning each to each,
 My lady stirr'd with low, impassion'd speech
The silence, saying, " If we now could die,
Both loving so, were it not well? " but I,
 Who dreamed of fairer heavens within my reach,
 Said, " Nay, not yet, for Love hath still to teach
Us sweeter secrets ere we put life by."

Then she, who saw our souls clothed in such peace
 As wraps the hills at sunset, turned her face :
  Ah, God ! if we had made that thought our prayer,
It might have been that, kneeling at her knees,
  My lips on hers, Death had made answer there,
And bound us in the bonds of our embrace.

TOO LATE.

Love has its morn, its noon, its eve, its night.
　　We never had the noontide, — never knew
　　The deep, intense, illimitable blue
Of fervid, mid-day heavens, making bright
With princely liberality of light
　　Waters the water-lily trembles through ;
　　But, in the evening's shadow did we two
Set out to gain Love's farthest, fairest height.

O love ! too late, too late for this we met ;
The goal was near, the nightfall nearer yet.
　　One star of Memory lightens in our track,
　　And all the rest is dark ; I will go back, —
　　　　Back to the paths we walked in, and there stay,
　　　　Until I change them for the silent way.

LOVE MET BY DEATH.

Love put our hands together, saying this, —
　　" Follow my steps, and I will bring your feet
　　Through paths that more than summer maketh sweet,
Unto the lordliest of my palaces ;
　　There will I fill ye full of fiery bliss ;
　　There, in deep groves and gardens shall ye meet,
And through mysterious twilights, to the beat
　　Of mystic music find it good to kiss."

But even, while we followed in his track,
　　A dark form came between us ; then it was
　　I felt her turn from me, and watch'd her pass
To the far country whence no soul comes back.
　　　　Now where our paths diverged, I stand, I wait,
　　　　Till Death in sleep my life shall consummate.

THE SOUL'S YEARNING.

THOUGHTS of clasp'd hands and unrememb'ring eyes,
   White breathless lips, and all the signs that show
   The weary soul at length has done with woe ;
The silence after death, the peace that lies
Upon the veilèd lids of whoso dies, —
   These thoughts, that but a little while ago
   Seem'd sad and bitter, now most tender grow ;
And sleep but hints what death can realize :

And yet sometimes the soul, unsatisfied,
   Will cry, " When I for so long time have striven,
   Endured so much, and overcome so much,
Shall no love clasp me on the deathward side ? "
   Such thoughts are hard to bear with, and yet such
   Point more, I think, than any creed to Heaven !

HOW MY SONGS OF HER BEGAN.

GOD made my lady lovely to behold, —
   Above the painter's dream he set her face,
   And wrought her body in divinest grace ;
He touched the brown hair with a sense of gold ;
And in the perfect form He did enfold
   What was alone as perfect, the sweet heart ;
   Knowledge most rare to her He did impart,
And filled with love and worship all her days.

And then God thought Him how it would be well
   To give her music ; and to Love He said,
" Bring thou some minstrel now that he may tell
   How fair and sweet a thing My hands have made."
   Then at Love's call I came, bowed down my head,
And at His will my lyre grew audible.

BEYOND RECALL.

My soul that cannot serve her now at all,
 I said is worthless ; she who made it fair,
 Can have for it no longer any care.
Why should I keep it, I will let it fall,
Nor reck of where it lies ; and therewithal,
 I fain had flung it from me in despair,
 But a voice said within my heart, " Forbear !
Thy soul was hers, is hers beyond recall.

" Is not the rose long dead, she wore an hour
 Within her breast, kept by thee for her sake ?
 Holds thy soul less of her than this poor rose ? "
 " Thy speech," I said, " unto my spirit shows,
 Of what it had been guilty ; I will take
My soul and keep it as I keep the flower."

VAIN COMFORT.

Because one voice is silent, and because
 The world is poorer by one queenly face,
 Wilt thou for this, say all thy nights and days
Are altogether desolate ? Alas !
Gone joys what God shall bring again to pass ?
 Lo ! Art stands near thee, live to gain her grace ;
 To ultimate joy and peace, are many ways.
Thou yet shalt live to say of grief, it was.

O thou vain comforter, do men bereft
 Of sight, and all the glory of the day,
In their first blindness, turn to what is left ?
 Nay, rather the bird's songs through flowery May,
 They hate, — divining from that rapturous mirth.
 How lovely the precluded sights of Earth.

AS THOU WILT.

IF she should come to me from far away,
　How would she come?　Should I upon some night
　Wake suddenly, and see a mystic light
Enshrining face and form, what would she say?
What sweet thing do?　As in the old, dear way,
　Would she bow over me, and first, with light,
　Sweet kisses, touch my brow ; then, as the might
Of love grew stronger, closer cling and lay

Her lips to mine, in one long passionate kiss?
　Or would she kiss me not, but stand aloof,
And say, " Rise ! work without the aid of bliss,
　Lest grief in time thy manhood should disprove ? "
　　Kiss me, refrain, or chide me, O my own,
　　But leave me not as now, alone ! alone !

AN INVOCATION.

O THOU my love ! my queen ! my life ! my all !
　By these my songs, and every song a cry ;
　By all love's hopes and fears ; by every sigh
Of joy and sorrow ; by the rise and fall
Of breasts drawn close together ; by the thrall
　Grief weaves about me ; by what shall not die, —
　The cherished anguish of thy memory, —
I do beseech thee, hear me when I call.

Hear me, O my belovèd, if thy soul
　Hear anything at all in that dim place.
My path is steep, — my path without a goal, —
　I never more may meet thee face to face ;
　　And all the prayer then of my life is this,
　　To gain, in dreams, one dear accomplished kiss.

9

SAD DREAMS.

For all my dreams of thee are sad, not sweet.
  I see thy face; but on thy face I see,
  The shadow of the end. I call to thee,
Come close to thee, yet never may I greet
Thy form with an embrace. My pulses beat
  With old remembered hopes; then suddenly,
  Hope stops, and thou, I know, art gone from me.
I strive to follow, but with failing feet;

Or else I dream that I, with heart on fire,
  Wait in some darkened ante-chamber's gloom,
    Till one shall lead me forth, to hear once more
    Thy words of love: the visionary door
  Begins to move; I see the dim-lit room,
And wake through over-stress of great desire.

THE ONE QUESTION.

This time last year we parted, — she and I.
  "The day of meeting soon will come," we said;
  And hand in hand, unto the last we stayed:
Then, when to love no more might love reply,
Starless to both became the star-lit sky.
  And now, that longer parting has been made,
  And she, released from love, in sleep is laid,
I stand where she stood, having said, "Good-by."

And as I come through paths she knew so well,
  The winds cry out to me, "Where is she now?
What has Love done with her? Speak thou, and tell."
  "Where is she?" moans the streamlet in its flow.
    "Where, where is all thou lovest?" fills the air;
    And I, O God! I can but echo, "Where?"

REBUKED OF LOVE.

SOMETIMES, I think Love doth my heart rebuke.
   I fancy that he calls to me and says,
   "What right hast thou to grieve? Go, hide thy face!
Say, wert thou worthy in her eyes to look,
Thou, whom God cursed, and even I forsook,
   Till she reclaimed thee, and transformed thy days?
   Say, hath she touched thee, hath one seen her gaze
Upon thee tenderly? Say, did she brook

Thy kiss upon her mouth, thou wretched one?
   Unworthy on thy knees to kiss the ground
      Her feet had sanctified, be still for shame!"
And I, I can but answer, if she found
      Me fit for acceptation, I may claim
Grief's bitter privilege to dwell alone.

THE NEW RELIGION.

THEY shall not be forgotten, these my lays;
   I know that they shall live when I am dead.
   A thousand things I might have sung and said,
And no man hearkened to my blame or praise;
I might have moved the veil from off the face
   Of awful Destiny; I might have spread
   Rebellion through a land misused, and made
My song the weapon of an injured race,

And men forgotten all the same, — but now
   I come among ye, and to each I cry,
      "He that hath ears to hearken, let him hear,"
   I sing of love, made manifest in her.
I preach the Gospel of her life, and so
   I feel these words, though mine, not born to die!

FATED !

STAND, fated house, forevermore, alone !
   Stand, 'mid thy barren gardens, wild, and swept
   By winds that wailing through thy trees have kept
The tune of grief. Be thou of joy unknown :
For in thy walls, now dank with oozing stone,
   My lady turned her face from me and wept,
   And gave me her last parting kiss, and slept
The sleep from which none wake to laugh or moan.

The summer misbecomes thee, O dread house !
Glad songs of birds sound alien in thy boughs !
   Death keeps thy doors, thy passages are full
   Of ghosts that sorrow makes not beautiful.
     Forlorn, barred, silent — keep thy secret well,
     That none who pass may guess what thou could'st
       tell.

A FAIR THOUGHT.

'MID very many bitter thoughts, I found
   One which seemed fair and gracious, and I said,
   "This thought shall prosper in the inner shade
Of being, where the wells of life abound."
And so I plucked it from the common ground,
   And set it where it should not be dismayed
   By winds and scorching heats, and near it laid
All sacred things which did my life surround.

"And when it is," I said, "full grown and strong,
   My chosen ones shall view it in its pride,
And I will fold its fragrance in a song."
   I left it in a quiet eventide,
Scarce breathing, lest my breath should do it wrong ;
   And yet because it was so frail, it died.

DIVINE COUNSEL.

AND if her soul has gained some place divine ;
  If even now she sits in heaven, and sees
  All round her ranged its shining companies, —
Has not God turned her heart from loving mine?
Has He not said to her, " A soul like thine
  Will find more sweet companionship in these
  Who, being peaceful, know how sweet is peace,
Than in the offspring of a stormy line? "

Yea, He has called that love of hers a sin,
  And purged her of it, and that love is dead !
Thus, even if some place near her I win,
  She will not say the things on Earth she said,
    God having turned her heart from me ; and so,
    What I have known I never more can know.

BITTER POSSESSION.

OUR raptures and our sorrows are our own,
  Most false it is to say we sympathize ;
  What man can see as with another's eyes?
The song of one man drowns another's moan ;
A man in sorrow always is alone !
  He pours his heart out 'neath unpitying skies,
  And tells his trouble to the night, and tries
To feel some message with the wind is blown.

He hath his anniversaries of woe ;
He walks o'er verdure that hides death below ;
  He gives to no man, as he takes from none.
    The life he lives, none hinder or control ;
  Only the hearts of lovers beat as one,
    For theirs is knowledge, absolute and whole.

UNCONFESSED WORSHIP.

You worship God.   I fail to recognize
   In aught the God you worship ; but I see
   How, broken-hearted, you wait patiently
Upon His will, and deem that He replies
In mercy to your sharp and passionate cries.
   You worship Art, a fair divinity ;
   And you — your God is holy Liberty,
Enduring as the ocean and the skies.

And all the worship of my soul is given
   To her whose life these songs commemorate.
Yet, if indeed there should be God and heaven,
   By loving solely what is pure and great,
      All that we deem in life is loveliest, —
      Is not the worship His, though unconfessed?

A PARABLE.

THERE was a certain man who thought to raise
   A temple reaching well-nigh to the skies ;
   And well, indeed, his plans he did devise,
And solidly and firmly wrought the base,
And worked with a brave heart for many days.
   And when the walls to a great height did rise,
   Fair things he put therein, and with proud eyes
Watched men in wonder on the structure gaze.

" Surely the gods," he said, " my labors bless."
   And higher still, and higher did he build ;
   The temple with pure images he filled, —
When, lo ! it reeled ; and, crushed beneath the press
     Of tottering walls and towers, he buried fell !
     Yet, do I think he planned, and builded well.

A LOST JOY.

A MAN who having loved for many days
  Some woman gracious, goodly to behold,
    With looks that all his yielding will controlled,
Love being dead, views with calm eyes her face,
Admiring, yet not thrilled, and sadly says,
  " How is my heart to all this beauty cold,
  Lasts there no charm my spirit to enfold?
Valueless now the long-desired embrace,"

When, lo! her face in the old, dear, lovely way
  She turns, and speaks; and then his soul perceives
    For what he loved her, though the love is dead;
So, walking lonely, on one April day,
  Noting the promise of unfolding leaves,
    I thought as he, and as he says I said.

LETHARGY.

BEHOLD, Grief came, and stood against my bed,
  And touched me with pure hands, and with calm
    eyes
  Looked on my face, and said to me, " Arise!
And do Life's bitter work." Whereto, I said,
" Forbear a little; she, my love, is dead,
  And all the wretched life within me dies."
  She passed, — and then, with sweet voluptuous sighs,
A crown of shining roses on her head,

Came one most fair, and cried to me, " Awake!
  Am I not fair, behold my lips and breast?"
But she passed on, because no word I spake.
  Then came a fiend, whose power my blood possessed,
And she the purpose of my life may shake;
  Yet on these two, Grief's likeness was impressed.

AN UNKNOWN TONGUE.

BECAUSE my life is dark and desolate,
  Like some gray, uninhabitable land,
  Which hears forever on its wreck-strewn strand
The roar of waves inimical as fate;
Because I cry life's bitterest cry too late;
  Because pale Grief, with her relentless hand,
  Leads me up paths most steep, until I stand
Alone before the shut and shadowy gate

Which opens once to each, and only once, —
  Would I make your lives sad, all ye who say
  " Bright are the skies above, and fair the way;
Darkness may come, the present is the sun's ! "
    Love knows I would not; fear not then my song.
    I speak strange words; ye know not yet the tongue.

THE DEAD HOPE.

THE mother who has lost her only child,
  Thinking of all it should have been to her,
  What time strange voices in the breezes stir,
Sits in the Autumn twilight, gray and wild,
Remembering how the dead lips spoke and smiled.
  And as she sits, her child full grown and fair,
  Large eyed, with glory of up-gathered hair,
Comes in a vision exquisitely mild.

So, sometimes, as in dreams, I seem to see
  That joy arisen to full height — that life,
That hope which died in shining infancy.
  The mother yet may be a fruitful wife
    And bear fresh children; but for me there springs
    No second hope from out the womb of things.

WEDDED MEMORIES.

AND if my memory live when I am dead:
    When all whereby men knew me turns to dust;
    When deaf and dumb, and sightless, I am thrust
Into dank darkness, where the worms are fed
By Death's gaunt hand, that breed in my cold bed;
    When I, at last, with life and love break trust;
    When the soul's yearnings and the body's lust,
Are ended wholly, as a tune out-played, —

If then, men name my name, and from these lays
    The depth and glory of thy soul divine,
    Shall not, beloved, my memory live in thine? —
Our memories moveless 'mid the moving days,
    Intense and sad, like changeless stars that shine
On ruined towers of a predestined race.

SAD MEMORIES.

IF two who love, when I am gone from hence
    To some far distant land across the seas,
    Should in this room, possessed by memories,
Sit wrapt in love's calm, holy and intense,
Feeling their passionate kisses recompense
    Their hearts for doubts and fears now lost in peace
    That manifold embraces but increase,
Aware in all of Love's omnipotence, —

Would they not, sitting silent, feel the weight
    Of some unknown despair upon them press?
Would they not taste the sorrow of our fate?
        Would not some black foreboding smite them
            there?
    Would they not feel and hear the tireless stress
        Of phantom wings through the love-bewildered air?

DEATHWARD WAYS.

ALL men and women walk by various ways
    To Death's dark land ; and some with song and mirth
    Beguile the time which lies 'twixt death and birth ;
Some, joyous and full blooded, through a maze
Of splendid passionate nights and dreamy days,
    Gain soon their goal ; and some who find a dearth
    Of joy in all, poor strangers on the earth,
Plod on their path, and yield nor prayer nor praise.

But, look you, I will walk with none of these,
    I walk a straight and solitary path, —
    A way which no sweet scent, or verdure hath ;
And as I walk, like strong and rising seas,
    I hear my whole past surging on my track,
    And would return, yet never may go back.

WAS IT FOR THIS?

WAS it for this we met three years ago,
    Took hands, spake low, sat side by side, and heard
    The sleeping trees beneath us touched and stirred
By some mild twilight wind as soft as snow,
Though with the sun's late kisses still aglow?
    Was it for this the end was so deferred ?
    For this thy lips at length let through the word
That saved my soul, as all Love's angels know?

Was it for this, that sweet word being said,
    We kissed and clung together in our bliss,
And walked within Love's sunlight and Love's shade ?
    Was it for this — to dwell henceforth apart,
    One housed with death, and one with beggared
        heart ? —
    Nay, surely, love, it was for more than this.

MISTRUST.

I FELL before Love in my heart, and cried,
  "O Love, Love, Love, am I cast out from thee?
  These that once held me in captivity
Rise up again about me on each side.
Have I so long their deadly charms defied,
  To fall now, heedless of my life to be?
  O Love! dear lord, hast thou forsaken me?
Dost thou thy face in sore displeasure hide?"

Then said a voice, "Thou dost me wrong, O son,
  Thou art not fallen yet. Does not this prove
  That thou art wholly mine, that I am Love,
And I am with thee? Of thyself alone,
    What strength hadst thou to battle with their
      spell?
    I am thy sword, and buckler; it is well!"

A MESSAGE FROM LOVE.

I DO not come among you as Christ came,
  To preach eternal life, for well I know,
  The soul and body both one way must go.
But on my heart this message, as in flame,
Was written: Go thou forth, now! and proclaim
  Love's glory, for the folk rebellious grow;
  My sacred images they overthrow,
And do blaspheme against my holy name.

Dante, and he who served with equal heart,
For love, the poet and the painter's art,
  They make their jest of; Love is dead, they say,
  And other gods we worship in this day.
    Better than love is lust; love made men sad,
    And we who labor, labor to be glad.

LOVE'S PRE-VISION.

No thought of me, I deemed, was in her soul
   When those sweet eyes, that did all eyes transcend
   In glory, saw Death waiting as a friend.
She heard no sound of Earth ; no distant roll
Of bitter waters o'er a sunken shoal ;
   No raving of mad winds that break and bend,
   And hurry to its black and brackish end,
The ship whose course no pilot may control.

'T was well : one thought of me had marred her rest,
   And made her soul, through pity, loth to go.
     She took my love, and wore it as a flower ;
     And, lest some thorn should wound her in that hour,
   I ove took it gently, when she did not know,
And laid it after on the cold, sweet breast.

SORE LONGING.

My body is athirst for thee, my love :
   My lips, that may not meet thy lips again,
   Are flowers that fail in drought for want of rain ;
My heart, without thy voice, is like a grove
Wherein no bird makes music, while above
   The twilight deepens as the low winds wane ;
   My eyes, that ache for sight of thee in vain,
Are hidden streams no stars make mirrors of.

I see thee but in memory, alas !
   So some worn seaman, restless in his sleep,
   In time of danger, o'er the raging deep
Sees visionary lights, and cries, " We pass
     The prayed-for land ; reverse the helm, put back ! "
     Yet still the ship bears on her starless track.

DIVINE POSSIBILITY.

BECAUSE no man who lives can surely tell
   What thing comes after death ; each night and day,
   Unheard of any save of Love, I say,
" O Love, my lord and master, from the spell
Of bitter sweetnesses that end in Hell
   Keep thou my soul ; strange forms beset my way,
   And as I pass, they whisper to me, ' Stay !
And rest with us, and life shall yet be well.'

" So guide me, Love, that if at end of all
   I should awake, and to my eyes be shown
Her face in heaven, and her voice should call,
     My soul to her, that soul then free from stain,
     Strengthen'd by love, and purified by pain,
   May answer, and reclaim her for its own."

VAIN DREAMS.

I AND my love are parted ; many days,
   Sad days, must be before we meet again ;
   But surely we shall meet, and all the pain
Of separation die as we embrace, —
When on her bosom lies again my face,
   And lips dissevered reunite and strain
   Together in a kiss that shall enchain
Our souls too much for any speech of praise.

And when at length we speak, I think I know
   Of what our speech shall be. Oh, vain my soul !
Put by these dreams, take up thy load and go ;
   Each lot, however bitter, hath its goal :
     Thy goal is death, not life ; and when life ends
     The night that hides thy love on thee descends.

DEAD !

"Dead, my belovèd, what means this word?" I say
    Over and over, as I fain would wring
    Some hidden meaning from it; let me bring
My soul to comprehend it.   Gone away !
Asleep, to wake no more on any day?
    Nay, not asleep, awake, and wandering
    Through lands of bloom in a continuous Spring !
I seek for light, yet find no certain ray ;

But this I know, again we shall not meet ;
    We never more shall sit as we have done,
Breathless with love, in twilight hushed and sweet ;
    Upon no joy of ours shall set the sun, —
       Nor more nor less than this it means ; and yet,
       Can I remember all, and thou forget?

GRIEF'S ASPECTS.

Grief does not come alike to all, I know.
    To some, grief cometh like an armèd man,
    Crying, "Arise, and strive with me who can !"
And some are brought to heavenly peace through woe,
And watch a new life from the old life grow ;
    And some there be who strive beneath the ban,
    And, having struggled hotly for a span,
Tread on the fallen body of their foe.

My grief has taken hold of me, and led
    My feet to lands of any spring unknown.
There has he bound me in strong chains, and said,
    "Behold, we are forevermore alone !
Drink from my hand thy wine, and eat my bread
    At last, I have thee solely for my own."

IMPOSSIBLE JOY.

WHAT of that place, my dearest, the far place
  We should have seen together, planning so,
  Before the Autumn winds had strength to blow,
And Summer turn'd from us with lingering gaze,
As one who, parting, yet to go delays?
  Ah, very strange, it seems to me, to know
  That seasons in that place still come and go
Though we come not; if down the talked-of ways

My solitary steps are ever led,
I shall seem surely as some man new-wed,
  Who finds the loved one absent from his side,
  And seeing she returns not, opens wide
The bridal chamber, and bows down his head
  Upon the couch where should have lain the bride.

A PARABLE.

THERE was a man who bore for many days
  Pains, sore to bear, that would not let him rest;
  Meanwhile, great fear of death upon him prest,
Till, lo! he dreamed and slept. And full of grace
The dream was; for a strange and holy place
  Was open'd to him, and on God's own breast
  He lay, with all his sins and fears confest,
Having Christ's saving kiss upon his face.

"And very sweet it is," he said, "to know
  That life at length is over, and grief done."
Then fell the dream away from him, and lo!
  He woke to find another day begun;
    Yea, woke to bear more agony and dread, —
    Death bending with gaunt face above his bed.

THY VOICE.

THY voice is in the sea's voice, when it makes
  A melancholy music to the beach.
  Thy voice is in the winds, when birds beseech
The twilight time with song.   The stream that takes
Its way from out the hill by flowery brakes,
  Has in its tones the sweetness of thy speech:
  At night — when all is still, and faint sounds reach
The ear of one who, having slept, awakes

Full of his dream — thy voice floats through the night,
  In music sad, as Autumn winds that blow
'Mid yellowing woods in the sun's waning light,
  Compassionate, persistent, clear, and low.
And, when the world is fading out of sight,
  Thy voice shall whisper peace, and bid me go.

RESTLESS SORROW.

I, WHO was once of love insatiable,
  And groaned, through sorrow humbled, — I, who said
  What time the hand so loved in mine was laid,
Give me the lips, and let my kiss compel
The answer that shall trance as with a spell
  My heart, which now through doubting is dismayed;
  And, when the prayer was granted that I prayed,
Still found fresh wants my spirit to impel, —

Should I, if thou couldst come but once again
  To me, — allowed to sit unseen, and hear
    Thy voice, — ah, say, should I be satisfied,
  Forbid to kiss, or even touch thee, dear?
Oh, mad, unreasoning heart, be still, and gain
    Contentment, that thy prayer has been denied.

THE DARK WAY.

WHEN first I knew this trouble of my days,
  This unrelenting grief, I was like one
  Who, suddenly made blind, walks not alone,
Nor yet for any other guidance prays,
But silent sits, conjecturing of the ways
  That he must tread, the perils he must shun,
  Unaided by the light of star or sun :
And as at length, with set and vacant gaze,

He rises, stumbles, stops, moves on again,
  Trusting, withal, his feet a path have found,
  Distinguishing the day from night, by sound ;
So I, through tortuous paths no light makes plain,
    Having less even than the blind man's faith,
    With outspread hands, grope my dark way to
      Death.

HIDDEN EVIL.

I LOOKED where many flowers grew, and I said :
  "The way I walk is barren, yea, and long ;
  Surely one hour of rest can do no wrong."
And so 'mid thickest of the grass I laid
My limbs ; the blossoms met above my head,
  And as I lay, half-eased, I heard a song,
  Which seemed to me a psalm, and then among
The flowers, with a faint halo round her shed,

Came singing a fair woman with drooped eyes.
  Oh, perfect soul, she touched me where I lay ;
She softened all my life's sad memories ;
But even while she soothed me with her sighs,
  A fiend possessed me, that I might not stay :
  Her breast I bruised, then turned, and went my way.

10

LOVE'S WORDS.

I.

"A MAN will give his life for me," Love saith.
  "His heart and brain and body will I take,
  And if Fate wills so, for that man, will make
A pleasure-house of life. Men shrink from death;
Yet I, by even a look, a tone, a breath,
  Can make the death-hour lovely for my sake.
  All things for me, a lover will forsake,
And verily I will reward his faith;

"But if a man have sorrow at my hand,
  If Death the life of all he loves destroys,
  And he should seek for any other joys,
Or search for consolation, I will brand
  That man with shame, and utter with my voice
The words that bid him from my sight, my land."

II.

"THEREFORE, O son," Love saith to me, "be wise!
  Think not thy sorrow how to mitigate;
  But rather, how to patient bear, and wait.
Thou hast loved well; I treasure all thy sighs,
And hear thy prayers: I cannot stay thine eyes
  As yet from weeping, or reverse the fate
  That God hath sent on thee, unbar the gate
That shuts her soul from thine, or bid her rise

To tell thee that these words are words of truth:
  But have thou faith, O son, believe in me;
And I will some day make the path more smooth
    For treading of thy pierced and weary feet.
  It may be late or soon, but thou shalt see,
    How sorrow borne for love, can make death
      sweet."

THE STRANGERS.

BECAUSE the time is Spring, when flowers should be,
  The Strangers wander through my land and say,
  "Surely some flower must blossom by the way.
The path should now be fair with greenery,
And birds make music in each flowering tree.
  Is only this land blossomless in May?
  Come, let us watch the first transforming ray
Of sudden light, that makes it fair to see."

They know the atmosphere they breathe is chill;
The gray wood songless, and the meadow still,
  They see no exultation of the Spring; and so
    They say Spring's sweetness is not yet begun.
  Alas! alas! how little do they know —
    The Spring-time and the Summer, both are done.

GRIEF AGAINST GRIEF.

BETTER, my love, than this, to love in vain, —
  To feel, what time my heart was sad for love,
  Thy soul unpitying stand from mine aloof;
Better to bear the torment and the pain,
Of lips that from all worship must refrain,
  So I might feel thy sweetness near me move;
  Touch thee, and see thee, find some way to prove
That souls can love, themselves not loved again.

But thus to sit without thee, and to know,
  No grief the past can ever recreate;
    To seek, and not to find thee; to awake,
And face the haggard day that can bestow
    No gift of love, — these are such griefs as make
Man feel he is but man, while fate is fate.

IN HEAVEN.

My lady sits at Beatrice's feet,
   Holding her hands, and gazing in her eyes,
   Breathing against her bosom all her sighs
For one who doth by day and night repeat
Her name, he finds so sad yet finds so sweet.
   And she, in her Italian voice, replies,
   " Nay, sister, have no fear, Love never dies !
And Love will lead him here, and ye shall meet."

I know when Dante, in his lady's ear,
   Murmurs his last sweet lay of her, my love
Sits silent, thinking of a by-gone year,
   When one, so speaking, sought her heart to move ;
     Then Beatrice understands, and bows,
     And kisses tenderly her lips and brows.

COMPLETE SACRIFICE.

I DO not ask thee, Love, to make life sweet ;
   All thou hast laid upon me I must bear ;
   Nor do I ask again for any share
In things I once held dear ; but when I meet
With sore temptation, and my pulses beat
   With bodily desire, and so despair
   Half drags me from the path, and makes me fare
Like men whose lips her lips did never greet, —

In such an hour, stand close, and hear my call,
   Lighten my darkness and sustain my feet ;
     Chain me in chains which, if they bruise, control ;
   That I may make this sacrifice complete,
Which is, indeed, no sacrifice at all,
     Except I yield the body with the soul.

FATE.

GOD knows I had no hope before she came,
　　And found me in the darkness, where alone
　　I sat, even then, and brooded o'er things flown.
She touched my hand, she called me by my name,
She turned my night to day, and smote with flame
　　The heights and depths of life, till I was shown
　　Where possible heavens lay, and things long known
As things transfigured in that light became.

I sought my heaven, her love, at whose white gate,
　　"O my belovèd, take me in," I cried.
　　　　A little while the answer was delayed;
　　　　And then her voice, from out the glory, said:
　　"Enter! and be at peace;" and Fate replied:
"Thy love is strong, but stronger is my hate!"

UNSEEN WORSHIP.

MY face is from the world, and turned mine eyes
　　Upon the sacred image of my past, —
　　Still as a sculptured saint, whose shade is cast
On some cathedral aisle.　Sad music sighs
About its placid silence; on it lies
　　That fleeting light divine, too rare to last,
　　Our Wordsworth caught, entranced.　From sins that
　　　　blast,
No soul to this calm saint for refuge flies;

But none of all Christ's votaries who fall
　　In mad excess of worship on the rood
　　　　That bears His image crucified, and lay
　　　　Their lips in kisses to the sacred wood,
Have worshipped as my soul, apart from all,
　　　　Worships unseen, its idol, night and day.

PROPHETIC MOMENTS.

As when one wandering in a wood by night,
   Hearing the owls cry down the dark for prey,
   Seeing no star to light him on his way,
In those dread moments feels the entire might
Of some great, distant grief his whole soul smite
   With sickening apprehension of a day,
   The fruit of years unborn, till waste and gray
His far life looks in the soul's prophetic sight;

So sometimes, through the horror of my days,
   The sights and sounds of ghostly memories,
     I stray; but the mysterious sadness through
   My soul is reached by breaths of some high peace;
     Airs from a fair far land I never knew, —
A land wherein she walks with Love, and prays.

LOVE'S BIRTH–HOUR.

WHAT was the day when, sweet, I loved thee first?
   The day when my heart trembled at thy tone
   Almost as much as would my lips have done
Could they have slaked at thine their new-born thirst?
When did this passion into full flower burst,
   As a bud into a rose, beneath the sun?
   When felt I first my body and soul as one?
Life with thee bless'd, without thee, empty and curs'd?

Who notes Love's birth-hour, then?   In sooth not I.
   Though Love like all things hath its birth and
       growth, —
     And love at first sight is a short-lived thing;
Nor shall I know the hour when Love must die,
   For that will be my death-hour too, and both
     Will pass where there is no remembering.

TREASURED THOUGHTS.

IF one you loved had tarried 'neath your roof,
   And wrought with her sweet fingers many a change,
   Would you, when she had left you, disarrange
Her handiwork, the veritable proof
Of her late presence? Nay, for very love
   You would not; but in memory would range
   Through rooms her dear touch had left sweet and
      strange,
And nought from where she placed it would remove :

So, when she came into my life's dark ways,
   Her soul gave many a saving thought to mine,
And all she gave of her abundant grace,
   I treasure in my heart, as most divine !
That if we meet again, in far-off days,
   They may be found as offerings on a shrine.

HER MESSENGERS.

AND could I think my dreams her messengers, —
   My dreams wherein she is, — should I not say,
   Waking upon some desolate new day,
As one who with a chosen friend confers
She did instruct this chosen dream of hers;
   Hers the sweet mouth that bade it wing its way,
   Through lands where dreams and sleeping spirits
      stray,
And sad lips laugh, and glad eyes fill with tears,

Until it found me? — Did she say, " O dream,
   Flying to him as swallows o'er the sea
     Fly on to summer, say some tender thing,
Kiss longing lips and eyes, and let him deem
   That I awhile am with him, bodily,
     Nor come back hither with a broken wing?"

WASTED SPRING.

ONCE more, though late, comes back to us the Spring!
   May's sunbeams waver in the wavering trees,
   And leaves and grasses sing in the singing breeze;
The time hath come for nightingales to sing, —
And suddenly, one day in June may bring
   From fields wherein 't were good to lie at ease,
   Life-giving as the perfume of blown seas
The warm, keen smell of hay, bewildering

The sense with its sharp sweetness; but to-day,
   Notes solemn, and sad, and measured have I heard, —
   The cuckoo's desolate cry presaging ill,
Telling of falling leaves, cold skies, and gray:
   Make the Spring hopeless then, prophetic bird,
   Since that one voice eternally is still!

A TERRIBLE SUGGESTION.

IF, after all, there should be Heaven and Hell,
   How shall it be with me upon that day,
   When God's voice calls me, and I answer, "Yea,"
To wait the doom I feel inevitable?
Shall He who made my life most memorable
   Through unexampled sorrow, turn and say,
   "Thy tears, O son, have washed thy guilt away,
And here within my Heaven shalt thou dwell?"

Yet even if He said this, and mine eyes
   Met hers again, and saw therein no love,
   Only, instead, a look of sad reproof,
Should I not stand forlorn in Paradise,
   And being by her spirit unforgiven,
   Sadden the saints, and so unmake God's Heaven?

ARRESTED SPRING.

THE Spring has been here ! thus much ye can tell.
  Behold these half-unfolded leaves that lie
  Upon the path, beneath an ashen sky.
Within these boughs, transfixed as by a spell,
Songless the song-birds sit ; there is a smell,
  Of Spring about, but that sweet breath shall die,
  As streams the west wind freed sink stagnantly,
Because, last night, a blight on all things fell.

What will ye hope, then, in this desolate place?
  Will ye entreat the Winter to make good
His promise ; and with cold and lustrous grace,
  Change to a chrysolite the tender bud?
      Not so, all energy that change could bring
      Lies mute, — arrested, with the arrested Spring.

AUTUMN QUIET.

THE splendors of the summer-time are done,
  And though the roses linger for a space,
  Soon will they fade on paths and garden ways.
The russet leaves lie thickly, and the sun
Wakes late now, and his course is swiftly run.
  No passionate summer storm the night dismays
  With flame and thunder ; these veiled nights and days
We would not seek, and yet we may not shun.

Then said a voice, I knew for Love's, " Even so
  May thy life be, dost thou my will and hers, —
A passionless existence that shall flow
Like some tamed stream which men have wrought to go
    Forever in one course ; which no wind stirs
    To speed or wreck the burden that it bears? "

PRAYER.

O LOVE, behold how steep the path has grown, —
  Almost too steep for any feet to tread,
  To thee I call, to thee I bow my head:
In solitude, with men, but still alone,
My heart hath made perpetually its moan.
  Yea, as the living call upon the dead,
  Stretching their empty arms across the bed
Where lies what yesterday they called their own,

So have I called on thee; but what avails!
  Sorrow, grown mad and impious, dominates,
And memory in the darkness sits and wails;
  At every step some foe in ambush waits
    To snare my feet. O Love, rise up, awake,
    And save me swiftly for thy mercy's sake.

THE ONE GRACE.

I KNOW my strength of singing scant and brief;
  Nor can I hope that men my words shall heed
  When I, in death, of love have little need.
I have not taught you wisdom out of grief;
And in myself have I had no belief,
  Said few wise words, and done no worthy deed;
  Too faint to follow, powerless to lead, —
A helmless vessel dashed from reef to reef.

But if, dear friends, you speak of me at all,
  Say in my favor this, and this alone:
    That when Love was in Her made manifest,
I knew her for my queen, and, leaving all,
    Followed the noblest and the loveliest
  Until I knelt before her at Love's throne.

MEMORY.

I STOOD once at the gates of Paradise ;
  I, even I — who now may chance on hell —
Stood there and heard the things unutterable
Love showeth once to all. And those dear eyes
Looked into mine, and then, as one who sighs
  For joy of peace, I sighed, nor broke the spell
  By any word. My kisses served to tell
My utter love ; her kisses for replies.

Oh, sweet, how sweet, all I had even then !
  And great the promise of the years to be.
Now must I stand deserted amongst men ?
  Nay, not deserted while thy memory,
    O love, hath still in its supreme control
    The failing body and the aspiring soul.

LIFE AND DEATH.

How is it then with her? I think 't is well :
  She hath no memory of days that were ;
  Her soul is vexed by no importunate prayer.
Love bowed beside her when on sleep she fell ;
No wanderer knocketh at her gates to tell
  Of things she would not know. She hath no care
  For any love. Our lives lie waste and bare
Like lands whose losses make them memorable,

And still she heedeth not ; yea verily,
Oh, life and love, if such a thing could be,
  That we for one brief minute should forget,
  She would not sigh or smile to know. And yet,
    While life is sad and death is even thus,
    Can all be well with her, and ill with us?

JUNE.

O JUNE, thou hast too many memories !
 Ghosts walk by daylight 'neath thy steadfast sun,
 And people thy warm darkness ; can I shun
These faces of dead joys, and pitiless eyes
That look in mine till my pierced spirit cries, —
 " Forbear — pass by !" and makes its desolate moan
 For pity of its sorrow spent and prone ?
Amid these ghosts my heart lies faint and dies.

O summer twilight, sad beyond all telling !
 O nights made once for love, made now for grief !
  Come, winter, with thy formidable array
Of frost and storms the gray cold ocean swelling !
 Yet wherefore come ? Thou canst bring no relief ;
  Hold'st thou not too the memories that dismay ?

WHAT PROFITS IT?

ALAS, my God ! what profits it at all, —
 The passionate love, the grief, the short-lived bliss,
 The pregnant silence after the long kiss,
The words half uttered and half heard, the fall
Of bitter tears, the long unanswered call
 Of heart to heart, the anguish and the fear ;
 And then the life lived after, chill and drear
As one long winter day when no sun is, —

The hourly strife with unseen enemies,
 The pitiable armistice, and then
The strife resumed, failures and victories,
 And yet no rest to either side, till when
 Death, that is mightier than the loves of men,
Makes all at once an everlasting peace ?

VAIN DELAY.

In every thought of comfort I essayed,
  I found some subtle evil, some base thing
  Unclean, most virulent, and sharp to sting :
Surely too long with these I have delayed ;
Yea, as a child who far from home has strayed,
  In some great forest lost and lingering,
  Expectant of the birds that will not sing,
When night comes on grows terribly afraid

And cries for home, — so seems to me my soul.
  Surely the child returned will no more stray?
  Surely my heart once more in the right way
Will keep most steadfastly in view its goal?
    Yet cry, lost child, for one to lead thee back ;
    And thou, Love, point my soul again its track.

LETHARGIC SORROW.

Surely to-night some mist hangs on my brain?
  My soul, grown blind, can only grope its way ;
  "Yes, thou art desolate," I hear one say, —
" For thee spring's sweetness all is turned to pain,
Art thou not bound and bruised by this, thy chain? "
  " Yea, I am bruised," I answer, in dismay.
  Yet now I can recall an ancient lay
Of a poor bard who deemed he loved in vain,

One queenliest of queens ; but she bowed low,
  And took and loved him for a little space,
  Then left him for a far and unknown place,
Where he, for all his longing, might not go.
    Now the mist fades, my soul regains its sight,
    And all shows plain in the old, unpitying light.

DESOLATE LOVE.

I saw Love sitting by a dry well-head;
   No crown was on his hair, and in his hand
   He had no sceptre, but a warrior's brand;
With blood his hands and feet and robes were red,
And ever as he bowed his face he shed
   Most bitter tears, and cried, "Where is my land;
   And all my subjects that might not withstand
My perfect will and the sweet words I said?

"Lo! men have turned from me in these dark days,
   The temples that I reared they have cast down."
Then close by his shone out my lady's face;
   I saw her bow, and knew she spoke with him;
   And when he raised his eyes they were not dim,
And on his hair was glory of a crown.

BY THEIR FRUITS YE SHALL KNOW THEM.

And if I say I love, and yet forbear
   To do her will, what does my love suffice?
   Barren it is, and all my songs are lies.
Yea, though I touch the limit of despair,
And breathe in sorrow, as I breathe the air,
   Find the earth waste, and gray the sunlit skies,
   A void where once I dreamed of paradise,
A bitter end of every hope and prayer,

Yet slight her least command, my love were vain, —
   A pitiful and unregarded thing,
   And I unworthy of her fame to sing, —
Too strong to fall, too feeble to attain.
      But if I do her will my life shall prove
      The depth and glory of her saving love.

THE TWO TEMPTATIONS.

Two met with me upon a weary day.
   One said, " I am Love's servant fair to see,
   And I have alms which I will give to thee."
But though most fair she seemed, I answered, " Nay,
I serve the master, pass thou on thy way,
   For, lo ! Love's servant gives no alms to me."
   The second cried, " I am Love's enemy,
And certes no wise fair ; let me essay

" To guide thy steps." " I walk alone," I said.
   But he seized hold of both my hands and cried, —
     " A little come with me, then stand aloof."
Love's foe he is and mine, a false, false guide ;
Yet must I bear with him, or bow my head,
     Serving Love's servant and betraying Love.

PAST AND PRESENT.

WHEN I conceive of things that might have been, —
   Of joys that now no God can reinspire,
   And all the melancholy years require, —
I turn my face and front my life unseen.
Stately she was, and like an Eastern queen,
   Only her soul was as a kindling fire.
   She comprehended every heart's desire
And was desire's bound.   O matchless mien,

O face of sleeping passion and grave eyes
   That grew Love's own when his soul kindled them ;
   O wide white brows that bore his diadem ;
O voice which now no more to mine replies ;
     O sweet, my love, my own in spite of fate, —
     Is the lamp quenched, my bride, and am I late?

THE RIGHT TO LOVE.

"O Love, be merciful to me," I cried,
  "Turn thou, oh, turn to me, my lady's face ; "
  And, as a dying man for new strength prays,
I prayed to Love and Love's own voice replied, —
"The prayer is granted, be thou satisfied."
  Ah me ! the pity and glory of those days,
  The lovely, mystic, unfamiliar ways
Of bliss wherein my spirit did abide !

Ah me ! the roar of that dark sea and cold,
  The flowerless paths, and heavens bereft of light !
O Love, and O my love, I was too bold !
What right had I thy love to seek or hold?
  Yet now Love saith from his unmeasured height, —
  "Let thy life show thou hadst alone the right."

AFFINITIES.

SOMEWHERE, I do believe, — though where, who
    knows ? —
  One like my lady dwells. Should I not see,
  If I could come upon her suddenly,
The queenly face and eyes whose depths disclose
Passionate rest, great thoughts, and the repose
  Of natures wrought for wise, sweet mastery?
  Yea, I do feel, though incommunicably,
That round my life, in this life, hers yet flows,

And she will read these lays, and all her soul
  Will yearn toward me to comfort and sustain.
  Others will read to find their truth in vain ;
    She only will entirely understand.
    O soul twin-born with hers, stretch out thy hand
And lead the pilgrim till he reach the goal.

QUANTUM MUTATUS!

WITH emptied, outstretched hands and downcast eyes,
   Love walks alone and walks uncomforted ;
  And if the aureole gleam about his head,
I hardly know ; his lips are full of sighs,
And they who question him gain no replies.
   Only to me he saith, " My feet have bled
  From many a thorny path ; and I have said
Such grievous words as make the swift tears rise.

" But never since men knew my awful name
   Have I walked thus by such precipitous ways,
Seen such deep darkness, and illusive flame
  Which leaves no track. O great ancestral days !
   For I am he whose mighty power and peace
  Crowned Helen, consecrated Beatrice."

DREAMING LOVE.

I SAW Love in a strange and hidden place ;
   His face was as the face of one who dreams,
  Yea, as some weary slumberer's who seems,
By the glad smile which lightens all his face,
To walk once more 'mid old loved country ways,
   What time the tender April twilight teems
  With songs, and breath of lilacs, and the streams
Run with the sound of wind through some green maze.

Love's hands were folded on his quiet breast, —
   But, lo, a far-off voice called, " Love, arise ;
  The night is ended and the dream is done."
Then Love unclosed his fair and mournful eyes,
Took up his staff, and turned him from his rest,
   And as he went shone round his path the sun.

LOVE AND DEATH.

" My gracious lady talks with Love," I said,
  " Yet hath perchance no thought of me. O sweet
See now I put my heart beneath your feet,
Having no crown to set upon your head :
Is the gift too unworthy?"   Then Love led
  My lady up to me, and bade her greet
  My lips with hers, that body and soul might meet :
We kissed, we clung together, comforted.

" My lady talks with me," I said ; " Love's grace
  Hath made us now forevermore as one."
    My lady turned aside, and, lo ! one saith, —
    " Lover, behold thy lady talks with Death."
I turned to clasp my sweet, but in her place
  Death towered before me and eclipsed the sun.

LOVE'S SERVANTS.

THERE came to me who cried, " Arise and wake
  And follow us, beholding we are Love's, —
  His chosen ones who haunt his secret groves,
Wherein are streams where thou thy thirst may'st slake ;
Ah, be well pleased with us thy home to make."
  The voice of her who spoke was like a dove's,
  When with her tenderest pleading she most moves
Her mate to love in some dim, tangled brake ;

A ripe seduction lurked in every curve
  Of her lithe body.   Then the second spake,
    Gayer her tone ; the third, with jeers and cries,
    Besought and threatened, — but I closed my eyes,
For these were all Love's servants, for whose sake
Shall they who knew the Master stoop to serve ?

LOVE'S SUFFICIENCY.

IF love be unsufficient, what avails?
　If love abideth not, then what thing stays?
　One prayed-to wearies as the one who prays;
The exquisite delight of passion fails;
No joy endures; the brightest beauty pales;
　And though to art we give our nights and days,
　We know our brows unworthy of their bays, —
Wreckt men whose eyes see visionary sails.

And is love insufficient, O my queen?
　Did we not say, when in love's sweet control
We stood, each bound to each, " For what hath been
　　This hour suffices?" O belovèd, see
　　It hath sufficed. Love's saving memory
Has interposed 'twixt ruin and my soul.

DEAD JOYS.

THE joy in sunset, and the large delight
　Of rains abundant, falling after heat;
　The passionate joy it was to break and beat
With strenuous limbs the blown waves warm and white;
The vital peace that fills the summer's night;
　The pensive joy, just touched with dreamy pain,
　Of autumn twilights when dim woods complain
And the past summer haunts the inward sight;

The joy of travel and acquaintanceship
　With lordly towns and many a sung-of place
Whose names are in man's ear and on his lip, —
　　All these for me are over now and done,
　　Since that essential life which lit the sun
Death has eclipsed, darkening my lady's face.

THE HIGHER SELF.

THAT higher self her spirit raised in me,
  Pressed in life's fight, desponding shrank away;
  And then, in irresistible array, —
Threatening to have me in captivity, —
Of tempters came a mighty company.
  Then did I turn myself to Love and pray;
  Yet still I felt my strength wane day by day,
And still I said, " Must these have mastery?"

And when it seemed, indeed, that I must fail,
  Came back that higher self and shook the door
    Of my shut soul, and smote the tempters down;
And said to me, " Does not her love prevail?
  Is she not one with thee, forevermore,
    That Death may crown thee with Love's perfect
    crown?"

A MESSAGE FOR THE OLD YEAR.

SOON shall we have the New Year in his place;
  With empty hands and unexpectant eyes
  I sit and ponder while the Old Year dies;
" Lo! from the stainless cold of the first days,
To this most gentle night, through all thy ways
  Have I not walked unchanged? With songs like cries,
  Wrung out of sorrow which Love deifies,
I have assailed thee. Now as one who prays,

" Hoping for acceptation of his prayer,
  I pray thee, dying year, that shouldst thou meet,
    In that dim place where all our sweet dreams be,
    The ghosts of years that knew even her and me,
  Thou say how one, forlorn, with weary feet,
Treads the dark path that leads he knows not where."

A PARABLE.

THERE was a certain man who thought to dwell
  Apart from all, in loveless solitude ;
  None roused him or had power to change his mood.
" Within the world, endowed with many a spell,
A sorcerer, whose name I will not tell,
  Waits me," he said ; and no man understood.
  So, for long months he dwelt in lonelihood,
Nor heeded how the seasons rose or fell.

He bore with memories, — a ghastly throng
  That filled his sleepless nights and desolate days.
    But, lo ! that sorcerer, subtle as a flame,
    Wound to him, hissing forth his awful name.
  Then he, the man, so hunted, turned his face
And sought his kind that they might keep him strong.

LOVE AND SORROW.

SORROW, of Love begotten, fought with Love
  And bruised the mother's breast, and in her ear
  Hissed bitter words and base ; then Love had fear.
But still with that rebellious one she strove,
Till Sorrow, seeming humble, sought to move
  Love's heart with sophistry, and cried, " Ah, dear !
  What can we hope for now?   Behold, quite near
Is many a mystic cave and magic grove,

" Wherein we may forget, at least one day,
  Our sad relationship ; fear thou no snare : " —
  So Sorrow, kneeling, prayed her impious prayer.
    But mightier was the mother than the child,
    Who owned her sin ; and these two, reconciled,
Now help each other on the tedious way.

CONCERNING THE NEXT BOOK, TO BE CALLED "THE PILGRIMAGE."

MORE have I spoken of myself than her.
　　I feel you do not know my lady, yet;
　　But those who knew her once may not forget.
I am a pilgrim, — no mere wanderer
Upon life's way, — and often I confer
　　With those I would not; but my face is set
　　Towards that high goal where love and grief are met,
And each becomes the other's minister,

And memorable sorrow makes love memorable.
　　Then, when I have o'ercome the weary way,
　　I will for you go back to that first day
When first I saw her face, of her to tell,
　　And make to all a sanctity of pain
　　For that she was and shall not be again.

A PARABLE.

THERE was a man who thought to dwell alone
　　In a fair house. "My lady sleeps," he said,
　　"Resting forever in the eternal shade;
But, lo, this place which should have been her own
I still will keep as hers; let Memory moan
　　Through sculptured passages for sweet things fled."
　　Only one dwelt with him, around whose head
The aureole shone, and he for Love was known.

Then to that house, in lamentable estate,
　　Came wanderers, craving shelter from the cold,
　　And these the master pitied for their pain;
But spoilers they, whom Love at length controlled,
Scourged, and cast forth, and closed in wrath the gate,
　　Where now for entrance angels cry in vain.

PAST SUMMER.

When first the summer-time seems gray and cold,
  Though sad, we are not hopeless, for we say, —
  "No summer yet has been all cold and gray;
Warm days shall come, e'en as they came of old;
Yea, days of bounteous sunlight shall enfold
  The longing earth. In paths where now none stray
  We yet shall wander, singing by the way;
And though the nightingale long since hath told

"Her tale to every green and wind-swept glen,
  In sumptuous summer nights we shall repose
    'Neath gold-touched leaves that have not lost their
      green.
But when the darkened summer finds its close, —
When we have had such days and nights, — 't is then
  We know what may not be by what has been."

SUMMER TWILIGHT.

Some natures seem, like days in early spring,
  Soft and most changeful, fair with light and shade;
  And some are like gray autumn days that spread
A chill on all they meet; and others bring
A sense of patience and mute suffering,
  Like summer days whereon the heat has laid
  Such sudden silence, that the wind seems dead,
And the sun's light is veiled from everything:

But her deep nature I may liken to
  A bounteous summer twilight, when one knows
  An unimagined heaven of repose,
From which a new heaven opens to the view,
  While there unfolds within the heart the sense
  Of some divine, unknown omnipotence.

THE BITTEREST.

Love took me by the hand, and said : " Arise,
　To know this last and bitterest thing, O son ! "
I bowed my face, and said : " Thy will be done ; "
And then he brought me where, beneath warm skies,
A gracious land unfolded to mine eyes.
　" A goodly land it is," he said, " but none
　May ever dwell therein." " Then I will shun
The sight of it," I cried ; but, with deep sighs

Love answered me, and said : " Nay, son, not so ;
　But thou must gaze forever on this land,
　　For thus thy lady wills that it shall be,
　　Seeing the far-off peace thou canst not see."
　I said, " I do not seek to understand ;
Only, Love, give me grace her will to know."

THE UTTERED SOUL.

If God to me had given the heart and brain
　Of some musician skilled above the rest,
　Her soul in music had been manifest.
Perchance some painter, frenzied to sweet pain
By her deep loveliness, through stress and strain
　Of great desire to be through life possessed
　Of all that beauty, had been crowned and blessed,
And, spent yet living, seen the light strike plain

Upon her deathless loveliness, and died !
　But Music could alone her spirit render ;
　　Long waves of passionate melody that roll
　　Wave after wave all tending to one goal,
　Pure notes, intense, beyond all language tender,
Her soul in music, Music deified !

LOVE'S QUEST.

LOVE walks with weary feet the upward way,
   Love without joy and led by suffering.
  Love's unkissed lips have now no song to sing ;
Love's eyes are blind and cannot see the day ;
Love walks in utter darkness, and I say :
   " O Love, 't is summer," or " Behold the spring,"
   Or, " Love, 't is autumn, leaves are withering,"
And, " Now it is the winter bleak and gray,"

And still Love heedeth not. " O Love," I cry,
   " Wilt thou not rest? — the path is over steep : "
Love answers not, but passeth all things by ;
   Nor will he stay for those who laugh or weep.
    I follow Love, who follows Grief; but, lo,
    Where the way ends, not Love himself can know.

AND THOU SLEEPEST.

With no speech in thy lips, and no light in thine eyes,
　　Thou liest, and sleepest in sleep so profound,
That my heart when it breaks, and my voice when it cries,
　　　　Do not vex it with sound.

But my soul, in the depth of its grief, can rejoice
　　That, for me, but for me, is the anguish of days
That shall know nevermore the too dearly-loved voice,
　　　　Nor see the loved face.

The days wax and wane, the stern winter is over,
　　While, with carols new-born and perfumes that cling,
As a maid, as a lovely compassionate lover,
　　　　To earth comes the spring.

Oh, thy sleep is serene, more serene than a sea
　　Lying under the passionless light of the moon ;
Thou forgettest all raptures that were, and to thee
　　　　The night is as noon.

O my love ! my sole love ! O thou one best beloved !
　　Have my songs and my kisses no part now in thee ?
Is thy soul by the storm of my sorrow unmoved ?
　　　　O love, can this be ?

My spirit goes back to the day of our meeting,
　　When thy name was no more than a name to my ears ;
O name so belov'd now, of which the repeating
　　　　Brings passionate tears.

Dear name, which, in speaking, the voice would grow
  tender, —
  Name beloved of my voice, as thy face of my sight ;
As thy lips of my lips, wont in kisses to render
      Delight for delight, —

Now rendered no longer, for kisses are done ;
  Embraces are over ; glad music played out.
Our joy was at noon ; now set is the sun,
      And night is about.

Yes, night is about me, a night without star,
  Blackest night with no moonlight to lighten its gloom ;
But here at Love's shrine, where Love's memories are,
      My heart makes its tomb !

Memories, pale memories, sad memories that move
  All around me, in front of me, go where I will, —
Are these ghosts, then, the all life has left me of love,
      Love that heaven could fill?

Crown'd ghosts of dead queens that, forsaking their
  tombs,
  Haunt the groves and the palaces once that were theirs,
Wander weeping through desolate banqueting-rooms
      No festival cheers.

With a great lamentation they fill, day and night,
  The fair chambers unpeopled, fair halls that were once
Glad with dancing and melody, flooded with light
      Outshining the sun's.

And is this, then, the end of our beautiful dream, —
  Our dream that was song ; our dream that was fire ?
Peace lives not for me ; and time cannot redeem
      My soul from desire, —

From the infinite longings for days that are past,
　　When thy hands were in mine, and thy breath on my
　　　　hair,
When I sat at thy feet, and beheld Love at last,
　　　　As tender as fair.

Oh, then, Love he was kind to me, Love that for days
　　I had prayed to, and sang of, songs bitter to sing,
For I said, "Not for me, not for me is his grace,
　　　　But only his sting."

I reviled him, defiled him, made light of his name,
　　Disdained him, profaned him, besought him to cease ;
And, in infinite pity, to pardon he came,
　　　　And said, "Be at peace!"

Of treasures, the rarest he had in his keeping,
　　He gave to my soul ; and my soul, newly living,
As a spirit awake that too long has been sleeping,
　　　　Confessed him forgiving.

What gift did he give to me?　Who shall declare?
　　The depth of the nature to my nature given, —
Will ye fathom the deep sea, and measure the air,
　　　　Or estimate heaven?

Then I said, "Has He altered, the God of the years,
　　Who established the darkness no less than the light,
Who controlleth the winds, and unfailingly bears
　　　　The day to the night?"

He bids kingdoms arise ; He appeaseth the wars.
　　The storms work His will which the thunder proclaims ;
He spreads out the heavens, and lights them with stars
　　　　Which He calls by their names.

Cried the soul of the Psalmist, in sorrowful strength,
 " Hath God to be gracious forgotten?" I said,—
" He has pitied our long lamentations at length :
   His anger has fled."

" Ah, His mercy endureth forever ! " you say.
 Not His mercy, but wrath, for no mercy He hath ;
For as slayers stand full in the path of their prey,
   Stood Death in Love's path.

Then Love clasped all her joys and her visions of
  peace,
 As the mother her babe in her bosom would hide
When avengers draw near, and in terror she sees
   The foe on each side.

And my life now is mine, love, to use as I will ;
 If I ruin my soul, will thy sweetness reprove me?
If with glory the days of my life I should fill,
   Would that, my love, move thee?

If I come from the battle defeated and weak,
 Will thy tenderness lull, and take sting from defeat?
If I triumph, will pride in thy voice, on thy cheek,
   Make triumph more sweet?

Let them lose, let them win, there is work to be done,
 Mighty battles to fight, fierce conventions to slay,
Ere the glorious battle of freedom be won,
   And Right have her way.

But for me, not for me, is the conqueror's crown,
 Nor the trench of the fallen ; I share in no strife ;
I have buried my dreams ; by their grave I sit down,
   And watch out my life.

And thou sleepest, beloved, and thy rest is so deep,
 That no dream comes to mar thine enduring repose;
I, too, at the end, after sorrow shall sleep,
  Hands fold, and eyes close.

Pale the realm that I look for, and bloomless and still;
 Love leads me, but Love shall relinquish my hand,
When I pass the dark portals, nor shrink at the chill
  Of the summerless land, —

A land without song, and a land without light;
 But the angels, that stand in its gateways, can hear
A sound of lamenting that comes day and night
  Through the colorless air:

The crying of mourners who weep as they come;
 And the wind brings the sound of their weeping before,
Till they gain it, the land where all voices are dumb;
  Then, they weep nevermore!

And thou sleepest as they; as thou sleepest, shall I;
 I shall not remember, I shall not forecast;
Shall feel not, shall see not, shall know not, but lie
  Asleep at the last.

AFTER.

I.

A LITTLE time for laughter,
 A little time to sing,
 A little time to kiss and cling,
And no more kissing after.

II.

A little while for scheming
 Love's unperfected schemes;
 A little time for golden dreams,
Then no more any dreaming.

III.

A little while 't was given
  To me to have thy love;
  Now, like a ghost, alone I move
About a ruined heaven.

IV.

A little time for speaking,
: Things sweet to say and hear;
  A time to seek, and find thee near,
Then no more any seeking.

V.

A little time for saying
  Words the heart breaks to say;
  A short, sharp time wherein to pray,
Then no more need for praying;

VI.

But long, long years to weep in,
  And comprehend the whole
  Great grief that desolates the soul;
And eternity to sleep in.

DE PROFUNDIS.

I HAVE no strength at all, Love, save through thee, —
Man helps me not, and God, if God there be,
Has turned His face in anger; help me then,
O thou who governest the lives of men!
I have blasphemed against thy name, and said,
"Love is as other gods, a god to dread,
A mighty, uncompassionating god;
A god who scourges with a fiery rod,

A wrathful god, who desolates our years,
Filling the breast with sighs, the eyes with tears, —
Hot, bitter, blinding tears that bring no ease."
Such things I said ; yea, bitterer things than these,
But never said thou wast not, or denied
In any way thy godhead.   I had died
Before thee, speaking impious things and base,
Hadst thou not turned a favorable face ;
Hadst thou not raised me up, and bade me see,
In her I worship, thy divinity.
O Love ! from whom no secret thought is hidden,
Thou knowest well how bitterly, self-chidden,
I fall before thee in my heart, and cry,
Love, save me, or I perish !   Life goes by, —
Each day the thing I would not, that I do,
Because I am so worthless.   Oh, renew
A righteous spirit in me.   Let me say,
When I from life's sad memories pass away,
At least, I am more worthy ; if we meet
In any unknown kingdom, strange and sweet,
I shall not turn my face, as if in shame,
But answer, when She calls me by my name,
And tell her, how not all in vain I strove
To keep my whole life stainless for her love.
O Love ! I do conjure thee, by her grace,
By all the anguish of a last embrace,
To keep me in the way that I would go,
To give me strength to conquer, and to show
Her glory in my life, till all men see
What love can do for love.   Love, strengthen me !
What man another's thoughts shall understand ?
I am become an alien in the land.
I am like those who hear not, and as one
Who, being blind, discerneth not the sun.
I am like one whose lips were sealed from birth,
And like a man who falleth to the earth
Because his strength is wasted utterly :
But breathe thou on my eyes, and I shall see ;

Unclose my ears, and I shall hear; unseal
My lips, and let me with my mouth reveal
Thy wondrous works. Increase my strength withal,
That I may walk uprightly, and not fall, —
Fall not, nor stumble, though the way be long,
Led by thy hand, and in thy strength made strong.
Thou gavest, and Death took; and I am left,
Of every joy and every hope bereft,
Save this, — that I be able, at the last,
To look unshamed upon a bitter past.
My sorrow is not hidden from thy sight;
Have I not called upon thee in the night,
And in the day? "Love, Love!" have I not cried,
And hast thou not from thy far heaven replied?
Yea, thou hast answered me, and said, "Be strong!
Perchance, the way is not so very long;
O son, be firm, and I will send thee aid.
Have I not heard, and wilt thou be afraid?"
O Love! make haste to help me, or I fall;
Without thy aid, I cannot strive at all.
I shall be trodden under foot, and shamed,
Whenever with my name her own is named.
'T is knowledge of thy laws for which I pant —
Oh, teach me, thou, to keep thy covenant.
Men fall from thee by reason of their grief,
And think that other gods can grant relief.
Thou art the only god compassionate,
Oh, give me strength and patience, Love, to wait.
We know not what comes after death, but trust
That no fresh sorrow quickeneth in the dust.
No man can tell for certain what shall be;
Death lies before us like a sombre sea.
It may be, land is on the farther side;
But none come back across the awful tide
To bear us revelation. We must stand,
And watch the dark waves mounting up the strand.
Thou couldst not keep them from her; did she go
As one who trembles and holds back? Not so,

12

Thy light was in her heart; thy saving grace
Made lovelier even that divinest face.
She preached thy gospel; through her life I came
To comprehend the glory of thy name.
Now by the joy that was, and grief that is,
By every sacred unforgotten kiss,
By all the bitterness of unshed tears,
Help me to bear the burden of the years;
Give me fresh courage, and sustain my soul;
Purge me of all uncleanness, make me whole,
That I may show thy wonders fitly; then,
Glory to thee, O Love, in all.   Amen.

BEFORE SLEEPING.

WHEN I sleep, Love, be thou near;
   Let me hear
In my heart thy voice, and say,
   " All the day
I have done thy will and hers."
   Sleep confers
Many blessings; but, to me,
   What shall be
Half so sweet as dreamless rest?
   That is best !
If she come in any dream,
   And I seem
To embrace her while I cry,
   " Thou and I·
Are together once again,"
   How the pain
Of awakening should I bear?
   O Love, hear !
Keep all evil dreams away;
   Only say,
" By thy side my watch I keep,
   Sleep, son, sleep ! "

WASTED.

I WOULD it were done with and over,
　　This life with no goal, —
That bountiful darkness might cover,
　　My body and soul.

I 'm weary of living and loving;
　　I 'm weary of strife,
Of shadows incessantly moving
　　In light of my life.

I 'm weary of night-time and day-time,
　　Of things that go by;
I 'm weary of winter and May-time,
　　The sea, and the sky.

I look to the rest that comes after, —
　　The peace that endures,
Of a land wherein tears are as laughter,
　　And no love allures.

By no thought of a lady beloved,
　　But never possessed;
Is the spirit again ever moved
　　When lost in that rest?

On that day when you bid me farewell,
　　And no word I say;
You may bow yourselves o'er me, and tell
　　Of times gone away.

You may show me her portrait, and lay it
　　Here, just on my heart;
The poem she said, ye may say it,
　　And I shall not start.

You may say that she loved not at all,
    Or loved overmuch ;
You may say, " If love held him in thrall,
    We knew not of such, —

" Had he striven and lived long enough,
    This thing had not been ;
We had found him another fair love,
    To be his soul's queen."

I shall not assent nor deny, —
    Say, do, what you will, —
On that day when I bid you good-by,
    And my heart becomes still.

O my love, in whose love I abided,
    Whose soul, like a star,
Shone out from the distance, and guided
    My life from afar,

Having lived out my life for thee solely,
    Renounced all for thee,
The death which I die shall be holy
    And gracious to me.

O most beautiful, languishing face !
    O peaceful gray eyes !
That beheld with prophetical gaze
    The shadows which rise

'Twixt spirits that life could not sever,
    Death only divide, —
Taking one where the lovers meet never,
    Nor bridegroom claims bride, —

It is sweet through the wintry hours,
    When thick the snow lies,
To think of warm airs, and fair flowers,
    Green fields, and clear skies.

'T is sad when the summer is dying,
  And nights become chill,
To think how the snow shall be lying
  On valley and hill.

'T is sweet for the lovers that sunder,
  If but for a day,
To think of their meeting, and wonder
  What words each shall say.

So, love, through these dark hours of sorrow,
  How peaceful it seems,
To think of the night without morrow,
  The sleep without dreams.

On that day when Death bids me arise,
  No longer to grieve,
I shall follow, nor look with sad eyes
  On things that I leave ;

I shall sleep, and forget altogether
  Your voice and your face.
The passionate, splendid June weather,
  Long nights, and long days,

Will come, and I shall not awaken
  To think of the night,
The June night, when my soul was first shaken,
  And thrilled by love's might.

Yet I see it so clearly to-day,
  That night when I loved ;
I remember the tree-covered way,
  The sound, as you moved,

Of your robes sweeping over the grass ;
  The sound of your voice —
O my love, my own love, let them pass,
  These ghosts of dead joys.

O Death ! let me join them, and follow
   Where no sorrows thrill :
Where to chambers all silent and hollow,
   Comes nought that is ill ;

Comes nought that is lovely or gracious ;
   Comes nought that can move.
The chamber, though narrow, is spacious
   And lofty enough

For the tenant who lies without motion,
   Mere ashes and dust,
No longer the thrall of emotion —
   So, Lord, do we trust.

We trust, that is all ; but who, living,
   Hath knowledge to say
What gifts we may have of God's giving,
   When life 's put away?

Who can say, after all, we shall sleep?
   I may find death is vain.
I may wake to remember, and weep
   To feel the old pain

As keen in my spirit as ever ;
   To long for love's joys :
For the music that comes again, never, —
   The sound of your voice ;

For the passionate lips that could thrill me ;
   The beat of the breast ;
The peace of the soul that could still me,
   And wrap me in rest.

Shall I thirst for old touches and kisses?
   Ah, what shall I see?
Shall that possible life be as this is ;
   Or worse, it may be?

We may rove, being dead, through gray places,
   With twilight above, —
Worn ghosts with pale, hungering faces,
   Souls yearning for love, —

In lands where the wind never ranges,
   The light never veers, —
A kingdom that knows not of changes
   Through infinite years.

There, Dante, stern-featured, may wander
   With sorrow suppressed,
And look o'er gray seas, and say, " Yonder,
   My queen, does she rest?

" Or moves she, like me, among shadows,
   And sighs, ' We were wrong ;
Are these then the heavenly meadows
   Proclaimed in thy song?' "

I may long, as I now long for quiet,
   For trouble and strife,
The discord, the fever, and riot
   Of actual life, —

Any sound that should free for a minute
   My soul from that sound
Of a voice with my heart's music in it,
   A voice that I found

Surpassing all Fancy invented,
   A voice, the heart's cry,
A voice, wherein Laughter repented,
   And failed in a sigh.

In the utter, eternal dismay
   Of life never stirred,
Time may seem like one petrified day,
   Transfixed at God's word.

But all this is barren of reason,
　　And useless as prayers;
We must live on, and wait for Death's season,
　　To know what it bears.

AT A WINDOW.

THIS is the window at which she read,
　That day in June when the heat-mist rose,
Veiling the light of the sun o'erhead, —
　The poem my heart the loveliest knows.
And here I sat at her feet, and fed
My soul with the exquisite present, and said,
" The future may give, it may take away,
But she, she is with me one whole June day."

She read, I listened, and oft there came
　The roses' scent from the paths below;
My lips inaudibly named her name,
　And, so great did the passionate worship grow,
It seemed I must weep to quench the flame,
Kindling and thrilling through all my frame;
When her voice in compassionate music folded
The thoughts my heart to its longings moulded.

And here, one twilight in summer, too,
　I who had dreamed of her all the day,
Hearing the exquisite voice come through
　The music of Nature, — striving to say
A part of my love in lays I knew
That her spirit should one day own for true, —
Was suddenly, rapturously made aware
That she I dreamed of was with me there.

She bade me tell her my rhymes, and so
   I told them over, her mood to please ;
My heart was full, and my voice was low,
   I knew she would speak, when my voice should
     cease.
She spoke : one minute I seemed to know,
All my life might be, if her life could flow
As one with mine, till the end were attained,
All grief and joy done with, the great rest gained.

And here I sit by myself to-night,
   Utterly lonely, hopeless of heaven ;
Hearing no voice, discerning no light.
   Were not my life and my life's love given
Into her keeping, my sole delight? —
And now she is far out of reach, out of sight,
What deed shall I do, what word shall I say?
What song shall I sing, and what prayer shall I pray?

" Dream thou no dream, though thy sleep be long ; "
   To her I will say, "sleep fast, and well,
I — I will turn from the great world's wrong,
   Henceforward, alone with my grief to dwell.
I will pray to Love, I will sing a song
That love shall keep pure, and passion make strong,
And the song thus born of my love shall be,
The star of my lady's divinity."

HOPE AND MEMORY.

HERE Hope, with strenuous wings that shone like fire,
Drew after, in his flight, a love's desire ;
And here gaunt Fear snatched at Hope's shining wing,
And plucked it back, and held it fluttering ;
Here with the sound of wind and wash of waves,
Came tones and glimpses of the love that saves ;

The place is still the same, — this place whereto
I brought the dream my lady's face came through.
O guardian cliffs, and thou, enduring sea,
Once part of Hope as now of Memory, —
Hope, which accomplished, all lies cold and dead,
While Grief and Memory take hands and wed.
They walk where phantom feet and faces pass;
They speak of Hope that was, of Joy that was;
Unknowing and unknown, alone they move,
Sad and undying ministers of Love.

THE SEASON'S ASSOCIATIONS.

Soft white wings in a whirling wind,
   Shivering trees, and sad gray skies,
   Bitter kisses and long, long sighs,
Eyes by passionate tears made blind,
   A fire of hope that waxed and waned,
   Words that soothed, and words that pained,
And hot, strange light in the aching eyes, —

Waters flashing beneath the sun,
   Songs of birds, and the scent of May,
   Grief for a loved one far away,
Pain of a hope that is all but done,
   A thought of meeting, bitter as sweet,
   Lips that by night in dreams repeat
The one sad prayer they have left to pray, —

Breathless heavens and blinding noons,
   Friends that loiter 'neath garden trees
   Two together, a sense of peace,
Long still nights and the great sweet moons,
   Love victorious, crowned at last,
   Bliss exalted and grief downcast,
And a calm as deep as of summer seas —

Dead leaves drifting down garden ways,
  Fear in place of a fair delight,
    Wind and rain through the day and night,
Hands outstretched, and a half-turned face,
  Words from lips that will soon be still,
  Hopes that cower and thoughts that kill,
And death that triumphs in love's despite.

A DREAM.

I DREAMED I sat one evening all alone,
  In chambers haunted by old memories, —
No hope of star, or prophecy of sun
  Lightened the grayness of the autumn skies,
My heart was full of sorrow, great and keen,
For there my love one year with me had been ;
There first my soul confessed her for its queen,
  There had we mixed our kisses and our sighs,
There first to me her inmost heart was shown.

The wind outside was sweeping from the trees
  Their few remaining leaves, as in some hall,
Where men have late held great festivities,
  One plucks the faded glories from the wall,
Because the giver of the feast lies dead,
And those for whom the festal board was spread
Stand with sad faces round his silent bed,
  And all the lamps that lit the festival,
Untended, burn a little space, and cease.

Then suddenly I heard a voice, and lo !
  That voice was like the wind's voice having speech :
It said to me, " Rise up, dost thou not know
  Thy lady waits outside, and doth beseech

For entrance ; shall she cry and thou not hear? "
I looked but saw no living creature near ;
Only that voice kept whispering in my ear, —
 "She calls to thee, to thee her hands outreach,
Lo, by thy name she calls thee, even now ! "

I made no answer, but flung open wide
 The door, and faced the light with eager eyes ;
I called her name with all my strength, I cried
 On that belovèd name, as one who tries
To make men hear, when in vext sleep hè seems
To fly from pale avenging forms, and deems
He sleeps, but cannot waken from his dreams ;
 I looked, and saw above the sad gray skies,
And the gaunt poplars standing either side.

And this was all I saw ; and all I heard
 Was sad, protracted moaning of the wind
And piteous crying of some twilight bird
 That came a nest in leafless boughs to find.
"O false, false voice," I said, and turned away,
And shut the door upon the dying day,
And in the evening, desolate and gray,
 Sat still as one whom sorrow maketh blind,
And in the silence with my heart conferred.

And as I sat, I heard that voice again,
 And "Lo ! " it cried, "be not discomfited,
Knocks she so loud, and calls she so in vain?
 Go forth once more, and speak, nor be afraid
Of any fresh disaster.   Heavenly state
She leaves for thee, and at thy very gate,
Worn in the wind and twilight, doth she wait."
 " I have no hope, for all thy words," I said ;
"And yet I could not, if I would, refrain."

Then, as a man who, being near to die,
  Knowing men cannot save him, turns his face,
And called on God, in his extremity,
  To lengthen yet a little while his days,
And, calling, feels, withal, he calls in vain, —
So by her name I called her once again,
Then listened, and I heard the rush of rain,
  And sweep of winds down leaf-strewn garden ways ;
I saw the blown clouds hurrying through the sky.

I looked, and listened, but no answer came ;
  No form or phantom stood beside the door ;
Only the wind, in moaning, moaned her name ;
  Only my footsteps echoed on the floor ;
And now the daylight died and darkness fell.
I did not know I dreamed, and yet the spell
Of dreaming seemed upon me ; who shall tell
  If dreams are only dreams, or something more ? —
Who lights the depths of sleep with any flame ?

And now that voice was silent ; so I thought, —
  " It is no voice at all that I have heard."
And now the wind and rain together wrought
  Wild sounds, and sweet, wherewith the night was
      stirred.
The hours bore on their dark and destined course ;
Glad hearts and sad hearts slumbered, and the source
Of joy flowed on unnoticed, and the force
  Of grief was felt not ; but my heart recurred
To that strange voice, whose tones the wind had
      caught.

Then, as I sat and pondered, suddenly
  In exultation woke again that voice ;
It cried, " Rise up, go forth, for verily
  Thy love, she waits to clasp thee ! Hope decoys,
And men grow sick of hope, but this is truth ;

Thy kiss shall warm anew her cold, sweet mouth.
She left thee, but she kept with thee her troth ;
   And now she comes from very far to thee,
And brings thee back with increase all thy joys."

Stung by those words I could but count as vain,
   I flung the door back, as in last disproof :
And there withal rushed in the wind and rain,
   And there I saw the bleak night's starless roof,
And there and then I heard a voice divine,
And there two cold, sweet hands took hold of mine,
And there a stormy star shone out for sign
   That all things were accomplished. " O my love,
Meet we so even in my dreams again ! "

I brought her in, and hardly could believe,
   For joy, what was ; I know I could not speak ;
I know I wept, yet not as those who grieve ;
   I know her breath and lips were on my cheek ;
I know I could not for a little space
Lift up my eyes and look upon her face ;
I know at last we met in wild embrace ;
   I know I felt her lips to my lips cleave,
And how I fell by joy's excess made weak ;

And how my hands were fain her hair to stroke,
   Soft hair and bright ; and how she bowed, and
      said, —
And these, I think, were the first words she spoke, —
   " O love, lay back upon my breast thy head ;
Great love alone is changeless amid change.
Love hath the utmost universe to range ;
And hearts that love even death cannot estrange."
   At that word — death — afresh the old wounds bled ;
I turned to clasp her once again, and woke.

And long I pondered on the dream gone by,
  As men will ponder on an ancient scroll
That holds the key to some great mystery,
  Whose hidden meaning they would fain unroll.
Then said a voice unto me, without sound,
  " So may the hope, long sought and never found,
Come when the last great darkness closes round, —
  Come, and be apprehended by thy soul,
That thou mayst say, ' So meet we, she and I.' "

TO CICELY NARNEY MARSTON.

WHAT were I, dear, without thee? Let me look
  Back on my earliest days, to-night, as he
Who having thoroughly read through some book,
  Re-reads the opening pages lovingly.
In days when we were children, who but I
  Should know how thy soul turned from tender things,
How thy girl's heart would girlish joys put by,
  To share the boy's uncouth imaginings?

If then those days were sweet, who more than thou
  Made them so fair, blending thy life with mine !
What books we read together, then, as now, —
  Books that boys love, full of sea-winds and brine :
Dost thou remember that pet place of ours
  We called our haunt? Not beautiful it was,
Not musical with birds, nor gay with flowers,
  But from it we could watch the mad trains pass,

Whirling to places that we knew not of.
  Some vision in its smoke we must have seen ;
Heard music in its voice, now shrill, now rough,
  Or, there, our wanderings not so oft had been.

Oh, days wherein all songs of birds were sweet, —
    The birds that mock us now with boisterous mirth, —
Days when we laughed for joy of summer-heat,
    Nor laughed less well when snow made white the
        earth !

Ah, precious days we knew not how to prize !
    If they were slighted then, 't is now their turn
To slight, and look with sad, reproachful eyes,
    And whisper with white lips : " In vain you yearn ;
You longed for other days, and they are come.
    Now, you look back ; so, Dives, deep in Hell,
In torture looked at Lazarus, where, at home,
    He lay in Abraham's broad bosom.   Well,

" A gulf as deep is set 'twixt us and you ;
    We cannot give you back the dream, the peace."
Alas ! we know their cruel words are true ;
    We never can re-capture one of these.
Did we not share our sorrows and our joys
    In later years, when we awoke, to find
Passion and sorrow in the deep sea's voice,
    A mighty mystery saddening all the wind ?

Have we not loved the sea together, dear?
    Not as they love who come one hour a day,
To breathe its life, and then come not too near,
    Lest the waves take them in the face with spray ;
But, when the July sun, through waste blue skies,
    Declared the summer in her majesty ;
When no sweet air, like a divine surprise,
    Came up from the scarce-stirring, breathing sea ;

Yea, when the heat a fiery scourge became,
    And myriad shafts of sunlight charged the main,
In all that soundless violence of flame
    That made the shore one charr'd and smoking plain, —

We did not fail at all !   Our eyes could pierce
   Between the blinding air and steaming beach,
To where, weighed on by summer, fair and fierce,
   The sea lay tranced in bliss too deep for speech.

Oh, silent glory of the summer day !
   How, then, we watched with glad and indolent eyes
The white-sailed ships dream on their shining way,
   Till, fading, they were mingled with the skies.
And how we watched that sea, on nights that steep
   The soul in peace of moonlight, softly move
As a most passionate maiden, who in sleep
   Laughs low, and tosses in a dream of love?

And when the heat broke up, and in its place
   Came the strong, shouting days and nights, that run,
All white with stars, across the laboring ways
   Of billows warm with storm instead of sun, —
In gray and desolate twilights, when no feet
   Save ours might dare the shore, did we not come
Through winds that all in vain against us beat
   Until we had the warm sweet-smelling foam

Full in our faces, and the frantic wind
   Shrieked round us, and our cheeks grew numb, then
      warm,
Until we felt our souls, no more confined,
   Mix with the waves, and strain against the storm?
Oh, the immense, illimitable delight
   It is, to stand by some tempestuous bay,
What time the great sea waxes warm and white,
   And beats and blinds the following wind with spray !

Have we not loved our France together? — yea,
   More than our northern mother, be it said, —
For there, oh, fuller is the life of Day,
   And all the earth seems sweeter to our tread.

13

We always grieved to leave her, always laughed
   For mere delight to see her face once more,
Tasting as wine the stainless airs that waft
   The sea-scents to the odors of the shore.

And we, together, have seen Italy;
   In kingly Genoa our steps have strayed,
And wandered by the famed and tideless sea, —
   Through Florence, in all loveliness arrayed,
Pure as a virgin, regal as a queen,
   Made great by many memories, — a place
To see and die, contented having seen!
   Have we not worshipped her?　O nights and days,

Unlike our English nights and days; for there
   Each day's a sumptuous summer, and each night
A large and passionate caress of air,
   And Heaven grows one with Florence in God's sight!
And Venice we shall not forget, I deem;
   Ah me! the night we gained her, and you said, —
" Weird as a city vision'd in a dream!"
   The winding, watery streets before us spread;

On either side we saw the houses stand,
   Mystic and dark!　Of them I yearned to sing;
You said, "They seem built by no mortal hand,
   Yet wear a look of human suffering!"
And then I knew my song might not avail
   More than those words to compass; and that we,
When most remember'd things with Time turn pale,
   Should vision still those houses by the sea!

Oh, in what things have we not been as one?
   Oh, more than any sister ever was
To any brother!　Ere my days be done,
   And this my little strength of singing pass,

I would these failing lines of mine might show
    All thou hast been, as well as all thou art.
And yet what need? — for all who meet thee, know
    Thy queenliness of intellect and heart.

Oh, dear companion in the land of thought,
    How often hast thou led me by thy voice,
Through paths where men not all in vain have sought
    For consolation, when their cherished joys
Lie dead before them, never more to rise
    And sing their souls to sleep; or in some place,
Busy with all life's work, with sudden eyes
    To flash upon them, till a rapturous space

Their souls yearn up, and lo ! the lover sees
    His lady's face, where folded in love's calm
She waits at sunset 'neath her garden trees,
    Till they stand mouth to mouth and palm to palm.
Now ebbs my song from thee, but as a waif
    The tide, receding, leaves upon the beach,
So, even this, my song's retreating wave,
    Leaves my soul nearer thine.   O poor, vain speech

That fails so sadly when the heart o'erflows !
    Yet love me, dear, a little, for love's sake.
Shine thou upon my spirit till it grows
    Not all unlovely.   If my life could take
Color from thy life, I might learn to live,
    With no joy come to fruit; perceiving this, —
It is not what we take, but what we give,
    That brings the peace more durable than bliss.

Bear with me, dear, a little longer yet ;
    Forsake me not, if I forsaken stand.
Remember me ! when others shall forget ;
    Thy love to me is as thy precious hand

Might be upon my forehead if it burned
  In Hell, of some last fever; hold me fast,
O thou to whom in joy's full noon I turned
  As now I turn, the glory being past.

WIND-VOICES.

PURE SOULS.

PURE souls that watch above me from afar,
  To whom as to the stars I raise my eyes,
  Draw me to your large skies,
Where God and quiet are.

Love's mouth is rose-red, and his voice is sweet,
  His feet are winged, his eyes are as clear fire;
  But I have no desire
To follow his winged feet.

Friendship may change, or friends may pass away,
  And Fame 's a bride that men soon weary of;
  Since rest is not with Love,
No joy that is may stay.

But they whose lives are pure, whose hearts are
        high, —
  Those shining spirits by the world untamed, —
  May at the end, unshamed,
Look on their days gone by.

O pure, strong souls, so star-like, calm, and bright,
  If even I before the end might feel,
  Through quiet pulses, steal
Your pureness, with purged sight

I might Spring's gracious work behold once more :
 Might hear, as once I heard, long, long ago,
 Great waters ebb and flow ;
Might smell the rose of yore ;

Might comprehend the winds and clouds again,
 The saintly, peaceful moonlight hallowing all,
 The scent of leaves that fall,
The Autumn's tender pain.

Ah, this, I fear, shall never chance to me ;
 But though I cannot shape the life I would,
 It surely still is good
To look where such lives be.

CÆDMON.

SEVENTH CENTURY.

(Cædmon relates his dream before the Abbess Hilda.)

BECAUSE I had no power in me for song,
But songless sat, the singing folk among,
And had no joy to see the harps draw near,
But felt my want as keen as shame or fear,
I turned away dejectedly my face,
And came alone to guard the lonely place.
The night was silent and the level air,
Which had day-long the summer heats to bear,
Seemed by the moonlight cooled and purified ;
And from the hall, by glad folk occupied,
I heard the voices with the music blend.
Then, as one friendless, yearning for a friend ;
Or as a blind man made a prey to night,
Mad, almost, with sick longing after light ;

Or as a deaf man, with men singing round,
Dead to the dear companionship of sound;
Or as a dumb man, speechless all his days,
The tongueless sorrow pleading in his face;
Or as a lover who may never press
Close to his heart his loved one's loveliness, —
Even as one and all of these I seemed,
Till, weary with my grief, I slept and dreamed.
But through my sleep I felt my sorrow still,
As one, tormented by some bodily ill,
Has consciousness of pain through deepest sleep;
My eyelids quivered, but I could not weep,
When suddenly one called me by my name,
And all my sleep was lightened as with flame.
Then lifting up my eyes I looked, and, lo!
One stood beside me whom I might not know.
His face was fair and tender, grave and wise;
The mouth had patience, and the large, clear eyes
Had exaltation of the seer's gaze,
Noting, from far, inevitable days.
"Cædmon," he said, "I charge thee now to sing."
And I made answer, my voice faltering, —
"Dost thou not know for this I have no power;
Can lighten never thus the heaviest hour?
My heart is even like a dry well-head
That holds no water man's sore thirst to stead;
My life is like a lamp which, being broken,
Lies, of the light that should have been a token.
My soul is like a harp, with harp-strings shivered,
Ere once to music keen as pain they quivered;
Lonely I am, and most exceeding friendless,
And as my grief seems, so my days seem endless."
Oh, those strong, steadfast eyes that gazed on mine,
With what unwonted splendor did they shine!
Under their irresistible control
New life began to pulsate through my soul,
Till for some inner, nameless joy I smiled,
As smiles the mother when the coming child

First stirs within her; and I said: " O thou
Who dost this vision to my soul allow,
Whom all the companies of dreams obey,
A little longer let this sweet dream stay."
Then silent did I lie, a rapturous space,
With eyes that fed upon the stranger's face.
Again he called aloud: " O Cædmon, sing ! "
I answered, humbly, no more faltering, —
" Of what, my master, shall I sing, forsooth?
What theme is fit for my untutored mouth? "
" Sing of Creation, and the matchless might
That shaped the world and gave it day and night, —
The day for labor and the night for rest."
Such was his answer, such his high behest.
Then as a woman when her hour has come,
For splendid, sovereign pain, is no more dumb,
But cries out in her travail, and is torn
Spirit from body till the babe be born,
I cried in pain, a mighty, passionate cry,
The travail of my soul to testify;
Then wept, then laughed, with some divine, strange
    mirth;
Then Heaven fulfilled me, and the song had birth,
And sleep was rent as with a thunder-stroke,
And with my song upon my lips I woke.
And all the night they stayed with me, those words,
Nor did they leave me with awakening birds
In virginal, cold daybreak; and I knew
The utmost wonder of my dream come true;
And what the words were, if ye will it so,
Most fain am I that you and all should know.

AT PARTING.

I PUT my flower of song into thy hand,
 And turn my eyes away, —
It is a flower from a most desolate land,
 Barren of sun and day,
  Even this life of mine.
As two who meet upon a foreign strand,
 'T was mine with thee to stray, —
I put this flower of song into thy hand
 And turn my eyes away,
  And look where no lights shine.

By phantom wings this desolate air seems fanned,
 Where sky and sea show gray —
I put my flower of song into thy hand
 And turn my eyes away,
  But to no other shrine.
My hopes are like a little Christian band
 The heathen came to slay —
I put this flower of song into thy hand
 And turn my eyes away, —
  Keep thou the song in sign.

Some day, it may be, thou by me shalt stand
 When no word my lips say,
And, holding then this song-flower in thy hand,
 Shalt turn thine eyes away,
  And drop pure tears divine.
We part at Fate's inexorable command ;
 We name no meeting day —
I put my flower of song into thy hand,
 And turn my eyes away, —
  These eyes that burn and pine.

Thy way leads summerwards; thy paths are spanned
    By boughs where spring winds play —
I put my flower of song into thy hand
    And turn my eyes away
        To Life's dark boundary line.
Fair are thy groves, thy fields lie bright and bland,
    Where evil has no sway —
I put my flower of song into thy hand
    And turn my eyes away
        To meet Fate's eyes, malign.

Sometime, when twilight holds and fills the land,
    And glad souls are less gay,
Take thou this song-flower in thy tender hand
    Nor turn thine eyes away,
        There in the day's decline.
My life lies dark before me, all unplanned;
    Loud winds assail the day, —
I leave my song-flower folded in thy hand,
    And turn my eyes away,
        And turn my life from thine.

A BALLAD OF BRAVE WOMEN.

OFF SWANSEA — JANUARY 27, 1883.

WITH hiss and thunder and inner boom,
White through the darkness the great waves loom,
And charge the rocks with the shock of doom.

A second sea is the hurricane's blast;
Its viewless billows are loud and vast,
By their strength great trees are uptorn, downcast.

At times, through the hurry of clouds, the moon
Looks out aghast; but her face right soon
Is hidden again, and she seems to swoon.

Hark to the voice which shouts from the sea,
The voice of a fiendish revelry !
For the unseen hunters are out, and flee

Over the crests of the roaring deep,
Or they climb the waves that are wild and steep,
Or right through the heart of their light they leap.

Roar of the wind and roar of the waves,
And song and clamor of sea-filled caves !
What ship to-night such a tempest braves ?

Yet see, ah, see, how a snake of light
Goes hissing and writhing up all the night !
While the cry, " Going down ! " through the winds'
    mad might,

Through the roar of the winds and the waves together,
Is sent this way by the shrieking weather ;
But to help on such night were a vain endeavor.

See ! a glare of torches, and married and single,
Men and women confusedly mingle ;
You can hear the rush of their feet down the shingle.

Oh, salt and keen is the spray in their faces ;
From the strength of the wind they reel in their paces,
Catch hands to steady them there in their places.

How would a boat in such seas behave ?
But the lifeboat — the lifeboat — the lifeboat will save !
She is manned, with her crew of strong fellows, and
    brave.

See ! They ride on the heights, in the deep valleys dip,
Until, with a cry which the winds outstrip,
Their boat is hurled on the sinking ship.

Its side is gored, for the sea to have way through, —
"It is over!" they cried. "We have done all men may
     do!
Yet there's one chance left!" and themselves they threw

Right into the wrath of the sea and the wind.
It rages all round them, before and behind;
Their ears are deafened; their eyes are blind.

There in the middlemost hell of the night,
Yea, in the innermost heart of the fight,
They strain and they struggle with all their might, —

With never a pause, while God's mercy they cry on;
Their teeth are set, their muscles are iron, —
Each man has the heart and the thews of a lion.

Wave spurns them to wave. They may do it! Who knows?
For shoreward the great tide towering goes,
And shoreward the great wind thundering blows.

But, no! See that wave, like a Fate bearing on!
It breaks them and passes. Two swimmers alone
Are seen 'mid the waves, and their strength is nigh gone.

Quoth three soldiers on shore, "They must give up all
     hope.
Neither swimmer nor boat with such surges could cope,
Nor could one stand steady to cast a rope.

"For he who would cast it must stand hip-high
In the trough of the sea, and be thrown thereby
On his face, nevermore to behold the sky."

But a woman stept out from those gathered there,
And she said, "My life for their lives will I dare.
I pray for strength. God will hear my prayer."

And the light of her soul her eyes shone through,
But the men they jeered, and they cried, " Go to !
Can a woman do what we dare not do ? "

Spake another woman : " I, too !   We twain
Will do our best, striving with might and main ;
And if what we do shall be done in vain,

" And the great sea have us to hold and hide,
It were surely better thus to have died
Than to live as *these* live.   Haste ! haste ! " she cried.

They seized a rope, and with no word more,
Fearless of death, down the steep of the shore,
They dashed right into the light and the roar

Of the giant waves, which sprang on them there,
As a beast on prey may spring from his lair,
While the roar of his triumph makes deaf the air.

Oh, loud is the Death they hurry to meet ;
The stones slip shrieking from under their feet ;
They stagger, but fall not.   Beat, mad billows, beat !

They raise their arms, with their soul's strength quivering ;
They pause, " Will it reach ? "   Then they shout and fling ;
And straight as a stone driven forth by a sling,

Driven far afield by a master hand,
The rope whizzes out from the seething strand.
A shout : " It is caught !   For land, now, for land ! "

A crash like thunder !   They drop to their knees
But they keep their hold in the under seas.
They rise ; they pull ; nor falter ; nor cease.

The strength of ten men have these women to-night,
And they shout with the rapturous sense of their might, —
Shout as men shout when they revel in fight.

They reel, but they fall not.   The rope winds in, fast ;
Then a shout, a near shout, answers their shout at last, —
" That will do !   We touch ground."   God, the danger
    is past !

They turn them, then, from the raging water
With the two they have snatched from its lust of slaughter ;
But their feet flag now, and their breath comes shorter.

Hardly they hear in their sea-dinned ears
The sound of sobs, or the sound of cheers ;
Their eyes are drowned, but not drowned with tears.

When deeds of valor Coast vaunts over Coast,
As to which proved bravest, and which did most,
Two Swansea women shall be my toast.

ESTRANGED.

SOME day she will come back, my poor lost dove, —
My dove with the warm breast and eager eyes !
How did it fail toward her, my passionate love ?
Where was the flaw ? — since flaw there must have been,
Or surely she had stayed with me, my queen.
Her heart was full of inarticulate cries,
Which my heart failed to catch ; and yet she strove
To cleave to me — ah, how she must have striven,
Praying, perchance, ofttimes for strength from Heaven !
But no strength came ; and so, one fatal day,
Despairing of all help, she went away.

And there her half-completed portrait stands, —
The fresh young face, the gray eyes brimmed with light !
I painted her with flowers in her hands,
Because she always seemed so bright and good.
I never thought the studio's solitude
Would weary her so much.   I thought the sight
Of painted forms and unfamiliar lands
Would be enough for her.   She was too mild,
Too patient with my painter's life, poor child !
Had she complained at all, by look or tone, .
Had she but said, " I seem too much alone,

" I grow half fearful of these painted eyes,
That never change, but, full of sad reproof,
Haunt me and watch me ; and these Southern skies
Reflected in deep streams ; and that dark boat
From which a girl with bare, sweet breast and throat
Droops, willow-like, and dreams of life and love ;
And that youth's dying face, which never dies ;
And then, again, that picture of Christ there,
Christ fallen in an agony of prayer,
And His disciples near Him, stern and dumb,
Like men who know the fated hour is come."

Had she said this, and added, " Take me, dear,
Away from these sad faces ; let me stand
Once more within life's shallows, and there hear
Light laughter of the surf upon the beach,
For here the very sea is without speech,
So still it is, and far away from land.
I want life's little joys ; this atmosphere
Oppresses me, — I cannot breathe in it.
The light that lights your life leaves mine unlit," —
I should have answered tenderly, and sought
To carry out, in all, her slightest thought.

She knew I loved her, through those winter days, —
Did it not comfort her at all, my love ?

14

It was such joy to look upon her face,
I sat for hours, content to be quite still,
Feeling her warm, bright, breathing beauty fill
My soul and brain; fearful lest she should move,
Or speak, or go; but when she met my gaze
I turned away, as if I had done wrong
In looking on her loveliness so long.
I rarely kissed her, rarely took her hand;
And now I think she did not understand.

Perchance she thought my love was passionless, —
Wanted what I withheld, yet longed to give.
She did not know my silence a caress,
Since passion was by reverence controlled,
And so she deemed my ways of love were cold.
Ah me! the lonely life she had to live;
And I knew nothing of its loneliness.
Hers was a nature quick to give and take, —
A nature to be broken and to break;
She loved confiding valleys, sun-kissed rills,
But saddened at the solemn peace of hills.

All things had been so different had I known
Her nature then as now; and yet, and yet,
If she came in as I sit here alone,
The April twilight failing through the room,
And all the pictures lapsing into gloom, —
Came in, knelt down, and prayed me to forget,
Forgive her, and reclaim her for my own,
I should be glad, and draw her to my heart,
And kiss the rising tears away, and part
The sweet hair back, and fold her to my side,
Yet leave, perchance, some want unsatisfied.

But ah, she comes not! I must wait and bear;
Live on, and serve my art as best I may.
If I can catch the color of her hair,

And the neck's poise, and set beneath, her name,
Shall not her loveliness have deathless fame?
Oh, help me, Art, upon my difficult way!
Now lights shine out along the London square,
O dreary place! where no joy comes at all.
There! I must turn the easel to the wall,
I cannot bear her face as yet — O Love!
O wounded of my hands! my wounded dove!

THY GARDEN.

I.

PURE moonlight in thy garden, sweet, to-night, —
  Pure moonlight in thy garden, and the breath
Of fragrant roses! O my heart's delight,
  Wed thou with Love, but I will wed with Death.

Peace in thy garden, and the passionate song
  Of some late nightingale that sings in June!
Thy dreams with promises of love are strong,
  And all thy life is set to one sweet tune.

Love wandering round thy garden, O my sweet!
  Love walking through thy garden in the night, —
Far-off I feel his wings, I hear his feet,
  I see the eyes that set the world alight.

My sad heart in thy garden strays alone, —
  My heart among all hearts companionless;
Between the roses and the lilies thrown,
  It finds thy garden but a wilderness.

Great quiet in thy garden, now the song
  Of that last nightingale has died away!
Here jangling city-chimes the silence wrong;
  But in thy garden perfect rest has sway.

Dawn in thy garden, with the faintest sound, —
   Uncertain, tremulous, awaking birds !
Dawn in thy garden, and from meadows round,
   The sudden lowing of expectant herds.

Light in thy garden, faint and sweet and pure,
   Dim noise of birds from every bush and tree,
Rumors of song the stars may not endure,
   A rain that falls, and ceases suddenly !

Morn in thy garden, bright and keen and strong !
   Love calls thee from thy garden to awake :
Morn in thy garden, with the articulate song
   Of birds that sing for love and warm light's sake !

II.

Wind in thy garden to-night, my love,
   Wind in thy garden and rain ;
A sound of storm in the shaken grove,
   And cries as of spirits in pain !

If there 's wind in thy garden outside,
   And troublous darkness, dear,
What carest thou, an elected bride,
   And the bridal hour so near ?

All things come to an end, my sweet, —
   Life, and the pleasure in living ;
The years run swiftly with agile feet,
   The years that are taking and giving.

Soon shalt thou have thy bliss supreme,
   And soon shall it pass away ;
So turn thyself to thy rest, and dream,
   Nor heed what the mad winds say.

III.

Snow in thy garden, falling thick and fast, —
  Snow in thy garden, where the grass shall be !
What dreams to-night? Thy dreaming nights are
    past, —
  Thou hast no glad or grievous memory.

Love in thy garden boweth down his head ;
  His tears are falling on the wind-piled snow ;
He takes no heed of life, now thou art dead ;
  He recks not how the seasons come or go.

Death in thy garden ! In the violent air
  That sweeps thy radiant garden thou art still ;
For thee is no more rapture or despair,
  And Love and Death of thee have had their will.

Night in thy garden, white with snow and sleet, —
  Night, rushing on with wind and storm toward day !
Alas, thy garden holdeth nothing sweet ;
  Nor sweet can come again, and thou away !

THE OLD CHURCHYARD OF BONCHURCH.

(This old churchyard has been for many years slipping toward
the sea, which it is expected will ultimately engulf it.)

THE churchyard leans to the sea with its dead, —
It leans to the sea with its dead so long.
Do they hear, I wonder, the first bird's song,
When the winter's anger is all but fled ;
The high, sweet voice of the west wind,
The fall of the warm, soft rain,
When the second month of the year
Puts heart in the earth again?

Do they hear, through the glad April weather,
The green grasses waving above them?
Do they think there are none left to love them,
They have lain for so long there, together?
Do they hear the note of the cuckoo,
The cry of gulls on the wing,
The laughter of winds and waters,
The feet of the dancing Spring?

Do they feel the old land slipping seaward, —
The old land, with its hills and its graves, —
As they gradually slide to the waves,
With the wind blowing on them from leeward?
Do they know of the change that awaits them, —
The sepulchre vast and strange?
Do they long for the days to go over,
And bring that miraculous change?

Or love they their night with no moonlight,
With no starlight, no dawn to its gloom?
Do they sigh : "'Neath the snow, or the bloom
Of the wild things that wave from our night,
We are warm, through winter and summer ;
We hear the winds rave, and we say, —
'The storm-wind blows over our heads,
But we, here, are out of its way'"?

Do they mumble low, one to another,
With a sense that the waters that thunder
Shall ingather them all, draw them under, —
"Ah, how long to our moving, my brother?
How long shall we quietly rest here,
In graves of darkness and ease?
The waves, even now, may be on us,
To draw us down under the seas !"

Do they think 't will be cold when the waters
That they love not, that neither can love them,
Shall eternally thunder above them?
Have they dread of the sea's shining daughters,
That people the bright sea-regions
And play with the young sea-kings?
Have they dread of their cold embraces,
And dread of all strange sea-things?

But their dread or their joy, — it is bootless:
They shall pass from the breast of their mother;
They shall lie low, dead brother by brother,
In a place that is radiant and fruitless;
And the folk that sail over their heads
In violent weather
Shall come down to them, haply, and all
They shall lie there, together.

BETWEEN JOY AND SORROW.

BETWEEN joy and sorrow,
As 'twixt day and morrow,
    I lay for a space;
And I heard, so lying,
My old Grief sighing
    From her far-off place.

I said, "Thou art over,
And where dreams hover
    Thou hoverest now;
In the land of thy dwelling
What waters are welling,
    And blossoms what bough?

" Old tears are its rivers ;
The wind that there quivers
    Is breath of old sighs ;
Wreck-strewn are the shores there ;
And sunset endures there
    Through infinite skies.

" But all there is quiet ;
There no wave makes riot
    On the waif-cumber'd coasts,
Where thou movest banished,
But not quite vanished, —
    A ghost among ghosts."

THE TWO BURDENS.

Over the deep sea Love came flying ;
Over the salt sea Love came sighing —
    Alas, O Love, for thy journeying wings !
Through turbid light and sound of thunder,
When one wave lifts and one falls under,
    Love flew, as a bird flies, straight for warm Springs.

Love reached the Northland, and found his own ;
With budding roses, and roses blown,
    And wonderful lilies, he wove their wreath ;
His voice was sweet as a tune that wells,
Gathers and thunders, and throbs and swells,
    And fails, and lapses in rapturous death.

His hands divided the tangled boughs ;
They sat and loved in a moist, green house,
    With bird-songs and sunbeams faltering through ;
One note of wind to each least light leaf :
O Love, those days they were sweet but brief, —
    Sweet as the rose is, and fleet as the dew !

Over the deep sea Death came flying;
Over the salt sea Death flew sighing:
  Love heard from afar the rush of his wings,
Felt the blast of them over the sea,
And turned his face where the shadows be,
  And wept for a sound of disastrous things.

Death reached the Northland, and claimed his own;
With pale, sweet flowers, by wet winds blown,
  He wove for the forehead of one a wreath;
His voice was sad as the wind that sighs
Through cypress trees under rainy skies,
  When the dead leaves drift on the path beneath.

His hands divided the tangled boughs,
One lover he bore to a dark, deep house,
  Where never a bridegroom may clasp his bride, —
A place of silence, of dust, and sleep;
What vigil there shall the loved one keep,
  What cry of longing the lips divide?

UNGATHERED LOVE.

WHEN the autumn winds go wailing
  Through branches yellow and brown,
When the gray, sad light is failing,
  And the day is going down,
I hear the desolate evening sing
Of a love that bloomed in the early Spring,
And which no heart had for gathering.

I and my lover, we dwell apart, —
  We twain may never be one;
We shall never stand heart to heart,—
  Then what can be said or done,

When winds and waters and song-birds sing
Of a love that bloomed in the early Spring,
And which no heart had for gathering?

When day is over and night descends,
    And dank mists circle and rise,
I fall asleep, and slumber befriends,
    For I dream of April skies;
But I wake to hear the silence sing
Of a love that bloomed in the early Spring,
And which no heart had for gathering.

When the dawn comes in with wind and rain,
    And birds awake in the eaves,
And raindrops smite the window-pane,
    And drench the eddying leaves,
I hear the voice of the daybreak sing
Of a love that bloomed in the early Spring,
And which no heart had for gathering.

JUST ASLEEP.

For a space the shadows lift now,
    Now that we are nearly met;
By what windings shall we drift now,
    To what shore our keel be set?
Dearest Sleep, so long denied me,
To what regions wilt thou guide me?

Let us leave behind old sorrow,
    In the room where Death has been;
Let it bide there till to-morrow,
    Let it stalk, of no man seen.
Though to-morrow it will find me,
Yet to-night 't will stay behind me.

Ah, to-morrow, iron-hearted
   As the hearts of all my days,
We shall be no longer parted, —
   No more travelling by strange ways ;
But together, whom forever
Death alone can really sever.

Thou shalt show me fair dream-spaces,
   Where my dead ones do not seem
Dead with dust upon their faces,
   Underground where comes no dream ;
But with living lips to cheer me,
And with ears that love to hear me.

Thou shalt take me to the shining
   Happy, precious, fleetest past,
When the heart had no divining
   Of what life could be at last,
Driven out of all its courses,
Beaten back by viewless forces :

From the terror and the passion,
   And the loneliness and strife,
Take me in soft, tender fashion
   To the old sequestered life ;
Let me move in the old places,
Let me look on the old faces.

Close against thy deep heart press me
   Till thine inmost soul I see ;
With thy loveliness caress me,
   Who am tired of all but thee, —
So, belovèd, till the morrow
There shall be no thought of sorrow.

NIGHTSHADE.

(The following poem is founded on the conclusion of Oliver
Madox Brown's "Dwale Bluth," as designed though not completed
by himself. In one or two particulars I have deviated from his
expressed intention; but the tragic tale of the lady and her blind
lover, with its tragic ending, belongs to him.)

WHEN she had gone, who was his light of life,
Back to her lord, — yet not to be his wife,
But rather Death's, — her lover, knowing this not,
Alone in darkness wailed his hapless lot.
Most men have joy in stars and moon and sun, —
Joy when the lengthening days are well begun ;
And love to mark, as birds take heart to sing,
The sweet, transitional processes of Spring, —
Love well the delicate, various flower-faces ;
Of wild-wood plants the free, untramelled graces.
But he in all these things had no delight,
And walked by day in fastnesses of night.
She was his love, his Spring, earth, moon, and sky,
His soul's one goal, and light to seek it by.

Lest questioning should make her lot more hard
His lips forbore ; so through sad days, debarred
From joy and her, he roamed about the land,
Remembering how her cool and subtle hand
Could make the grateful blood leap in each vein,
What time his lips of her lips were so fain ;
When of his life love made so sweet a thing,
It grieved not for the unbeholden Spring,
Nor longed so very much to see by night
The distant stars, the moon's immaculate light,
While they two loved, and time flew fast and faster,
Till that dread night of infinite disaster

When he — the strange, hard man for years deemed dead,
Sunk with his ship to some deep salt sea-bed,
The man to whom her girlish hand was wed,
Whereof had come such sorrow to them both —
Stood there and claimed her by her marriage troth,
Seeing that the woman was fair, and very his,
And that of old her lips were sweet to kiss.

And when he bade her come, saying : " Right or wrong,
This blind man with his lips just closed on song,
The song he sang you of his love's delight,
Falls in one moment from this rocky height
To instant violent death, if you delay.
By chance he fell ; nought else shall any say."

Then for *his* sake — not seeing without her life
Could be for him but a most bitter strife.
Vain strife with all the black-plumed powers of night,
And memories wailing for a lost delight —
She stayed her trembling voice, and said, " Good-by, —
God keep you, dear ; " and dark against the sky,
The sunset sky, she, turning, saw him stand,
Sightless and wordless, with his out-stretched hand.
Then, knowing well his way about that part,
He crept along, with his wrung, broken heart.
At length he sank in some soft, leafy place,
Nor knew the moon shone full upon his face ;
And, lying there, he moaned, but could not weep,
And far from him was any comfort of sleep.

In that green place, with many trees girt round,
The nightingales had tranced the night with sound.
Ah me, ah me, what melody they made
Within the moon-thrilled, palpitating shade !
Hark, the exultant joy of each high note
Sent gushing from the unseen, singing throat !
The exultant music mocked him ; but the long

Low, passionate, tender pleading of the song,
Appealing vainly 'gainst some ancient wrong, —
He heard his heart's cry uttered in that strain !
So poets into music pour their pain.

Chill turned the air ; the singers ceased their tune,
Between the climbing dawn and sinking moon.
From fields near by there came a low of herds
And soft, consenting murmuring of birds,
Which grew and strengthened, till a blackbird came,
And through that dim sound flashed his song like flame.
Then into singing all the others broke ;
Out shone the sun, and all the world awoke.
And then, above all notes that morn in May,
Now sometimes near, and sometimes far away,
He heard the violent cuckoo high in air —
He saw it not, yet felt the day was fair.

'Twixt him so sad, now, and his lost delight,
There lay but one brief, singing, moonlit night ;
But 'twixt himself and self of yesterday,
A gulf more wide than gulf of death there lay.
Morn being come, he rose and took his road.
He entered not in any man's abode,
Until, one day, sore worn and scant of strength,
He came upon a narrow path, at length ;
And leaning there, against the wall behind,
He heard a sound of wailing on the wind.
It came close by.   Close by him was the fall
Of heavy steps that tend a funeral, —
So near they came, they brushed him with the pall.
"Whose funeral?" he cried, with dread surmise ;
And one made answer, mingling words with sighs.

They bore to church *her* body, who had been
Of all his life, of all his heart, the queen.

He let them pass, and followed with the rest ;
His lips set fast, and hands together prest.
And when the coffin was lowered into the ground,
And on the lid he heard the dull earth sound,
Men saw him tremble ; but he kept his place,
Bent o'er the void, as if his spirit's gaze
Could see therein that dear and worshipped face
His hands and lips had loved so well to cherish,
Which now, forever, from his life must perish.

That day he was no more by any met ;
But when he felt the warm May sun had set,
He sought the churchyard and the grave new-made,
On which he stretched himself, yet no word said ;
And lying there he knew a storm was nigh,
For thunder heavily rolled along the sky.
Vain throes of death, or throes of some strange birth, —
Which horror was it so constrained the earth?
The air was dumb, as if in dread affright,
Save when the thunder shuddered along the night.

Then tardy rain-drops came down, one by one,
As from some wound the large, slow blood-drops run.
The lightning flashed out bright and fitfully ;
The waxing thunder seemed more near to be.
Then a dread, soundless, flameless interval ;
Then a fierce blaze of light, enkindling all ;
And then — as if God, roused to wrath at length,
Had smitten with almighty, vengeful strength
The old, wrong-doing world, that, stricken so,
Cowered and reeled beneath the pitiless blow —
Fell the loud thunder, crashing through the heaven,
And all the night with fire and storm was riven.
Then, suddenly, a stormy wind up-sprang,
And wild and shrill the song was that it sang,
And with a rush and roar came down the rain,
To save the earth, and make her whole again ;

And soon that place where death held sway, alas !
Smelt fresh and sweetly of the growing grass.

Then he who lay upon the grave found there
A sprig of that dread plant she loved to wear
In her abundant tresses.   Who would braid
But she her locks with deadliest nightshade?
And one who knew how well she loved the plant
Had placed that sprig there, as to fill some want.
" At last ! " he cried, and ate with bated breath, —
For him dear buds of life, not buds of death.

" Sweetheart," he cried, " I come, I come to thee,
And when we meet again may it not be
With unsealed eyes I may thy beauty see?
At least, if all else fail, I shall have rest,
Though it should be no more upon thy breast.
Whether to light, or deeper night, I go,
I cannot tell — this thing no man may know."

His body above, and hers unseen, beneath, —
Only an earth-mound severing death from death, —
So shone the morning sun upon them both
Who had kept thus in death their life's dear troth.

A LAMENT.

OLIVER MADOX BROWN — Born 1855, Died 1874.

My friend has left me, he has gone away ;
   Before his time — so long before — he went.
Bright was the dawn of his unended day ;
   But love might not, yea, nothing, might prevent
The hand of Death from striking.   O fair Art !
First mistress of his intellect and heart,
Of this our common sorrow bear thy part,
   Bow down, and weep now for the words I say.

His lips are mute, and stilled is the great brain;
　　The strong heart beats no more; the strife is done.
So near the goal, he reached it without pain;
　　We crowned him, then he went beyond the sun.
But though he has gone out from us, his name
Shall lessen not with time; and his young fame
Shall burn forever, an enduring flame, —
　　A steadfast light, that may not wax or wane.

Lo, that first work whereby we bowed to him,
　　Calling him master, though he was so young! —
Shall intervening centuries make dim
　　Those sea-tossed lovers who together clung,
What time they had for common enemies
The blasting tropic suns and treacherous seas,
And torture of long thirst they might not ease,
　　Till hearts began to fail, and brains to swim?

The years that might have been, I seem to see;
　　I know the great work ended, and I hear
Rumors of storms, and voice of waves that flee;
　　I breathe a fierce and fervid atmosphere;
I see strong warriors meet, and armed for war,
I see each helmet shining like a star,
I hear the shock of weapons near and far,
　　And in the densest of the strife is he.

My friend, my friend! He strikes with confident hand,
　　I hear the blows ring on opposing shields,
And none, I know, his prowess may withstand;
　　I know the shield he bears, the sword he wields.
Before his strength I see his foes give place;
And in my heart I see a spectre race
Look with glad eyes upon his lifted face, —
　　They who inhabit now the flowerless land.

15

O friend and brother, if this thing might be,
　That souls live after death, the great elect
Should throng the portals to give hail to thee ;
　And they thy wandering footsteps should direct, —
Should take thee where the fairest gardens glow,
Should take thee where the deepest rivers flow,
Should show thee all the faces thou wouldst know,
　And linger with thee by the jasper sea.

But perfect rest is now thine heritage ;
　For though the labor of thy hand and brain
Had made thy life triumphant, none engage
　To point the world new paths without the strain
Of long and arduous fighting.　Oh, my friend,
Not thine our loss, — this unimagined end.
Life is not sweet, but sharp with thorns that rend ;
　And the soul's thirst what springs in life assuage?

Fame is not always good, — remember this,
　All ye with whom I mourn, who mourn with me ;
Nor is love always a sure path to bliss,
　And time works many changes sad to see.
Between the dearest friends estrangements rise,
Across wide gulfs they look with longing eyes ;
But they have done with questions and replies,
　And sad and very hard to bear this is.

London I never loved for London's sake ;
　Her crowds oppressed me more than solitude.
But some strange music his fine ear could take
　Mine failed to catch ; yea, since he found her good, —
Loved the strong ebb and flow of fluctuant life,
The night's uneasy calm, the day's loud strife ;
Found all her ancient streets with memories rife, —
　Shall I not love her too, asleep, awake?

O friend, my friend, there is so much to tell, —
 Since that September night when we met, last,
Dreams have passed by, and hopes have said farewell.
 O love that lives, and life that soon is past !
From where he is he may not make reply ;
Too far away he is to hear my cry.
Love weeps for us ; for him love may not sigh ;
 And grief saith but one word, — irreparable !

We talked about our future, many times ;
 Planned work together, jested and were grave ;
And now he will not listen to my rhymes.
 My sorrow breaks above me in one wave,
For he has left me, he has gone away
To lands that do not know the night from day ;
Where men toil not, neither give thanks, nor pray ;
 Where come no rumors from the sounding climes.

O men and women, listen and be wise ;
 Refrain from love and friendship, dwell alone,
Having, for friends and loves, the seas, the skies,
 And the fair land, — for these are still your own.
The sun is yours ; the moon and stars are yours ;
For you the great sea changes and endures,
And every year the spring returns, and lures :
 I pray you only love what never dies.

For life hath taught me with much diligence
 How bitterest sorrow springs from things most fair, —
Remorseless Fate that calls those loved ones hence,
 Who living gave us strength our cross to bear ;
The failure of high purposes ; the death
Of fairest inspiration ; the quick breath,
The ebbing light, and the last words one saith ;
 Then dust and sleep and death, for recompense.

I know it was of his a favorite creed,
　　That when the body dies the existing soul
Of other souls becomes a fruitful seed,
　　Changing, surviving through the years that roll ;
Flashing continually from state to state,
Not ceasing with the lives that terminate, —
A part of life, of destiny, of fate,
　　The germ and the fulfilment, thought and deed.

Here, where I stumble, he walked, sure of foot ;
　　And here more clear than mine his spirit's sight ;
His high thought sprang from no uncertain root ;
　　His intellect was like the broad noonlight ;
He stemmed the tide of passion, strong and deep ;
He walked most confidently up paths most steep ;
And, in the path he loved, he fell asleep,
　　And of his life we gather now the fruit.

I clasp another sorrow in my soul ;
　　I take another memory to weep,
To love and cherish, while the seasons roll,
　　To think of while I wake or fall asleep.
The weary winter-time shall pass, and Spring
The patient earth at last revisiting,
With soft and flowerlike skies, and birds that sing,
　　Shall come most hearts to gladden and make whole.

But mine she shall not gladden ; I, for one,
　　By all her sweets will not be comforted.
The summer days shall glow with stress of sun ;
　　The placid light of golden stars be shed ;
With dew, at eve, the roses shall be sated ;
And all the earth by slumber softly weighted, —
But love shall keep its sorrow unabated
　　Till all the fears and pains of life be done.

Alas ! what can be said ?   What can we do ?
　　Ah me ! we have no words ; we can but wait,
Wait and remember, while the years wear through.
　　Life is at longest but a brief estate ;
As a flower of the field, the Psalmist saith,
It blooms, and the fashion of it perisheth ;
We cannot tell when we may chance on death,
　　To be resolved into the light, the dew.

O friends, who sit together, well content,
　　Throwing your personal news out pleasantly,
Or meeting hotly in some argument,
　　Or interchanging deepest sympathy,
Prize well the precious moments ; for indeed
You cannot tell when you may sorely need
The friendly talk and counsel.   Take good heed
　　Your lips let through no word they might repent.

Sleep well, my friend, the sleep that no dreams break !
　　I, too, some day, of sleep shall take my fill ;
But now I live, and work for mere work's sake,
　　Missing the strength of thy controlling will.
I know my soul, through all, shall thirst and fret
For thee, for thee whom time may not forget ;
And when I see dear friends together met,
　　I know my heart will fail in me and ache.

IN MEMORY OF ARTHUR O'SHAUGHNESSY.

DIED JANUARY 30, 1881.

THAT day returns which took thee from our sight
　　And did forever hush that voice of thine.
　　Thine eyes beheld, through thy youth's fair sunshine,
And not so far away, the end of light ;
And not from far thy young ears heard Death say, —
" It shall be good to rest with me some day ! "

Singer and seer, who, ere the end of all,
   Didst turn thy back on death, and look past birth
   To where, in terror of the life on earth
And all the griefs to which it should be thrall,
Thine unborn soul did in sublime despair
Assail " En Soph " in unavailing prayer !

This year that bears us on to storm — or what? —
   Has no acquaintanceship with thee, O brother,
   Gone home, now, to the earth, our common mother.
Men come and go ; things are remembered not :
But I shall think of thee, O parted friend,
Till, even as thou, I reach the journey's end.

First come of us, to leave the first thou wert, —
   To fall from out the ranks of us who sang.
   How clear along the ranks thy full note rang
With individual sweetness, lyric art ;
Thou who hadst felt John's spiritual stress,
What time he tarried in the wilderness.

May not thy soul in song embodied be,
   As patriots dead, who once strove here with wrong,
   Bequeath their souls to make new patriots strong?
May not all spirits in their own degree
Be unseen sources, feeding evermore
The causes which on earth they labored for?

Thy day of death was Landor's day of birth ;
   And, while all hearts that revel in his might,
   Rejoicing in that soul's immaculate light
Which was so long as sunlight on our earth,
Give thanks, I will keep mute upon this day
On which thy singing spirit passed away.

Often when in my room I brood alone
   With weary heart, bowed down to death almost,
   Hearing waves break upon an unknown coast
Where be great wrecks of ships that were mine own,

With all their freights of precious merchandise
That comes alone from ports of Paradise,

I seem to hear a step, a voice I know;
　　Almost I feel a hand; and then my heart
　　Thrills and leaps in me with a sudden start,
Then sinks again, because this is not so.
Here, where thy feet so many times passed o'er,
Again thy footstep shall fall nevermore.

When through these outer and unpitying ways,
　　With all their loud and lacerating noises,
　　Thunder of wheels, and jar of unknown voices,
I walk alone, I think of those past days
When arm-in-arm we walked the same way through,
Talking and laughing as good comrades do.

Thou wert so full of song and strength and life,
　　Hadst such keen pleasure in small things and great,
　　It hardly can seem real to know thy state
Is with the ancient dead, where jars no strife,
Where very surely I shall come some day,
Hands torn, and feet left bleeding from the way.

Take thou this song, as yet another wreath
　·To those we dropped into thy resting-place,
　　Each bending low, with eager, hungering gaze,
Knowing it was thy dust that lay beneath;
Knowing thy fair, fleet, singing life was done,
Thy light extinguished, and thy bay-wreath won.

A BURDEN.

Have I not dreamed of you all night long,
          Love, my Love?
Shall I not tell my dream in a song,
          O my Love?

Have I not worshipped you six long years,
          Queen, my Queen?
Have I not given you bounteous tears,
          O my Queen?

Have I not said, when the spring was here, —
          " Sweet, my Sweet,
More than the pride and flower of the year,
          O my Sweet "?

Have I not said, in the dawning gray, —
          " Heart, my Heart,
I shall see my lady ere close of day,
          O my Heart "?

Have I not said, in the silent night, —
          " Dove, my Dove,
So soft of voice and rapid of flight,
          O my Dove "?

Have I not said, in the summer hours, —
          " Rose, my Rose,
Greatly exalted above all flowers,
          O my Rose "?

Have I not said, in my great despair, —
          " Soul, my Soul,
Love is a grievous burden to bear
          O my Soul "?

Have I not turned to the sea, and said, —
    " Life, my Life,
If she be not mine, be thou my bed,
    O my Life " ?

Have I not dreamed of your eyes, and cried, —
    " Light, my Light,
Lead me where love may be satisfied,
    O my Light ! "

Have I not trodden a weary road,
    Saint, my Saint?
And where, at last, shall be my abode,
    O my Saint?

Sometimes I say, in an hour supreme,
    " Bride, my Bride !
I shall hold you fast, and not in a dream,
    O my Bride ! "

CAUGHT IN THE NETS.

A.D. 1180. — " This year, also, near unto Orford in Suffolk, certain fishers took in their nets a fish, having the shape of a man in all points, which fish was kept by Bartholomew de Glandeville in the Castle of Orford six months and more. He spake not a word; all manner of meats he did gladly eat, but most greedily raw fish. Oftentimes he was brought to the church, but never showed any sign of adoration. At length, not being well looked to, he stole to the sea, and was never seen after." — Sir Richard Baker: *Chronicle.*

" Would I were back, now, in my own sea caves !
  Curse that March twilight, and those stormy waves
  Which rioted above me till I said
  I too must rise and frolic, so I sped
  Up dim green twilights of the under sea ;
  And louder seemed the waves to call to me,

Until I dashed their foam apart, and, lo !
The sky above with fire seemed to glow,
And in the waste, wide glare of crimson light
Made merry the mad waves, all vast and white,
And each to each roared loud some secret thing ;
And the Wind seemed a strange new song to sing,
And wantoned with the waves in violent play,
As great sea-monsters do, then fled, and they
Roared after, and made haste upon her track ;
Then, suddenly turning, she would hurl them back,
And they, with their own speed and rage made blind,
Wild, rent, and staggering before the Wind,
Fell, and in falling dashed high up their spray,
As with it they would drown the eyes of day.

" Being of hearing quick, it seemed to me
I heard strange sounds abroad upon the sea,
That cursed March twilight ; yea, but it was fun
To swing in the waves and see the blood-red sun
Strike sharp their white and hurrying heights between,
And when the Wind would cut too strong and keen,
Just for a moment the waves dive under,
And go, as it were, through the heart of the thunder.

" How sweet the weed smelt, by the wave washed warm !
Ah, could I smell it now, and hear the storm
Make white and loud the sea above my head,
I would not leave again my soft sea bed,
And coral groves the dear sea-girls come through,
Singing the songs I love to hearken to.
That last time that I went through a great wave
Something did catch about me ; and some waif
Of monstrous floating weed it was, I thought ;
But when about my head and feet it caught
And seemed to bear me forward, surely then
I knew myself snared in the nets of men, —
The nets wherein our simple fish are taken.
Then, with great fear the heart in me was shaken ;

My one hope was, I knew, to break the net.
For this I strove, while, with my face down set,
Through all the interposing sea I prayed
That some bold merman would make haste to aid.
But all were in their homes; none answered me, —
Only, at times, most friendly seemed the sea,
When a great wave would with a mighty blow
Send me afield; but in the fall and flow
I spun round helplessly, half choked and blind,
Hearing, above, the singing of the wind.
Then franticly the net I strove to rend,
But, being weak, came suddenly the end, —
A strain, a rush, the wind cold on my breast,
No sea, then light, then darkness was the rest,
Until I found myself here, and breast high
In dead sea-water, and above no sky,
Nor light of sea, but something hard and black;
Ah me! if I could only once go back!

" I heard a mighty noise about me; then
I looked into the faces of cursed men.
Right hard they stared.   They questioned me, I knew;
But never word from me their cunning drew.
They gave me food, of which I was full glad;
And strange it was, and sweet, so that I had
Some joy in eating it; and fish they gave, —
Dear fish, that smelt and tasted of the wave;
And then they left me dark and lonely there.

" There was no sound at all upon the air;
The awful silence filled me with such dread
I violently dashed with hands and head
The water round me, that some sound might be,
Some littlest whisper from the far-off sea;
But with the light of day came noise again,
And strange it was to me, and bitter pain,
To hear the wind outside, but not the sea.
Then came fresh faces and looked hard at me,

In the cold, pitiless glare of the new day.
I heard them say it was the time to pray ;
And one man cast a chain my neck about,
And with a mighty grasp he dragged me out, —
Right out into the sunlight and the wind, —
And some men walked before, and some behind.
So on we wended, till we reached a hall,
Where all around upon their knees did fall,
And made together a most dismal noise.
Then one cried to them, in a louder voice ;
Whereat more wail upon the air they poured,
Then rose.   Next in their midst a monster roared,
Whereat they yelled ; yea, all they yelled as one,
So that I thought by fear they were undone ;
And much I marvelled that they kept their ground,
For still that monster made the dreadest sound.
Then ceased he, and they ceased ; and one man rose
And shouted to them, and with many blows
Did beat himself, and long and loud he screamed ;
And like some fearful dream that I had dreamed
It seemed to me, and full of dread I was,
Not knowing well what next might come to pass.
But back they took me to my lonely place ;
And here go by the dreary nights and days.
O shining home, wherein are all things fair ;
O sea, O world of mine, where art thou, where?
O deep sea caves, wherein strange, rare things are,
And great sea-shells, that praise the sea from far !
Green hills of slippery seaweed, wet and high,
Where green-haired mermaids love full length to lie,
Their faces in the wet weed buried deep,
Till, by their gambols tired, they fall asleep !

" What joy it was to dance among the rocks,
  And startle, unaware, the mild sea flocks ;
  Or, from afar, that low, long sound to hear,
  Whereby that cruel whaling-ships are near
  One whale warns all the whale-fields, and all start,

Nor rest until they reach a safer part ;
To see the waves above, now green, now blue,
With light of silver fishes flashing through.

" Here through a chink I watch the evening sky ;
Sometimes I think my bar is not so high
But I could overleap it, and be free,
And so go forth to seek and find the sea.
Even now the gate stands open which leads out ;
I hear no sound of any man about !
Shall I not do it?   Gently !   It is done.
Released I stand.   Ah, which way shall I run?
Straight on, I think.   Ah, now be swift, my feet !
The sky is full of light ; the air is sweet.
Fly fast, my feet, and faster, and more fast,
Until my long lost home be found at last.

" What sound is this ahead?   O joy of joys !
It is the sea's and my own people's voice.
And as more fast I run, more loud it comes ;
Mermaidens call me from their deep sea homes.
And now upon the verge of my own land
And yet within this world of men I stand.
A vast and empty place it is — ah me !
But I shall sleep to-night beneath the sea,
And wake to hear the great dear waves wash over,
And some sea-girl shall have me for her lover,
And wind about me with her cold, green tresses,
And comfort me with damp and salt caresses.
O world of men, good-by, I love ye not,
Mine is a wilder and a happier lot ;
White in the moonlight shines the flying foam,
O joy ! O joy, now I make haste and home ! ''

THE BALLAD OF MONK JULIUS.

MONK JULIUS lived in a wild countrie ;
And never a purer monk than he
Was vowed and wedded to chastity.

The monk was fair, and the monk was young ;
His mouth seemed shaped for kisses and song,
And tender his eyes, and gentle his tongue.

He loved the Virgin, as good monks should ;
And he counted his beads, and kissed the rood ;
But great was the pain of his manlihood.

" Sweet Mary Mother," the monk would pray,
" Take thou this curse of the flesh away, —
Give me not up to the devil's sway.

" Oh, make me pure as thine own pure Son !
My thoughts are fain to be thine, each one ;
But body and soul are alike undone."

And, even while praying, there came, between
Himself who prayed and Heaven's own Queen,
A delicate presence, more felt than seen, —

The sense of woman though none was there,
Her beauty near, her breath on the air,
Almost the touch of her hand on his hair ;

And when night came, and he fell on sleep,
Warm tears in a dream his eyes would weep,
For strange, bright shapes that he might not keep,—

The fair dream-girls who leaned o'er his bed,
Who held his hand, and whose kisses were shed
On his lips — for a monk's too full and red.

O fair dream-women with flowing tresses
And loosened vesture !   Their soft caresses
Thrilled him through to his soul's recesses.

He woke on fire, with rioting blood,
To scourge himself and to kiss the rood,
And to fear the strength of his manlihood.

One stormy night, when Christ's birth was nigh,
When snow lay thick, and the winds were high
'Twixt the large light land and the large light sky,

Monk Julius knelt in his cell's scant light,
And prayed, " If any be out to-night,
O Mother Mary, guide them aright."

Then there came to his ears, o'er the wastes of snow,
The dreadest of sounds, now loud, now low, —
The cry of the wolves, that howl as they go.

Then followed a light quick tap at the door ;
The monk rose up from the cell's cold floor,
And opened it, crossing himself once more.

A girl stood there, and " The Wolves ! " she cried.
" No danger now, daughter," the monk replied,
And drew the beautiful woman inside, —

For fair she was, as few women are fair,
And tall and shapely ; her great gold hair
Crowned her brows, that as ivory were.

Her deep blue eyes were two homes of light,
Soft moons of beauty to his dark night, —
What fairness was this to pasture sight?

But the sight was sin ; so he turned away
And knelt him down yet again to pray ;
But not one prayer could his starved lips say.

And, as he knelt, he became aware
Of a light hand passing across his hair,
And a sudden fragrance filled the air.

He raised his eyes, and they met her own, —
How blue hers were, how they yearned and shone !
Her waist was girt with a jewelled zone ;

But aside it slipped from her silken vest,
And the monk's eyes fell on her snowy breast,
Of her marvellous beauties the loveliest.

The monk sprang up, and he cried, " O bliss ! "
His lips sought hers in a desperate kiss ;
He had given his soul to make her his.

But he clasped no woman ; no woman was there —
Only the laughter of fiends on the air ;
The monk was snared in the devil's own snare.

RENUNCIATION.

HERE in my sheltering arms at rest she lies,
Her head upon my shoulder, and one hand
About my neck ; sleep has sealed fast her eyes.
The pensive twilight gathers round the land,
The first star ventures forth into the skies,
The air is gentle, and the month is May,
And peaceful is the death of the fair day ;
And with the dying day my life's hope dies, —
It sinks, it sets, — and then alone I stand.

How breathes she, like a little child at rest !
Above her brown hair's warmth I lean my face.
Ah me ! the day when first my glad lips pressed
Her answering lips, and in a long embrace
I felt against my own her throbbing breast !

First day of love, first gathered fruit of bliss, —
O day made memorable by the first kiss,
Pressure of hands, sweet secret things confessed !
Art thou not holy, day above all days?

O Love ! between that first kiss and this last
How many kisses were, — how sweet they were !
Still, Love, within my arms I hold you fast,
My tears and kisses fall upon your hair ;
Your sleep and this brief hour will soon be past.
Then shall my heart grow strong in its endeavor ;
Then shall I put you from my arms forever,
Saying, " We part, we part, and the wild blast
Sweeps over all my life, and life lies bare."

Indeed I know you thought you loved me, sweet ;
You pitied me, and loved my love of you ;
In all I said you heard my heart's swift beat.
" This heart that loves me so is warm and true,
A flower to wear, not trample 'neath my feet," —
Thus to yourself you thought, that dear, dead day,
We sitting in the twilight still and gray,
Your hands in mine.   When hands of lovers meet,
Not long, O Love, before the lips meet, too.

Because my kisses thrilled your eager blood,
I thought I found love in your ardent kiss,
And said, " She loves ! "   'T was but your womanhood,
With all its great capacities for bliss.
Without a word, in time I understood, —
You did not love me, though I saw you strove
To think you were returning love for love.
O my beloved, so passionately wooed,
In your new freedom, sweet, forget not this, —

That he who loves you gives you liberty
And joy transcendent, when the rightful lover,

16

Predestined by mysterious powers to be
Heart of your heart, the days at length discover.
Then, fast in Love's divine captivity,
In twilights like this twilight, or some night
When earth lies still beneath the moon's large light,
Think then a little, not untenderly,
Of one who walks where only sad ghosts hover.

About my life strange winds begin to rouse, —
I hear strange voices call me from afar ;
Outside the moonbeams rain through moveless boughs,
And heaven grows stronger with each confident star.
God's very peace encompasses the house ;
But what have I to do with peace or Heaven?
To the outer seas let my lone bark be driven :
One last kiss laid on mouth and fair broad brows,
Then let me go where storm and shipwreck are.

HIS VIEW.

Do you think she dreams of me for a minute,
Would care, were I out of the world, or in it?
            Not she, — no, no.

I might do my best, or my worst in evil ;
Be enshrined as a saint, or damned as a devil,
            And she not know.

Yet of all the many that love and tend her
She will find no heart so true to befriend her,
            Though she does not know.

But I think some day when the ninth wave takes her,
Grips her and lifts her, batters and breaks her,
            Then she may know.

UNCOMPLETED LIVES.

At last we stand again upon the heather here.
Just where we stood five years ago to-day, my dear:
The morning is all round us, — wind and light and scent ;
    Above us are the high, blue, foreign, summer skies ;
That way lie cornfields and rich, pastoral content ;
    In front the great sea shines, and almost blinds the eyes.

You hear the ripple, stirring shell and pebble, —
A pleasant sound, that delicate, tremulous treble ;
The air is warm with the sun, and keen with the sea ;
    And cliffs and sky and summer are the same :
But we are greatly changed ; we twain can never be
    As we were when we last this path together came.

That day we let our dreams fly far away like birds ;
Fools were we, surely, for a few impatient words
To give up all the joy which had been ours, indeed, —
    The perfect spiritual community,
The rapture of a passion naught might supersede,
    The unapproachable, divinest ecstasy

Of being wholly one with one you love the best ;
For love with sweetness does the simplest things invest.
How fair it looked to us ! — that life we cast away ;
    And yet we are not wretched, neither you nor I.
You have your children and their interests, to-day ;
    And I paint pictures that find men to praise and buy.

Sometimes I have forgotten you ; and yet at hours, —
And mostly when Spring comes with all her birds and
        flowers, —
At twilight, when the winds are gathered into rest,
    A vision of you, as I saw you last of all,
Fills my poor lonely room, and leans upon my breast,
    Till for passionate self-pity the tears begin to fall.

And I call you from my deep and desolate heart,—
From the life in which you have no longer any part;
But silence only mocks my bitter discontent,
    And the cruel darkness sweeps away the vision,
And I sicken at the roses' potent scent,
    And the moon and starlight laugh me to derision.

And now we stand together, and I hear your voice.
We had our time for choosing once,—we made our choice;
We chose to part; we twain in Love's sight did this sin.
    Has Love forgiven it to us?—consider well:
You know he has not, for we only now begin
    To know the meaning of that word—"irreparable."

It is our punishment that we should meet to-day;
And do you bid me help you, find some word to say
To heal our wounded spirits with, and stanch regret?
    Too late it is for words our stricken lives to heal;
Deep in your soul, as deep in mine, the pain is set
    Which hardly to each other yet we may reveal:

No great despair,—so noble and intense
It elevates the heart, is its own recompense,—
But dull, continuous ache of incompleteness,
    Persistent sense of failure in life's highest good,
Echoes of songs, and breaths of parted sweetness,
    From lands we may not now re-enter though we would.

Come on, to where the little wind-blown chapel stands,
With all its quaint inscriptions carved by seamen's hands.
Last night, when I came in from wandering by the sea,
    And saw you sitting lonely in the *salon* there,
Your face bent down, and sweet eyes never seeing me,
    The lamplight falling on your shining, golden hair,

The knowledge of your actual presence in the place,
The sight, again, of your fair, often-dreamed-of face,
Overcame me ; and I stood there, only knowing
    In a moment more perchance we should be meeting;
And I ceased to hear the summer sea-wind blowing,
    And louder than the seas I heard my own heart beating.

You must have risen, though I did not see you rise,
For, a moment more, I was looking in your eyes,
And I heard your voice, low and sweet and nothing
        changed, —
    The strangely quiet, deeply passionate voice ;
And so we met again, whom fate had long estranged,
    Who loved, yet in this meeting hardly could rejoice.

Then in the fresh, sweet darkness we sat upon the
        beach, —
We twain, and he, your husband, weak of will and speech ;
I took your hand, and my eager blood turned fire,
    As a great flame that a great wind drives before it ;
My heart turned to you with a cry of wild desire,
    But my lips kept mute, and I wonder how I bore it.

And all night long I lay awake, and heard the sea
Under the light, dry summer wind sound fitfully, —
Now soft among the pebbles, stirring stone by stone ;
    Now vehement with hiss and bubble of spray ;
Now soft again, in some most tender undertone ;
    Now loud and very near, then faint and far away, —

And the thought of you so filled me that I could not sleep ;
And the moonlight bright and broad lay over shore and
        deep ;
And I told my passion to the moon and to the sea ;
    And every way I looked I seemed to see you there,
The head bent back, and sweet eyes never seeing me ;
    The lamplight falling on your shining, golden hair.

And now we stand alone together, you and I, —
We twain who saw Love come, and let him pass us by, —
Give me your hands, and listen, dearest. We must wait,
    And bear the trouble of our days as best we may ;
And when we are both older, passion shall abate,
    As summer winds that at the sundown fall away,

And leave the earth to feel the moon's pure light, —
The great, compassionate quietude of night.
You say that day seems distant? Yes, but come it will, —
    As surely as our death-day it will come to pass, —
When we may meet as friends, without a single thrill,
    And smile at all the joy and all the grief that was.

But here is the chapel, smelling damp as any cell ;
We have it wholly to ourselves, though ; that is well.
Rest here, my dear ; you understand now all it meant,
    That day you let the scorn break out of lips and heart,
And then the deep, unutterable discontent, —
    Your life divorced from mine, of which your life was
        part.

But now, before we part forever, I and you,
One kiss upon the lips to last my whole life through, —
One draught of joy, one blessèd glimpse of paradise,
    With sound of shining angels singing round Love's
        throne.
O lonely place ! O moment that Love deifies !
    I hold you to my heart now, mine, and mine alone.

O my divided life, my first and only love !
O sweet. pale Northern flower ! O fairest, fluttered dove !
Alas ! there is no help in life for our great pain ;
    The winter winds must blow, and summer suns must
        burn,
The tides obey the moon, all things fulfil their reign,
    And we must bear to walk apart, and vainly yearn.

HE AND SHE.

SHE (*to herself*).

O LOST to me, lost more than if by death!
Why did I let him take me back at all?
      Did I not know
He never could forgive my perjured breath?
      Could he forego
From height of his proud faith to scorn my fall?

I loved that other man, and that God knows;
I know it, to my bitter shame and cost.
      O fair and cruel face,
Which like a baneful and false beacon rose,
      And by its rays
Lit me to shipwreck, where, then, all was lost!

Do I not hate him, now, cast off by him?
Surely I do, with all my strength of heart;
      As tired and cold,
In this man's strange forgiveness, bleak and grim,
      My wings I fold,
And ache for love of which I once was part.

O happy, shameful, shameless days gone by,
As warm with sun as these are cold with snow!
      False love! And yet
Did he not build for me new earth and sky?
      Can I forget
The joy he made my body and soul to know?

Doubtless, as I this evening sit and shiver,
Here in the twilight by the flickering fire,

Those lips of his
Make other women's lips with joy to quiver,
As 'neath their kiss
Mine trembled, while my blood was all desire.

Do I not hate him? Yea, with heart and soul;
But am I sure that if he came in now, —
Came in and turned,
With the old air of confident control,
Or looked and yearned
Into my eyes, or touched my cheek or brow,

My scorn would strike as I would have it do?
O vanished heaven of love in which I was,
Could I resist,
If once again my face towards his he drew
And my lips kissed,
And things that were should come again to pass?

There sits my husband, thinking what? Who knows
What thoughts are busy in his working brain?
He kept his word,
And took me back, to shelter from the crows
A wounded bird,
With draggled plumage, on its breast a stain.

HE (*to himself*).

Yes, if this case goes rightly, it will make
A difference to my fortunes certainly.
If they can only nurse the patient well!
Much hangs on them in this — more than on me;
And yet a cure would seem a miracle:
So save we folks for our and not for their sake.
Still sitting there, poor, punished, contrite thing!
And can *she* be the woman for whose love
I once had given all that men most prize?
It seems she has no heart in her to move,

But sits and gazes with those great, sad eyes,
And sad, strained lips that never smile or sing !
O pale and changed !   No longer proud of mien,
Who held herself with such a stately grace
That scarce your utmost praises could beguile
A faint, pink flush to the all-perfect face,
Or stir the cold composure of her smile, —
Fair are you still ; but not as once, my queen !

Nay, queen no more of mine !   Queen of what, then?
Queen of dishonor and all treachery —
But why upbraid?   Has she not borne her part?
Her life went down with mine beneath that sea,
Whose depths close over many an eager heart,
Whose wrecks are ruined lives of women and men.

I have not thought enough of her, I fear,
Pondering my own profession and my fame ;
We have not spoken this long afternoon ;
'T is hard to leave her to her speechless shame.

(*Aloud.*)

Come, now, and play me some slow, sleepy tune,
And as you pass me, stay and kiss me, dear.

COME, BUY.

Some things which are not yet enrolled
In market lists are bought and sold.
                                    ROSSETTI'S *Jenny*

" WHO will buy my roses,
    Roses red and white,
Sweetest of all posies
    For a man's delight?

" Who will buy my gold grass,
　　Feathery, sweet, and tall, —
Buy, ere the summer pass,
　　Sweetest thing of all?

" Who will buy my violets,
　　Fresh from warm, wet earth?
He who stops to buy them gets
　　All his money's worth."

" I will buy your roses,
　　Roses red and white,
Sweetest of all posies
　　For a man's delight.

" I will buy your gold grass,
　　Feathery, sweet, and tall, —
Buy, ere the summer pass,
　　Sweetest thing of all.

" I will buy your violets,
　　Fresh from warm, wet earth,
Since he who buys them gets
　　All his money's worth.

" Violets, grass, and roses,
　　You are mine to-day, —
When you 're faded posies,
　　Then I throw away."

FALSE REST AND TRUE REST.

I.

" AND thou hast taken from me my fair faith,
Which like a star lit the waste night of death, —
A light I thought no blast could ever kill.
O friend of mine, was it for me so ill
To fancy that my lips when void of breath
Should open in that land one entereth
Through portals of the grave, — how dark, how chill?

II.

" What hast thou set me in my dear hope's place
But thy stern Truth, with white, implacable face,
Cold eyes, shut lips, clenched hand, and barren breast?
I stand, of all my sweet faith dispossessed, —
Discrowned of my belief. Death hath no grace,
But seems a thing to shudder at. My days
Are joyless, and my nights are void of rest.

III.

" I thought that I, in some far paradise,
Should hear the old, sweet voices, and that eyes
Of those I loved and lost my eyes should greet.
O visionary fields that felt the feet
Of my impatient thought, which no more flies
From you to me, but in my cold heart lies
Quite cold and dead, once warm with my heart's heat !

IV.

" Oh, life was full of comfort in those years, —
Sweet things I dreamed of the impossible spheres ;
I had a haven. If the winds were strong,
Above their roar I caught from far the song

Of beckoning angels.   Now no light appears —
No song at all my heart, desirous, hears ;
The day is short, but oh the night is long !

v.

" Oh, long, oh, dreary long, that night of death !
No dawn it hath, no star that lighteneth.
There comes no love, no passionate memory
Of all the dear delights that used to be.
Shall one see God there, lying without breath ;
Or shall the dead give thanks? — the psalmist saith.
Nay, if the dead thank, they thank silently."

VI.

" There is no dreariness in death for one
Who sets his eyes on Truth, — that cold, calm sun,
By whose impartial and unvarying light
Men might walk surely, who now grope in night.
Who fears, when labor of the day is done,
To rest and sleep?   Then wherefore should ye shun
The sleep no dream, no waking, come to spite?

VII.

" Lift up and fix on Truth thy timorous eyes,
Till they can tolerate her awful skies.
Thy rest was warm and sweet, but could it save?
Would thy hope's torch have lasted to the grave?
How suddenly the grim mistrusts arise, —
' My soul, wilt thou find hell or paradise?
Pray, dear life, keep me till I grow more brave.

VIII.

" ' Oh mighty mystery of mysteries !
I venture forth upon the unsailed seas.
I go to face the awful, the unknown ;
O Death, how full of terror art thou grown !
I trust I go to lands of perfect peace,
Wherein are all the mighty companies
Of the illustrious dead, and those, my own, —

IX.

" ' My own, whose loss was such sharp gall to drink.
I trust !   Yet what are we, that we should think
Eternal peace and rapture must be ours?
Again by fear appalled my spirit cowers
In abject terror on the grave's dark brink.
Can I believe that through a coffin-chink
From dust of me it breaks anew and flowers?

X.

" ' But, nay, I do believe and will attest
That God is good, and on my Saviour's breast
I shall lie safely, when this life is over,' —
So say thy lips ; but thy soul sees above her
No visible heaven of deep joy and rest ;
She knoweth not the end of her long quest,
And deathly fears once more about her hover.

XI.

" That music which of old so loud did seem
Comes faint, as from a dawn-receding dream.
How has it paled — thy hope of future bliss !
Lo, by chill winds thy light extinguished is —
Not quite, for by its fluctuating gleam,
Its little, wandering, insufficient beam,
Death has a ghastly look, not really his.

XII.

" Were it not best all thought to concentrate
Upon this life in which we work, and wait,
And love, and grieve, and bear?   Life is a day ;
And death the night that follows it? — nay, nay,
If, when our days of toil we terminate,
We go to be a very part of fate,
Or, no end serving, simply pass away.

XIII.

" How shall death be, or night be, when we know not
That life has ceased in us ; that wild winds blow not
For us again ; for us no more the sun
Fulfils the earth, when winter-time is done ;
For us the tender things of Spring they show not ;
For us the birds are mute, the rivers flow not, —
What pain is there in this sweet dissolution? "

XIV.

" A slothful soul, in time of war, I slept.
While other men their dangerous outposts kept ;
And when you did command me to arise,
And with the light and air familiarize
My spiritual senses, I had crept
Back to my lair, by wholesome winds unswept,
Had you not fixed on Truth my coward eyes.

XV.

" If life be full of comfort, fair and sweet,
I will be meekly thankful that my feet
Are spared the stones that wound, and as I may
Try to make smooth for others a rougher way ;

But should life bitter prove, and incomplete,
This pain of living it is very fleet,
And rest will come, with quiet set of day.

XVI.

" I feel an ardor never felt till now, —
A stimulus to work, to keep the vow
I take to help each weary woman and man.
There was no room before in my life's plan
For this, — my dreams and visions filled it so ;
But now I know the way my soul shall go,
Shall I not use it here as best I can?

XVII.

" Death holds no longer any fear for me,
Now that my hopes and doubts cease equally.
I know, at length, the place I journey to,
I know the work in life I have to do.
This rest of ours is true rest, verily.
O power of undeniable Truth, set free
All souls that from false rest a false joy drew ! "

MY GARDEN.

O my Garden, full of roses,
    Red as passion and as sweet,
Failing not when summer closes,
    Lasting on through cold and heat !

O my Garden, full of lilies,
    White as peace, and very tall,
In your midst my heart so still is
    I can hear the least leaf fall !

O my Garden, full of singing
　From the birds that house therein,
Sweet notes down the sweet day ringing
　Till the nightingales begin !

O my Garden, where such shade is,
　O my Garden, bright with sun ;
O my loveliest of Ladies,
　Of all Gardens sweetest one !

PARTED LOVERS.

O Love, the way is steep,
And dark the night and deep,
And rest is not in sleep,
　　　Where evil dreams roam free.

O hearts no longer glad,
But worn with pain and sad,
Because the joy they had
　　　Perchance no more may be.

O Love, so far away,
Out of this night-like day
One lifts his voice to say
　　．His thoughts are all of thee,

Even as streams that blend
Only to one goal tend,
And ever, in the end,
　　　Eventuate in the sea.

O lonely, loveless lover,
Walking where dream-things hover,
Whose lips no more discover
　　　How sweet her sweet lips be, —

Does she at all desire
Once more Love's subtle fire,
That thrilled her as a lyre
      Is thrilled when tune goes free?

O parted, weary lives
The cruel billow rives,
The pitiless storm-wind drives
      To where all wrecked lives lie.

For all are wrecked at last,
Though long delayed the blast,
Though long withheld the vast
      Ninth wave that cries Death's cry.

There, done with smiles and tears,
Desires and hopes and fears,
Under the whelming years,
      At length at rest they lie.

Heart of his heart, sweetheart,
He feels of her grief the smart,
And sighs as he walks apart, —
      "Only less sad than I !"

A GRAY DAY.

FORTH from a sky of windless gray
Pours down the soft, persistent rain;
And she for whom I sigh in vain,
Who makes my bliss, now makes my pain,
Being far from me this autumn day, —
      So far away.

17

Upon the waters void and gray
No floating sail appears in sight;
The dull rain and the humid light
No wind has any heart to spite,
This dreary, weary, autumn day,
    With love away.

No gull wings out 'twixt gray and gray, —
All gray, as far as eye can reach;
The sea too listless seems for speech,
And vaguely frets upon the beach,
As knowing she, this autumn day,
    Is far away.

Ah, like that sea my life looks gray;
Like a forgotten land it lies,
With no light on it from her eyes
Lovely and changeful as those skies
'Neath which she walks this autumn day
    So far away.

But they shall pass, these skies of gray,
And she for whom I sigh in vain,
Who makes my bliss and makes my pain,
Shall turn my gray to gold again,
Being not, as now, that future day,
    So far away.

A SONG'S MESSAGE.

To her to whom all sweetnesses belong,
In whom all deep and opposite charms unite,
Who is at once the shadow and the light,
    I send my pilgrim song.

Say unto her how I am fain to be
Where she is, who is all my life's desire,
For whom my love is pure as vestal fire,
    And deep as the deep sea.

Say unto those whom now she moves among, —
"Though for a while you in her days have part,
Ye have no habitation in her heart,
    As I, a little song."

Yet be thou humble, song, for her dear sake,
Knowing thou hast no grace at all but this, —
To sing of her for whose transcendent kiss
    Hearts of all men might break.

THE SWEETEST DREAM. .

FOLD, white arms, about me ;
    Cling, sweet lips, to mine !
Sweetest sweet, without thee
    I but waste and pine.

Lean, dear face, above me ;
    Soft hands, hold mine close ;
Let me look and love thee,
    O my very rose !

Comfort me with kisses
    That your soul comes through ;
Let the old dead blisses
    Breathe and burn anew.

Lean upon my bosom
    Till I feel yours beat,
And your mouth's sweet blossom
    Passion make more sweet.

O my sweet one, sweetest,
    Love of loves supreme,
This has been the fleetest,
    Sweetest, bitterest dream.

IN EXTREMIS.

Now that Hope lies sick to death,
  Come and weep ;
None can stay her parting breath ;
  Dark and deep
Let her grave be, — cool and quiet
Under all the summer riot.

At her head let roses be,
  For a sign
Of Love's ardent wreath that she
  Might not twine ;
And, for Peace, she might not meet with,
Lilies cover her white feet with.

Now that she is dead and dumb,
  Stay your tears ;
In the years that are to come,
  Sunless years,
She again will never move you,
Only hopeless sorrow prove you.

All your weeping is in vain, —
  She is dead !
Her no tears can make again, —
  Lift her head.
Dearest, most divine deceiver,
Say your last farewell, and leave her.

AT HOPE'S GRAVE.

WE said that Hope was dead
   So many years ago ;
We planned to make her bed
   Where all the sweet flowers blow ;
To lay her quiet head
   Where the long grasses grow.

But while with tearful eyes,
   Though tears must fall in vain,
And just permitted sighs
   To ease our weary pain, —
Deeming she should not rise
   Nor speak to us again, —

While thus we sat, behold !
   She stirred ; she was not dead !
Take off the wreath ; unfold
   The shroud ; raise up her head, —
Not yet beneath the mould
   And flowers shall be her bed.

But now when Spring is here, —
   This day, this heavy day,
When skies are pure and clear,
   And earth with flowers is gay, —
We clasp sad hands, my dear,
   And turn our eyes away,

Our burning eyes away,
   Because not by Hope's bed
We sit this young Spring day,
   And fancy she is dead,
And find soft words to say,
   And roses for her head ;

But by her very grave,
  Whereon the earth we heap,
Knowing no thing can save, —
  That this *is* death, not sleep, —
We stand, but do not rave,
  Too numb at heart to weep.

SOLITARY.

My thoughts have been with you the whole night long ;
  I wonder did you know, my dear?
My heart went flying to you, in a song ;
  I wonder, sweetheart, did you hear?

Here, where I kissed your hands and lips and hair, —
  Here, where I held you to my heart,
While passion thrilled and kindled all the air,
  Till hands and lips and lives must part,

I have lain, weary, at Sleep's shadowy gate,
  Which would not ope to let me in
Where happy dreams of you I knew must wait,
  So that I might some rapture win.

I have been weary for your voice, your touch,
  The desperate sweetness of your kiss, —
The joy which almost thrills me over-much,
  O sweet, my sweet, so sweet it is.

I strove to think you leaned above me here,
  Laid lips to mine, then found to say
The dearest words, — as dear as love is dear ;
  But, O Love, you were far away.

Only for me this drear, ghost-haunted room,
    And noises in the street outside ;
Only for me to go from gloom to gloom,
    And at the end, dark Death for bride.

FROM FAR.

" O Love, come back, across the weary way
Thou wentest yesterday, —
      Dear Love, come back ! "

" I am too far upon my way to turn :
Be silent, hearts that yearn
      Upon my track."

" O Love ! Love ! Love ! sweet Love, we are undone,
If thou indeed be gone
      Where lost things are."

" Beyond the extremest sea's waste light and noise,
As from Ghost-land, my voice
      Is borne afar."

" O Love, what was our sin, that we should be
Forsaken thus by thee ?
      So hard a lot ! "

" Upon your hearts my hands and lips were set, —
My lips of fire, — and yet,
      Ye knew me not."

" Nay, surely, Love ! We knew thee well, sweet Love !
Did we not breathe and move
      Within thy light ? "

" Ye did reject my thorns who wore my roses ;
Now darkness closes
                    Upon your sight."

" O Love ! stern Love ! be not implacable.
We loved thee, Love, so well !
                    Come back to us."

" To whom, and where, and by what weary way
That I went yesterday,
                    Shall I come thus ? "

" Oh, weep, weep, weep ! for Love, who tarried long
With many a kiss and song,
                    Has taken wing.

" No more he lightens in our eyes like fire ;
He heeds not our desire,
                    Or songs we sing."

"LOVE HAS TURNED HIS FACE AWAY."

Love has turned his face away
                    Weep, sad eyes !
Love is now of yesterday.
                    Time that flies,
Bringing glad and grievous things,
Bears no more Love's shining wings.

Love was not all glad, you say ;
                    Tears and sighs
In the midst of kisses lay.
                    Were it wise,
If we could, to bid him come,
Making with us once more home ?

Little doubts that sting and prey,
    Hurt replies,
Words for which a life should pay, —
    None denies
These of Love were very part,
Thorns that hurt the rose's heart.

Yet should we beseech Love stay,
    Sorrow dies ;
And if Love will but delay
    Joy may rise.
Since, with all its thorns, the rose
Is the sweetest flower that blows.

"LOVE LIES A–DYING."

COME in gently, and speak low,
    Love lies a-dying ;
By his death-bed, standing so,
    Hush, hush your crying.

Once his eyes were full of light,
    Who now lies a-dying ;
Round about him falls the night,
    Hush, hush your crying.

Ghostly winds begin to blow,
    Love lies a-dying ;
Hark where distant waters flow,
    Hush, hush your crying.

From a Land of Lost Delight —
    Now he lies a-dying —
Visions come to haunt his sight,
    Hush, hush your crying.

From a land he used to know —
    Love lies a-dying —
Ghosts of dead songs come and go,
    Hush, hush your crying.

Perished hopes like lilies white —
    Now he lies a-dying —
Leave beside him, in Death's night,
    Hush, hush your crying.

Round about him, to and fro —
    Now he lies a-dying —
Phantom feet move soft and slow,
    Hush, hush your crying.

Sharply once did sorrow bite, —
    O Love lies a-dying ! —
Tears and blood sprang warm and bright,
    Hush, hush your crying.

Pain is done now ; strength is low, —
    Love lies a-dying, —
Let him gently languish so,
    Hush, hush your crying.

AT LOVE'S GRAVE.

Now we stand above Love's grave,
    Shall we weep, —
We who saw and would not save ?
    Let him sleep.

Shall we sing his requiem?
  Ah, for what?
Better stand here, cold and dumb;
  Vex him not.

He was young and strong and fair,
  Myrtle-crowned;
Now no myrtle wreathes his hair,
  Cypress bound.

Did *we* slay him?   Nay, not we;
  We but said,
"Doubts and bitter words *must* be."
  He is dead!

Of those doubts and words he died.
  Hush, keep still!
Late regrets would but deride.
  One calm will,

Perfect peace, and perfect faith,
  Had these been,
He had never chanced on death,
  Never seen

Darkness of the under night
  Where he lies,
No song on his lips, no light
  In his eyes.

Leave him where he lies alone,
  Void of care;
Only carve upon his stone, —
  "Love *was* fair."

LOVE'S RESURRECTION SONG.

I MADE a grave for dead Love to lie in;
　　And I dug it deep in a grassy place,
With trees above it for winds to sigh in,
　　Or birds to make song in through blithe Spring days.

Then I stretched myself on the grave in sorrow,
　　Remembering Love, and how fair was he;
Yesterday poisoned the thought of the morrow,
　　The blank morrow, in which no Love should be.

And I cried, "O Love, thou wert full of splendor
　　And pomp and dominion but yesterday,
Thy voice was kind and thine eyes were tender;
　　But all, now, all, has been taken away.

"Love, canst thou hear?" But the wind moaned only,—
　　Only the grass on Love's grave was stirred;
In the trees above sang, faint and lonely,
　　One sad, little, bright-eyed, unmated bird.

The twilight fell as I lay and wept there;
　　And dew dropped silently, wetting my face;
Alone my weary vigil I kept there,
　　Till the moon arose in its placid grace:

And the air was charged with her benediction;
　　And my desolate heart was soothed and filled
With a spirit of some divine prediction, —
　　And suddenly all my weeping was stilled.

Then I beheld, in the moonlight tender,
　　A presence more bright than the moon's pale fire;
For there stood Love, with increase of splendor,
　　And my heart was made one with my heart's desire.

A SONG OF MEETING.

I LOOK down days and nights,
And see Love's beckoning lights
Shine from his fairest heights.

On winds that come and go
I hear, now loud, now low,
The song my heart loves so.

I know the way shall end, —
The weary way I wend ;
I know that God shall send

A great, propitious day,
When she I love shall say,
" Rest here, with Love to stay."

As ships to harbor bear,
Through seas and deeps of air,
Through darkness and despair,

I bring to Love's high goal,
To his supreme control,
My body and my soul.

O joy of day begun,
O joy of day just done,
Lessening the days by one,

Until her lips meet mine,
Until we drink the wine
Of Love's most hidden vine !

Oh, in Love's land with me
Will my belovèd be?
Shall our eyes live to see

Those dim and mystic ways
Haunted by many a face
Of lovers from old days?

O Love, those ways are sweet, —
Their stillness so complete
We hear our own hearts beat.

And there forever blows
Of roses, the one rose
Whose leaves for us unclose.

Love, from thy distant place,
Lift up thy loveliest face
To greet the passing days, —

Each day a wave that sweeps
Back to the sunless deeps
Where Life forgotten sleeps.

O thou for whose love's sake
New souls in men might wake,
And harp of sweet song break

To know itself so slight, —
Forgive Song's failing flight,
Bow, Love, from thy fair height !

CHANGED LOVE.

When did the change come, dearest Heart of mine,
  Whom Love loves so?
When did Love's moon less brightly seem to shine,
  While to and fro,
  And soft and slow,
Chill winds began to move in its decline?

When did the change come, thou who wast mine own?
  When heard the rose
First, far-off Autumn winds begin to moan,
  At sunset's close,
  When sad Love goes
About the Autumn woods to brood alone?

When did the change come in thy heart, Sweetheart,
  Thy heart so dear to me?
In what thing did I fail to bear my part,
  My part to thee,
  Whose deity
My soul confesses, and how fair thou art?

Alas for poor, changed Love!   We cannot say
  What changes Love.
My love would not suffice to make your day
  Now gladly move,
  Though kisses strove
With answering kisses, in Love's sweetest way.

But though I know you changed, right well I know
  That, should we meet,
Deep in your heart some love for me would glow;
  Though not that heat
  Which made it beat
So fast with joy, two years — one year ago.

TOO LATE.

LOVE turns his eyes away.
    He had so long to wait
Before the words we say,
    But say, alas, too late, —
He turns his eyes away.

"Oh, pity our dismay,
    Our sad and fallen state;
Ah, pity us, we pray,
    Let it not be too late ! "
He turns his eyes away.

"O Love, up some dark way —
    If so thou wilt — and straight,
Lead us; but on some day
    Let our hands meet ! " — Too late !
He turns his eyes away.

"Our sky is cold and gray,
    Our life most desolate,
If we no more may lay
    Gifts on thy shrine." — Too late !
He turns his eyes away.

Down drear paths we must stray,
    Each faring separate,
Because Love would not stay,
    But cried "Too late ! too late ! "
And turned his eyes away.

NEW GARDEN SECRETS.

———◆◇◆———

BEFORE AND AFTER FLOWERING.

BEFORE.

FIRST VIOLET.

Lo here! how warm and dark and still it is;
Sister, lean close to me, that we may kiss.
Here we go rising, rising — know'st thou where?

SECOND VIOLET.

Indeed I cannot tell, nor do I care,
It is so warm and pleasant here.   But hark!
What strangest sound was that above the dark?

FIRST VIOLET.

As if our sisters all together sang, —
Seemed it not so?

SECOND VIOLET.

More loud than that it rang;
And louder still it rings, and seems more near.
Oh, I am shaken through and through with fear —
Now in some deadly grip I seemed confined!
Farewell, my sister!   Rise, and follow, and find!

FIRST VIOLET.

From how far off those last words seemed to fall!
Gone where she will not answer when I call!

18

How lost? how gone?   Alas! this sound above me, —
" Poor little Violet, left with none to love thee ! "
And now, it seems, I break against that sound !
What bitter pain is this that binds me round,
This pain I press into !   Where have I come?

AFTER.

A Crocus.

Welcome, dear sisters, to our fairy home !
They call this Garden ; and the time is Spring.
Like you I have felt the pain of flowering ;
But, oh, the wonder and the deep delight
It was to stand here, in the broad sunlight,
And feel the Wind flow round me cool and kind ;
To hear the singing of the leaves the Wind
Goes hurrying through ; to see the mighty Trees,
Where every day the blossoming buds increase.
At evening, when the shining Sun goes in,
The gentler lights look down, and dews begin,
And all is still, beneath the quiet sky,
Save sometimes for the Wind's low lullaby.

First Tree.
Poor little flowers !

Second Tree.
                    What would you prate of, now?

First Tree.
They have not heard ; I will keep still.   Speak low.

First Violet.
The Trees bend to each other lovingly.

CROCUS.

Daily they whisper of fair things to be.
Great talk they make about the coming Rose,
The very fairest flower, they say, that blows!
Such scent she hath; her leaves are red, they say,
And fold her round in some divine, sweet way.

FIRST VIOLET.

Would she were come, that for ourselves we might
Have pleasure in this wonder of delight!

CROCUS.

Here comes the laughing, dancing, hurrying rain;
How all the Trees laugh at the Wind's light strain!

FIRST VIOLET.

We are so near the earth, the Wind goes by
And hurts us not; but if we stood up high,
Like Trees, then should we soon be blown away.

SECOND VIOLET.

Nay; were it so, we should be strong as they.

CROCUS.

I often think how nice to be a Tree;
Why, sometimes in their boughs the Stars I see.

FIRST VIOLET.

Have you seen that?

CROCUS.

   I have, and so shall you
But hush! I feel the coming of the dew.

NIGHT.

SECOND VIOLET.

How bright it is! the Trees, how still they are!

CROCUS.

I never saw before so bright a Star
As that which stands and shines just over us.

FIRST VIOLET (*after a pause*).

My leaves feel strange and very tremulous.

CROCUS AND SECOND VIOLET TOGETHER.

And mine, and mine!

FIRST VIOLET.

O warm, kind Sun, appear!

CROCUS.

I would the Stars were gone, and day were here!

JUST BEFORE DAWN.

FIRST VIOLET.

Sister! No, answer, sister? Why so still?

ONE TREE TO ANOTHER.

Poor little Violet, calling through the chill
Of this new frost which did her sister slay,
In which she must herself, too, pass away!
Nay, pretty Violet, be not so dismayed;
Sleep only, on your sister sweet, is laid.

First Violet.

No pleasant Wind about the garden goes,
Perchance the Wind has gone to bring the Rose.
O sister ! surely now your sleep is done.
I would we had not looked upon the Sun.
My leaves are stiff with pain.   O cruel night !
And through my root some sharp thing seems to bite.
Ah me ! what pain, what coming change is this?

(She dies.)

First Tree.

So endeth many a Violet's dream of bliss.

THE ROSE'S DREAM.

I.

O sisters, when last night so well you slept
I could not sleep; but through the silent air
I looked upon the white Moon, shining where
No scent of any Rose can reach, I know.
And as I looked, adown the path there crept
A little trembling, restless Wind, and lo !
As near it came, I said, " O little breeze,
That hast no strength wherewith to stir the trees,
What dost thou in this place? "   It only sighed,
And paused a little ere it thus replied, —

II.

" I am the Wind that comes before the rain, —
Which, even now, bears onward from the west,
The rain that is as sweet to you as rest.
When all the air about the day lies dead,
And the incessant sunlight grows a pain,
Then by the cool rain are you comforted.

O happy Rose, that shall not live to see
This summer garden altered utterly, —
You know not of the days of snow and ice,
Nor know the look of wild and wintry skies."

III.

Then passed the Wind, but left me very sad,
For I began to think of days to come,
Wherein the Sun should fail and birds grow dumb,
And how this garden then should look, indeed.
And as I thought of all, such fear I had
I cried to you, asleep, though none would heed;
And so I wept, though none might see me weep,
Till came the Wind again, and bade me sleep,
And sang me such a small, sweet song that soon
I fell asleep while looking on the Moon.

IV.

And as I slept I dreamed a fearful dream : —
It seemed to me that I was standing here,
The sky was sunless, and I saw anear
All you, my sisters, lying dead and crushed.
I could not hear the music of the stream
That runs hard by, when suddenly there rushed
A giant Wind adown the garden walk,
And all the great old Trees began to talk,
And cried, " What does the Rose here?   Bid her go,
Lest buried she should be in coming snow."

V.

I strove to move away, but all in vain;
And flying, as it passed me, cried the Wind,
" O foolish, little Rose, and art thou blind?
Dost thou not see the snow is coming fast?"
And all the swaying Trees cried out again,
" O foolish Rose, to tarry till the last!"

Then came a sudden whirl, a mighty noise,
As every Tree that lives had found a voice ;
And I was borne away, and lifted high,
As birds that dart in summer through the sky.

VI.

And then the great Wind fell away, and so
I felt that I was whirling down and down,
Past Trees that strove, with branches bare and brown,
To catch me as I fell ; and all they cried, —
" She will be buried in the cold, deep snow ;
Ah, would she had like other Roses died ! "
Then, as I thought to fall, I woke to find
The cool rain dropping on me, and the Wind
Singing a rainy song among the Trees,
Wherein the birds were building at their ease.

VII.

FIRST FLOWER.

A fearful dream, indeed, and such an one
As well may make you sad for days to come.

SECOND FLOWER.

A sad, strange dream !

THE ROSE.

Why is the Lily dumb?

THE LILY.

Too sad the dream for me to speak about !

THE ROSE.

I fear, this night, the setting of the Sun.

A Tree.

Nay, when the Sun goes in the Stars come out.
You shall not dream, Rose, such a dream again;
Forget it, now, in listening to the rain.

The Rose.

I would the Wind had never talked to me
Of things that I shall never live to see !

THE FLOWER AND THE HAND.

I.

Just after Nightfall.

I HEARD a whisper of Roses,
　　And light, white Lilies laugh out —
" Ah, sweet when the evening closes,
　　And Stars come looking about ;
How cool and good it is to stand,
Nor fear at all the gathering hand ! "

II.

" Would I were red ! " cried a White Rose,
　　" Would I were white ! " cried a red one.
" No longer the light Wind blows,
　　He went with the dear dead Sun.
Here we forever seem to stay,
And yet a Sun dies every day."

III.

A Lily.

" The Sun is not dead, but sleeping,
　　And each day the same Sun wakes ;
But when Stars their watch are keeping,
　　Then a time of rest he takes."

MANY ROSES TOGETHER.

" How very wise these Lilies are !
They must have heard Sun talk with Star ! "

IV.

FIRST ROSE.

" Pray, then, can you tell us, Lilies,
    Where slumbers the Wind at night,
When the garden all round so still is,
    And brimmed with the Moon's pale light? "

A LILY.

" In branches of great Trees he rests."

SECOND ROSE.

" Not so ; they are too full of nests."

V.

FIRST ROSE.

" I think he sleeps where the grass is ;
    He there would have room to lie ;
The white Moon over him passes ;
    He wakes with the dawning sky."

MANY LILIES TOGETHER.

" How very wise these Roses seem,
Who think they know, and only dream ! "

VI.

FIRST ROSE.

" What haps to a gathered flower? "

Second Rose.

" Nay, sister, now who can tell?
One comes not back a single hour,
   To say it is ill or well :
I would with such an one confer,
To know what strange things chanced to her."

VII.

First Rose.

" Hush ! hush ! now the Wind is waking —
   Or is it the Wind I hear?
My leaves are thrilling and shaking —
   Good-by — I am gathered, my dear !
Now, whether for my bliss or woe,
I shall know what the plucked flowers know ! "

GARDEN FAIRIES.

Keen was the air, the sky was very light,
Soft with shed snow my garden was, and white,
And, walking there, I heard upon the night
     Sudden sound of little voices,
     Just the prettiest of noises.

It was the strangest, subtlest, sweetest sound, —
It seemed above me, seemed upon the ground,
Then swiftly seemed to eddy round and round,
     Till I said : " To-night the air is
     Surely full of garden fairies."

And all at once it seemed I grew aware
That little, shining presences were there, —
White shapes and red shapes danced upon the air ;
     Then a peal of silver laughter,
     And such singing followed after

As none of you, I think, have ever heard.
More soft it was than call of any bird,
Note after note, exquisitely deferred,
      Soft as dew-drops when they settle
      In a fair flower's open petal.

" What are these fairies ? " to myself I said ;
For answer, then, as from a garden's bed,
On the cold air, a sudden scent was shed, —
      Scent of lilies, scent of roses,
      Scent of Summer's sweetest posies.

And said a small, sweet voice within my ear, —
" We flowers that sleep through winter, once a year
Are by our flower queen sent to visit here ;
      That this fact may duly flout us, —
      Gardens can look fair without us.

" A very little time we have to play,
Then must we go, oh, very far away,
And sleep again for many a long, long day,
      Till the glad birds sing above us,
      And the warm sun comes to love us.

" Hark what the roses sing, now, as we go ; "
Then very sweet and soft, and very low —
A dream of sound across the garden snow —
      Came the chime of roses singing
      To the lily-bell's faint ringing.

Roses' Song.

  " Softly sinking through the snow,
To our winter rest we go,
Underneath the snow to house
Till the birds be in the boughs,
And the boughs with leaves be fair,
And the sun shine everywhere.

Softly through the snow we settle,
Little snow-drops press each petal.
Oh, the snow is kind and white, —
Soft it is, and very light ;
Soon we shall be where no light is,
But where sleep is, and where night is, —
Sleep of every wind unshaken,
Till our Summer bids us waken."

Then toward some far-off goal that singing drew ;
Then altogether ceased ; more steely blue
The blue stars shone ; but in my spirit grew
    Hope of Summer, love of Roses,
    Certainty that Sorrow closes.

SONNETS TO C. N. M.

THE NINTH WAVE.

Lo, now, the end of all things come at last !—
    The great ninth wave, whose coming none might
        stay ;
    A bitter wave made strong to ruin and slay !
I stretch my hopeless hands out to the past
From which it whirls me ; and I hear a blast
    Of melancholy music sweep this way,
    That makes my very soul afraid to pray,
And all my life shrink fainting and aghast.

O dead mute mouths and unrecording eyes ;
    Dead hearts that loved me, — is it well with ye ?
    Is death made sweeter, now that even she
For whom alway my spirit thirsts and cries —
Who, going, took the light from out of my skies —
    Has joined your high and silent company ?

BEREAVEMENT.

WHAT words have I for thee o'er whom I bow,
　Whose soul has reached the undiscovered land?
　In densest midnight of my life I stand, —
The light which lightened it is darkened now.
Thy love cruel Death would not to me allow;
　Once more went forth the inexorable command,
　And in thy place he sets at my right hand
A still sad ghost, thine absence to avow.

To-day I look away from Death, and see
　The bitter days thy love sustained me through;
Bright days thy love made brighter — let them be;
　I move about a world I never knew —
A sunless, soulless world that knows not thee
　From whose dear life my life took strength and grew.

ALONE.

NOT as of old times do I come, to-day,
　To breathe the strength and freshness of the sea
　Until as part of it I seemed to be, —
Part of the sea-wind and the blowing spray:
She who once came with me is far away,
　For Death was kind to her, though cruel to me,
　And all my empty life drifts aimlessly,
Like vessels that no more their helm obey.

O sea, that had my childish love and hers,
　What message from my dead one dost thou bring?
Surely with me through thee her soul confers,
　In some inexplicable way, to wring
　Mine eyes with bitterest tears, remembering
What no more lights my dark, disastrous years.

THY BIRTHDAY.

To-day it is thy birthday; but we twain
  Are not together as in days gone by, —
  Silence and darkness gird thee round, and I
Apart from thee for a brief while remain.
Some little joy; perhaps some strange new pain;
  Some doubt; some wonder, — then my spirit's cry
  To which my bitter singing made reply,
Shall cease, and leave me what the gods ordain.

What that may be, indeed, we cannot know:
  Silence and patient night, methinks; and yet
No man can surely say that this is so.
  Thy heart to-day may on past days be set,
Even as mine is, wandering to and fro
  In sunset lands where tongueless ghosts are met.

EIGHT YEARS AGO.

To-night for the first time, eight years gone by,
  We stood in Dante's Florence, and felt beat
  Our hearts to know we passed where fell his feet.
To-night I walk beneath an English sky,
And round me, meek and very peacefully
  Our English country stretches. Oh, how fleet,
  How fair with dreams accomplished, heavenly sweet,
Was that, our sovereign month in Italy!

I wonder if your soul has been, this hour,
  To lean with mine where sacred Arno flows,
So much, to-night, the Past asserts its power.
  Nay, no dream comes through your divine repose
Deep under grass and many a watching flower;
  'T was but my love that feigned it drew thee close.

FIVE YEARS AGO.

FIVE years ago to-day, since Death, thy friend,
　　Hushed all the music of thy noble life
　　With his long, icy kiss, and called thee wife ;
And I am five years nearer to the end,
When with the stars and winds my life shall blend.
　　This loud and populous world to-day is rife
　　With thoughts of thee.　O wild and tragic strife
Of one who wars with memories that rend !

Dear heart, which for so long beat close to mine,
　　Nor quailed before the darkness, and could bear
　　With bitterness and violence of despair,
Rest, in these later days, deep rest is thine ;
　　And I, bereft of hope, too sad for prayer,
Still kneel, in soul, and worship at thy shrine.

AFTER READING IN INGRAM'S MONOGRAPH
ON OLIVER MADOX BROWN
THE CHAPTER ENTITLED "FRIENDSHIP."

I.

WALKING my way, with face to sorrow set,
　　A voice, most like the wind's voice when it says
　　Some grieving word within a pine-thronged place
Spake low to me ; and turning round, I met
The eyes my spirit never may forget,
　　Then for long time unseen ; and down the ways
　　A spectral band, the ghosts of my old days,
Came to me sighing, " Ah, not forgotten yet ! "

And some looked sad, and some were garlanded
   With flowers that long ago made fair the land ;
   And in the midst there came, hand clasped in hand,
My friend, and those to whom my life was wed.
   "But ah, what shape," I cried, "now heads the
      band ? "
"What shape but thine old self?" the wind's voice
   said.

II.

AND did it really live, that far-off day,
   That day in March, so memorably sweet,
   When to the country went our hastening feet,
And small spring flowers made blithe the country way,
And birds sang to us of the coming May ;
   And in the soft, blue air, with song replete,
   We felt glad presage of the longed-for heat,
When summer should be come in brave array?

Now only one of us can ever go
   To give Spring welcome where skies show more clear,
   When birds attest the glad youth of the year ;
And grief is not quite unassuaged, while so,
On winds that, whispering, wander to and fro,
   Spring's inner message the hushed heart can hear.

MISCELLANEOUS SONNETS.

BEYOND REACH.

Dear Love, thou art so far above my song,
   It is small wonder that it fears to rise,
   Knowing it cannot reach my Paradise ;
Yet ever to dwell here my thoughts among,
Nor try its upward flight, would do thee wrong.
   What time the lark soars singing to the skies,
   We know he falters, know the sweet song dies,
That fain would reach Heaven's gate, sustained and strong :

But angels bending from the shining brink
   Catch the faint note, and know the poor song fails,
     Having no strength to reach their heavenly height ;
So listen thou, belovèd, and so think —
   More for the earth than Heaven his song avails,
     Yet sweetest heard when nearest to God's light.

I, LEAST OF ALL.

No man is worthy of her favoring grace,
  I, least of all, on whom the gods have laid
  A heavy hand; who live with soul afraid,
As one who walks by dark, precipitous ways,
Knowing on either side lie death and space.
  Yet in a desperate mood my whole heart prayed
  'That she by whose least touch my blood is swayed,
Whose soul is as a high and heavenly place,

Would love me, seeing how wholly I was hers.
  Behold, she did accept my prayer: even she,
Ringed round by bands of goodly worshippers,
  Stept from their midst to sit alone with me
  Under the shadow of my dark yew-tree,
Where, parted, still her soul with mine confers.

LOVE AND MUSIC.

I LISTENED to the music broad and deep:
  I heard the tenor in an ecstasy
  Touch the sweet, distant goal; I heard the cry
Of prayer and passion; and I heard the sweep
Of mighty wings, that in their waving keep
  The music that the spheres make endlessly, —
  Then my cheek shivered, tears made blind mine eye;
As flame to flame I felt the quick blood leap,

And, through the tides and moonlit winds of sound,
  To me love's passionate voice grew audible.
Again I felt thy heart to my heart bound,
  Then silence on the viols and voices fell;
  But, like the still, small voice within a shell,
I heard Love thrilling through the void profound.

LOVE'S STRESS.

About my love, O love, why do I sing?
   Canst thou by my weak words my great love know?
   Or can I hope that any words should show
That exquisite interchange of June with Spring
That makes thy sweet soul the divine, sweet thing
   Of which no man the memory lets go,
   Once having known?   What breath have I to blow
The clarion of thy praise to echoing?

I sing, not for thy sake, nor for men's sake, —
   I do but sing to ease my soul from stress
   Of love, and thy deep, passionate loveliness ;
So, in some great despair, our hearts must break
   But for our bitter sobs and frantic cries,
   Sent out against the inaccessible skies.

CROWNING LOVE.

Am I not very part of thee, O Sweet,
   Even as a soul is part of the great sun?
   In days before I knew thee, life had run
With me to barren wastefulness ; no heat
Informed my days : I only heard the beat
   Of Death's dull sea no traveller may shun, —
   I did not fear to meet it, being as one
Who goes with head downcast and flagging feet ;

When, lo, between me and Death's wave a light,
   A sudden heat and splendor in the air !
   Thy soul from far caught the importunate prayer
For dawn of one who wrestled with the night ;
And, as mine eyes, my soul had instant sight
   Of things divine and strange, for Thou wert there.

OUTER SADNESS.

I HELD my Love against my heart, and knew
  The deep delight of loving her ; yea, all
  The maddening sweetness, when beyond recall,
Her lips through mine my longing spirit drew
And uttermost heaven opened to my view,
  Where she and I with Love kept festival.
  But with the calm that followed, and the fall
Of gentler kisses, soft and sweet as dew,

Came in the March wind's melancholy voice,
  A weary monster seeking after prey ;
And farther off I seem to catch the noise
  Of waves that hiss and thunder while they slay, —
A sudden terror seized me 'mid my joys,
  And " Death " was all the word Love found to say.

REMEMBERED HOURS.

Not here at all, nor in thy far-off place,
  I stand to-day in heart ; but by those seas
  Which two years back made choral symphonies
To Love's great hymn of rapture and of praise ;
I stand and hear the clamor of old days, —
  The days of sun, and winds that made no peace
  At dusk, but through the night's wide radiances
Fought on, before the moon's affrighted face ;

And o'er the confluent thunder of the deep,
  The infuriated shrieking of the gale,
  I hear the sweetness of thy tones prevail.
Ah, how the blood thrills, and the pulses leap,
  When all Love's burning memories assail
This heart which only meets thee, now, in sleep !

A DREAM.

HERE, where last night she came, — even she for whom
   I would so gladly live, or lie down dead, —
   Came in the likeness of a Dream, and said
Such words as thrilled this desolate, ghost-thronged
     room,
I sit alone now, in the absolute gloom.
   Ah, surely on her breast was leaned my head !
   Ah, surely on my mouth her kiss was shed,
And all my life broke into scent and bloom.

Give thanks, heart, for thy rootless flower of bliss ;
   Nor think the gods severe, though thus they seem —
Though thou hast much to bear and much to miss —
   Whilst thou, through nights and days to be, canst deem
One thing, and that thing veritably this,
   Imperishable, — the memory of a Dream.

ALIEN HOURS.

THESE days that bring no word of hope to me,
   From her whose presence turns my dark life bright,
   Are guests with whom one may not live aright,
Because they enter not that sanctuary
Of intimate, perfect, dearest secrecy,
   As friends to whom one speaks without affright
   Of Love, and Love's immaculate delight,
Knowing their heart's unuttered sympathy.

These days — though fair enough, with Summer's soul
   Reflected in their eyes, and in their tone
   The deep sea's chime — are yet to me unknown.
Depart from me, — your goal is not my goal !
Come that dear day, to make my spirit whole,
   Which brings me word of her, my queen, my own !

THE HEAVEN OF HEAVENS.

Not to the general heaven take thy flight,
 O happy, happy, happy song of mine ;
 But to the heart of innermost heaven divine ;
O'er fields of day, to privacies of light,
Take thou thy way, and being come aright
 To that fair place which is my heaven and thine,
 Where my thoughts throng, as pilgrims to a shrine, —
Even to her heart, whose love is my soul's sight, —

Say unto her that other songs are free
 To sound about the world and win men praise ;
 Thy greater glory is this sovereign grace
To live alone in her sweet memory, —
 To have thy heavenly and abiding place
In her deep heart, Love's holiest sanctuary.

SOON TO MEET.

When a man sails to far-off, longed-for ways,
 With many days to pass 'twixt sea and sky,
 At first he heeds not time, and seeks thereby
To mock its power ; but after weary days,
When one cries, " Land in sight ! " he takes his place
 With others on the deck, and can descry
 The outlines of the land ; then feverishly
He counts the minutes till he win their grace.

So when my venturous life put forth alone —
 Yourself the lovely land it steered unto —
I dared not count the hours that now are flown,
 All but these last remaining, lessening few ;
And these, being few enough to count, have grown
 As painful ages till they bring me you.

LOVE'S LOST DAY.

WHEN thou and I are parted, presently,
   This dead day's ghost, with white, accusing face,
   Shall walk among our harsh, unpitying days,
Saying, " For tenderness Love fashioned me ;
And, lo ! ye did defame my deity,
   Reft me of sweetness, took away my grace,
   And set a horror in my fair self's place, —
That self no tears can make again to be."

But when, for one of us, vain days go by,
   The while the other sleeps beneath the flowers,
   Heedless of sunshine, or soft, April showers,
" Look ever in my eyes," this day shall cry,
" Wherein, as in deep streams, reflected lie
   Love's murdered, irrecoverable hours ! "

OTHER TWILIGHTS.

O LOVE, does she recall the far-off place, —
   The place we loved in, but two years ago,
   And through gray twilights heard the sea-winds blow,
And thunder of the sea that shines and slays?
I walk alone, now, by still, inland ways ;
   The time is Autumn, and the light is low,
   Through which a wind like that we used to know,
Comes, like the voices of those other days, —

Those other twilights, thronged with dreams and hopes,
   When all my way with flowers seemed fair to see,
Who now must go by harsh, unflowering slopes,
Through night with which no least light ever copes,
   Until some blessed day I come to be
   Where all my silent dead ones wait for me.

TWO PALACES.

Lo, now, how well, at last, all things come right !
　We thought a lordly pleasure-house to raise,
　But, shaken by the shock and change of days,
It fell ; and now we build upon its site
Another palace of more moderate height, —
　Not large, or lordly, but a pleasant place,
　With quiet paintings, and a waving grace
Of leaves for June, when suns are over-bright.

"How fair it is !　How better in all ways
　Than that we strove to build before !" we muse,
Both silently ; yet o'er some buried trace
　Of that first palace both to bend might choose,
Saying : "This last is worthy of most praise,
　Yet here was something that we loved, and lose."

TWO LIVES.

In a still twilight one sits very still, —
　There is no light of rapture in her eyes,
　But they are peaceful as the twilight skies.
Life's joy is past ; past also is Life's ill ;
Soon sleep with dreamless rest her heart shall fill.
　Through sunset wastes, where many a wild bird flies,
　Thrilling the lurid glow with short, sharp cries,
Wheeling above great waves made strong to kill,

Up a precipitous, unflowering way,
　Where salt sea-grasses shiver drearily,
　One labors on, toward the disastrous sea,
Moaning, "We were together in Life's day,
　But now the night is on us, where are we?"
And the waves, answering, thunder, "Where are they?"

HOPE.

I SAID, "Who art thou, with the flower-crowned hair
　　And shining eyes?"　She answered, "I am Hope,
　　Thy friend for life, with all thy foes to cope."
Sweet songs she sang me, of far lands and fair;
Her face made starlight in a starless air;
　　But once, as down a dark and flowerless slope
　　That heard the sea, we strove our way to grope,
A sudden terror came upon her there;

She fell, — the strength ebbed from her, and she died.
　　Above her, dead, in body and soul I bowed,
　　While with strange tongues the darkness was endowed;
And well I knew the thing they prophesied:
　　Then up the shore came the waves large and loud,
And my life answered, tide to bitter tide.

AT THE END.

IF now, indeed, O Love, the end be near,
　　And thou and I — who for so many days
　　Have struggled on, up steep and perilous ways,
Crying "Good cheer," when there was no good cheer —
Gain now this topmost summit, steep and sheer,
　　And see below that sad, abysmal place
　　Where all fair lost things are, whereof one says,
"They rise not ever, who lie buried here," —

If this be so, once more take hands and kiss;
　　Let our souls rush together as two flames
Of which the wind makes one flame.　By Love's bliss,
　　By all his saddest, most memorial names,
We swear that no love ever, after this,
　　Shall claim us, till ourselves Death, mightier, claims.

LOVE'S INFINITY.

WHEN to thine arms myself I do consign,
   And yield thee with my body all my soul,
   Why seems it that I give not yet the whole, —
That by some way thought hardly may divine
I might be more irrevocably thine, —
   More utterly subject to thy heart's control?
   Oh, far away, before I reached Love's goal,
Lie the dead days which were and were not mine,

Being days that saw not, heard not, felt not thee.
   Now, wailing, unconsolable ghosts of days,
They would anew their lives re-live in me,
   That so thou might'st have all in thine embrace :
Nay, were it thus, would Love's infinity
   Not yearn for gifts of still more lavish grace?

MY LOVE.

My Love is like great music when it fills
   Man's heart and brain with high, all-hail delight ;
   My Love is like some still, immaculate night,
When through the hushed and sleeping earth there
      thrills
God's very peace ; my Love is like the hills
   That welcome first the dawn upon each height, —
   For is she not as pure as they and bright,
With eyes like sunlight upon wind-kissed rills?

But ah, my song, that thou canst never say
   How fairer far she is than all these things, —
My governing moon by night, my sun by day,
   My nightingale, in whom the whole choir sings,
   My summer of women, in whose beauty clings
What men to pluck would give their souls away !

WHAT TWO SAW.

I HEARD thunder of drums, and the trumpet's blast ;
   And I saw red banners that waved on the air ;
   And I heard the shouts of those fighting there ;
I saw fires blaze, saw the tents o'ercast,
Saw cannon front cannon, deep, deadly, and vast ;
   Heard the conqueror's shout, the cries of despair
   Of falling and wounded, who died with the glare
Of flame on their features, distraught, and aghast.

You stood beside me, but what did you see ? —
   No field of battle, but one sown with corn,
Yellow corn, which in time man's bread should be ;
   You heard not the cry of the hope forlorn ;
You heard not the feet of the hosts that flee, —
   But my soul at your feet lay dead, down borne.

BESIDE THE DEAD.

SAD seems the room, and strangely still, where lies
   Some form now motionless, in which of late
   Glad life exulted.   Mark the changed estate,
The helpless hands, clasped in such peaceful wise,
The speechless lips, and unbeholding eyes
   Which might not look into the eyes of Fate ;
   And as about the bed you watching wait,
What pleading pity to your spirit cries !

But, surely, yet a sadder thing is this
   To look upon Love's face, where Love lies dead,
While all his memories of pain and bliss,
   Thorn-crowned and rose-crowned, watch beside the
      bed.
    Sped souls may live again, no man can tell ;
    But dead Love shall not break Death's awful spell.

SPRING SADNESS.

O SPRING, and art thou here again, as one
  Who, bearing erst the tidings of high things,
  And echoes of that song that no man sings,
Com'st now, with all thy promises foredone?
Thy clear, fresh wind, thy clouds surprised by sun,
  Swallows that wheel and dart in mazy rings,
  Thy charitable wall-flower scent that clings,
And noise of streamlets carolling as they run, —

Are these not sweet as in the far-off days,
  When the heart answered some mysterious call,
And eyes discerned the fair, indefinite face,
  Of future things to be memorial?
Aye, sweet; and yet, alas for one who says:
  "Ghosts of the vanished Springs! and is this all?"

IN EARLY SPRING.

WITH delicate wind, clear light of the warm sun,
  Surely I know the subtle charm of Spring,
  The earth and man's worn heart revisiting.
I would not have thy brief existence done,
And yet I would, O new-born Spring, that one
  Might meet thine eyes without their mirroring
  The ghost of many a sweet and bitter thing, —
Old dreams, old hopes, too frail to lean upon.

O last descended of a hostile race,
  Though in thyself so gently, softly fair,
Within thine eyes ancestral Springs I trace!
Thus some wronged woman, in her baby's face
  May shuddering see its father's likeness there,
  While parted raptures thrill through her despair.

MAN AND SPRING.

WHEN love upon the man's side falls away,
    And delicate finger-tips and the slow kiss
    Which kindled once such wild, delirious bliss
As no words seemed intense enough to say,
And dear, low voice, and eyes that seemed to pray
    For Love's reply, — when, at the last, of this
    Only the unavailing memory is, —
" Once it was sweet ; once, on a far-off day — "

Is there in life, indeed, a sadder thing? —
    I answer, there is one thing even more sad, —
To greet with loveless heart and eyes the Spring,
    In which of old such pure high joy we had ;
To grieve anew, when all her glad birds sing,
    Remembering that we too — we once were glad.

VOID SPRING.

THIS placid day, here at the Winter's end,
    This day of temperate sunshine and mild air,
    Filled with high promise of glad things and fair,
Is unto me like some dear, chosen friend, —
Loved well by twain whose two lives might not blend
    Because Death called the worshipped woman where
    Is no delight in love or love's sweet care,
Where neither prayers nor songs nor sighs ascend.

If any comfort to the lover's heart
    Yields the dear friend who holds so much of her
At whose light footfall he no more shall start,
Such comfort to my soul these hours impart ;
    I greet of Spring the Spring-like harbinger,
    Knowing with me Spring's self may not confer.

YOUTH AND NATURE.

Is this the sky, and this the very earth
   I had such pleasure in when I was young?
   And can this be the identical sea-song,
Heard once within the storm-cloud's awful girth,
When a great storm from silence burst to birth ;
   And winds to whom it seemed I did belong
   Made the keen blood in me run swift and strong
With irresistible, tempestuous mirth?

Are these the forests, loved of old so well,
   Where on May nights enchanted music was?
   Are these the fields of soft, delicious grass ;
These the old hills with secret things to tell?
O my dead youth, was this inevitable,
   That with thy passing, Nature, too, should pass?

A JUNE DAY.

THE month is June, but all the sky is gray,
   And to the weary earth seems leaning low ;
   There is no little breath of wind to blow
The searching perfume of these flowers away
That climbing round my window peer and stay ;
   The thrush sings, where the branches thickly grow ;
   The day moves by, with heavy feet and slow ;
" Death endeth all," the stillness seems to say.

But Love shall come before Death's nuptial hour ;
   There sits my queen, and silent — pondering what?
Sees she, as I, Love's joy-environed bower,
   Where sweet, conspiring things one sweeter plot ;
Or does she hear, 'neath some grave's guardian flower,
   Sad sighing of dead loves remembered not?

A JULY DAY.

To-day the sun has steadfast been and clear;
   No wind has marred the spell of hushful heat,
   But with the twilight comes a rush and beat
Of ghost-like wings; the sky turns gray and drear,
The trees are stricken with a sudden fear.
   O wind forlorn, that sayest nothing sweet,
   With what foreboding message dost thou greet
The dearest month but one of all the year?

Ah, now it seems I catch the moan of seas
   Whose boundaries are pale regions of dismay,
Where sad-eyed people wander without ease;
   I see in thought that lamentable array,
   And surely hear about the dying day
Recorded dooms and mournful prophecies.

MOMENTS OF VISION.

I.

One came to me, and led me by the hand,
   And took me from the city far away;
   Bright was the sun, and loud with wind the day,
And on we wended till we took our stand
Where mighty waters broke against the land.
   Bright in the sunlight shone the shivering spray,
   While, loud as monsters roaring after prey,
Roared the strong waters laboring up the strand:

And through their roar an inner note I caught
   Of passionate remembrance; and mine eyes
Beheld a light long lost and vainly sought.
   My heart was stormed by a divine surprise;
For, lo! this was the sea, — even she who wrought
   For the dead boy miraculous ecstasies.

II.

So once in Summer walking 'mid the hills,
   What time the twilight clothes them with her peace,
   And birds fly home to rest in deep-leaved trees
Through which a last, low song one moment thrills,
Then ceases ; and the unobtrusive rills
   Babble along their ways, and small winds cease,
   And in their soft, blue spaces stars increase
Before the moon of Heaven her light fulfils, —

Through that deep peace, long seen though unfelt long,
   As from a land divine and most remote
Wherein alone do pale-mouthed dreams make song,
   The ancient peace of boyhood seemed to float ;
     O heart of Heaven ! deep rest and undefiled
     Needs the man less than the untroubled child ?

III.

THEN spoke a low, clear voice to me and said :
   " What knew the boy of the hot strife for fame,
   Or love that often slighted turns to shame ?
Ambition's curse you drew upon your head,
And with strange food unnatural hungers stayed ;
   Then ghosts, with tongues against you to declaim,
   With cruel, deriding lips, and eyes of flame,
Filled all your sleep with sorrow and sick dread.

" Good gifts I, Nature, gave you, — storm and rest,
   Sundawn and sunset, and the shade profound.
   'Good gifts !' you laugh, 'but man must be renowned,
So I will forth, nor weary in the quest
   Till mighty gods my ambitious brows have crowned.'
Lo, the lost child !   Lo, the forsaken breast ! "

PARABLES.

I.

I BUILT a house for quiet and dim peace, —
   A place whereto when weary I might go,
   To sit alone and let the pent tears flow,
And feel a little while their bitter ease.
I built my house, I ringed it round with trees,
   And often, when the sun and winds were low,
   I sat and mused there, while there seemed to grow
A rest begotten of dear memories.

But strange, unholy shapes with snake-wreathed brows
   Did throng my refuge and defile my grove, —
   So now no more about that house I move.
Still it looks peaceful through its shadowy boughs;
   But voices from within the calm disprove:
What say you, then — shall I not burn my house?

II.

A MAGIC circle holds me round, to-day, —
   The air is vital with the young, sweet Spring;
   In the fresh wind the leaves and grasses sing;
The songs of birds are blown from spray to spray;
The time is pure, and ardent, and how gay!
   Now falls the saintly dusk; low whispering
   The gentle wind goes by with flagging wing,
The sun to follow, on his downward way.

Great quietude of moonlight holds the land;
   Now if one word I whisper to the air,
If one way turn, or even reach my hand,
   The spell is broken, and my Spring to scare
Comes Winter back, and shivering I stand,
   Once more the old blast of his old winds to bear.

III.

I WALKED in Summer through green, pleasant ways,
   And heard a soft wind singing as I went,
   And casual songs of birds ; sweet was the scent
Of wild things prospering in a sheltered place ;
But suddenly chill rain-drops smote my face,
   And, like the sad, melodious discontent
   That wakens in the wind-played instrument,
The low wind sighed, recalling other days.

I passed into a churchyard filled with dead ;
   And all the graves, it seemed, had separate tongues,
For over each a bird poised, wings outspread,
   And sang sad things of those deaf, eyeless throngs :
"What may this mean?" I cried, and one there said,
   "These be thy griefs of old, and these thy songs."

IV.

THOU sayest, "The skies are dark above my head,
   Destroying waves break loud upon my strand,
   Wild winds and ruining blight infest my land :
'T is Summer still, but Summer flowers lie shed
On wind-scourged paths ; my song-birds all are dead :
   Only the oldest trees may hope to stand
   Against this mad wind's devastating hand,
There will I house me till its wrath be sped."

Thou fool ! Thou shalt awake some day to see
   Thine oldest trees crash round thee, every one ;
   To meet no darkness, but the insatiate sun,
    A beast with eyes of flame, and thee for prey ;
   And slight, indeed, on that disastrous day,
Will seem this dead day's harsh calamity.

V.

SHE sits at home in lordly palaces,
　With glowing eyes, and flowing, vine-wreathed hair,
　And dainty, white-rose body left half bare ;
And they who find life glad and full of ease
Make love to her, and sweet she is to these ;
　And they who know the blackness of despair
　Turn to her, seeing she is surely fair,
And from their pain she gives them swift release.

The same she is who walks the populous street,
　A painted, brazen harlot without shame ;
But all her lovers, poor and rich, shall meet
　There where she leads them, — where in lurid flame
Those gone before her fiery kiss entreat,
　Gnash teeth, and dying execrate her name.

THREE SONNETS ON SORROW.

I.

A CHILD, with mystic eyes and flowing hair,
　I saw her first, 'mid flowers that shared her grace ;
　Though but a boy, I cried, " How fair a face ! "
And, coming nearer, told her she was fair.
She faintly smiled, yet did not say " Forbear ! "
　But seemed to take a pleasure in my praise.
　She led my steps through many a leafy place,
And pointed where shy birds and sweet flowers were.

At length we stood upon a brooklet's brink, —
　I seem to hear its sources babbling yet, —
She gave me water from her hand to drink,
　The while her eyes upon its flow were set.
　"Thy name?" I asked ; she whispered low, "Regret,"
Then faded, as the sun began to sink.

II.

WE met again, as I foresaw we should;
 Youth flooded all my veins, and she had grown
 To woman's height, yet seemed a rose half-blown.
Like sunset clouds that o'er a landscape brood
Her eyes were, that they might not be withstood;
 And like the wind's voice when it takes the tone
 Of pine-trees was her voice. I cried, " My own ! " —
And kneeling there I worshipped her and wooed.

O bitter marriage, though inevitable, —
 Ordained by Fate, who wrecks or saves our days !
 Lo, the changed bride, no longer fair of face,
And in her eyes the very fires of hell !
" Thy name ? " I cried ; and these words hissing fell :
 " Anguish and madness come of my embrace."

III.

WHAT thing may be to come I cannot know.
 Her eyes have less of Hell in them, meanwhile ;
 At times she almost smiles a ghastly smile,
I have in all things done her bidding so.
Chill are the rooms wherein no bright fires glow,
 Where no fair picture doth the eye beguile ;
 Once awful laughter shook the gloomy pile ;
Unholy, riotous shapes went to and fro.

There is no sound, now, in the house at all,
 Only outside the wind moans on, alway :
 My Lady Sorrow hath no word to say,
Seems half content ; for well she knows her thrall
Shall not escape from her ; that should God call
 She would rise with him at the Judgment Day.

IN PRAISE OF SLEEP.

I.

THERE is a Land where nightly I repair,
　　At whose dim gate I put my cross aside,
　　Stretch out my arms toward Rest as toward a bride,
And am withal assuaged.　Ah, even there,
Beyond false hope, beyond the stress of prayer,
　　Beyond the hurt and smart of broken pride,
　　With no more hunger for sweet things denied,
My heart has rest and respite from despair.

O land of mystic shapes and languid pleasure,
　　Waste field of poppies without track it seems !
　　O scentless lilies, by the voiceless streams
Where come my ghosts and dance a silent measure,
　　Hold my last joy, now ! — only in dear dreams
Give back to me, sometimes, my buried treasure !

II.

I HAVE no heart in me for Love's delight :
　　How sweet the Summer was !' How strong its spell !
　　I care not, now, what stars may have to tell ;
To me the day is void, and void the night.
Upon her dim and inaccessible height
　　Fame stands above me, robed and crowned. Ah, well !
　　Let those who love her find her pleasurable ;
She hath no grace or merit in my sight.

I am in love alone with tender Sleep, —
　　Dew on my sad, unfruitful flower of life
Of which no man the memory may keep.
　　O most divine forgetfulness of strife,
My sky is not too dark, my path too steep,
　　While Thou art mine, for Friend, for Love, for Wife !

MY LIFE

To me my life seems as a haunted house,
 The ways and passages whereof are dumb ;
 Up whose decaying stair no footsteps come ;
Lo, this the hall hung with sere laurel boughs,
Where long years back came victors to carouse.
 But none of all that company went home ;
 For scarce their lips had quaffed the bright wine's foam,
When sudden Death brake dank upon their brows.

Here in this lonely, ruined house I dwell,
While unseen fingers toll the chapel bell ;
 Sometimes the arras rustles, and I see
 A half-veiled figure through the twilight steal,
Which, when I follow, pauses suddenly
 Before the door whereon is set a seal.

HAUNTED ROOMS.

Must this not be, whate'er the years disclose,
 When I and those in whom my heart has vent,
 From whose dear lives soul-light to mine is sent,
Lie at the last 'neath where the long grass grows,
Made one, in one interminable repose,
 Not knowing whence we came or whither went, —
 Done with regret, with black presentiment
Of greater griefs, or more victorious foes, —

Must this not be that one then dwelling here,
 Where one man and his sorrows dwelt so long,
 Shall feel the pressure of a ghostly throng,
And shall upon some desolate midnight hear
 A sound more sad than is the pine-trees' song,
And thrill with great, inexplicable fear?

WORTH REMEMBRANCE.

OF me ye may say many a bitter thing,
   O Men, when I am gone, — gone far away
   To that dim Land where shines no light of day.
Sharp was the bread for my soul's nourishing
Which Fate allowed, and bitter was the spring
   Of which I drank and maddened ; even as they
   Who wild with thirst at sea will not delay,
But drink the brine and die of its sharp sting.

Not gentle was my war with Chance, and yet
   I borrowed no man's sword, — alone I drew
   And gave my slain fit burial out of view.
In secret places I and Sorrow met :
So, when you count my sins, do not forget
   To say I taxed not any one of you.

A LIFE.

HE walked 'midst shadows, and he nursed at heart
   A grief that set strange poison in his blood ;
   He lived, and was of no man understood.
In all glad things that be he had no part ;
And wearily he turned unto his art,
   But of his labor had he little good.
   Comfort he sought in cheerless solitude ;
But visionary faces made him start.

Wrong things he did, was quick of thought and speech,
   For grievous sin had grievous punishment ;
Missed Love, missed Fame, both once within his reach,
   Nor might succeed in any high intent ;
   And when he died had on his monument :
"All that Life taught him, Lord, let Death unteach."

ANTICIPATED DEATH.

Let none be sad for this man when he lies
   Alone and out of torment, — past the sting
   Of all his various agonies, — but bring
The brightest flowers to lay upon his eyes.
With no high, glad, triumphant chants surprise
   His perfect quietness; bend low and sing
   Some wistful song, soft as winds whispering
Through leafy branches under twilight skies.

And if when death was on him he had yearned
   Once more to try his desperate chance, and so
     Had died with life and death unreconciled, —
     Think of him only as a wayward child,
   Who craves ill things because he does not know;
The rest which shall be his he will have earned.

PRISONED THOUGHTS.

O soul of Song, hast thou forsaken me?
   Thoughts journey through my spirit night and day,
   And throng the gateways of my soul, and pray
That thou, who holdest in thy hand the key,
Would'st let them forth, that they may wander free.
   Listen, O distant soul, to what they say:
   "We wander up and down, yet find no way
To lead us forth from our captivity.

"Lo! we have messages for those outside,
   And all day long we beat against the gate."
   Come then, O Song, my thoughts to liberate;
Make thou, in turn, each one thy fruitful bride, —
   Through life else must they daily watch and wait,
And in dark places of my soul abide.

IRREVOCABLE.

BECAUSE it did not yield me shade enough,
   Because the time seemed long till fruit should be,
   I smote at root my flowering apple-tree:
It was the fairest tree in my scant grove,
And fell with little sound. I watched above
   And viewed it where it lay, content to see
   My fearful handiwork, and angrily
I shook its boughs, and plucked the leaves thereof, —

Poor leaves that never a deep shadow made,
   Yet were so fair ! I dropped them, one by one ;
   And then I wept, for what I cannot say, —
   Unless my heart conjectured of some day
When I should stand alone, and no such shade
   Should interpose between me and the sun.

MY LAND.

I WALK 'neath sunless skies ; by flowerless ways
   With failing feet and heavy heart I go, —
   Through leafless trees vague winds of twilight blow.
A strange, still land this is : ghosts of old days
Rise up to meet me ; a beloved, dead face
   Emerges on my path ; or sweet and low
   The accents of some voice I used to know
Fall on my heart, where only sorrow stays.

My ghostly Land, wherethro', myself a ghost,
   I journey ever toward that stranger strand
By which no ships from this world ever coast, —
   Ah, there shall I remember, still, my Land?
   Nay, God, — if any God indeed there be, —
   Grant me, in Death, release from Memory.

THE TEMPTRESS.

I.

Unto the awful Temptress at my side,
 From whose embrace comes madness at the end,
 I said, "I will not yield, but will defend
My weary soul till body and soul divide."
"Art thou so much in love with grief?" she cried,
 "That thou wilt have no other love or friend?"
 I answered her, "In guile thou dost transcend
All other foes who have my strength defied."

"Once thou didst tarry in my halls," quoth she,
 "And to fair chambers were thy footsteps led."
 "Blood-red and hot thy kisses were," I said,
"Thralled was I, then, who now, at least, am free;
 But if again those floors my feet should tread,
Then thou and Hell should have me utterly."

II.

Because she stands so fatally close to me;
 Because I breathe in anguish with each breath,
 Who may not face the awful eyes of Death,
Nor 'scape the pitiless eyes of Memory;
Because my soul is deaf, nor may it see;
 Because within my ear the Temptress saith:
 "Am I not fair, crowned with my fragrant wreath?
Have I not pleasant gifts to give to thee?"

Because I know the sweet mouth only lies,
 Yet surely know that she is very fair, —
I venture not to look into her eyes,
 As in a lighter mood I might have done,
 Nor touch her hand, nor idle with her hair,
 Seeing of this could come no end but one.

III.

" Look at me once again," she pleaded yet ;
  " Come thou with me, and be no more alone ;
  Why should thy heart perpetually make moan?"
She took my hand.   Then, being so beset,
I spoke no word, but turned, and our eyes met.
  My blood leaped in me, as a flame wind-blown.
  " Call me again," she said, " thy very own,
And teach thy heart its sorrow to forget."

I gazed, and gazing saw that she was fair,
  And full of grace ; but while I looked, behold
Her beauty like a robe fell from her there,
  And left her standing, wrinkled, lean, and old :
  " Go hence," I cried, " base mother of sins untold,
And leave my soul its undefiled despair."

WARFARE WITH THE GODS.

This man was full of strength once, hope, and fire ;
  And when the gods derided him, he said :
  " O Gods, your curse lies heavy on my head ;
Against my peace I know that you conspire ;
But, lo ! I can defy you.   Will ye tire
  Yourselves with warfare?   Shall my soul fall dead
  Because scant blessings on her path are shed?
Some things are left still, dear to my desire ;

" And these shall give me courage in despite."
  " Thou fool ! " the gods laughed, and with wrong on
      wrong,
  As seas come wave on wave when winds are strong,
They came against him, and laid waste his might,
Till, utterly humbled, prostrate in their sight,
  He fell, and moaned, " My Masters, oh, how long? "

LIFE.

PRISONED I was within a noble hall,
　Ringed round with many gracious images,
　And through it floated strains that might appease
The soul's sore thirst for music.　On each wall
Fair pictures hung to hold the eye in thrall, —
　High mountains clothed in cold, immaculate peace,
　A light of water between wavering trees,
Wild seas wherefrom drowned mariners seemed to call.

A table stood there, heaped with fruits and wine,
　But, lo, the fruits turned ashes at my gaze,
And to my taste the gold juice seemed like brine :
　Here must one die, then, with no chance for strife,
　Loathing the impotent beauty of the place ? —
　Then these words shivered past me, "This is
　　Life !"

A WISH.

I DO but ask a little time of peace
　Before the end of all.　I crave no bliss ;
　I crave no love, nor fame ; but only this, —
On summer days to bask beneath old trees,
Or half asleep to lie by gentle seas,
　Hearing the waves that whisper ere they kiss,
　Then break and babble ; or, when twilight is,
And one by one the birds from singing cease,

Wander the patient, tranquil hills among,
　And languish in an exquisite regret,
And hear a sad but not discordant song
　Possess the air ; and when the sun is set,
Lie down with thankfulness to know, ere long,
　All things that ever were I shall forget.

A QUESTION.

IF I had been in love with Life, had Death
　　Seemed any ghastlier, more full of dread,
　　Or I shrank more from thought of being dead,
Sightless and still, and in my lips no breath,
Night all about me, and the dust beneath?
　　Not so, I think, for then I should have said:
　　" I have been glad, though now I make my bed
Where dead folk lie, and never a word one saith."

Harder seems this, — to die and leave the sun,
　　And carry hence each unfulfilled desire.
　　　　I heard one cry, "Come where the feast is
　　　　　　spread;"
But when I came the festival was done;
　　Somewhile I shivered by the extinguished fire,
　　　　And now retrace my steps uncomforted.

MAN'S DAYS.

FROM sorrow unto sorrow man progresses,
　　If length of days be his; till, come at last,
　　Nigh to that realm unknowable and vast,
Which hides the whole world's dead in its recesses,
Where iron night on every sleeper presses,
　　In its strange neighborhood he moves aghast;
　　Remembering intermittently his past,
Lulled sometimes by a gentle ghost's caresses.

He moves down ways and by-ways listlessly, —
　　A traveller who, having paid his score,
　　Knowing therewith he hath to do no more,
Waits till the ship already in sight be free
　　To bear him back to his far, natal shore,
Back though the darkness and the awful sea.

VAIN FREEDOM.

I SAT between two shapes with eyes of fire :
   All there was dark except those eyes of flame ;
   Each shape spake severally its dreadful name ;
Through them was life made barren of desire.
I heard a sound as of a stricken lyre,
   And lust of power and song upon me came ;
   But they cried out, " For thee shall be no fame ;
Kneel down, now, and cast dust on thine attire."

Silent I knelt, in my most abject woe,
   Till from my lips there brake a passionate prayer.
Then Love's voice called me, and I strove to go.
   They freed me, with wild laughter on the air ;
I struggled forward to the light, and, lo !
   Not Love it was, but Death who met me there.

EVEN FOR THEE.

THY feet are weary, and thy strength is low ;
   Life's brightness is behind thee, and thy face
   Is set against the darkness.   For a space
Sad winds about thy path shall moaning blow,
And ghosts on either hand with thee shall go.
   Great dread shall be upon thee, in those days, --
   Dread of the darkness and the uncertain ways,
Such dread as man again may never know.

But even for thee shall come at last the end,
   And Death thy soul with slumber shall assuage.
No painful thought of altered or dead friend
   Shall hurt thy heart again, nor impotent rage
At Fate's blind mysteries thy soul shall rend ;
   But rest shall be thy well-earned heritage.

THE PRISONER.

GLOOM girdeth gloom, and in the central gloom,
    Yea, in the inmost sanctuary of despair,
    Lies one who knows the impotence of prayer,
Waiting, perchance, yet more disastrous doom.
Outside his night fair women and sweet flowers bloom,
    And doubtless laughter and glad song are there ;
    No music ever trembles on this air,
But phantoms wail, dread ghosts that burst their tomb.

He broods in solitude, remembering
    He once was free about God's world to go ;
He once kept holiday with Love and Spring ;
    He once felt Summer in his glad veins glow :
But now, but now, what hope of anything
    Save this, — to cease, to pass, and *not* to know !

THE LONG WAY.

STILL the old paths and the old solitude,
    And still the dark soul journeying on its way,
    A little nearer to its goal each day.
About it does an awful silence brood,
Nor may it know what dread vicissitude
    Shall overwhelm it, ere of it men say :
    " It is not ; and the place of its dismay
Shall know it never more, and this is good."

" But, ah, poor Soul, how long ? " I questioning cry.
    " Already thou hast journeyed very long,
By barren ways, beneath a dumb, dark sky.
    Once light was with thee, yea, and birds made song,
    And voices cheered thee ; but of all that throng
What voice to thy voice shall to-day reply ? "

BURIED SELF.

WHERE side by side we sat, I sit alone,
　But surely hear the absent voice, — as one
　Who, playing, when the tune he plays is done,
Hears the spent music through the strings yet moan.
I rove, through places that my soul has known,
　Like the sad ghost of some departed nun
　Who comes between the moonrise and the sun,
To sit beside her monumental stone.

So by my buried self I take my seat,
　And talk with other ghosts of vanished days,
And watch gray shadows through the twilight fleet,
　And half expect to see the buried face
　Of my dead self rise in the silent place,
To look at me with mournful eyes and sweet.

MY GHOSTS.

WHEN dark days come, and winds are charged with sleet,
　And strong men shiver with cold as if with fear,
　Then will I ponder by my bright fire here
On things gone by, — half drowsing seem to meet
Fair, gracious comers, who the silence cheat;
　And, as the twilight gathers, seem to hear
　About the room, and near me and more near,
Soft stir of robes and fall of phantom feet.

But now, to-day, to-day, when it is Spring,
　And larks are almost mad with their delight,
Shall I not go where I can hear them sing,
　And send my spirit following on their flight? —
Though still within mine ear old tones shall ring,
　And from Spring woods ghosts steal upon my sight.

21

DREAM–MOONLIGHT.

DREAM-MOONLIGHT, which for me sometimes makes
    bright
  And fair and wonderful the vales of sleep,
  Where spirits come in dreams to laugh or weep,
Is, more than that which floods the actual night,
A secret, subtle message to the sight.
    Sometimes it shines upon a pale dream-deep,
    Or on untrodden fields no reapers reap,
Or some unscaled and inaccessible height ; —

Sometimes it falls 'twixt branches of dream-trees,
  Where the soft light and shade divinely blend.
O fair dream-moonlight, which dost give surcease
  To this sore heart from memories that rend,
If death were but to languish in thy peace
  How could one stay and battle to the end ?

BIDDEN.

ONE man at Life's feast sat an honored guest, —
  Fame on his left hand, Love upon his right,
  And Fame and Love were goodly in his sight ;
But while those feasting there waxed merriest,
Sudden his smile flagged far behind the jest.
  Then in his eyes altered and failed the light ;
  For one stood there, vast, garmented in night,
Against whose presence men in vain protest.

Another had gall for wine, and stones for bread ;
  By Fortune buffeted and overthrown,
  Knew neither Fame nor Love, but dwelt alone.
To him, " Come hence with me, O Son," Death said :
Now which seems worse, since all must bow the head ;
  To know and leave, or never to have known?

LIFE'S UNCERTAINTY.

MAN draws his fleeting breath in utmost dread,
　　Not knowing from what ambush ill may start
　　To plunge another dagger in his heart.
He scarcely knows his living from his dead ;
The skies are dark with gloom above his head ;
　　He hears night-birds upon their meek prey dart, —
　　O Night, of whom he is a very part,
How long is he his dubious path to tread ?

Sometimes he hears, and this appals him most,
　　Ring through the night a chiming wedding-bell.
It is the signal summoning to its post
　　A new despair to lead his steps to hell, —
So 'twixt wild seas and some implacable coast
　　Men, sailing, know their doom inevitable.

VAIN WAITING.

ONE waits and watches all his days away
　　For what may never come.　So looks alone
　　Some man, upon a desert island thrown,
For sails that pass not ; till, too faint to pray,
He folds his hands, and waits the eventful day
　　When Death, unintercepted, claims his own,
　　Bids hope lie down by fear, stills the long moan,
And folds the weary feet, no more to stray.

None knew of his sad life and death, till, lo,
　　Men voyaging from afar, by fierce winds driven,
　　Cast anchor on that isle, where tempest-riven
They see a log-propped hut, by which they know
　　That one has lived and died there, hoped and striven ;
They shed their unavailing tears and go.

FATAL DELAY.

THERE sat with Love who feasted and were glad, —
    Strong men whose lids through love wax warm and wet,
    And amorous women whose soft looks beget
Most poignant passion. There, not richly clad,
Sat one, remote, and on his robes he had
    Dust of long journeyings ; his fingers met
    About Love's goblet, but he sighed, " Not yet,"
Though often through great thirst he was nigh mad.

He held the goblet up against the light,
    And saw the sparkling wine therein was good ;
But sudden darkness settled on his sight ;
    The guests were gone ; he sat in solitude ;
The goblet clanging fell, with all its might,
    And now he moistens his charred lips with blood.

DEAD LOVE.

AND will you now cry out upon dead Love,
    Inform the lifeless clay with new, warm breath?
    I tell you that Love sleeps the sleep of death.
Cry out, wring hands, and weep ! You will not move
Those lips to any speech : yea, though you clove
    With yours to his, enfolded him with faith,
    He would not stir your word or kiss beneath ;
His soul now dwells from pain and joy aloof.

What time Love lay a-dying you stood near,
    With lips shut tight, and cold, confronting eyes ;
Love's voice had then no music for your ear,
    You had no pity, though one cried, " Love dies ! "
And now, behold, as to another sphere
    You call on Love, and lo ! no voice replies.

LATE LOVE.

WITH two who might have loved each other well
   Had they met earlier who meet too late,
   How does it fare?   Do they keep separate,
Each one with feelings incommunicable;
Or are they as dear friends content to dwell
   In heart together till they change this state?
   Or may their sad and unaccomplished fate,
Instead of joining, wound them and repel?

So when, unjust, a father wills away
   His land and fortune from his rightful heirs,
They, wronged, incensed, come after set of day,
   And thief-like gain the house, and scale the stairs,
   And slay the invader, spite his threats and prayers;
Yet there for fear of judgment may not stay.

LOVE AND DESPAIR.

ONE came to me with sad, sweet eyes, and said,
   A mighty sorrow trembling in his voice,
   "Weep now, poor heart, for all thy dreams and joys,
For, lo, thy very hope of them lies dead."
And as he spake, withal, he bowed his head,
   And for a little while there was a noise
   As of one weeping, when fell Chance destroys
The life whereby his following life was led.

And he who spake to me for Love I knew,
   Though cypress leaves were bound about his hair:
Then close to us another form there drew, —
   Stern was his aspect, surely; nowise fair;
Yet round me a strange, awful rest there grew.
   "Thy name?" I cried; and he replied, "Despair!"

LEAST LOVE.

THIS small least love of mine, which can but creep
　　Between the twisted stems of joy and pain,
　　Is warmed by sun and bathed by every rain.
Last night, transplanted to the fields of sleep,
It blossomed so I could not choose but weep,
　　Knowing the sweet, familiar scent again.
　　Mostly it grows unnoticed, fair, and fain
In depths of sunlit air its leaves to steep ;

But there are times when every fairer flower
　　Looks cold, unsympathetic, in my sight ;
Then am I glad to turn, in such an hour,
　　To this my blossom, neither red nor white,
Holding the fragrance of the last warm shower :
　　But gather it, it fades before the night.

BITTER-SWEET.

WITH roses, lilies, and the eglantine,
　　Love filled our hands ; and from the grapes that hung
　　Above his garden, quick with scent and song,
He pressed a sweet and sleep-begetting wine ;
And melody intense, remote, divine,
　　For our delight from his own harp he wrung :
　　And when sense failed, so many sweets among,
And very passion threatened to decline,

He plucked for us the sharp and bitter brier,
　　Wherewith our aching brows he garlanded,
And made a sudden discord with his lyre.
　　Then with new color lips and cheeks grew red,
And pain was straight converted to desire ;
　　" For thus my bitter turns to sweet," Love said.

BRIDAL EVE.

HALF-ROBED, with gold hair drooped o'er shoulders white,
　　She sits as one entranced, with eyes that gaze
　　Upon the mirrored beauties of her face ;
And through the distances of dark and light
She hears faint music of the coming night ;
　　She hears the murmur of receding days ;
　　Her future life is veiled in such a haze
As hides, on sultry morns, the sun from sight.

Upon the brink of imminent change she stands,
　　Glad, yet afraid to look beyond the verge ;
She starts, as at the touch of unseen hands ;
　　Love's music grows half anthem and half dirge.
　　　　Strange sounds and shadows round her spirit fall,
　　　　Yet to herself she stranger seems than all.

THE SOUL'S PREGNANCY.

IF all be irrecoverably lost,
　　Why linger here to watch the dull days out,
　　To greet the meaningless spring, or hear the shout
Of winds and waves upon some stormy coast,
To wither in the winter's deadly frost,
　　To think on Death, to speculate, to doubt,
　　To move in funeral train, or festive rout,
'Mid living presences a very ghost?

'T is that the pain-wed soul is conscious of
　　Some in-wombed child of spiritual good
　　　　The heart, before the end, would recognize,—
　　So some young widow, feeding with her blood
Her own and her dead husband's fruit of love,
　　　　But lives that she may see her baby's eyes.

ATHEIST TO PANTHEIST.

No future, separate life, — such is your creed, —
    But general life of which you grow a part ;
    A heart-beat of the universal heart ;
A rose, perchance, or poor, unnoticed weed ;
A fraction of the brilliance and the speed
    Of starlit, gusty nights, when meteors dart
    Down all the brightening wind ; a pulse of Art ;
A portion of man's speech, and actual deed :

And thus, absorbed in all-pervading God,
    You think to live, conscious, yet knowing nought
    Of all the past with pain and joyance fraught, —
An atom, where the atoms onward plod.
        What you call God, I Nature name, and hence
        Am Atheist ; but where the difference ?

TO PAUL HAMILTON HAYNE.

NOT in this life shall we meet, O my friend, —
    My friend unseen, but not unknown of me, —
    My friend so far away beyond the sea,
To whose sequestered home my thoughts oft tend.
Nor dare I trust that some new life shall blend
    Our lives together ; yet strange things may be,
    And sweet for thinking is the phantasy
That some new life this failure might amend ;

And I might hear a voice, unheard till then,
    And clasp a hand, till then unclasped of mine.
    At once should I not know them to be thine, —
Poet, and man " who loves his fellow-men,"
    Whose thoughts are pure and limpid as star-shine,
    And greet thee by thy name, that happy when ?

NO DEATH.

I saw in dreams a mighty multitude, —
   Gathered, they seemed, from North, South, East, and
     West,
   And in their looks such horror was exprest
As must forever words of mine elude.
As if transfixed by grief, some silent stood,
   While others wildly smote upon the breast,
   And cried out fearfully, " No rest, no rest ! "
Some fled, as if by shapes unseen pursued.

Some laughed insanely. Others shrieking, said :
   " To think but yesterday we might have died ;
For then God had not thundered, ' Death is dead ! ' "
They gashed themselves till they with blood were red.
   " Answer, O God ; take back this curse ! " they cried,
But " Death is dead," was all the voice replied.

WITHOUT PASSION.

Yes, I am changed. When passion warmed my blood,
   What time your kisses thrilled me through and
     through,
   There was no thing I would not dare or do
Because your manhood stormed my womanhood.
You were my lord, and all you did was good ;
   Through you, it seemed, my very breath I drew ;
   My sun-god, in whose bountiful light I grew.
Now that no more my being with joy you flood ;

Because the altered blood flows tranquilly,
   For the first time I see you with clear sight, —
Changed, now, indeed from Passion's deity, —
   Selfish of heart, ambitious, prone to spite,
   Mostly at fault, occasionally right,
Your soul's one claim, your steadfast love of me.

LOST SOULS.

Ah, fair, lost Love, I thought once to make mine,
  Till you chose God, and turned your face away !
  Not cruelly, but firmly did you say :
" I must be God's, none other's, — at no shrine
But His bow knee ; God only is divine."
  And so you left me, and behold, to-day,
  While fair among the rest you chant and pray
Where fumes the incense and the tapers shine,

I, who with you had walked unblamed as most,
  I, whom you cast off in your heavenly zeal,
    See my own face, grown old before its time,
    Scarred deep by grief and many an unguessed
        crime, —
My own lost soul, and those my soul has lost
  At the last day against you shall appeal.

AT THE LAST.

Because the shadows deepened verily ;
  Because the end of all seemed near, forsooth, —
  Her gracious spirit, ever quick to ruth,
Had pity on her bond-slave, even on me.
She came in with the twilight noiselessly,
  Fair as a rose, immaculate as Truth ;
  She leaned above my wrecked and wasted youth,
I felt her presence, which I could not see.

" God keep you, my poor friend," I heard her say ;
  And then she kissed my dry, hot lips and eyes.
Kiss *thou* the next kiss, quiet Death, I pray ;
  Be instant on this hour, and so surprise
My spirit while the vision seems to stay ;
  Take thou the heart with the heart's Paradise.

JONATHAN SWIFT; HIS LAST ILLNESS.

THOU sawest from far the curse thou might'st not stay,
  Most mighty spirit, strong to love and hate.
  For what great sin, sinned in some former state,
Was thy soul forced to contemplate that day
Which should not at one blow take life away,
  But on each vital sense shut gate by gate, —
  Until thy lord's unfathomable hate,
Supreme, relentless, and which none gainsay,

Left thy great brain confounded in black night,
  And wild with pain? Yea, thou wert all alone,
  Shut fast in night, as in a living tomb
Where no sound was ; Death quenched thy spirit's light
  So long before, oh, racked in uttermost gloom,
  He made thy poor, dark, tortured body his own.

TO ARTHUR O'SHAUGHNESSY.

ON THE SECOND ANNIVERSARY OF HIS DEATH, JANUARY
30, 1883.

AGAIN returns this day, and still, my friend,
  I listen for a step that comes not near,
  And hearken for a voice I may not hear
Save in my dreams, where many memories blend.
Two years have passed, and still the days extend,
  Void day on day. He, too, has gone away
  Who loved thy lyric work ; his praise a bay
For which all songs most gladly might contend.

April, that came and found him with us yet,
  And took him hence, makes sad the heart of Spring,
And January days shall not forget
  That then it was thy sweet lips ceased to sing,
And we who loved thee, knew our feet were set
  In paths where thine were no more journeying.

TO JAMES THOMSON, AUTHOR OF "THE CITY OF DREADFUL NIGHT."

I.

BROTHER, and fellow-citizen with me
　Of this great city whose tremendous gloom
　Weighed on thee with the heaviness of doom, —
I walk its ways to-day, and seem to see
Thy saddest eyes; again with thee to be
　As on that day when, in this very room,
　Thine eyes and ours who watched thee saw Death
　　loom,
A mighty monarch, strong to set thee free.

Still, still the same, this "City of Dreadful Night," —
　Still does it hear a sound of lamentation,
　As of a conquered, broken-hearted nation;
Still glowers the Sphinx, and breaks us with her might
Of unresponsive front.　There is no light;
　There is no hope; God, there is *no* salvation.

II.

No tears of mine shall fall upon thy face;
　Whatever City thou hast gained, at last,
　Better it is than that where thy feet passed
So many times, such weary nights and days.
Those journeying feet knew all its inmost ways;
　Where shapes and shadows of dread things were cast,
　There moved thy soul, profoundly dark and vast,
There did thy voice its hymn of anguish raise.

Thou wouldst have left that City of great Night,
　Yet travelled its dark mazes, all in vain;
But one way leads from it, which found aright,
　Who goes by it may not return again.
　There didst thou grope thy way, through thy long pain;
Hast thou, outside, found any world of light?

IN MEMORY OF D. G. ROSSETTI.

WHAT wreath have I above thy rest to place,
   What worthy song-wreath, Friend, — nay, more than
     friend?
For so thou didst all other men transcend
That the pure, fiery worship of old days —
That of the boy, content to hear, to gaze —
   Burned on most brightly; though as lamps none tend
   The lights on other shrines had made an end,
And darkness reigned where was the festal blaze.

Far from us now thou art; and never again
   Thy magic voice shall thrill me, as one thrills
When noblest music storms his heart and brain.
   The sea remembers thee, — the woods, the hills,
   Sunlight and moonlight, and the hurrying rills, —
And Love saith, "Surely this man leads my train!"

A LAST HARVEST.

LYRICS.

———◦•◦———

LOVE'S LOST PLEASURE-HOUSE.

Love built for himself a Pleasure-House, —
    A Pleasure-House fair to see :
The roof was gold, and the walls thereof
    Were delicate ivory.

Violet crystal the windows were,
    All gleaming and fair to see ;
Pillars of rose-stained marble up-bore
    That house where men longed to be.

Violet, golden, and white and rose,
    That Pleasure-House fair to see
Did show to all ; and they gave Love thanks
    For work of such mastery.

Love turned away from his Pleasure-House,
    And stood by the salt, deep sea :
He looked therein, and he flung therein
    Of his treasure the only key.

Now never a man till time be done
    That Pleasure-House fair to see
Shall fill with music and merriment,
    Or praise it on bended knee.

LOVE'S LADY.

To-day, as when we sat together close,
A great wind wakes and thunders as it blows, —
    We were together then beside the sea,
And now instead the sea between us flows.

O day that found us on that wind-swept coast,
And did such brave things for the future boast, —
    Though in thy voice a note of warning was, —
This day, so like thee, seems thy very ghost !

O parted, precious, memorable days,
When sudden summer kindled all my ways,
    When Love reached out his blessing hand to me,
And turned on mine the glory of his face !

And thou, my Love, in whose deep soul my soul
Lay for a little season and grew whole, —
    Thou who wert heat and light and sun and shade, —
Thou who didst lead me to Life's fairest goal ;

Whose sweetest lips Love, kissing, made to sing, —
Ah, at what bright unfathomable spring
    Was thy life nurtured, in the far-off land
Through which the unborn host go wandering ?

In stately body God thy soul did clothe, —
Thy perfect soul, — that so thou might'st have both
    To take away the hearts of men, withal ;
And tenderness to strength He did betroth ;

And in thy beautiful and luminous eyes
The wayward changefulness of April skies
    He set for sovereign charm ; and made thy voice
A sweet and a perpetual surprise.

Alas, what song of mine can demonstrate
The love that came between me and my fate, —
    That would have saved me from despair and Doom
Had Destiny but been compassionate?

As high as Heaven it was, deep as the sea,
And mystical and pure as lilies be,
    And glowing with the glory of the June,
When birds and flowers and light make revelry.

Steadfast it was, as stars whereby men steer;
Tender as twilight, when the moon is near,
    And all the gentle air is warm with hope,
And we the Summer's hastening feet can hear.

How can my single, singing strength suffice
To worship thee, my Love, my Paradise?
    My song falls weak before thee, and abashed,
Nor ever to thy spirit's height may rise;

Yet even by its failure men shall see
How more than all loves was my love of thee, —
    Thou, who didst overflow my life with Heaven,
Making that life Love's miracle to be!

And, though my little note of music pass
As barren breath one breathes upon a glass,
    And I be numbered with the numberless throng
Of whom men say not, even, "This man was,"

Oh, yet, from thee, in whom all beauty blent,
My Rose of women, from thy heart there went —
    From thy deep, splendid, perfect, passionate heart —
A love to be, in death, my monument!

ALAS!

ALAS for all high hopes and all desires !
　Like leaves in yellow autumn-time they fall ;
Alas for prayers and psalms and love's pure fires, —
　One silence and one darkness ends them all !

Alas for all the world, — sad fleeting race !
　Alas, my Love, for you and me, Alas !
Grim Death will clasp us in his close embrace ;
　We, too, like all the rest from earth must pass.

Alas to think we must forget some hours
　Whereof the memory like Love's planet glows, —
Forget them as the year her withered flowers, —
　Forget them as the June forgets the rose !

Our keenest rapture, our most deep despair,
　Our hopes, our dreads, our laughter, and our tears
Shall be no more at all upon the air, —
　No more at all, through all the endless years.

We shall be mute beneath the grass and dew
　In that dark Kingdom where Death reigns in state, —
And you will be as I, and I as you —
　One silence shed upon us, and one fate.

MY LIFE PUTS FORTH TO SEA ALONE.

My life puts forth to sea alone ;
　The skies are dark above ;
All round I hear gray waters moan, —
　Alas, for vanished love !

" O lonely life that presseth on
  Across these wastes of years, —
Where are the guiding pilots gone, —
  Whose is the hand that steers?"

The pilots they are left behind
  Upon yon golden strand ;
We drift before the driving wind ;
  We cannot miss the land, —

That land to which we hurry on
  Across the angry years ;
Hope being dead, and sweet Love gone,
  There is no hand that steers.

FLOWN LOVE.

So far Love has flown we cannot find him ;
  All joy is past :
We may not follow, regain and bind him,
  He flies so fast.

" And where has Love flown, if flown he be?
  Can you not say?
Across what mountains, and over what sea?
  Which way?   Which way?"

O'er viewless mountains and seas you know not,
  To lands unknown,
Where winds are still, and where waters flow not :
  There has Love flown.

" And when did Love leave you alone, alone?
  Heart, say this thing."
In the autumn-time, when the wet winds moan,
  And dead leaves cling ;

When the night was wildest, the sky most black,
    At dead of night,
Right into the wind, on his trackless track,
    Love took his flight.

"Oh, wait till the summer the earth redeems
    From winter's spell:
Then Love shall return and fulfil your dreams,
    And all be well."

Nay, Love shall not come with the lengthening light, —
    O Love flown far,
Right into the land, deep into the night
    That knows no star.

A BAGATELLE.

NOT all the roses God hath made
    Can love the sun aright:
The white rose is too chastely staid
    To praise his warmth and light, —
But great red roses, they can love
With their deep hearts their king above.

Nor nightingales by night that sing
    Can love alike the moon;
Nor all the flowers that come with Spring
    Can praise aright her boon, —
One nightingale most feels Night's power;
And Spring is dearest to one flower.

Not all the gulls that skim the sea
    Delight alike in storm;
And never man, Sweetheart, to thee
    Gave love so true and warm
As mine, that Heaven ordained on high
To worship thee until I die.

A CASTLE IN SPAIN.

To that country fair and far,
Where so many castles are,
    Go, Song, on thy way !
Grand my castle once to see, —
Home of light and revelry, —
    What is it to-day?

Round its turrets, fallen, lonely,
Dreams and songs now wander only,
    Dreams and saddest song :
Dreary looks it in the noonlight ;
Ghosts possess it in the moonlight,
    When the night is long.

O my castle, fallen, lowly,
Fittest home for melancholy,
    Sad, deserted place,
In your cold and crumbling halls,
Never now her footstep falls,
    Never smiles her face !

A SONG FOR TWILIGHT.

Now the winds a-wailing go
  Through the sere forsaken trees ;
Now the day is waxing low,
    And above the troubled seas
    Faint stars glimmer, and the breeze
    Hovers, sad with memories.

Now the time to part has come,
　　What is left for us to say?
Shall we wander sad and dumb
　　Down this garden's leaf-strewn way;
　　Or by tossing waves and gray
　　Hand in hand together stray?

In this garden shall we stand,
　　In the day's departing light, —
Here, where first I touched your hand
　　On that unforgotten night,
　　When you stood, 'mid roses bright,
　　Dream, embodied to the sight?

Where we met, Love, shall we part?
　　In this garden shall we twain,
Mouth to mouth, as heart to heart,
　　Loving turn, and kiss again, —
　　In this garden shall we drain
　　Love's last bitter-sweet, and pain?

Nay, Love, let us leave this place;
　　Let us go, Dear, to the beach
Where in happy summer days,
　　Sleeping Love awoke to speech;
　　And his voice though low, could reach
　　To the deepest heart of each.

There the sea-winds drifting sweet
　　From some strange land far away,
And the blown waves as they meet
　　One another in the bay, —
　　These together haply may
　　Hint some word for us to say.

Let us kiss, then, Dear, and go
　　Down together to the sea ;
We will kiss, Dear, meeting so,
　　In the days that are to be . . .
　　If my heart should then be free,
　　If you should remember me !

THE RIVER.

SUGGESTED BY THE FIFTEENTH PRELUDE OF CHOPIN.

THE river flows forever ;
　　The moon upon it shines, —
One walks beside the river
　　With heart that longs and pines.

A breeze moves on the river ;
　　The moon shakes in its flow, —
He grieves and grieves forever,
　　For days of long ago.

The softly lapsing river,
　　It whispers in its flow
Of dear days gone forever,
　　Those days of long ago.

He listens to the river ;
　　A spirit seems to say :
" Forever, Love, forever,
　　Some day, some blessed day ! "

Between the moon and river
　　The spirit seems to glide, —
He cries, " To-night, forever,
　　I 'll clasp thee, O my bride ! "

And the happy pilgrim river,
    As it journeys toward the sea,
Sings, " Ever and forever,
    Together they shall be ! "

LOVE'S FLYING FEET.

OH, follow Love's flying feet, —
    They 're fleet as the Wind's and fleeter ;
Oh, honey indeed is sweet,
    But the kisses of Love are sweeter.

Oh, hark to the voice of Love !
    The song of the lark as he rises,
Or the cry of the bird in a grove
    That the light of a brooklet surprises

Is not so glad as Love's voice, —
    That voice that of all things is gladdest, —
For it whispers of delicate joys,
    And of raptures dearest and maddest.

Oh, look in Love's eyes that shine,
    Alight with the whole world's splendor :
They are stars, intense and divine,
    In a passionate heaven and tender.

Oh, worship Love while you may, —
    For never a love-dream may follow,
Where, hid from the light of the day,
    Man sleeps in his small earth-hollow.

TO SLEEP.

Ah, stay, dear Sleep, a little longer yet,
 Though Day be come to chase thee;
And let me in thy sheltering arms forget, —
 Dear Sleep, once more embrace me!

The time will come when thou and I must part,
 But now, Belovèd, linger,
And soothe once more the sad and weary heart
 Of me, thy lover and singer!

Dear Comforter, who reignest undefiled, —
 Within thy kingdom holy
The weary man is even as a child, —
 The lofty as the lowly.

Ah, when our nuptial day shall dawn on high, —
 With nuptial love-fires lighted, —
Then I forever in thine arms shall lie,
 By no fresh grief affrighted.

LOVERS.

Oh, what does the night-wind say to the rose?
Alas, there is never a heart that knows!
Oh, what does the nightingale there in the brake
Sing to his love, as he sings for her sake?

Be glad there is never an ear to discover —
O sweet wind-lover, O sweet bird-lover!
Your secret is safe, as mine own shall be
When the lips that I love have breathed it to me.

A REMEMBERED TUNE.

My hand strayed o'er the piano keys,
  And it chanced on a song that you sang, my dear,
When we roamed through the country stillnesses,
  Or stood by the sea, when the moon was clear,
      In that other year.

I forget the words you were wont to sing;
  But the tune was a sweet and a tender one,
And sad as the thought of youth and Spring
  To him who dreams, in the fading sun,
      That the sweet time 's done.

As I play, old hopes and old sorrows move,
  Till it almost seems that your voice I hear,
And my spirit goes forth, to-day, to rove
  Down the inland way where the sea was neai,
      In that other year.

      As a bird that finds its nest,
        When the winds are overstrong,
      With quivering wings and panting breast,
        Even so to-day this song
      Which your dear lips used to sing,
        From the days long left behind
      Enters now, and folds its wing
        In the still, remembering mind.

AFTER LOVE'S PASSING.

The awful stillness in two human souls
  Whence Love has passed away;
The dreary night no moon of joy controls;
  The undelightful day; —

The cruel coldness where was once Love's heat ;
  The darkness where was light ;
The burning, tearless eyes ; the weary feet
  That journey day and night ; —

The long, dark way that has no end but one, —
  That goal no man may miss ;
The winds that wail about the sunken sun
  For life's departed bliss ; —

The fearful loneliness that comes between
  Those souls erst one, now twain ;
The passionate memory of what has been ;
  The unavailing pain ; —

The springs that come, but bring no hope of change ;
  The cheerless, summer hours ;
With songs of birds grown old and harsh and strange,
  And scentless, bloomless flowers ; —

The fruitless autumn, with no garnered corn ;
  The dreary, winter weather ;
The two who walk apart, alone, forlorn,
  Who once kept step together ; —

The bitter sense of failure and regret ;
  The life without an aim ;
The unavailing struggle to forget
  The weakness, owned with shame ; —

These things make sad the night and sad the day,
  And hard are they to bear :
Yet let those souls whence Love has passed away
  Though sad, keep pure and fair :

Ah, let them say, " Great Love once tarried here
  Making his home divine, —
Though he has passed, yet let us still hold dear
  The temple and the shrine."

A QUESTION.

Once at this window, touched by climbing boughs
    Whose plenteous leaves were quivering listlessly
With some least breath of wind, through the still house,
    Borne from the dim, remote old library,
I heard the organ's music, slow, profound, —
A moon-thrilled, travelling twilight of sweet sound,
    Sad as the last breath of the leaves that lie
Thick, dead, and autumn-colored on the ground.

To-day a child with eager hands will try
    To gain the secret of the organ's soul,
And waking it to simple melody
    Smile with fond pride to think he has the whole :
Shall I, who know of old the stops and keys,
The pain and longing, the regret and peace
    That stronger fingers waken and control,
Hurt his young heart by mocking him with these?

HEART–BREAKS AND SONGS.

Heart-breaks and songs, —
    Fate, leave us these,
Since no man prolongs
    Love's joy and peace.

Summer was fair,
    Though it was fleet, —
Cold now the air,
    No breath is sweet.

Faint is the sun, —
    Roses are dead ;
Lingers not one,
    Dear, for your head.

Heart-breaks and songs, —
 Fate leave us these,
Since no man prolongs
 Love's joy and peace.

LOOKING FORWARD, IN FEBRUARY.

I LOOK across the brief, remaining space
 Of chill and wintry days,
Till March to sprinkle violets shall begin,
 And snow-drops white and thin.

I look through April, quick with scent and song,
 To where the shining throng
Of laughing, garlanded May days come on,
 With large light of the sun.

I look to June, — fair flower of all the year, —
 O month of months appear !
O ardors of the summer-time come close,
 With nightingale and rose !

Make haste to come, O time of all delight !
 Bright day, and tender night —
For then shall I within a Heaven dwell
 Whose name Love may not tell.

HER PITY.

THIS is the room to which she came that day, —
Came when the dusk was falling cold and gray, —
Came with soft step, in delicate array,

And sat beside me in the firelight there :
And like a rose of perfume rich and rare
Thrilled with her sweetness the environing air.

We heard the grind of traffic in the street,
The clamorous calls, the beat of passing feet,
The wail of bells that in the twilight meet.

Then I knelt down, and dared to touch her hand, —
Those slender fingers, and the shining band
Of happy gold wherewith her wrist was spanned.

Her radiant beauty made my heart rejoice;
And then she spoke, and her low, pitying voice
Was like the soft, pathetic, tender noise

Of winds that come before a summer rain:
Once leaped the blood in every clamorous vein;
Once leaped my heart, then dumb, stood still again.

GO, SONGS OF MINE.

Go, songs of mine, to bring her on her way
        With whisperings of love;
'T is bleak March now, but then it shall be May,
        With gentle skies above
And gentle seas below, what time she hears
Your little music chiming in her ears.

Cold, cold this day, and white the air with snow,
        And dark this place wherefrom
My hastening music ever loves to go
        To find its natural home, —
Its home with her to whom all charms belong;
Who is both Queen of Love and Queen of Song.

Shall glad spring come?   Shall May come with warm hours
    And laughter of clear light,
And blossoming trees, and festivals of flowers,
    And nightingales by night,
That pour their shuddering sweetness on the air, —
The music of an exquisite despair?

And shall she come, who is my Spring of springs, —
    Herself than May more fair?
Sweet is the song the Night's sad songster sings;
    But her tones are more rare, —
Ah, shall she come, who is Spring and Summer in one, —
To my sad life its star, its moon, its sun?

AFTER SUMMER.

WE'LL not weep for summer over, —
    No, not we;
Strew above his head the clover, —
    Let him be!

Other eyes may weep his dying,
    Shed their tears
There upon him, where he's lying
    With his peers.

Unto some of them he proffered
    Gifts most sweet;
For our hearts a grave he offered, —
    Was this meet?

All our fond hopes, praying, perished
    In his wrath, —
All the lovely dreams we cherished
    Strewed his path.

23

Shall we in our tombs, I wonder,
    Far apart,
Sundered wide as seas can sunder
    Heart from heart,

Dream at all of all the sorrows
    That were ours, —
Bitter nights, more bitter morrows;
    Poison-flowers

Summer gathered, as in madness,
    Saying, " See,
These are yours, in place of gladness, —
    Gifts from me?"

Nay, the rest that will be ours,
    Is supreme, —
And below the poppy flowers
    Steals no dream.

AT LAST.

REST here, at last,
The long way overpast;
Rest here, at home, —
    Thy race is run,
    Thy dreary journey done,
Thy last peak clomb.

'Twixt birth and death,
What days of bitter breath
Were thine, alas!
    Thy soul had sight
    To see, by day, by night,
Strange phantoms pass.

Thy restless heart
In few glad things had part,
But dwelt alone,
    And night and day,
    In the old way
Made the old moan.

But here is rest
For aching brain and breast,
Deep rest, complete,
    And nevermore,
    Heart-weary and foot-sore,
Shall stray thy feet, —

Thy feet that went,
With such long discontent,
Their wonted beat
    About thy room,
    With its deep-seated gloom,
Or through the street.

Death gives them ease ;
Death gives thy spirit peace ;
Death lulls thee, quite.
    One thing alone
    Death leaves thee of thine own, —
Thy starless night.

LAST GARDEN SECRETS.

ROSES AND THE NIGHTINGALE.

In my garden it is night-time,
But a still time and a bright time;
For the moon rains down her splendor,
  And my garden feels the wonder
  Of the spell which it lies under
In that light so soft and tender.

While the moon her watch is keeping,
All the blossoms here are sleeping,
And the roses sigh for dreaming
  Of the bees that love to love them
  When the warm sun shines above them
And the butterflies pass gleaming.

Could one follow roses' fancies,
When the night the garden trances,
Oh, what fair things we should chance on!
  For to lilies and to roses,
  As to us, soft sleep discloses
What the waking may not glance on.

Hark, now, how across the moonlight,
Through the warmness of the June night,
From the tall trees' listening branches
  Comes the sound, sustained and holy,
  Of the passionate melancholy,
Of a wound which singing stanches.

Oh, the ecstasy of sorrow
Which the music seems to borrow
From the thought of some past lover
 Who loved vainly all his lifetime,
 Till death ended peace and strife-time,
And the darkness clothed him over !

Oh, the passionate, sweet singing,
Aching, gushing, throbbing, ringing,
Dying in divine, soft closes,
 Recommencing, waxing stronger,
 Sweet notes, ever sweeter, longer,
Till the singing wakes the roses !

Quoth the roses to the singer :
"Oh, thou dearest music-bringer,
Now our sleep so sweetly endeth,
 Tell us why thy song so sad seems,
 When the air is full of glad dreams,
And the bright moon o'er us bendeth."

Sang the singer to the roses :
" Love for you my song discloses ;
Hence the note of grief I borrow."
 Quoth the roses, " Love means pleasure."
 Quoth the singer, " Love's best measure
Is its pure attendant sorrow."

FLOWER FAIRIES.

FLOWER fairies — have you found them,
 When the summer's dusk is falling,
With the glow-worms watching round them ;
 Have you heard them softly calling?

Silent stand they through the noonlight,
   In their flower shapes, fair and quiet;
But they hie them forth by moonlight,
   Ready then to sing and riot.

I have heard them; I have seen them, —
   Light from their bright petals raying;
And the trees bent down to screen them,
   Great, wise trees, too old for playing.

Hundreds of them, all together, —
   Flashing flocks of flying fairies, —
Crowding through the summer weather,
   Seeking where the coolest air is.

And they tell the trees that know them,
   As upon their boughs they hover,
Of the things that chance below them, —
   How the rose has a new lover.

And the gay Rose laughs, protesting,
   "Neighbor Lily is as fickle."
Then they search where birds are nesting,
   And their feathers softly tickle.

Then away they all dance, sweeping,
   Having drunk their fill of gladness.
But the trees, their night-watch keeping,
   Thrill with tender, pitying sadness;

For they know of bleak December,
   When each bough left cold and bare is, —
When they only shall remember
   The bright visits of the fairies, —

When the roses and the lilies
   Shall be gone, to come back never
From the land where all so still is
   That they sleep and sleep forever.

THE LONELY ROSE.

" To a heaven far away
　Went the Red Rose when she died : "
So I heard the White Rose say,
　As she swayed from side to side
　　In the chill October blast !
　　In the garden leaves fall fast,—
　　This of roses is the last.

Said the White Rose, " O my Red Rose,
　O my Rose so fair to see,
When like thee I am a dead rose
　Shall I in thy heaven be ? "
　　O the drear October blast !
　　In the garden leaves fall fast, —
　　This of roses is the last.

" From that heavenly place, last night,
　To me in a dream she came, —
Stood there in the pale moonlight,
　And she seemed, my Rose, the same."
　　O the chill October blast !
　　In the garden leaves fall fast, —
　　This of roses is the last.

" Only it maybe, perchance,
　That her leaves were redder grown,
And they seemed to thrill and dance
　As by gentle breezes blown."
　　O the drear October blast !
　　In the garden leaves fall fast, —
　　This of roses is the last.

" And she told me, sweetly singing,
 Of that heavenly place afar
Where the air with song is ringing,
 Where the souls of dead flowers are."
 O the chill October blast !
 In the garden leaves fall fast, —
 This of roses is the last.

" And she bade me not to fail her,
 Not to lose my heart with fear
When I saw the skies turn paler
 With the sickness of the year, —*
 I should be beyond the blast
 And the leaves now falling fast,
 In that heavenly place at last."

SUMMER CHANGES.

SANG the Lily, and sang the Rose,
Out of the heart of my garden close :
 " O joy, O joy of the summer-tide ! "
Sang the Wind, as it moved about them :
" Roses were made for the Wind to love them,
 Dear little buds, in the leaves that hide ! "

Sang the Trees, as they rustled together :
" Oh, the joy of the summer weather !
 Roses and Lilies, how do you fare ? "
Sang the Red Rose, and sang the White :
" Glad we are of the Sun's large light,
 And the songs of birds that dart through the air."

Lily, and Rose, and tall, green Tree,
Swaying boughs where the bright birds be,
　Thrilled by music, and trembling with wings,
How glad they were on that summer day!
Little they recked of skies cold and gray,
　Or the dreary dirge that a Storm-wind sings.

Golden butterflies gleam in the Sun,
Laugh at the flowers and kiss each one;
　And great bees come, with their sleepy tune,
To sip their honey and circle round;
And the flowers are lulled by that drowsy sound,
　And fall asleep in the heart of the noon.

A small, white cloud in a sky of blue;
Roses and Lilies, what will they do?
　For a Wind springs up and sings in the Trees;
Down comes the rain. The garden's awake:
Roses and Lilies begin to quake,
　That were rocked to sleep by the gentle breeze.

Ah, Roses and Lilies! Each delicate petal
The Wind and the rain together unsettle, —
　This side and that side the tall Trees sway:
But the Wind goes by, and the rain stops soon,
And the shadow lifts from the face of the noon,
　And the flowers are glad in the Sun's warm ray.

Sing, my Lilies, and sing, my Roses,
With never a dream that the Summer closes;
　But the Trees are old, and I fancy they tell,
Each unto each, how the Summer flies:
They remember the last year's wintry skies;
　But that Summer returns, the Trees know well.

A RUINED GARDEN.

ALL my roses are dead in my Garden —
    What shall I do?
Winds in the night, without pity or pardon,
    Came there and slew.

All my song-birds are dead in their bushes —
    Woe for such things!
Robins and linnets and blackbirds and thrushes,
    Dead, with stiff wings.

Oh, my Garden! rifled and flowerless,
    Waste now and drear;
Oh, my Garden! barren and bowerless,
    Through all the year.

Oh, my dead birds! each in his nest there,
    So cold and stark;
What was the horrible death that pressed there
    When skies were dark?

What shall I do for my roses' sweetness,
    The summer round, —
For all my Garden's divine completeness
    Of scent and sound?

I will leave my Garden for winds to harry;
    Where once was peace,
Let the bramble-vine and the wild brier marry,
    And greatly increase.

But I will go to a land men know not, —
    A far, still land,
Where no birds come, and where roses blow not
    And no trees stand:

Where no fruit grows, where no spring makes riot,
　　　But, row on row,
Heavy and red and pregnant with quiet
　　　The poppies blow.

And there shall I be made whole of sorrow,
　　　Have no more care, —
No bitter thought of the coming morrow,
　　　Or days that were.

SONNETS.

WHEN WITH THY LIFE THOU DIDST ENCOMPASS MINE.

WHEN with thy life thou didst encompass mine,
   And I beheld, as from an infinite height,
   Thy love stretch pure and beautiful as light,
Through extreme joy I hardly could divine
Whether my love of thee it was, or thine,
   Which so my heart astonished with its might.
   But now, at length, familiar to the sight
So I can bear to look where planets shine,

Ever more deep the wonder grows to be
That thou shouldst love me, while my love of thee
   Does of my very nature seem a part, —
   So, often now, as from a dream, I start,
To think that thou — even thou — thou lovest me,
   I being what I am; thou what thou art.

THE BREADTH AND BEAUTY OF THE SPACIOUS NIGHT.

THE breadth and beauty of the spacious night
  Brimmed with white moonlight, swept by winds that
    blew
  The flying sea-spray up to where we two
Sat all alone, made one in Love's delight, —
The sanctity of sunsets palely bright ;
  Autumnal woods, seen 'neath meek skies of blue ;
  Old cities that God's silent peace stole through, —
These of our love were very sound and sight.

The strain of labor ; the bewildering din
  Of thundering wheels ; the bells' discordant chime ;
  The sacredness of art ; the spell of rhyme, —
These, too, with our dear love were woven in,
    That so, when parted, all things might recall
    The sacred love that had its part in all.

WHICH IS IT, LOVE?

WHICH is it, Love, enthralls me more to-night,
  Quickening the pulses' throb and the heart's beat, —
  The memory of joy so subtly sweet
It wakes at thought, as when one plays aright
Some air to which Love's tones were wont to plight
  The dearest singing words, till with the heat
  Of passionate remembrance he can cheat
The heart that longs so even in Death's despite?

Or is it expectation of fresh bliss, —
  That bliss which Memory can so poorly feign,
Deep joy of the anticipated kiss
  Quickening the jubilant blood in every vein?
  Thought of past joy, or joy to come again ;
Confused by Love, I know not which it is.

HER ATMOSPHERE.

WHAT of her soul's immaculate atmosphere,
    Which all who know her breathe ; which he knows
        best
    Whose heart her love transfigured, saved, and blest ?
Buoyant as is the spring of the young year ;
Tender as twilight when the moon is near ;
    Ardent as noon, and deep as midnight's rest ;
    Pure as the air on heights no foot has prest,
That unto Heaven aspire, to Heaven are dear ; — ·

A rareness and a fragrance and a sweetness,
    A wonder and a glory without bound, —
Such is her atmosphere's divine completeness,
    A moving Paradise of sight and sound.
        Blest She, in whom dear Heaven, dear Earth
           combine —
        How shall they reach her, these weak words of
          mine ?

LOVE ASLEEP.

I FOUND Love sleeping in a place of shade,
    And as in some sweet dream the sweet lips smiled ;
    Yea, seemed he as a lovely, sleeping child.
Soft kisses on his full, red lips I laid,
And with red roses did his tresses braid ;
    Then pure, white lilies on his breast I piled,
    And fettered him with woodbine sweet and wild,
And fragrant armlets for his arms I made.

But while I, leaning, yearned across his breast,
    Upright he sprang, and from swift hand, alert,
        Sent forth a shaft that lodged within my heart.
Ah, had I never played with Love at rest,
        He had not wakened, had not cast his dart,
        And I had lived who die now of this hurt.

LOVE'S GHOST.

Is it the ghost of dead and buried Love
   Which haunts the House of Life, and comes by night
   With weary sighs, and in its eyes the light
Of joys long set?   I hear its footsteps move
Through darkened rooms where only ghosts now rove, —
   The rooms Love's shining eyes of old made bright:
   It whispers low; it trembles into sight, —
A bodiless presence hearts alone may prove.

I say, "Sad visitant of this dark house,
   Why wanderest thou through these deserted rooms,
A dreadful glimmering light about thy brows?
   Thy silent home should be among the tombs."
     And the Ghost answers, while I thrill with fear:
     "In all the world I have no home but here."

APRIL.

Between the sudden sunlight and the rain
   The birds sing gayly in the path wherethrough
   I walk, and note the sky's ethereal blue, —
Pure as the peace that 's won, at last, from pain.
The sunshine and the sun-bright showers ordain
   A festival of laughing flowers, whereto
   The bees go buzzing past me; trees renew
Their lives of green; the whole land smiles again.

O April, longed for so through cheerless hours,
   Thou who dost turn to silver winter's gray!
What is it ails thy skies, thy birds, thy flowers,
   Gives to thy winds a mournful word to say,
And brings a sound of weeping with the showers, —
   What, but the thought of Aprils passed away?

MY GRAVE.

For me no great metropolis of the dead, —
    Highways and byways, squares and crescents of
        death, —
    But after I have breathed my last sad breath,
Am comforted with quiet, I who said,
" I weary of men's voices and their tread,
    Of clamoring bells, and whirl of wheels that pass," —
    Lay me beneath some plot of country grass,
Where flowers may spring, and birds sing overhead ; —

Whereto one coming, some fair eve in spring,
    Between the day-fall and the tender night,
Might pause awhile, his friend remembering,
    And hear low words, breathed through the failing
        light,
In tone as soft as the wind's whispering :
    " Now he sleeps long, who had so long to fight."

HER IN ALL THINGS.

Unto mine ear I set a faithful shell,
    That as of old it might rehearse to me
    The very music of the far-off sea,
And thrill my spirit with its fluctuant spell :
But not the sea's tones there grew audible,
    But Love's voice, whispering low and tenderly,
    Of things so dear that they must ever be
Unspoken, save what heart to heart may tell :

And hearing in the shell those tones divine, —
    Where once I heard the sea's low sounds confer, —
I said unto myself, " This life of thine
    Holds nothing then which is not part of Her ;
    And all sweet things that to men minister
Come but from Love, who makes Her heart his shrine."

OF EARLY VIOLETS.

SOFT, subtle scent, which is to me more sweet
  Than perfumes that come later, — when the rose
  In all the splendor of her beauty blows, —
Here, even to this busy London street,
Thou bringest visions of the grace we meet
  When all-forgetful of the winter's snows
  The earth beneath the sun's kiss throbs and glows,
And answers to his strength with strong heart-beat.

Thou 'rt like his lady's voice to one who waits,
In the dim twilight at her garden gates,
  Her coming face ; thou art the trembling, rare,
    First note of Nature's prelude that leads on
    The Spring, till the great, splendid orison
  Of Summer's music vibrates in the air.

BELLS OF LONDON.

As when an eager boy, I heard to-night
  The selfsame bells clash out upon the air,
  It seemed not then a city of despair,
But a fair home of promise and delight, —
This London that now breaks me with its might.
  Is this the end of all sweet dreams and fair?
  Is this the bitter answer to my prayer?
The bells deride me from the belfry's height, —

"We clamored to thee in the old, far years,
  And all the sorrows of thy life forecast ;
And now, with eyes uncomforted by tears,
  And dry and seared as by a furnace-blast,
Thou walkest vainly where no hope appears,
  Between veiled future and disastrous past."

24

A COUNTRY'S GHOST.

SOME long dead Country's Ghost it surely is
   Which haunts these Western waters, — strange and
      bright
   With dazzling gold of the sun's setting light :
Fair hills and fields it shows, but more than this
We may not know, since all its bane and bliss
   Lie hidden in its cities out of sight, —
   Strange cities, haply wrapt in sleep and night,
Where phantom lovers come again to kiss :

Or Ghosts of weary men by stealth come back
   To climb the silent by-ways noiselessly, —
      Those ancient ways which no more dream of change,
      Where still, I think, dead with their dead must
         range —
Ghost ! seen a moment in the low sun's track,
   Now hidden again in the concealing sea.

TO ALL SAD OF HEART.

I HEARD one cry, " The day is well nigh done ;
   The sun is setting, and the night is near, —
   The night wherein no moon or stars appear,
And to whose gloom succeeds no joyful sun ;
The race is ended, and the prize is won, —
   What prize hast thou ? " I rose with heavy cheer,
   Stretched empty hands, and said, " No prize is here :
My feet were bruised, so that I might not run."

Of victors wreathed I saw a goodly throng ;
   But turned mine eyes from these to where, apart,
Sad men moved wearily, with heads down-hung.
   I cried, " O ye who know Grief's poisonous smart,
   Brothers ! accept me, now ; for from my heart
To yours I send the passion of my song ! "

TO ALL IN HAVEN.

ALL ye who have gained the haven of safe days,
    And rest at ease, your wanderings being done, —
    Except the last, inevitable one, —
Be well content, I say, and hear men's praise ;
Yet in the quiet of your sheltered bays, —
    Bland waters shining in an equal sun, —
    Forget not that the awful storm-tides run
In far, unsheltered, and tempestuous ways.

Remember near what rocks, and through what shoals,
    Worn, desperate mariners strain with all their might ;
They may not come to your sweet restful goals,
    Your waters placid in the level light :
Their graves wait in that sea no moon controls,
    That is in dreadful fellowship with Night.

FORECASTING.

SOME day, as now, the world shall reawake —
    The city from its brief, dream-tortured sleep ;
    The country from its rest so pure and deep —
To song of birds in every flowering brake ;
And men light-hearted, or with hearts that ache,
    Shall rise and go what they have sown to reap ;
    And women smile, or sit alone and weep
For life once sweet, grown bitter for love's sake.

But we, that day, shall not be here, — not we ;
    We shall have done with life though few may know :
Between us then shall awful stillness be,
    Who spake such words of bliss, such words of woe,
As winds remember, chanting fitfully —
    Chanting, as now — above us lying low.

FRIENDSHIP AND LOVE.

As feels the port for ships that come and go,
    That tarry for a night, and in the day
    Spread canvas and steer sailing far away
To other ports of which it may not know,
In unconjectured countries, even so
    Man feels for man ; nor long may friendship stay ;
    And little of its joy or its dismay
May any friend's heart to another show.

As feels the spirit of the melody
    That, slumbering in a viol, a touch will start ;
As feels the sun-thrilled sap within a tree, —
    So man and woman feel, when heart in heart
They live, and know this miracle to be, —
    In soul together, though to sense apart.

HERE IN THIS SUNSET SPLENDOR
DESOLATE.

HERE in this sunset splendor desolate,
    As in some Country strange and sad, I stand ;
    A mighty sadness broods upon the land, —
The gloom of some unalterable Fate.
O Thou whose love dost make august my state,
    A little longer leave in mine thy hand :
    Night birds are singing, but the place is banned
By stern gods whom no prayers propitiate.

Seeking for bliss supreme, we lost the track :
    Shall we then part, and parted try to reach
        A goal like that we two sought day and night,
        Or shall we sit here, in the sun's low light,
    And see, it may be through Death's twilight breach,
A new path to the old way leading back ?

ALL ROUND ABOUT ME IS THE
CITY'S NOISE.

ALL round about me is the City's noise, —
  The pitiless clamor of the London street,
  Wherethrough to-day I move with flagging feet :
Ah, shall I live, indeed, to hear thy voice ;
Once more in thy dear beauty to rejoice ;
  To feel thy heart with mine give beat for beat?
  Ah, Love, shall lips and hands and spirits meet,
Dear Love, once more, before grim Death destroys?

Or shall Death come beforehand, in Love's place, —
  His semblance dark be set for dreadful sign?
  O Love, if I no more should call thee mine,
Nor hold thee yet again in Love's embrace !
  O Love, if thou no more shouldst own me thine,
Nor even thy tears be shed on my dead face !

O YE WHO SAILED WITH ME.

O YE who sailed with me the evening seas,
  Take to your boats now and depart, I say.
  Ye know what winds and rains laid waste my day,
Yet how with even-song there came surcease ;
But it is ended here, my term of peace :
  The sun has set ; once more the sky turns gray,
  And giant waves in menacing array
Surge on, and thunder, while the winds increase.

I must away, and sail to breast their might ;
  I — who once dallied by the fair sea-side
Dreaming of stars, and gentleness of night —
  Must go, now, with the inexorable tide,
Straight on to shipwreck, past each beacon-light,
  Till Death, his prey, from all men's sight shall hide.

BELOVED OF HER.

THOSE people who are dear to her at all
   Are for her sweet sake very dear to me ;
   All places known of her divinity
Are loved by me, and hold my heart in thrall :
These flowers, that felt her pure breast rise and fall,
   Laid here apart where all her love-gifts be,
   Are fragrant with the passionate memory
Of a dear day lost now past Love's recall.

Books she has read ; least things her hands have touched ;
The very floor her garment's hem has brushed, —
   Being loved of me, shall I not love as well
     What she loved most, — to climb the upward way ;
   No longer in this poppied vale to dwell,
     But scale the heights where shines the perfect day ?

COULD IT BUT BE !

COULD the sheer weight of suffering be laid
   Upon my heart, — if I for both might bear
   The weariness, the horror, the despair,
The thoughts whereby the eyes become afraid
To close themselves in sleep ; by grief dismayed
   Watch the slow hours go by, while sobbing there
   With broken wing comes back each outcast prayer
The soul in its wild agony has prayed :

If so I might take all the pain, and see
   You walking happy with forgetful soul,
My image burned from out your memory,
   Your dear feet hastening to some shining goal, —
Then, surely, I could find grief ecstasy ;
   I could defy despair, your heart made whole.

NOT ONLY ROOMS WHEREIN THY LOVE HAS BEEN.

Not only rooms wherein thy Love has been
 Hold still for thee the memory of her grace,
 The benediction of her blessing face ;
But other rooms that never saw thy Queen
Are full of her. Has not thy spirit seen
 A vision of her in this firelit place,
 That never knew the witchery of her ways,
The perfect voice, the eyes intense, serene?

Ah, stood she not before the mirror there,
 Her loveliness all clothed in soft attire,
 Then turned to thee, low-kneeling by this fire,
And laid a gracious hand upon thy hair,
 While thy heart leaped to her, thy heart's desire,
And thy kiss praised her, and thy look was prayer?

WHAT WAILING WIND.

What wailing wind of Memory is this
 That blows across the Sea of Time to-day,
 Blending the fragrance of a long-dead May
With breath of Autumn — agony with bliss?
What phantom lips are these that cling and kiss,
 And, kissing, clinging, find old words to say?
 What parted days, in sad and glad array,
Rise up to haunt me from the grave's abyss?

Their tones subdue me, and their eyes confound,
 So that I may not look from them to where
 Each with its special message of despair,
In darkness habited, with darkness crowned,
 Come on the days that rend, and will not spare,
Till in Death's sleep I, too, at last am bound.

I THOUGHT THAT I WAS HAPPY
YESTERDAY.

I THOUGHT that I was happy yesterday;
  For, though apart, we stood soul close to soul,
  So joined by infinite Love's supreme control
That happy spring danced with us on our way;
But now the brooding sky has turned to gray,
  And heavily the clouds across it roll:
  Oh, to what awful, unconjectured goal
Are our feet tending, — my beloved one, say?

I dare not speak, — dare hardly think of Love:
  I am as one who not being dead yet hears
  A sound of lamentation round his bed,
Feels falling on his face his friends' hot tears;
And, though he struggles inly, cannot move,
  Or say one word to prove he is not dead.

WHEN THOU ART FAR FROM ME.

WHEN thou art far from me while days go by
  In which I may not hear thy voice divine,
  Or kiss thy lips, or take thy hand in mine,
I walk as 'neath a dark and hostile sky,
And the Spring winds seem void of prophecy,
  Nor is there any cheer in the sun's shine;
  But present Grief and mocking Fear combine
To overthrow me when on Love I cry.

I am as one who through a foreign town
  Journeys alone, some wild and wintry night,
And from the windows sees warm light stream down,
  While there, for him, is neither heat nor light;
  But far, far off, he has a lordlier home,
  Whereto, one day, his weary feet shall come.

FOUR PARABLES.

I.

HEIGHT UPON HEIGHT.

HEIGHT upon height, all washed by heavenly air
  And crowned of heaven, I saw them rising free, —
  Those heights of Love, where I was fain to be, —
And there I knew Love reigned, benign and fair,
With noble gifts for whoso enters there.
  But, since between those heavenly heights and me
  Stretched weary miles, with no compassionate tree
To shade me from the noon-tide's pitiless glare,

I paused brief while in a cool, wayside lane,
  Under green boughs, and heard a strange bird sing;
But when I fain would struggle on again,
  Lo, round me Elfin things had drawn their ring,
    And clouds shut out from me Love's shining height,
    And Fate's strong sword flashed threatening in my
      sight.

II.

ABOUT THIS LAND MOVES MANY A SAD-EYED GHOST.

ABOUT this land moves many a sad-eyed ghost;
  And there is wail of weeping all night long,
  And sounds by day of melancholy song:
Weird is the land, and beautiful, almost;
But wrecks of mighty ships strew thick the coast,
  Though now the sea looks innocent of wrong,
  And low, soft waves the deep sea-caverns throng,
Where sirens sing, and Death waits at his post.

Rise, rise, my soul, that we may strive with fate,
   And flee the baneful beauty which delays
   Us through warm, weeping nights and hectic days ;
Spread sail and steer where fresh life may await.
   But, ah, what words sigh down these trackless ways, —
What words but these : "Too late — Too late — Too
   late " ?

III.

I WALKED ONE SPRING DAY, WHILE YET WINDS WERE COLD.

I WALKED one spring day, while yet winds were cold,
   Between the waning day and waxing night,
   And the boughs strained and whirled in the wind's
     might.
I took a simple wild-flower in my hold,
And fair it was and delicate of mold,
   And sweet to smell, and tremulous with light ;
   And something lurking in its petals white
Meant more to me than even its fragrance told.

Full long I held that flower, until one day
   I came where queenliest, reddest roses grew ;
   Then from my hand afar the flower I threw,
     Roses to gather.   But, behold, this hour,
When roses and their thorn-stems strew the way,
   I vainly seek for my lost woodland flower.

IV.

BEFORE THIS NEW LORD CAME.

BEFORE this new Lord came into my house
   It was a quiet place, — within its halls
   Were gracious pictures that made glad the walls
With hints of Southern slopes and olive boughs,
Or saints that wore bright halos on their brows;
   But now that here the new Lord's footstep falls,
   Now that his voice the ancient peace appals
Where once from dreams soft music did arouse :

Lo ! all is changed.   Gone the fair, pictured things,
   And in their stead are many a grinning face,
And loathly shapes, and hurry of strange wings.
   Shrieks rend the air, and blood-stained are the ways :
Yet — heard by me alone — a spirit sings,
   This Lord shall not forever hold the place.

LOVE'S DESERTED PALACE.

REGARD it well, 't is yet a lordly place;
   Palace of Love, once warmed with sacred fires,
   Sounding from end to end with joy of lyres,
Fragrant with incense, with great lights ablaze.
The fires are dead now, dead the festal rays;
   No more the music marries keen desires,
   No more the incense of the shrine aspires,
And of Love's godhead there is now no trace.

Yet if one walked at night through those dim halls,
   Might it not chance that ghostly shapes would rise,
And ghostly lights glide glimmering down the walls;
   That there might be a stir, a sound of sighs,
And gentle voices answering gentle calls,
   And wayward, wandering wraiths of melodies?

SPRING AND DESPAIR.

THE cold spring twilight fills his lonely room, —
    There is no warmth, no fragrance on the air, —
    No song, but roll of traffic everywhere ;
He dwells apart, in his own separate gloom,
Borne down by dread, inevitable doom.
    The bitter winds have left the young trees bare ;
    So wind-swept is his soul, no longer fair,
And withering slowly in a mortal tomb.

The early cold of spring shall pass away,
    And June come on, of all sweet gifts possest,
    With noons for rapture, and deep nights for rest ;
But never any vivifying ray
Shall change for him one hour of any day
    Till death's dark flower be laid on brow and breast.

LETHARGY.

THIS is no midnight rent with thunder and fire,
    Charged by mad winds, and wild, bewildering rain ;
    Here is no great despair, no splendid pain,
But misty light, in which near things retire
And things far off loom close.   No least desire
    Is here : Why race ? — There is no goal to gain ;
    Only one lethargy of heart and brain,
Which now not even Grief can re-inspire.

A sense of unseen Presences, that throng
    The lonely room, the loud and populous street ;
A sound from days long past, half wail, half song ;
    Death hurrying on, with swift, approaching feet,
      Showing the man, as in a vision dread,
      His cold, dead self stretched stiff upon a bed.

FROM LONDON STREETS.

How fares it with my Love, in her far place?
  I hear along the streets, this afternoon,
  Thunder of wheels and melancholy tune
Of church bells clashing over crowded ways.
To her of peerless heart and perfect face, —
  In whom is April wedded unto June, —
  Go now, my song, and breathe some mystic rune,
That she may think of far-off, lovely days.

Oh, for my love's sake, and my soul's deep woe,
  Be as a kiss upon dear lips and eyes;
Be warm about her, that her heart may know
  The heart of one who is so little wise
That for the dreams and days of long ago
  He seeks still with the spirit's diligent eyes.

OUT OF SLEEP.

FROM out dream-haunted coverts of dim sleep
  A spirit staggers blindly toward the day,
  Once more to face the old, unchanged dismay, —
Once more to climb Life's desolate road and steep;
To sow his difficult field, and not to reap;
  To look far up the dark and tedious way,
  To see Death waiting at the end; to pray
That he may know prayer's worth; to watch and weep;

To linger in the once familiar place;
  To talk with ghosts, — frail ghosts that come and flee,
Some with kind eyes, some with reproachful gaze, —
  To see his unburied past stretched wretchedly
Across his path; and still forever face
  Each pitiless day, till days no more shall be.

RESIGNATION.

I THOUGHT in life to meet with Happiness,
    And when, instead, Grief met me by the way
    Most strange and bitter words I found to say;
But still I thought, through all the strain and stress
Of sorrowful living, — through my life's excess
    Of grief and loss, — " Pain shall not always stay,
    And fair may be the closing of my day;
Clear light and quiet may my evening bless ! "

Then Happiness was shown me like the sun, —
    One flash and glory of triumphant light
    Lit all my sky : but swiftly came the night
      With waste winds wailing on the dead day's track;
And I am silent, now the day is done,
      Knowing no words can bring its lost light back.

TO-MORROW.

I SAID, "To-morrow ! " one bleak, winter day, —
    "To-morrow I will live my life anew," —
    And still " To-morrow ! " while the winter grew
To spring, and yet I dallied by the way,
And sweet, dear Sins still held me in their sway.
    "To-morrow ! " I said, while summer days wore
      through ;
    " To-morrow ! " while chill autumn round me drew ;
And so my soul remained the sweet Sins' prey.

So pass the years, and still, perpetually,
    I cry, " To-morrow will I flee each wile ;
To-morrow, surely, shall my soul stand free,
    Safe from the siren voices that beguile ! "
    But Death waits by me, with a mocking smile,
And whispers, " Yea !   To-morrow, verily ! "

SORROW'S GHOST.

I SAW one sitting, habited in gray,
　Beside a lonely stream ; and in her eyes
　Was all the tenderness of twilight skies
In middle spring, when lawns are flushed with May.
" Mysterious one," I cried, " who art thou?　Say ! "
　She answered in low tones scarce heard through sighs :
　" Look on this face !　Dost thou not recognize
A face well known once, in another day? "

Then on the air these words grew audible :
　" The same she is who scorched thine eyes with tears,
　But changed now by the sovereign force of years,
And piteous grown, and no more terrible :
　Look on her now, who once thy life opprest, —
　Called bitterest Sorrow then ; but now named Rest."

LONDON, FROM FAR.

AFAR from all this country peace it lies,
　Tremendous and inscrutable for gloom, —
　The dreadful, fateful City of my doom
I know its lurid, fog-invested skies ;
I know what pestilential odors rise
　From court and alley, each a living tomb ;
　I know the tainted flowers, by night that bloom
Along its wayside, — flowers men spurn and prize.

I know the strife and the unceasing din, —
　The utmost blackness of its heart I know ;
I hear their shrieks and groans who toil within,
　And cries of those it murdered long ago, —
Yet 'mid the twisted growths of Shame and Sin,
　One woodland flower of memory shall grow.

UNSHELTERED LOVE.

LIKE a storm-driven and belated bird
   That beats with aimless wings about his nest,
    Straining against the storm his eager breast,
So is my love, which by no swift-winged word
May enter at her heart, and there be heard
   To sing as birds do, ere they fold in rest
    Their wings, still quivering from the last sweet quest
When with their song and flight the air was stirred.

Oh, if some wind of bitter disbelief,
   Some terrible darkness of estranging doubt,
    Has kept it from thee, now, sweet Love, reach out
Thine hand and pluck it from this storm of grief;
   It takes no heed of homeless nights and days.
   So in thy heart it find its resting-place.

WHEN IN THE DARKNESS I WAKE UP ALONE.

WHEN in the darkness I wake up alone,
   To face the loveless, desolated day,
    What thought shall comfort, or what hope shall stay?
Ah, Love, dear Love, Sweetheart that wast mine own,
Thou wilt not hear my spirit's bitter moan, —
   Thou wilt not see the terrible array
    Of foemen marching on my destined way,
With ruthless hands and hearts more hard than stone.

I shall be left in those old ways to tread
   Where Love and Sorrow walked with thee and me :
For thee, ghosts of old days, unquiet dead ;
   Days glad in life, and sad in memory, —
For me, to bow down weary heart and head
   On dead Hope's grave, till I be dead as she.

A PRAYER TO SLEEP.

O SLEEP, to-night be tender to my Love ;
   Hold her within thy clasp, so dear and deep ;
   Press gently on those sweetest eyes, kind Sleep :
Let no sad thought of me intrude, to move
Her heart to grief ; but through some fair dream-grove
   Where faint songs steal, and gentle shadows creep,
   And mystic stars and moons of dreamland keep
Their fond, persistent vigil, let her rove :

And if a dream of me must come, at all,
   Oh, show me to her glad with love and strong ;
Let on her mouth my garnered kisses fall,
   And to her ears make audible that song
      I sang her once, when at her feet I lay,
      At close of one divine, love-laden day !

I WALKED IN LOVE'S DESERTED ROOM.

I WALKED in Love's deserted room alone,
   And saw the lampless shrine, and in Love's place
   Not Hope's transcendent light, nor met her gaze
Who, Queen of Love, made all my heart her own ;
But a strange shape, as cold and hard as stone :
   And round it pressed in that most desolate place
   A phantom band, each one with ghastly face,
And each for some especial grief made moan.

I saw my Soul there, reigning in Love's stead,
   And it cried out, " Depart, ye clamoring throng !
   While Joy or Grief was mine I gave ye song,
But now, behold my last song-word is said :
   Love is a frail thing ; Death alone is strong, —
And Hope and Joy and Grief with Love lie dead."

25

TO THE SPIRIT OF POETRY.

ALL things are changed save thee, — thou art the same,
  Only perchance more dear ; as one friend grows
  When other friends have turned away.   Who knows
With what strange joy thou didst my life inflame
Before I took upon my lips the name
  Which vows me to thy service ?   Come thou close ;
  For to thy feet, to-day, my being flows,
As when, a boy, for comforting I came.

Thou, whose transfiguring touch makes speech divine ;
  Whose eyes are deeper than deep seas or skies, —
Warm with thy fire this heart, these lips of mine,
  Lighten the darkness with thy luminous eyes,
Till all the quivering air about me shine,
  And I have gained my spirit's Paradise !

OLD MEMORIES.

WHAT olden memories are these that throng
  To greet me on the threshold of this day, —
  Of buried hours what melancholy array ?
Dull, now, the eyes that once were clear and strong,
Their lips but whisper that once thrilled with song ;
  Their grave-clothes are upon them, and they say :
  " Know'st thou us still, and by what winding way
We led thy steps ; nor did that path seem long ? "

Yea, verily, I know ye but too well :
  Your loving kindness once indeed was sweet,
Your deep joy subtler than a man may tell ; —
  But why, with hearts that can no longer beat,
Why come ye back, and weave the olden spell
  To daze my senses and perplex my feet ?

GOOD-NIGHT AND GOOD-MORROW.

THE fires are all burned out; the lamps are low;
   The guests are gone; the cups are drained and dry.
   Here there was somewhat once of revelry;
But now no more at all the fires shall glow,
Nor song be heard, nor laughter, nor wine flow.
   Chill is the air; gray gleams the wintry sky:
   'Through lifeless boughs drear winds begin to sigh.
'T is time, my heart, for us to rise and go

Up the steep stair, till the dark room we gain
   Where sleep awaits us, brooding by that bed
On which who lies forgets all joy and pain,
   Nor weeps in dreams for some sweet thing long fled.
     'T is cold and lonely now; set wide the door;
     Good-morrow, my heart, and rest thee evermore!

AFTERMATH.

SONNETS.

—◦◦—

SORROW'S KINSHIP.

Day after day — as wave on wave — goes by,
   And still I sail the old familiar seas,
   Like him of old who never might find ease,
Or rest, 'twixt barren sea and barren sky,
Till she were come whose love would not deny
   Her very life to compass his release : —
   O Captain of pale spectral companies,
Kinship of sorrow knits us, thou and I !

On shore — in every seven years — three days
   Thou hadst to seek her who might not be found ;
   As still I find Her not, whose love had crowned
     Even Love himself anew. Sail on, sad ghost ;
But I, past reefs and straits and roaring bays,
   Shall anchor, some day, on a still, dark coast.

LOVE REFT OF HOPE.

As one whom Hope hath failed, Love walks alone, —
  No more on festivals his godhead shines ;
  Nor bides he where lamps burn before his shrines ;
But in gray twilights by chill breezes blown,
Where waters sob, and hapless voices moan,
  He strays, and with their wail his voice combines :
  His voice, now sad as sound of wind through pines,
That once with triumphing music called his own.

See how the wreath has faded round his head, —
  His weary head, that droops upon his breast ;
  His thorn-pierced feet are weak, yet may not rest.
Ah, dig beneath the willow-tree his bed :
  His one dear Hope being slain, were it not best
He should himself with that lost Hope lie dead?

CONSOLATION.

I FRONT the Present with the Past, and say :
  " Which reckons more, the anguish or the bliss ;
  The joy that was, or agony that is ;
The path I trod when life was glad with May,
Or this gray sky, and lone, unlovely way ;
  The deep delight of many a long, close kiss,
  The pressure of warm, clinging arms, or this
Fierce fire of thirst, that wastes me night and day? "

I think of thee, lost Love, and testify
  The present pain cheap price for the dear past :
Though Fate through life all comfort should deny,
  And after death my loneliness still last,
  'T is better to have held thee once so fast,
Than die without thy love, as others die.

UNDESCRIED.

WHEN from her far New World she sailed away,
  Right out into the sea-winds and the sea,
  Did no foreshadowing of good to be
Surprise my heart? That memorable day
Did I, unwitting, rise, think, do, and say,
  As on a day of no import to me?
  Did Hope awake no least low melody, —
Send forth no sign my wandering steps to stay?

Oh, could our souls catch music of far things
  From some lone height of being undescried,
Then had I heard the song the sea-wind sings
  The waves; and through the stress of storm and
      tide,
As soft as sleep, and pure as lonely springs,
  Her voice, wherein all sweetnesses abide.

LOVE'S SUNSET.

BEHOLD, the glory of the day is done !
  Now lies she dying 'mid her fading flowers,
  While twilight winds moan through her desolate bowers.
The sky is gray, forsaken of the sun, —
I muse upon this day whose course is run :
  What rose-hued splendor bathed her morning hours ;
  What golden glory crowned her noontide towers,
Fallen, now, in widespread ruin, every one !

Yet on the ruin a placid moon shall rise,
  And winds be hushed, and steadfast stars appear :
  Thus now at Love's sad sunset pale with fear,
Let moon and stars of Friendship light our skies ;
  So can we wait, the night through, for the cheer
Of some new world, and a new day's surprise.

COULD THIS THING BE ?

COULD she come in to-night, from her far place,
  And sit beside me in the firelight here,
  And all be as it was that other year,
When love made fair and fragrant all our ways
With such rare flowers as hearts may fitly praise,
  Before the day that brought our heavy cheer,
  And overthrew all that we held most dear,
Whereof the memory only now dismays, —

Could this thing be, how should the dreary room
  Where now I dwell with Sorrow, my pale mate,
Like some sweet sudden rose burst into bloom,
  And the heart's music grow articulate,
And joy-bells ring, and the loud cannon boom,
As when a queen sweeps through her realm in state !

FALLEN LOVE.

IF Love has fallen into disrepute,
  And they who fought for him now conquered bleed,
  And they who once believed forswear his creed,
And spurn his shrine with sacrilegious foot,
Fell his fair tree and trample on the fruit, —
  What joy is left?   What glory for our meed?
  Where shall we turn for comfort in our need?
What voice shall answer when Love's voice is mute?

Whose mocking cry is this that rends the night,
  And shouts, " Rejoice that conquering Love is dead ;
Dethroned, defamed, cast out of all men's sight, —
Now is the time for rapture and delight !
  Come one, come all ! where Pleasure's feast is spread ;
Since Love is dead, and Pain is put to flight ! "

REMEMBERED GRIEF.

LIKE some persistent ghost Grief's memory broods,
  An awful Presence in his lonely room ;
  Sometimes it swathes him in tremendous gloom,
Then scourges him to Frenzy's maddest moods :
It bides by him in country solitudes ;
  It shouts through cities with the voice of doom ;
  At night beside his bed he sees it loom,
A mocking Fiend no subterfuge eludes.

The Grief itself has passed ; and fair things hide
  Its grave, — where grasses grow and wild flowers spring.
  And soft winds come and go, and glad birds sing, —
But its stern shadow fareth at his side,
  With pitiless eyes and wan lips whispering :
" Lo ! I am with thee still, although I died."

SHIPWRECK.

The night is dense ; the waves climb wild and high ;
  Our ship drives on, to shipwreck speeding fast.
  How could it stand before these waves, this blast
That whirls between white billows and black sky ?
Comrades, the end is near, and we must die !
  No beacon light upon our way is cast ;
  We cannot see rude rocks and quicksands vast ;
Though well we know the snares that wait near by.

When will it suck us in, that fatal sand ;
  Or the rock rend us through the boiling wave ?
  Alas, man cannot, and God will not save ; —
Yet if strong Love but took the helm in hand,
  Then not for us the wide sea's clamorous grave,
But sudden summer, in some fair, far land.

DREAMS.

I.

COME to me in a dream, O Love of mine !
　　Come to me, Sweetest, from thy far-off place, —
　　Stand close and lean above me thy fair face :
Within my fingers let thy fingers twine,
And kiss mine eye-lids till they quiver and shine
　　With passionate joy, and all sleep's mystic ways
　　Are lighted with the bright propitious rays
'That beam from Love's own moon, — Love's star
　　　　divine.

O Love, for God's love, and for love of love,
　　Send forth thy soul across the weary way,
And find me, where through sleep I blindly rove,
　　Seeking my buried treasure, — ah, but stay
　　　　Here at my side till I have felt again
　　　　The jubilant blood exult in every vein !

II.

SOMETIMES I seem to find thee in my dreams, —
　　I do not hear thy voice ; nor do I see
　　Thy face ; but, Sweet, I feel all silently
Thy Presence watch my sleep.   Sometimes it seems
I catch from far the shining of Love's streams,
　　Or hear once more his blithe, dear minstrelsy ;
　　But when I would draw near those streams and thee,
They mock my sight with their elusive gleams :

And then my spirit, baffled in desire,
　　Possesses only the blind realm of Sleep,
And wakes to face the hours that wound and tire,
　　Wherein no more the happy pulses leap, —
　　To see the hostile years rise, steep on steep,
While from no height shines forth Love's answering fires.

CITY BELLS.

KNEELING by her who is my Heaven, I heard
   The clamoring chimes of city churches fill
   The mid-May evening, warm and deadly still.
My soul recoiled within me, and recurred
To winter nights, when the black air was stirred
   By the same sound, — when she whose perfect will
   Is my heart's law, whose touch my soul can thrill,
Was far away, past reach of kiss or word.

So will they sound again, O God, when she
   Is far, once more, Black Winter in her stead;
So shall they sound again in Jubilee,
   When in some new-born spring our lips are wed;
So shall they sound, through days and nights to be,
   When we, at last, our last farewell have said.

PARTING WITH SUMMER.

ON DOVER BEACH. — AUGUST 31.

As friends who part, and know not if again
   They ever shall take hands, so this still day,
   By this still sea, I and the summer say
Our long farewell.   The air is soft with rain,
Tender with trouble of this parting pain;
   And sea and sky are of one pensive gray.
   The small waves seem to sigh about the Bay,
As if they feared what the stern Fates ordain.

Autumn will mock us for a little space
   With Summer's semblance; but too well we know
That hectic flush which burns while life decays:
   Oh, better the wild Winter winds that blow
   The sea-foam, like tumultuous banks of snow,
And in our hearts Summer's remembered grace!

AT END OF LOVE.

As one who dying in some alien place —
    Some Northern Land no lavish sun makes bright —
    Dreams, in the silent watches of the night,
How once it fared with him by other ways,
Through large blue eves and deep, warm, Southern days,
    And seems once more to see things out of sight,
    To hear old sounds that bring back old delight,
Yet knows, above them all, what words Death says:

So now, at end of Love, I ponder still
    On all Love's glory, which was once mine own,
And sweet elusive visions come to fill
    My dreams with beauty; and a long lost tone
Thrills through the dark: but in the dawning chill
    I shuddering wake, to know I am alone.

A FALLEN CITY.

Gazing upon some city wrecked by war,
    The stranger, standing in its desolate square,
    O'er which broods low the stagnant autumn air,
Marvels at thought that here was once the jar
Of clashing weapons, while from near and far
    The death-fires blazed, and in their lurid glare
    Gleamed awful faces: women shuddered there,
And raised frail hands their awful doom to bar.

Here, too, he ponders, was mirth once and song,
    And glad feet danced, and eyes with joy were bright:
So in my heart was music sweet and strong,
    In long-gone days, and festival and light;
Then strife and clamor; now darkness and the throng
    Of grieving ghosts that haunt the ruins by night.

ON HEARING OLE BULL IMPROVISE ON
THE VIOLIN.

WHAT note is this of infinite appeal
  That wakes beneath thy hand's inspired control?
  Is it a prayer from man's most secret soul
To those dim gods Death only can reveal, —
Whose hands we know can wound, yet hope may heal?
  Hark! — for between the prayer and the prayer's goal,
  From far away, where unknown planets roll,
Surely I hear — or do I subtly feel —

Down all the deep, untravelled, star-watched way,
Faint as the wind at dawn of a June day,
  Steal some divine response? Ah, yes! 't is here,
    And prayer is turned to passionate triumphing,
  And in thy music's moon-thrilled atmosphere
    My soul drinks deep from some immortal spring.

DURING BATTLE.

LET there be martial music loud and strong,
  And shock and clamor of bells, and everywhere
  A sudden flame of banners on the air:
Yea, let the people chant a mighty song,
And to the gate-ways of the city throng!
  In old and solemn churches, stilly fair,
  Let there be organ breath, and stress of prayer;
Let there be love of right, and hate of wrong: —

For lo! outside the city rages now
  A deadly conflict, between Wrong and Right.
O perfect, peerless, fervent heart, pray thou
  That Wrong be done to death, in all men's sight;
For if he fall not, he will triumph, — how
  Those only know who have beheld his might.

LYRICS.

LOVE STRONG AS DEATH.

Nay, say not, Sweet, that Love has turned away
        Because one day
He gathered alien flowers when it was May, —
For Love is Love, and cannot pass that way.

Though little loves there be that dance and sing,
        And kiss and cling,
And praise the light and laughter of the Spring,
But on dark days, like birds, forbear to sing, —

Shall Love that bore the blast and did not fail,
        Now cower and quail, —
Strong Love that blanched not then, to-day turn pale? —
Nay, Love is Love, my own, and cannot fail.

MY HEART.

I gave you my heart for your own to rest on,
    When the night was wild
    Round your life, poor child, —
My lily, by rain and darkness prest on.

You broke my heart with your weight of sorrow;
    But it failed not, Dear,
    Till the day shone clear,
And storms no longer assailed your morrow.

DEAD LOVE.

Lay white roses on Love's bier ;
　　Kneel there now and weep —
He was fair once, and how dear, —
　　He who lies asleep.

Yes, he sleeps a sleep so long
　　That it shall not break —
Like a white rose, leave this song
　　By him, for Love's sake.

In the glorious summer-time,
　　In the rose-red June,
As the sun began to climb
　　To the ardent noon,

Love went singing to the light,
　　Splendid in his pride ;
Wounded came he home at night :
　　Of that wound he died.

PRECIOUS COMFORT.

" Hast thou no comfort in thy nights and days,
　　Thou weary wanderer upon the earth,
Traveller by dark and unfrequented ways?
　　Circuitous thy road was from thy birth, —
　　　　Oh, does there lie, perchance, within thy breast
　　　　Some little hidden, secret spring of rest?"

" My life is not all comfortless," I said,
　　" For when the winds are wildest on my track,
Hunting through forests, where the leaves lie dead,
　　Above the yell of that insatiate pack
　　　　I hear a sound more sweet than bird-notes are,
　　　　More solemn than the sea's voice heard from far.

26

"On moonlit nights in June, when winds are low,
    And yet sonorously upon the beach
The level waves come in with tidal flow,
    And every cave is brimmed with the sea's speech,
        Love's very voice it is that calls to me,
        And says : 'I am become a part of thee.'

"Then there arises in my soul a ray
    By which my darkened life transfigured seems,
And I remember how, upon one day,
    Perfect beyond all visioning of dreams
        Stood one beside me, — one who said : 'Arise,
        And I will show thee where is Paradise.'"

ACROSS THE SEA.

Across the sea, the shining Southern sea,
Is she with whom I am so fain to be,
Though well I know her heart has turned from me.

Fly through this misty, rainy Northern air —
Fly, Love, to her !   Fly, eager Love, even where
The purple South smiles, warm and flushed and fair !

Stand by her, Love, where fast asleep she lies,
And drop for me on her dear lips and eyes
The kiss which for my longing must suffice.

Be thou to her as song and scent and shine, —
Let all thy dearest memories combine
To turn again that queenliest heart to mine !

IF YOU WERE HERE.

A SONG IN WINTER.

O LOVE, if you were here,
 This dreary, weary day;
If your lips, warm and dear,
 Found some sweet word to say, —
Then hardly would seem drear
 These skies of wintry gray.

But you are far away, —
 How far from me, my dear!
What cheer can warm the day?
 My heart is chill with fear,
Pierced through with swift dismay, —
 A thought has turned Life sere:

If you, from far away,
 Should come not back, my dear;
If I no more might lay
 My hand on yours, nor hear
That voice, now sad, now gay,
 Caress my listening ear;

If you, from far away,
 Should come no more, my dear, —
Then with what dire dismay
 Year joined to hostile year
Would frown, if I should stay
 Where memories mock and jeer!

But I would come away
 To dwell with you, my dear;
Through unknown worlds to stray, —
 Or sleep; nor hope, nor fear,
Nor dream beneath the clay,
 Of all our days that were.

WIND–GARDENS.

MIDWAY between earth and sky,
There the wild Wind-Gardens lie, —
Tossing gardens, secret bowers,·
Full of song, and full of flowers, —
Wafting down to us below
Such a fragrance as we know
Never yet had lily or rose
That in earthly garden grows.

O those Gardens, dear and far,
Where the wild Wind-Fairies are,
Singing clearly, singing purely,
Strains of far-off Elf-Land, surely ! —
Though we see them not, we hearken
To them when the Spring skies darken, —
We divine their wayward playing,
Through those far, strange Gardens straying ;

Plucking there the wild Wind-posies,
Lilies, violets, and roses,
Whose sweet breath like angels' pity
Finds us, even in the City,
Where we toiling seek as treasures
Dull Earth's disenchanting pleasures.
O those gales with Wind-flowers laden, —
Flowers that no mortal maiden

In her breast shall ever wear !
Flowers to wreathe Titania's hair,
And to strew her happy way,
When she marries some wind-fay !

O Wind-Gardens, where such songs are,
And of flowers such happy throngs are,
Though your paths I may not see,
Well I know how blest they be !

TO CICELY.

AH, my dear one, laid to rest
  In your lowly English bed,
With the grass upon your breast
  And the sweet flowers at your head ;
    Did you whisper now to me :
    " Dear, remember Italy ? "

Do you think I could forget
  How unto that hope most blest,
Like two ships with canvas set,
  Making for the sunlit West,
    Went we to our shining goal, —
    Heart in heart, and soul in soul ?

And to me, on my lone way,
  Still the glory of it cleaves,
As at close of some June day
  All the sky with sunset heaves, —
    Ah, but to this sunset light
    Comes a starless, moonless night.

Dear one, these are homesick words, —
  For our love's sake, and our past,
Flying home to you, as birds
  To the nest fly home at last,
    Their tired wings to fold and rest
    When the sun fails in the West.

CRITICAL OPINIONS

OF

PHILIP BOURKE MARSTON'S POEMS.

CRITICAL OPINIONS.

Concerning "Song-Tide."

THIS is a first work of extraordinary performance, and of still more extraordinary promise. The youngest school of English poetry has received an important accession to its ranks in Philip Bourke Marston, who will at once, by virtue of this volume, take a place alongside of Swinburne, Morris, and Rossetti. That the author of "Song-Tide and Other Poems" is a genuine and original poet cannot be doubtful to any reader of this book. . . . The "lyric cry" pervades every stanza. . . . It is a marvellous triumph of poetic expression. — *London Examiner.*

The book is undoubtedly the work of an original mind. . . . We have surely a new poet in our midst. —*Morning Post.*

A book of very beautiful poetry. — ROBERT BROWNING.

The truth and force of tragic sentiment in such poems as the "Christmas Vigil" have made their own singing notes for themselves, as all genuine lyric verse does. — ALGERNON CHARLES SWINBURNE.

An exquisite loveliness of sentiment and diction seems to me its prevailing characteristic. It has the nameless elegance of the Italian verse, but with the deeper and more latent sympathies which belong to the Northern genius. — LORD LYTTON.

Only yesterday evening I was reading your "Garden Secrets" to William Bell Scott, who fully agreed with me that it is not too much to say of them that they are worthy of Shakespeare in his subtlest lyrical moods. — DANTE GABRIEL ROSSETTI.

Concerning "All in All."

In circumstances which would shake the strongest, the intellectual courage of our author is remarkable. . . . If the conditions under which he has worked are taken into account, it may truly be said that his book is not only an interesting and beautiful one, but hardly to be paralleled anywhere. — WILLIAM M. ROSETTI, in *London Academy.*

Before going to bed, I read your "Dream" twice over. It is very beautiful throughout, — the strong and sure imagination keeping time, so to say, with the deep and subtle pathos in a quite triumphant manner. Other things in the volume confirm me in the assurance that it is altogether an advance in point of power and perception on your first book. — ALGERNON CHARLES SWINBURNE.

I should have thanked you earlier for your beautifully entitled volume, "All in All." You may be sure such verse is of a kind especially fragrant to me, belonging as it does in feeling to the small highest class, — the heartfelt; and excellent as it is in execution also. — DANTE GABRIEL ROSSETTI.

Concerning "Wind-Voices."

Emotion genuine and deep breathes from every line of this book. It is now so well known that Mr. Marston is blind, that the indelicacy would lie not in alluding to the fact but in ignoring it. His work, however, asks no indulgence on account of his physical infirmity. Even in pictorial power it can sustain comparison with the work of any of the subjective school to which the poet belongs. . . . Mr. Marston can, as in "The Rose and the Wind," produce a lyric that is absolutely perfect, — perfect in conception, and perfect in form. As a writer of sonnets, he is unequal, and yet capable of producing a perfect thing. — THEODORE WATTS, in *London Athenæum.*

It is as a sonnet writer that Mr. Marston is at his best. It is not too much to say that his sonnets are a permanent possession for English Literature. — *Glasgow Herald.*

We believe that no candid critic will be able to avoid the conclusion that the present book contains the weightiest and the most delicate work that its author has yet produced. . . . If we would feel how excellent this work is, we have only to read such melodious and lovely poems as "The Two Burdens," "At Hope's Grave," "Ungathered Love," "At Parting," and "Three Songs." . . . Toward the end of the volume we have in "New Garden Secrets," a little sheaf of verses dealing in an exquisitely light and graceful way with the imagined thoughts and speeches of the flowers. — *London Academy.*

The grief which finds so thrilling and sincere a voice in these poems is almost more poignant than any which we recollect in literature. . . . In this age of sonneteers, Mr. Marston is one of the best that we possess in England. . . . He is, perhaps, the poet who has used the sonnet in its most Italian form, — much more so, for instance, than Rossetti. His sonnets give the reader the impression, as so many Italian ones do, of being part of a great autobiography in sonnets, of which these only have been preserved. . . . The section called "New Garden Secrets" is full of lovely things; the speculation of the unblown violets, the good-humored derision of the trees for the ephemeral blossoms that pant with hope and passion at their feet and are silenced by one night of frost, the terrors of the over-wrought spirit of the rose, the garrulous chattering of the

crocus, the wonder of all the flowers as to what becomes
of the sun at night, with the rose's conviction : —

> "I think he sleeps where the grass is, —
> He there would have room to lie;
> The white Moon over him passes ;
> He wakes with the dawning sky."

All these are exquisite. — EDMUND GOSSE, in *Pall Mall
Gazette.*

Concerning "*A Last Harvest.*"

It is the fruit of the three final years of a life which was
one long bereavement. . . . Among the sonnets with which
the volume concludes there are some fine examples of a form
of verse in which all competent authorities allow that Marston excelled. "The Breadth and Beauty of the Spacious
Night," "To all in Haven," "Friendship and Love," "Love's
Deserted Palace," — these, to mention no others, have the
"high seriousness," which Matthew Arnold made the test of
true poetry. — THEODORE WATTS, in *London Athenæum.*

Marston was a poet of rare and delicate genius, often
with a note so poignant and exquisite that one realizes at
once how, in happier circumstances, he might have won a
great name and an enduring place ; and all to whom his
poetry appeals find in it a charm which is not to be gain-
said. . . . The finest of his sonnets are probably better than
the finest by any of his contemporaries, with the single exception of Rossetti. — WILLIAM SHARP, in the *London
Academy.*

The first question which will be asked is, "Is the volume,
or is it not, an advance upon Marston's previous achievements?" And to that question the answer is at once, "Yes,"
and "No." Yes, in the sense that a higher level of artistic
workmanship is sustained throughout ; no, inasmuch as it
contains, with one exception, no sonnet or lyric that is dis-

tinctively finer in its way than anything to be found in "Song-Tide," "All in All," or "Wind-Voices." The most notable poem in the collection is the opening one, — a lyric, which in the haunting witchery of its melody, recalls Edgar Allen Poe at his best. . . . The most remarkable feature in "A Last Harvest" is the high average excellence of the sonnet work. — COULSON KERNAHAN, in *The Gentleman's Magazine.*

www.ingramcontent.com/pod-product-compliance
Lightning Source LLC
Chambersburg PA
CBHW031055110726
47900CB00003B/935